MAJJIAN SPRINGS

MAGIC TO SPARE, BOOK 2

MICHELLE L. LEVIGNE

www.YeOldeDragonBooks.com

Ye Olde Dragon Books
6909 Ackley Rd.
Parma, OH 44129

www.YeOldeDragonBooks.com

2OldeDragons@gmail.com

Copyright © 2024 Michelle L. Levigne

ISBN 13: 978-1-961129-65-8

Published in the United States of America
Publication Date: June 1, 2024

Cover Art © Copyright 2024 Ye Olde Dragon Books

THANK YOU!

Many thanks to the members of my launch team for this book. I hope you had fun, and you'll be back for more book launches and adventures together!

Jean Alfieri
Tim Allen
Lindsy Arrowood
Rosemarie DiCristo
Pam Halter
Michelle Houston
Akaysha Mynes
Simona Rinfreschi
Kez Sharrow
Deborah Cullins Smith
Chris Wachter

CHAPTER ONE

"My dear Princess Merrigan ..." Bergomass, wizard and great-uncle to King Auberg of Williburton, shook his head as he looked her over, head to foot and foot to head. "You are a greater puzzle than you were when we first met."

"I don't understand," Prince Bryan said, and wrapped his arm around Merrigan, drawing her up against his side, even as he turned to put himself between her and the wizard. "I thought that Merrigan taking the cursed apple for Belinda, and everything else she has gone through, met the requirements of the seer's enchantment."

They had come up to Bergomass's tower to say good-bye, in preparation for leaving the capitol city of Alliburton early in the morning. A quest rested on them, to find Bryan's brother, Bayl, free their father's kingdom of Sylvanglade from a sleeping curse, and return Princess Belinda, Bayl's sweetheart, to her father's kingdom.

"It did, she did, however ..." The elderly enchanter shook his head. "The removal of the healing curse that Clara put on you has revealed other magics wrapped around you. Come, children, sit. I fear we shall be here for some time. We should be comfortable." He waited until Merrigan and Bryan settled in two deeply cushioned chairs facing him in the cozy sitting room in his tower at the palace. "I thought the vision of your inner being, your potentials and even shadows of your destiny would be clearer, but I fear that what I saw before ... hmm ... well, I can only speculate, since I have never run into so many layers of magic, spells upon spells. I think I was seeing the destiny that others tried to impose on you. I dare to speculate that you were cocooned with magic to separate you from the nourishing influence of the magical forces that surrounded you as a royal child, sitting on the edge of, I dare to say, one of the most important majjian springs in all of Armorica. You were insulated, I suppose, to make you vulnerable to whoever tried to impose that new destiny on you."

"So someone deliberately made me the royal brat?" Merrigan shook her head, her face warm. She hadn't meant to say that. It was ridiculous to want to blame someone, and yet at the same time, she felt a cool sense of relief. So perhaps all the selfish things she did growing up, all the stupid choices, her nastiness and rebellion, weren't entirely her own fault? Someone had influenced her?

"Hmm, in essence. Insidious, almost unimaginable, and yet ... Yes.

Making you the royal brat, as you say, certainly obscured the path that your parents tried to set you on and prayed to the Unseen to grant you. Your heritage was stolen, and someone tried to impose a different one on you." He smiled, mischief and something nastily triumphant glittered in his eyes, sharpened his voice. "Or rather, they tried, and failed. You must continue to fight. This battle is far from won."

"Why?" Merrigan shuddered, and Bryan wrapped his arm around her. "Why did they choose me?"

"What did they want to use her for?" Bryan said. "Yes, royal blood always has a stronger portion of magic. Prophecies and magical events always seem to need someone of royal blood as a cornerstone or anchor. But what could they want specifically with Merrigan?"

"I fear that cannot be determined until more of the cocoon has been unwound from you," Bergomass said with a weary sigh. The mischief and sharpness faded away. He was just a kindly old man again. "You will not find all your answers until you have returned home, and yet ... Some spells wrapped around you are like ... like parasitic flowers. They have entangled you in the spells, for good and for evil, that wrapped around those you have encountered. You are bound to Princess Belinda's quest as much as to Prince Bayl and Prince Bryan's quests. The quest to find Prince Bayl and free him is just as important as freeing you. And just as important as your mission to free Sylvanglade. There are too many tendrils of magic attached to you for me to advise you clearly which step to take, which path to follow, which spells are for good and which are for evil. The illusions are still falling away from you. Like vines deprived of root and water, shriveling up and turning to dust."

"Can you do anything to help her?" Bryan said.

"I can study the strands and try to find their sources, some clues to the ones who wove them and how long ago and where those magics first sank their roots into you. It will be uncomfortable, with no guarantee of swift answers. How long can we afford to delay, sitting here and searching? Setting about your quests immediately is vital. You must solve those problems because they are part of you now. Much as I would dearly love to say yes, go straight home to Avylyn, to your father's palace, find the vanished door into the queen's garden, free the majjian springs to flow ... I cannot be certain that is the wisest course of action."

Merrigan and Bryan agreed to the study. It only made sense to her, and her eyes prickled with tears when she saw how Bryan worried for her. What had she done to deserve his love, much less his care for her?

Bergomass settled her in his workroom, trying to make her as comfortable as possible. Bryan hurried down to the palace library. Bib and Crystal, the magic book and magic mirror were consulting maps and the most recent records of the kingdom and surrounding kingdoms, to help them on their journey. They would both be of great help in studying the magic tangling Merrigan.

She feared that having to sit still and say nothing, eyes closed, might be the hardest thing she had ever done. And thinking back on all the stiff, uncomfortable clothes she had worn to look the part as Leffisand's queen, that was saying a great deal. Why had she endured all that discomfort for him? So much of the deceptively helpful guidance he had sent her in those secretive letters when she was growing up had been training her, molding her into the selfish, scheming, cold queen he needed for his plans of conquest. He had trained her to believe he always knew best and mocked her when all her parents' teaching conflicted with his "greater wisdom."

Certainly after the torture of the tight clothes and rigid posture and the heavy weight of jewels, she could sit still for a few hours.

Bryan wasn't allowed to be there. His connection to Merrigan through true love's kiss, breaking the spell of the cursed apple, was strong enough to interfere. Especially if he got protective of her. After Bryan left, and Bergomass locked the workroom door, he admitted he didn't want to be interrupted with dozens of questions.

Sitting still was even harder than she had feared. She wanted to ask questions every time Bergomass and Bib and Crystal discussed the threads and webs and knots and tendrils of magic cocooning her, and whether it would be wise to try to snip apart various threads and uproot others. As the day progressed, Merrigan decided this was more like burial wrappings than a cocoon. A cocoon held the promise of something new and beautiful emerging, but she felt rather as if the person she had been born to be had been slowly smothered, on purpose, to kill her.

"Hah!" Bergomass said, after nearly twenty minutes of silence, during which Merrigan tried not to flinch and wriggle with every sharp prick and sting, like hairs were being pulled out, one at a time.

"Fascinating," Crystal said. "I never would have guessed, and yet I of all people should have seen it."

What? Merrigan wanted to shout. *Tell me. Don't leave me out.*

"What?" Bib said. "I can't see it."

"She's a water child," Crystal said. "Well, of course. Born in the palace guarding the largest and most powerful of all Armorica's majjian springs. She has strong ties to all majjian springs."

"I wouldn't be surprised if that is why she was targeted," Bergomass muttered. His tone of voice indicated he was thinking aloud rather than talking to his co-workers. "There are always attacks on the integrity of the majjian springs. To weaken the land and make it vulnerable to enchanters from other lands, or to try to take control of all the magic and ... "

He was silent so long, Merrigan's eyelids started fluttering, giving in to the temptation to peek and try to read his face.

"Let me try something. Now that I have an idea ... this might help." He patted Merrigan's hand, resting on the arm of the chair, making her flinch. "I'm sorry, my dear child, but this might sting a little."

Merrigan gripped the armrests in anticipation. When someone said something might sting, that meant it was really going to hurt. She swallowed hard, trying to close up her throat against a shout.

Pinpricks danced over her skin and then seemed to sink down to her bones. Heat spiraled through her blood and she felt as if she lay in a massive sieve, and something tried to press her through the holes. Before she could inhale to release that shout building in her belly, all the pressure vanished. She nearly opened her eyes, shocked by the relief.

"Yes," Bergomass whispered. He sounded tired. "Exactly. That must be at the root of it, and ... yes, that could explain much. And reveal an insidious plot. An ancient plot. Those with the illusion of immortality are willing to wait centuries for their plans to come to fruition."

"Water children are often targeted by the King of the Archipelago," Bib offered. *I'm sorry, mi'lady,* he said into Merrigan's thoughts. *I hear all those questions churning in your head. I will tell you everything. The telling will take a great deal of time because this despot has many cruel and sad stories attached to him. His history is long. If he is the villain at the core of this story, then we have half the threat and half the cure identified. You must return to your father's palace and open the door to the garden and free the spring. But not immediately.*

"Indeed," Bib continued aloud, "you are proven right, sir, when you said Merrigan and the others should deal with the other quests first. I wouldn't doubt that just like with Princess Belinda, alarms were triggered when some of the magic tangling Princess Merrigan was uprooted. Her enemies will be looking for her. And what could be more logical than to return home?"

"It makes perfect sense now," Crystal said. "Merrigan, you reconnected to the majjian springs when you healed the queen's garden in Seafoam. That started healing you."

"And if she is a water child, then that identifies another enemy, more readily at hand than the Archipelago," Bergomass said. "I detect some twisted, sour notes of magic. Very faint. Already being rewritten by the true song of the princess awakening after years of slumber. If I am right, those notes are the signature of a nasty, selfish band of rebels." He sighed, and patted Merrigan's hand. "You're probably ready to burst with questions. I will tell you this and leave the rest for Bib to inform you on your journey. There is a rebel band among the lower-ranked majjians spread across the world. When they fail to impose their standards of magic use and priorities on the entire world, they retreat, to sit in the shadows and silence and tend their poisoned mushroom garden of thoughts until another generation grows up, dissatisfied with their lot in life. Then they arise again."

"You're not explaining anything, and she's getting a little impatient with your eloquence," Crystal said with a chiming sort of chuckle.

Merrigan smiled, and a tickle of laughter relaxed her throat.

"I apologize. I'm still not used to having much of anyone to talk to. It's a lovely temptation and indulgence to have an audience." Bergomass patted her hand again. "A captive audience, so to speak." He chuckled, then took a deep breath. "As I was saying … These lower-ranked majjians want to control who gets to use magic, who benefits from magic. They want to decide who is worthy. They insist that magic is used too freely, too prodigally, and it is being wasted on the unworthy. They insist the majjian springs will go dry, like ordinary physical springs can go dry sometimes. They refuse to see that limiting the springs, building up walls around them, denying the natural flow of the water, only serves to pollute the water. And unlike natural, physical springs, if magic's flow is stopped up, if it is hoarded, it turns to poison and then dries up.

"They want to tame and guide the flow of magic. History proves that wild magic is far healthier than the pathetic, stingy stuff they prefer. They refuse to admit that the Unseen guides wild magic. They are among those who insist that the Unseen does not exist at all because the world does not proceed as they believe it should. Centuries ago, after their most ignominious defeat, when they should have learned their lesson for all time, the whining, self-righteous band believed the lies of the King of the Archipelago and became his minions."

Well, Merrigan admitted, that did explain a little bit what was going on. Should she feel flattered or worried that she was somehow being used by a group of sour old whining, demanding … She inhaled so sharply it was nearly a cry.

"What?" Bergomass said. "You thought of something."

"Think hard, Mi'lady, and I will tell the others," Bib said. "What did you think of? What did you remember?"

Images filled Merrigan's mind. Shriveled, sharp-voiced old women, standing in the palace courtyard, shrieking their demands, daring to argue with Queen Daylily. She remembered the chill and the sour smell that neither her sisters nor any servants had seemed to notice. Those old women finally stomped away in a huff because the queen would not give in to their demands. Merrigan remembered glimpses of those women, like fragments of nightmares, sneaking through the palace, wrapped in their rusty black clothes, searching for something.

They had been searching for the door to the queen's garden, Merrigan realized now. They kept coming. And when they couldn't find it, they had tried to bully servants into showing them the way. Then they had tried to coerce Merrigan into showing them the door. And not just show them the door, but open it for them.

She gasped, trying to muffle the sound, when she saw Nanny Tulip's face among those sour, snarling, demanding women. A different Nanny Tulip, sharper in features, vicious anger making her eyes like coals. Not the sweet-voiced, smiling, laughing Nanny Tulip who had come into her life and comforted her, and taught her how a true princess should act even in the deepest throes of grief, after her mother sickened and died.

"Oh, cruel, insidious," Bergomass whispered, when Bib spoke her thoughts and memories. "That answers so much ... and I fear shows me how correct I was. This is a tangle and a threat that must be dealt with slowly, cautiously. The best tactic in such tangled circumstances is to simply set forth and let the winds of fate and destiny guide you. Wander. Meet every challenge you face, do every good deed you can find to do, gather up allies, and every time you resist the urge to become the royal brat again—" He chuckled and patted her hand, when Merrigan flinched at the word. "Every time you resist, you will snap another cursed thread imprisoning you. This is vital, my dear. Every bit of enemy magic must be conquered, or it must be failing, fading, ready to die, by the time you walk through the doors of your father's palace. Until you are free of that magic that caused the door of your mother's garden to vanish in self-defense, that door will not appear and open for you. And you are the only one, I suspect, who can open that door." He cupped her cheek. "No more seeking is necessary. Get up and eat a light meal and go right to bed. You have an early day and a long journey ahead of you."

Merrigan opened her eyes. She was startled to look out the wide window shielded with magic and discover that night had fallen. She thought she had only been here for an hour or two. Not most of the day.

Bryan came hurtling up the winding stairs to the tower room before Merrigan had finished drinking the restorative potion Bergomass made for her. The searching had been draining on many levels for her. She was glad to lean into Bryan's support, his arm tight around her, as she finished drinking the potion.

"I have an idea," Bryan said. "Another layer of magic to protect us, I think. True love's kiss broke the—"

"The potential for true love," Bergomass said, waving an admonishing finger at them both. He smiled, a little wearily. "Yes, a good idea that under other circumstances, I would approve."

"What?" Merrigan said. She flinched when her voice came out too sharp. Well, she was tired, wasn't she? She didn't like it when people talked about her and she didn't understand what they were discussing.

"Let's seal our promises to each other. The ones we made as children, and our new ones." Bryan caught up both her hands between his. "If

Bergomass officiates, and Aubrey and Gilda stand with us, with the magic still radiating from their broken curses and their true love, that will grant us even more protection. And I'm sick to death of waiting for you, Merrigan," he added, his face reddening, looking like the boy he had been in their childhood adventures.

"Oh, yes, please," she whispered. She tugged her hands free to slide them around his neck, aching for another of those delicious kisses that sent tingling, bubbling magic through her blood.

"Ah, no, I'm sorry." Bergomass pressed gently on their shoulders to move them apart. "This must be done properly. All the rules. All the chances for blessing."

"But—"

"You must have her father's blessing. You must stand at her mother's tomb and let the tree blossom out of season and drop flowers on you. Again, to gain her blessing. You need to quest and build up the magic that comes from being heroes. And you must heal every majjian spring your path crosses, before you can stand in the queen's garden in Avylyn and release magic that will heal all of Armorica."

"I don't understand." Bryan's voice had just a touch of irritated rasp. Merrigan knew she was ridiculous to be so pleased at that.

"Much as I hate to delay true love, young love, love that has been denied so long and then restored so splendidly ..." Bergomass sighed, and finally sat down on the stool facing Merrigan's chair. Now he looked as tired as she felt. "I have heard rumors that majjian springs are drying up. If so much effort has been put into warping Merrigan's magical destiny, then it is even more imperative to proceed carefully. No shortcuts, no cheating, every step taken with all propriety and caution, and all the rules followed. The fate of not just this continent but all the majjian springs across the entire world could hinge on your patience and obedience."

~~~~~

Their traveling party left before dawn the next morning. Long after the walls of Alliburton had vanished behind the horizon, Merrigan remained silent. She couldn't think of what to say without whining or complaining. Or sounding like a spoiled child deprived of a treat she hadn't earned.

Bib, she thought to her friend and confidant and advisor, *I've already started this journey off on the wrong foot. Help me fix things?*

It was highly convenient and soothing to her pride that she could speak in her mind with the magic book. He continued to help her reform and shake off more and more aspects of being the self-absorbed, martyr-attitude brat. Even more convenient that she could have a conversation with him when he wasn't riding with her. Currently, Bib and Crystal were riding in a padded bag hanging off the back of Bryan's saddle. And Bryan
~~~~~

rode at the head of their little party, conversing with Captain Garan, head of the soldiers guarding them. They did have quite a lot to do: find Bayl, wherever Belinda's vicious enchantress sisters had sent him; reconcile Belinda and her father; and free Sylvanglade from a sleeping curse brought on it by the thoughtlessness of Bayl and Bryan's oldest brother, Branwell, and the scheme of his future in-laws to escape the sleeping curse put on their daughter.

Common sense said Bryan should ride with the captain, to discuss their plan of action. Except that they had left Alliburton with Bryan riding next to Merrigan, and she had the awful feeling he would still be riding next to her if she hadn't been so silent. She had probably been scowling since they rode out through the city gates. Why would Bryan want to look at her scowling and pouting all day? Yes, he loved her, but love didn't mean she had the right to inflict that misery on him.

He probably thought she was angry with him for suggesting they marry before heading out on their journey.

Not the idea of marrying right away, but the disappointment when Bergomass shattered that delightful proposal. She couldn't argue because she didn't want to be the demanding, selfish Royal Brat ever again, and what he said made such dreadful common sense.

It's not as bad as you think. Crystal's shimmering voice whispered through Merrigan's mind, startling her. The magic mirror chuckled, sounding like the tinkling of paper-thin glass wind chimes. *Yes, as long as I'm in contact with Bib, I can talk to you as easily as he does. Don't be so hard on yourself, Merry. You notice the boy hasn't tried to talk to you, either. It takes two to have a conversation. I think he's pouting too. And he feels a little guilty for making the suggestion.*

I thought it was lovely! Merrigan smiled at the nickname Crystal insisted on using for her. *Did he tell you that's how he feels?*

Heavens, Bryan has been gnawing on the problem since he kissed you goodnight. He's afraid to say anything and make you cry. I do admire a man who is paralyzed by fear of tears from the woman he loves.

Does he still love me? I really am the brat. How am I ever going to shake off this awful tendency to believe the world should revolve around me?

Utter nonsense. We need to levy on that wretched Nanny Tulip and her band of rebels due punishment for twisting your mind and soul when you were a helpless child. That's for starters, Bib said, with a comforting growl in his paper-whisper voice. *I agree with Bergomass. You were a tool in their agenda. It wasn't by accident she became your nanny and eventually your only friend.*

The tally at the bottom of the ledger is that you're both ninnies, each thinking the other is angry and not sure how to make things right, Crystal interrupted. *Do focus on the more important problem, Bib dear. Their attitudes are charming and frustrating at the same time.*

"Tell me something I don't know," Merrigan sighed.

"Are you all right?" Belinda raised her head from the book she had been trying to read. It rested on the brace on the saddle Bergomass had devised, to making reading while riding easier.

"No, she's not," Bryan said, startling both princesses. When he had dropped back in the short column of riders, Merrigan didn't know. "Crystal says we've both been ninnies. Again."

"She's right. I'm sorry," Merrigan hurried to say. She calculated she owed him ten apologies for every one he made her. If she had just ignored Nanny Tulip, she and Bryan would be married already.

"You've got nothing to be sorry about. And we can't even be angry at Bergomass. Blame Nanny Tulip and her friends. The whole tangled mess of being royal blood. Destiny and the fate of the entire world." One corner of his mouth twitched up in the soft, blue-black curls of his beard. "I should have just whisked you away for a private little ceremony days ago, when I first thought of it. Deed done."

"You did?" Her voice cracked and rose high enough to get ear twitches from several of the horses of their guards.

"But maybe that would have just made things worse, instead of better." He shrugged.

"Hmm ... yes ... that makes far too much sense." She tried to smile, but the effort made her mouth ache. Pouting was so much easier.

Honestly, would her reformation ever finish? When would it be all right to have a few flickers of selfishness and self-pity every once in a while, without the horrid risk of turning into a brat?

"But who ever promised that the sensible thing would be pleasant?" he said.

"I'm glad you're thinking ahead. The only practice I seem to have in thinking ahead is when I'm focusing solely on myself. Bib is right. We need to find Nanny Tulip and do something absolutely horrendous to her. What if she is responsible for Nanny Starling being sent away in disgrace? Or worse, for my mother's long sickness?" She shuddered deep inside, as if her belly had turned to ice. "I know she has to be responsible for losing the door to Mama's garden, and the thorns taking over her garden the way they did. Yes, I know I did something wrong. I tried to sidestep the magic and I broke rules. I accept responsibility and I know I have to undo what I did, no matter what the cost ... but I did it at her instigation. From her teaching." She clasped her gloved hands, to keep them from grasping and tearing and shredding something.

"Merrigan." Bryan caught hold of her hands in one of his.

It startled her every time he did that, emphasizing how small her hands were. She had done so much work with her hands in the years since she had brought Clara's curse on herself, they felt strong and large to her.

Nanny Tulip had to be infuriated, wherever she was, at the knowledge that the princess she had trained to demand constant attention and pampering enjoyed taking care of herself and giving to others.

Her nanny had deliberately turned Merrigan into a self-centered, vindictive little shrew who blithely justified every nasty, self-serving action she took. She believed with self-righteous fervor that Leffisand, her husband, had been right in stomping on the people his ancestors had vowed to nurture. Her own father had said often that a king was only king for the purpose of defending and healing and guiding his people.

"It's going to be all right," Bryan continued. "We have a good idea what happened and why, and that will help us fix things."

"You hope," Belinda said. She offered a lopsided little smile when they both flinched at the interruption.

Merrigan's face warmed enough she swore she could bake their morning bread in the heat. What must the guards be thinking of this conversation? It was the highest priority that soldiers especially think their leaders were infallible and always confident and ...

No, wait. That was Leffisand's teaching. Appearances were always far more important to him than anything else. Her stomach knotted at this further evidence that everything her dead husband had taught her about being royal, about leading a country and doing her blood-born duty was brutally, fatally wrong.

"What do you mean, we hope?" Bryan said.

"After yesterday's revelations, Bergomass gave me copies of reports he and other enchanters throughout the continent have been compiling for a few decades now. It takes time to see the pattern." Belinda stroked the cover of the book she had been reading. "This is a decline that has been happening everywhere. Gradually. The kingdoms affected don't even realize what is happening until someone comes from outside and points out all the changes, the decline, the drying up of the majjian springs, the blight creeping through their queens' gardens."

CHAPTER TWO

"It starts small," Belinda continued, "with the swans and frogs and other magical creatures vanishing from the gardens. The healing and purifying herbs slowly lose their strength and effectiveness. Thorns meant to protect the gardens from intrusion gradually turn against the chosen heirs, the next guardians, because they have become tainted in some way. The thorns only sense poison. They are unable to think or differentiate or communicate what has gone wrong and what needs to be done to remedy the damage. No one is sure what went wrong because it happened so slowly. They grew used to the decline and didn't feel or see until suddenly the pools were dry and the plants were dead, the swans hadn't returned in years, the doors into the gardens vanished, and people couldn't remember the last time they saw the doors."

That reminded Merrigan too much of what had happened with the royal family and the queen's garden in Seafoam. Could the vanity and silliness of a previous queen, who neglected the garden to protect her complexion, have been part of this insidious plot against all the majjian springs across Armorica?

What had been Nanny Tulip's goal when she set out to turn a daughter of the King of Avylyn into a brat?

"That's it," Merrigan whispered, and shuddered with a cold that had nothing to do with the snow sugar-frosting the landscape.

"You could be right," Bib said. "Why didn't I think of that before?"

"We've both been focusing on other problems, more personal ones," Crystal said. "Stop interrupting the girl. She's on to something brilliant."

"What is it?" Belinda said.

"What does the book say about the daughters and sons with the most magical potential in the family?" Merrigan said. "The youngest or the seventh child? What strong magical tales run in the families? Does it say if the child was ..." She shuddered with the effort to find the right word for what had happened to her. "Turned aside? Tainted?" Merrigan took a deep breath to brace herself. "What damage distracted the family, so they didn't realize an enemy had crept into the nursery until it was too late?"

Belinda shook her head. "I'm only at the beginning. I'm sorry. This is an introduction to what the book contains. Several books, actually."

"Reading while riding isn't easy, and this is something we all need to be studying," Bryan said. "Crystal, Bib, are you keeping notes?"

"Of course, we are. Keep thinking and speculating, dear boy. Make me proud," Crystal responded.

"Well, it's a good thing we have a long journey to get to your father's kingdom," Merrigan offered, trying for a light tone. "Plenty of reading to keep us entertained, sitting by the fire at night."

"Entertained." Bryan shook his head. His grin was crooked. "When I think of all the kingdoms Bayl and I wandered through, looking for Belinda and hoping we'd stumble across an answer to free Sylvanglade ... I wonder if Talithia's silliness was also part of this creeping blight."

"Maybe that's what happened to your sisters," she offered, nodding to Belinda.

"I wouldn't be surprised." Belinda's mouth flattened for a moment. Her glance shifted to the deceptively plain wooden box that served as the magical prison for her two nasty younger sisters, Bythia and Barbarina. "I pray when we get home, I won't discover something quite nasty has happened to Blossom. That's our youngest sister. Father named her that because the apple tree in Mother's garden burst into bloom the day she was born, late in the fall after all the leaves had already fallen. I betrayed her, running away like I did. I should have brought her with me, or made sure Great-Aunt Sophie was coming back, to protect her. Our other sisters were able to take care of themselves. At least, I hope so ..." She sighed. "I betrayed Father, too, no matter how unreasonable he was."

"We have all been betrayed," Merrigan said, reaching for her friend's hand. "And now that we know, we have a starting place to find the cure and the criminal. The guilty parties will pay, and we will stop the curse they have brought on Armorica."

"The question," Bryan said, "is how long these people have been sneaking into palaces and twisting the magic of the royal bloodlines. The majjian springs have been either blocked or diverted so they dry up ... and that doesn't happen overnight or even in a single generation."

"This looks like an organized effort," Belinda said, gesturing at the book on the saddle before her. "How many people are involved?"

"And how many royal children were turned into royal brats and made entirely useless?" Merrigan inhaled sharply. "Made fitting spouses for truly evil kings and queens. If Tulip was grooming me to marry Leffisand, specifically ... " She couldn't think of a punishment vile enough.

~~~~~

Belinda dove into studying the books and distilling all the depressing reports and theories into something usable. Merrigan was grateful. Belinda had something constructive to do. Better to obsess about finding some answers and contribute to the quest that lay before them than to slump in her saddle and weep over Bayl. They had no answers or ideas
~~~~~

yet what had happened to him. Merrigan imagined the heartache Belinda suffered. She knew exactly how she would feel if she had come so close to being reunited with Bryan, everything made right between them, only to have him snatched away.

She had been taught to take vindictive retribution for her every disappointment. Her response would have been to do something vicious to Belinda's wicked enchantress sisters. Knowing they had failed in destroying their sister, the heir to the kingdom, had to be galling for them. It wouldn't have been punishment enough to satisfy Merrigan.

She wanted to question them and find out if they had been influenced by someone like Nanny Tulip. The two sisters had displayed a propensity for magic from early childhood, according to Belinda. What could they have done for their father's kingdom if they hadn't focused on themselves, and punishing Belinda for being firstborn and the heir?

"That's on my list of questions, once we get home," Belinda said, when Merrigan shared her thoughts. "I think we're going to find a very clear pattern once we figure out the right questions to ask. Many more people like Nanny Tulip, sneaking into royal nurseries and libraries and gardens, twisting all that magical potential, keeping it from growing."

"Keeping it from taking root and tapping into the majjian springs," Bryan said. "Is this happening elsewhere in the world, or just Armorica?"

"I can write to my friends at the Bookish Mermaid," Merrigan said, thinking aloud. "They have contact with seafarers around the world." She shuddered. "Part of me hopes this is only happening here, that the plot to control all magic hasn't grown far enough to leave Armorica's shores."

"The question is how to find a way to stop them."

"We can't just stop them, we have to reverse what they've done. I tried to forget the curse put on me, that day I demanded magic to support my lie. But with majjian springs drying up ... I fear it will be too late for her to be any help."

"Who?" he asked and reached to take hold of her hand.

Merrigan caught her breath. Just a simple touch was so comforting. Her dignity as queen of Carlion had denied her even that, and she could throttle both Leffisand and Nanny Tulip for it.

"Clara, the seeress who cursed me. Part of me wants to go running to her for advice, for some insight. Another part of me argues that if a seeress didn't see this problem, then she isn't really that insightful and powerful, so what use is she?"

"What if people like her were the first targets?" Belinda said. "She is Clara of the Pools because her visions come from the water. If the water is tainted or cut off, then she loses her insight, she can't see around the world, she can't see anything."

Belinda took regular breaks from reading and making notes. Then their small group discussed the references to different kingdoms and the queens' gardens and the tiny changes that hadn't been visible until they grew numerous enough to become a pattern. Bib and Crystal also searched the books Bergomass had given Belinda. They kept her busy making notes of pages to study and patterns they had harvested, and requests for all sorts of magical texts to look up when they encountered caches of magical books. There were several hubs of learning for majjians scattered across the continent, all linked to deep majjian springs. Those locations were unknown to ordinary folk, and were supposed to be neutral territory, where all majjian folk could come to do research. The problem was that if the majjian springs were being attacked, then perhaps those deeper springs and the archives of learning might be damaged in some way. Possibly even fade away or become forgotten.

Merrigan searched memories of her childhood, before her mother died. The best ones were touched with a sense of wonder, centered on the queen's garden. She wasn't surprised when her dreams were filled with garden memories she hadn't thought of in years. They were equally divided between Viridian, the prince of frogs, who had been her friend, Honk, the ugly little duck who had been her constant companion, until her own nastiness had driven him away, and the thorns that had seemingly sprung up overnight after her mother died.

Muted honking echoed through the chilly air two mornings after that breakthrough discussion, waking Merrigan abruptly. She choked on a mixture of tears of regret and an aching need to call out to Honk and beg him to come back. All that fled when she realized Belinda wasn't curled up in the blankets next to her, in the little tent the soldiers put up for them. Panic had her scrambling out of the cozy nest of blankets and into the icy wet filling the air. The late winter weather couldn't settle between sleet or snow. She ignored the threat of ice coating her face and hair as she searched for Belinda.

While they were preparing for their journey, Belinda had begun walking in her sleep. It was one thing for her to creep through the orphanage warehouse in her bare feet and nightgown. She was safe there. It was another thing altogether to wander away from their camp. True, Bryan slept under a blanket overhang attached to the front of their little tent, and soldiers guarded them, and she wouldn't go far. Yet they were in unfamiliar country now. Brigands and highwaymen might be waiting for a chance to sneak into the camp and steal something. Or someone. If they knew two princesses rode in this company, what would they do or risk for the sake of profit?

Merrigan nearly raced past Belinda, seated by the fire, scribbling so madly in her journal she left spots of ink in her wake.

"Are you all right?" She barely managed to soften her tone.

"Sorry." Belinda sounded distracted and never looked up. "Too many ideas in my head. Didn't mean to wake you."

"You didn't." Merrigan sighed and settled down on the folding camp stool next to her friend. "I dreamed about Honk again."

In answer, more honking echoed through the sleety, dark sky overhead. It sounded much closer and clearer than the haunting call in her dreams. Merrigan shivered and looked upward, just in time for a gust of sleet to slap her. She wiped her face and tugged the blanket she still clutched up around her shoulders.

"Is there anything in that amazing, depressing book of statistics about the effect on swans?"

Now Belinda looked up. She paused in reaching to dip her pen in the inkwell and frowned. "Not that I can remember ... Why?"

"In Seafoam, the swans returned to the queen's garden after the frogs did. Their song haunted me. I woke a few times in tears. I dreamed but couldn't remember anything other than an awful feeling of regret. That achy, sort of sick feeling you get when you know you've done something horrid. You can't remember what you did, and you don't want to remember because you don't want to admit you've been so stupid and yet ..." She sighed. "What sort of magic is involved right this moment, to make swans fly in the winter? What sort of magical healing mission are they on, to be out and about now?"

"Healing," Bryan said, joining them. He held out Merrigan's cloak and gave her a teasing-scolding look until she wrapped it around herself and gratefully tugged up the hood.

"Thank you. I'm a much nicer person, but incredibly flighty. Is it really such a good trade?"

"When you're worrying about everyone else around you, it's easy to be distracted." He huffed a little as he donned his cloak and looked around their camp once before settling next to her.

Merrigan flinched, realizing the soldiers were stirring. Certainly they deserved every moment of sleep they could get, and now it appeared she had caused a ruckus and started their day sooner than usual. Any moment now, that incredibly talented Corporal Gorm would plop himself down next to the cooking fire and begin to assemble another one of those delicious meals he managed with the simplest ingredients. He had blushed and stammered the other day, when she asked if he would teach her to cook and let her help him. Merrigan hadn't been thinking about contributing to the comfort of their small traveling party, but about a dream she had. She and Bryan had retreated from the world and lived in a cozy little cottage, with no royal duties, no courtiers to deal with, no problems, just the two of them in simple solitude and bliss. She had thought about that dream and realized that if it were just the two of them, meaning no servants, she would need to learn to keep house. Learning to cook seemed like a good first step. She hadn't been thinking about her traveling companions at all until Gorm stammered and thanked her, and Bryan gave her that admiring look that made her melt inside.

Captain Garan joined them and offered some useful information. He had grown up near a sheltered valley full of streams and ponds where swans congregated in the winter. He had learned much from watching the swans, their habits and interactions.

"You're right, Mi'lady," he said. "Something's afoot if swans are stirring so early in the season."

"Has anyone thought to consult Bib and Crystal?" Bryan said.

"It might be wiser to wait until we're on the road again, with the noise of the horses slogging through the mud to muffle your voices."

Over breakfast, they discussed their dreams. That had become a habit, just on the chance that something they had discussed during the previous day had crystalized into a usable idea, or more questions to investigate. Merrigan squirmed a little when she had to admit her dreams included Bryan's visits to Avylyn when they were children, and how she had been so cruel to Viridian and Honk.

Several times during the discussion, she could have sworn she heard comments between Crystal and Bib. Fragments of words. A hint they were excited yet refusing to share what interested them. It was quite vexing, and she let it irritate her more than it should. She retreated to the clearing that had been set up with a bucket and blankets strung along branches for privacy, to give herself a private scolding. She took far too long, because when she emerged, she found Bryan was waiting for her, his face unreadable in the shadows of his cloak's hood. Merrigan braced herself for a scolding she had probably earned over the last few days.

That faint echo of swan honking overhead grew louder, as if the swans might finally drop through the gray, swirling cloud cover and come to land on the road. Was there a pond nearby, or a stream? Just how many swans were flying overhead, that the sound of their honking never seemed to fade away?

"Do you know what makes me grumpy the most?" he said, as she paused a half-dozen steps away from him.

"You're never grumpy."

"I'm grumpy all the time, because I feel like I should be properly courting you, and that's hard to do with escorts and scholarly discussions and our two friends listening in all the time and offering advice."

"Courting ..." She choked on what would be unladylike laughter, ragged with relief. "Bryan, you don't need to—"

"Yes, I do." He caught hold of her arms just above her elbows and pulled her up against him, close enough their hoods nearly touched, enclosing them in shadows. "I want us to have long walks where I come up with witty conversation that makes you laugh and tricks you into thinking I'm the wisest, most clever man in the entire world."

"There. See? Waste of time. I already think that, so —"

She squeaked as he lifted her so her toes nearly left the ground, and kissed her. Softly, gently, lingering, until she felt his pulse in his lips, until their hearts raced in perfect harmony. She managed to lift her arms and cling to him. When he ended the kiss, he tucked her head under his chin and wrapped his arms around her. Merrigan thought she could happily stand here like this all day. Who needed witty conversation? Although, a few more kisses would be nice.

"Every time I think about kissing you, I get angry." His voice rumbled in his chest right under her ear.

"Why?"

"Because Belinda is always there, and I feel guilty for being so happy. You're right here, close enough to kiss, and she's fighting not to despair over Bayl. And I feel guilty for not worrying right then about my brother and what those two hags might have done to him. I don't like feeling guilty, and I resent the big bite it takes out of being so happy that you're … you're mine."

"Well, don't forget that you belong to me, too. Fair's fair," she offered, wishing she could be witty and wise.

A long, raspy honk filtered down from directly overhead, making her flinch. How close was that swan? The heaviness of the air, the threat of sleet, the grayness that kept sunrise from reaching them, made all sounds muffled and hard to distinguish.

"What worries me the most is that part of me refuses to believe it's that easy, that we'll always be this happy."

"There was nothing easy about getting to where we are and what we have now." She fought down a need to laugh that threatened to turn into tears. "Bryan, how much time have we lost, how much time did I waste? Stolen from me, from us, by Nanny Tulip." She pushed away enough to lean back and look up at him. "I loathe her with such heat and fury that I never felt for anyone or anything. And that's saying something, because I was a truly selfish, nasty, vindictive little royal brat. I don't know how you can love me at all. You really don't know me." She caught her breath. "So maybe you're right. How can we be so happy? It can't last."

"And that's why we need to court each other. My mother and father always warned us to be careful of the kind of love that seems like a magical gift, easily bestowed, created by a spell. They said we needed to find someone we could argue with, and someone we could like when all the magic had worn out and faded away. We need roots."

"And that's also why Bergomass was right. We need to wait. In case after all the riding and talking and fighting for answers and breaking the sleeping curse on Sylvanglade we discover ... we're really not going to be any good once the quest is over."

"You keep making me fall in love with you." He brushed his fingers across her cheekbone, then frowned and tipped his head back. "Is that honking getting louder?"

"My lord and lady?" Captain Garan stepped into the clearing. "We're ready to mount up. Just a last few ..." He gestured beyond them, at the clearing that had been set up as the privy.

"Yes, of course." Bryan released Merrigan. He waited until the captain turned, then bent down and stole one last, quick kiss. Merrigan clutched at the front of his cloak, trying to prolong it, but the impression of something large dropping down on them had her stepping back, dodging, raising her arms to protect her head.

With a triumphant, rasping honk, a silvery-gray swan swirled down into the clearing and settled two steps away from Merrigan. The big eyes sparkled and the elegant head shook from side to side. The swan extended its neck, hissing, when Bryan put himself between it and Merrigan.

Then, oddly, the swan turned sideways to them to display a black mark on the left side of its neck where it merged with its muscular breast. Merrigan didn't realize she stepped around Bryan to get a closer look until he extended an arm to block her.

The black mark looked like an hourglass.

She gasped and went down on one knee. The swan honked three times and bobbed its head at her. Merrigan shook her head, then despite knowing this was ridiculous, this was impossible, she had to be dreaming still, she pressed her lips together and honked through her nose.

The swan tipped its head back and honked joyfully, again and again, massive wings spread and flapping so it rose half its height off the ground.

"Honk?" Merrigan's voice broke. "Is it really you?"

"Honk?" Bryan stumbled sideways a few steps.

"Are you all right?" Captain Garan stepped forward with one hand resting on the hilt of his sword.

"The duck?" Bryan asked.

"Honk. You were a swan all this time?" Merrigan burst into tears and held out her arms.

Honk nearly knocked her over as he lunged at her and curved his neck around her shoulders.

"I'm sorry. I'm sorry. I'm so sorry!" she blurted, enough times she didn't even try to count.

The faint honking that had haunted Merrigan for the last few days finally faded away into nothing. That sensation of watchful eyes bearing down on her faded as well. Had the swans been hunting for her, to help

Honk find her? Why had he come looking for her? How? What did it mean? And how was she going to convey to her old friend that they couldn't sit here on the snowy-muddy ground for much longer, hugging and honking and weeping, because they were on a quest and had to get into the saddle and go?

"I can't imagine how you're going to travel with us," she murmured, as she drew back and wiped at her teary cheeks with the back of her glove. "You do intend to travel with us, don't you? You're not going to make me leave everyone and go on some errand or other, to make up for all the stupid things I did, are you?"

Honk scooted back a few steps and bobbed his head from side to side, regarding her first with one large eye, then another. He folded his wings against his sides and conveyed the same sense of interest and understanding and excitement she had imagined she saw in him when he was just an oversized, awkward, scruffy duckling.

"I don't suppose he'd be willing to fly escort overhead?" Bryan stepped up closer behind her and rested a hand on her shoulder.

The swan turned his head, shifting his gaze between Bryan and Merrigan.

"Well … among all those amazing magical trinkets in that box, was there anything to translate and let us speak to animals?" he asked after a few moments of the three of them just sitting and waiting.

"Yes!" Merrigan struggled up to her feet, clutching at Bryan's cloak. "You are brilliant." She gave him a quick kiss, then beckoned for Honk to follow and hurried through the trees to return to their camp.

The magical box had been a gift from Morton, the chancellor of Seafoam. When Merrigan reached their camp, she found Belinda sitting by the fire, bent over the box. Her face wrinkled in distaste as she reached into it.

The problem and the blessing of the wooden box was that it could hold anything and everything. The pile of magical trinkets and useful items that could be stored in it was nearly endless. Among the many items Merrigan and Bib had discovered was a sleeping cap that made the wearer fall asleep and never wake up until the cap was turned inside out, and a ring that let her understand all the birds in the northern half of Armorica. The sleeping cap made it possible to imprison Belinda's two wicked enchantress sisters in the box for the long trip to their father's kingdom. Merrigan felt a flash of pity for Belinda, having to work around her two sisters to find whatever she was searching for.

"The problem is that I don't know which ring you need," Belinda said, raising her head from her task. "Crystal was watching you and told me…" Her eyes widened at the sight of Honk. Merrigan admitted he was a rather large swan. How had she ever made the mistake of thinking he was a scrawny, rather ugly duck? Blame whatever malign influence Nanny Tulip had been inflicting on her?

"How many rings did we find before?" Merrigan stepped up and exchanged places with Belinda in front of the box. She didn't look forward to the search, because none of them had needed to look inside the box since Bryan had imprisoned Bithia and Barbarina. They had been shrunk down by the box to the size of dolls.

Seven, Mi'lady, Bib answered. *Swans are nomadic, so perhaps both rings for talking with birds will help you talk to him. If so, then two of you can hear and talk to him at one time.*

"Yes, but what makes those two rings different from the others in this box? I don't particularly care to pick up the one that lets me turn everything I touch to gold." A nasty little snicker escaped her, at a sudden mental image of accidentally turning Belinda's two sisters to gold statues. It would serve them right, but it wouldn't help find Bayl.

They resorted to settling Bib, open, on Belinda's lap. When Merrigan found a ring, she put it on the book's page and he identified the ring. Belinda made wrappers of paper from the back of the blank journal, to write the name and function of each ring. Bryan suggested using a bit of stickum to attach the rings to the inside of the lid of the wooden box, so they wouldn't have to search if they needed them later in their journey. The third and fifth rings were the bird language rings.

"Hello, Honk, can we talk now?" Merrigan said softly, after slipping one ring on her thumb.

Images spilled into her head, so rapidly, so tangled, she found herself half-collapsed in Bryan's arms as he struggled to get her upright again.

The swan honked happily and bobbed his head.

Yes, yes, yes, we can talk now. I can help you. You can help. She needs help. They are angry. She deserves their anger, but she doesn't know what a mess she made and how much she has hurt them.

"Who?" The urgency spilling from Honk had Merrigan striding away. "Captain Garan, we must hurry! Someone is in danger."

CHAPTER THREE

Honk took a perch on the back of Merrigan's horse as their traveling party hurried to mount and climbed the short incline back to the road.

"I understand him." Bryan held up his hand, displaying the other bird ring.

Captain Garan gestured for them to take the lead, then maneuvered so he and Bryan bracketed Merrigan as their traveling party picked up speed. They were at one of those long gaps in the merchant road where there were no towns or inns or even waystops, so there was no other traffic at that time of the morning. No one to go around. No curious or belligerent or bored travelers to get in their way or try to follow them.

They traveled less than two miles, according to the gouged and weathered and moss-covered stone mile markers. Then Honk had them plunge off the road, following what Merrigan thought was an animal trail. She was grateful Bryan could understand Honk and verify what she heard, because from the deepening frown on Captain Garan's face, he didn't like this. What did he know about this section of the merchant road and the thick forests surrounding it, to make him so grim?

"Is there a reason why there are no villages along the road here?" she asked Garan, when their pace slowed. The hard-packed dirt and the debris of years of falling leaves made for slippery footing under the thin layer of snow that penetrated the thick canopy of branches tangled with dry vines.

"The common people suffer when their rulers make foolish mistakes and need punishing," he said after a frowning pause.

"Meaning?" Bryan said.

Silly bad girl. Disobedient girl. Won't listen and won't learn. Not evil, Honk said, his voice squeaking and clicking.

"How can bad girls not be evil?" Garan mused, when Merrigan translated.

"Children can be bad and not be evil," Belinda offered. "He did say disobedient, didn't he? Won't listen or learn?"

Honk bobbed his head in agreement so rapidly, Merrigan feared he would snap his neck. Her own neck ached from turning constantly to watch him, and her arm ached from reaching back to make sure he wouldn't fall off the horse behind her. The saddle wasn't made for two to share or ride pillion. Swans had magic, but she hadn't thought it would be used for such mundane things as staying on a horse maneuvering down a narrow animal trail in a forest.

"Who is she?" Bryan said. "What does she need rescuing from?"

She's going to ruin it. Not their fault. They wanted to help her. They won, they should be happy and safe, but the arrogant ones changed the rules. They stole the magic. They let the ugly ones back in. They are so close to winning, but she made them angry. Bear angry.

Despite the reputation of swans as majestic and wise, apparently they could be rather bird-brained when they were excited or upset.

"Who changed the rules?" Bryan said.

The ones stealing the water. Who make good girls selfish and mean. Honk stroked Merrigan's arm with his head. *Tricked my girl so she sent me away.*

"Stealing the water?" Belinda said, nearly choking on the words. "Do you think ... drain the majjian springs?"

"Honk, is there a majjian spring, a queen's garden near here?" Merrigan said.

Was. Dry now. Trolls made it sick. Trolls needed the prince. Tried to trick him to marry the troll princess and make her queen. The changers, cheaters, they brought a good girl to break their magic. Followed the rules to break the rules. She saved the prince. They should be happy. The changers took the water and took the troll magic and trapped them.

"Bib, Crystal," Bryan said, reaching back to rest his hand on the saddlebag where the magic book and mirror traveled together, "if there was a castle around here at one time, are there any remnants of books you can contact, to find out what happened?"

Before they could respond, their horses stepped out into a clearing around an odd sort of house. At first glance it looked like a pile of massive stones, partially buried in forest debris. Then a flutter of ragged cloth in a hole in the pile yanked Merrigan's perspective sideways, and she saw it as a curtain. Then she saw another hole with a curtain. A gap in the pile of stones at ground level, blocked with what looked like a wide slab of bark, looked like a door. She caught movement in the air and saw smoke curling up from a pile of stones and mud that could be a chimney.

"Do I smell porridge?" Belinda said. "Oat and nut porridge, with honey, rather than peas porridge?" A smile flickered across her face for a moment. While the shattering of the tracking spell meant she was no longer allergic to peas, she preferred to avoid them.

"Help me?" a tiny voice cried. "Please? They're so mean to me. I didn't do anything wrong. Well, I didn't mean to."

Don't listen to her, Bib said, while Merrigan was looking around the clearing, trying to find the source of the voice.

"Her who?" Bryan said, keeping his voice low. He stood up in the stirrups, trying to see into a tangle of branches and vines in a tree to the right of the clearing. Like an oversized bird's nest.

There are quite a few books in the den or cottage or whatever it is, Bib said. *They're quite relieved to have someone new to talk to, and none of them will shut up long enough for me to make sense. Give me some time to untangle things?*

That girl has come along at just the wrong crucial moment, Crystal said.

"What girl?" Merrigan said.

It's the typical troll trick, the mirror said with a sigh. *You'd better deal with the captain before he finds her and acts all gallant and makes the situation worse. The bears are going to come out any moment, and if someone laughs or if someone tries to shoot them, we're all going to be at the nexus point of several tangled curses and mangled spells going from bad to worse.*

"Stand down, Captain," Bryan said. "No one move, no one do anything, no matter what you see or hear. There's warped magic at work here and we don't want to make things worse." He slid out of his saddle and stepped over to offer Merrigan a hand to slide down.

Honk jumped off the horse, the force of his launch making it grunt and take a sideways step. The swan flew up into the tangle of branches. The branches shook and leaves and snow fell down as he landed on a massive branch that supported the clump of leaves and vines and branches. A dirty little face peered down at them, surrounded by a tangle of golden hair that glimmered despite the shadows.

Glittering bits filtered down through the branches. Merrigan tracked the girl's path through the tree with her gaze and found glittery handprints on the trunk, and indentations in the wood where someone had apparently cut gouges for rough steps.

"She has the golden touch," she said, trying to pitch her voice so only Bryan and Captain Garan heard. While King Auberg and the captain trusted the escort soldiers, she couldn't be sure how they would react to finding a child who turned everything she touched into gold. At the very least, she imagined the poor, dirty little thing shorn bald the moment she got within their reach.

Yes, and the books are in terror of her touching them, Bib said. *She's supposed to wear gloves, but she keeps losing them. Lucinda only has a few minutes at a time when she has hands instead of paws, so making new ones is nearly impossible.*

"What do you mean, she has hands instead of paws?" Bryan asked.

"Sir?" Garan looked around the clearing. "If you don't want the men to hear ..." He gestured at the saddlebag.

"Quite right," Belinda said. "You and your men can leave us to handle this. Surround this clearing but far enough away you can't see us." She glanced at the door of the cave, cottage, whatever this odd structure was. "And hurry, please."

"What is it?" Merrigan whispered, as her friend slid down to the ground to join her and Bryan. She kept her gaze focused on that little face and that amazing, potentially dangerous cloud of golden curls.

They're coming, Crystal said. *Can't those soldiers obey any faster?*

Bryan caught hold of the reins of their horses, likely bracing for something Crystal had shown him. His years with the magic mirror enabled her to put images in his head.

Honk trumpeted and plummeted from the nest where the girl had retreated out of sight again. Merrigan braced for the shock of finding he had been turned to solid gold. She let out a gushing breath of relief when he landed in the snow-dusted clearing beside her, still silvery-gray.

Bad girl. Silly girl. Help her. Take her away. She's hurting them. They're good. They're nice. When they aren't bears.

"Bears?" Merrigan blurted, as the massive sheet of bark for the door swung outward on hinges that looked like coarse rope. A huge, white bear shouldered its way through the opening.

The bear was almost too big for the gap between the boulders and tree trunks and what looked like clumps of mud filling the spaces between them. He took several seconds to come through on all fours and then stand up on his hind legs, so he rose half again the height of the horses' heads.

Oddly, the horses only snorted a few times, but didn't panic, didn't struggle to break free and flee. What did the horses know?

Another bear came out behind the first. The white bear's belly and lower regions were wrapped with sacking, held in place with a belt with a silver buckle. The second bear was glossy brown, and wore a vest and an apron, also of sacking, and what looked like rough attempts at embroidering flowers on the vest. A gold ring adorned the middle claw of her right forepaw.

"They're under some awful enchantment, aren't they?" Belinda murmured. "They're people." She glanced up at the nest where the girl hadn't emerged. "Did she do that to them?"

The brown bear—Merrigan assumed the apron meant she was female—turned to Belinda and let out a moan that sounded not at all bearish. She bobbed her head several times, then gave a grunt and shook her head. What was she saying yes to, and what was she saying no to?

"Well, at least they can understand us," Merrigan said.

Then she choked, near tears for a moment, as a little golden-brown bear cub toddled out of the doorway on all fours and pressed against the mother bear's back leg. His fur was wet and showed signs of having been combed. He wore a diaper and rough little booties on his hind paws, and he clutched what looked like a toy horse. A gold horse.

It looked like it had been made of cloth. The little bear nuzzled the horse and made snuffling noises that sounded like a child's whimpers. Like he was crying. Over a spoiled toy.

Merrigan tipped her head back to look up at the nest where the golden girl hid. "You did that, didn't you? That's why they're angry? You spoiled his toy?"

The white bear let out a creaking growl and bobbed his head. The brown bear bent to pick up the little bear and cuddle him.

"I just wanted to hold it," the girl said in a pouty sort of voice. "It's not my fault I lost my mittens again."

The mother bear barked, her head raised to focus on the nest. Merrigan clearly heard a familiar response from her nursery days, when Nanny Starling and her mother tried to correct her with loving firmness.

"I believe she is saying yes, it most certainly is your fault," she said. "Use some common sense, child. You have hands, they don't. Your golden touch is dangerous. I'm going to make a wild guess that they fed you and sheltered you, and this is how you repay their hospitality."

"Why is everybody always so mean to me?" the child wailed.

"Because you're a brat, and no one has any right to be a brat. I speak from experience!"

Bryan snorted. She glanced at him as he raised one hand to cover his mouth. Merriment danced in his eyes. She choked, fighting her own laughter.

"I have to wonder ..." Belinda curtseyed to the three bears.

The mother and father bear managed a bow and curtsey with a surprising portion of grace, despite their bulk and the fact that bear bodies simply weren't designed for courtly gestures.

"Did someone turn her into a brat on purpose?" Merrigan mused. "Did someone give her the golden touch and send her wandering through the forest to create havoc?"

"Please excuse our bad manners," Bryan said, bowing. "May we be of any help?"

"You can take us out," Bib said. "I doubt these enchanted bears will be at all surprised to see a talking book and mirror."

The white bear bowed and gestured through the door into the rock pile cave cottage.

"No, I think it might be wiser if we stayed out here and made sure your golden menace doesn't climb down and escape." Bryan gestured up at the nest. It rustled and golden bits of bark and glitter rained down.

"Bother," Merrigan said. "We need to take precautions ... Pardon me, but just how extensive is her golden touch?" she said, nodding to the mother bear. "Is it just her hands, or anything that touches her skin?"

After a moment of thought, the mother bear raised her paws and fanned her claws for a moment. Merrigan took that to mean just her hands.

"Good. That's some measure of safety. I have a spare pair of gloves. Fancy ones I intended to save for dressy occasions." She stepped over to her horse and began digging through her saddlebag. "My hands are rather rough and no one would believe I was a princess the way they ..." She sighed and was relieved when Belinda just smiled and didn't look exasperated with her. "I'm still reforming. Be that as it may ... Honk, would you take these gloves up to her? Child, I want you to put these gloves on and keep them on, and then I want you to climb down. It's very rude to force people to keep tipping their heads back and strain their eyes to try to see you."

She found the gloves and tried not to sigh too much at the loss of them. They were a gift from King Auberg, light and stretchy and decorated with fine embroidery so they looked like her hands were enclosed in lace. The kindly old king had understood how her hands were such a concern for her, though she tried not to be vain. Merrigan was proud of all the things she had learned to do for herself since Clara had cursed her to reform her mind and heart. At the same time, she truly did miss her pale, graceful hands that had inspired poems of adoration.

Granted, Leffisand had likely intimidated those poets into praising her. Did he ever truly love her? She suspected his had been the love of a craftsman for his creation. Not the way Bryan loved her.

"Woolgathering isn't helping us," she scolded herself under her breath. She shook her head and handed the gloves to Honk.

"Child, you come down here right now and let's fix this problem," Belinda said.

"My name isn't Child," the girl called, her voice even more pouty.

"What is it, then?" Bryan looked at the bears.

The white bear shrugged. The brown bear put down her cub and sent him toddling back into the cave cottage with a shove to his backside.

"They called me Gilda, but that's not my name."

"Who called you Gilda? Certainly not the bears," Belinda said.

"No. The mean old grannies who took me away when my hair turned gold." The child made some grunting noises. The nest shook. Merrigan held her breath, half-expecting it to fall apart and the child to plummet down through the branches.

She had the awful feeling all three of them would hesitate to rush to catch her, in terror she would touch them and turn them to gold.

Honk glided back down and honked softly. *Done. Smart. My princess is smart. Good girl now. Yes?*

"Yes, Honk, I hope I'm a good girl now," she whispered, and caught her breath against a sob when the swan rubbed her hip with his head.

"When did your hair turn gold?" Belinda said.

"I was thirsty! Nobody said why I shouldn't drink it. They just said nobody could drink it. Nobody ever tells me anything!" A louder rustling of leaves followed the petulant words.

Merrigan noted the falling leaves and bits of bark weren't gold now.

A golden shoe appeared through the shadows and branches overhead. Then a second shoe. Then a ragged dress streaked with gold, and dirty leggings. The girl clambered backward down the rough ladder cut into the massive trunk of the tree. She was tiny, but the way she spoke made Merrigan doubt she looked her age.

"What's your real name?" she asked, when the girl had climbed down about a quarter of the way. She noted that the gloves, which were large on the child and went halfway up her arms, weren't entirely gold. Was that a good thing?

"Coral."

"Why did the grannies take you away? Who did they take you from?" Belinda said.

"Nasties." The girl sniffled and rubbed her face.

"Who was nasty?" Merrigan tried to make her voice softer.

The bears stood in their doorway, watching.

"Everybody is nasty. My stepmother died and her new husband sold me to troubadours and they got nasty when their magic didn't work on me. They left me with a hedge witch and she got nasty when I drank the water and when my hair turned to gold the mean old grannies got in a big fight with her. I ran away and they caught me and—" Coral burst out in a shrieking sob and threw herself down on the snowy ground.

"What troubadour magic didn't work?" Bryan said, raising his voice.

"I don't know! They liked me because I'm little and my stepmother said I was half-faerie, and they wanted to put wings on me and have me fly around while they sang, and they were angry that I couldn't sing and every time someone tries to work a spell on me it doesn't work!"

"That could be it," Crystal said. "If she's a halfling, she could be immune to many spells. Or worse, there's something in the human side of her heritage that warps the magic, so both sides of her heritage are constantly fighting."

"Which explains why not everything she touches turns entirely to gold," Merrigan said, nodding. "Well, that's half an explanation. What did the mean grannies want with you?"

"Magic water," a low, grumbly sort of voice answered.

All of them turned to stare at the white bear. Merrigan shivered as she noted changes in him since she last looked at him. After all, it wasn't wise to take her eyes off a bear at close quarters, no matter how much he tried to look and act like a man.

"Oh … you're under a curse. I'm sorry. Bib, Crystal, do we have anything in the box to help them? The entire family is under a curse?"

"Curing. Takes time," the white bear said, nodding. Then his eyes, which looked much more human now, narrowed as he turned to look at Coral. "She breaks things."

"The books have been telling me the whole convoluted story," Bib hurried to say. "They ran afoul of the trolls trying to take over his kingdom by forcing him to marry their princess. Some hedge witches trying to become faerie godmothers made a bargain with the trolls just as Lucinda was fulfilling the conditions to break their spell on Prince Corwen. They were both turned into bears. Depending on the phases of the moon, they cycle between three-quarters bear and three-quarters human. They must entirely break the curse before their son, Larch, is a year old, or they'll be completely bears for the rest of their lives."

"What can we do to help?" Bryan said.

"Take." Lucinda, the brown bear, pointed at Coral. "We tried to help, but she breaks things. Anger ..." She rubbed her paws, furry human hands with claws instead of nails, down her sides. "Makes us more bear."

"They have to be as much human as possible," Bib supplied. "Dress and eat, read and cook, all the little tasks. Play with toys. Sing."

"Oh, and Coral makes it harder for them to do those things when she breaks ..." Merrigan caught her breath. "When she breaks their toys and makes it hard to read books because the pages are turned to gold, and turns their food to gold, so they can't eat human food and ... Bib, there isn't some sort of cure for things turning gold in that box, is there?"

"No, but there are several books written in an obscure tongue that Corwen retrieved from his castle library before it entirely vanished inside the cave. They have the answer, and I can translate. That should help," the magic book answered.

"Turned me into a bear before I learned that language," Corwen said, and offered a grin that showed too many bear teeth. There was something pitiful about his expression, rather than frightening.

"Do they have to do it all on their own?" Belinda asked. "If we left clothes and plates and other things with them, would that help? If our soldiers made the cave more of a house, would that help?"

"What about helping me?" Coral whined.

CHAPTER FOUR

Merrigan nearly laughed, to realize they had all forgotten about the child. Yes, Coral was a brat, but life had certainly been hard on her. Merrigan wouldn't be at all surprised to learn Coral had deliberately broken things in the bear family's home, in plain and simple spoiled brat nastiness, despite the bears trying to help her.

"How old are you really?" she asked. "You look like you're maybe six at the most, but I doubt that's your true age."

"Fourteen." Coral sighed and leaned back against the tree and raked her hands through her hair, which didn't want to behave like normal hair when brushed away from her face.

Merrigan winced, guessing how it had to feel to have stiff gold wire for hair. Finding a reversal spell to at least fix her hair would greatly improve the girl's temperament. Then they could figure out what to do with her on-again, off-again golden touch.

"What did you mean by magic water?" Bryan said, turning back to Corwen.

"Lodestone. Magic water. Majjian springs." The white bear gestured at the cave house behind him, and then down at the ground. "The trolls and the old women tried to break the protective magic in the queen's garden and dry up the majjian spring. They needed me to marry their princess, to make her my queen. Give her power over the garden. The old women tried to trick Lucinda into putting the entire contents of the pool into a pitcher, the day we married. They fought and she overheard them, so we closed the doors of the garden to hide it from everyone. The old women got angry and cursed us. Little by little, everything has vanished. We had more days when we were nearly human, until she came." He bared his teeth at Coral, and his features shifted back into bear.

Then sorrow and visible pity touched his eyes and softened them and made them human again.

"It's not her fault," Lucinda said. "Those old women stole her to use her to hurt people. Who wants to be used as a weapon?"

Merrigan shuddered. Wasn't that what Nanny Tulip had been trying to do with her?

"Yes, but she still chose to be a brat," Merrigan said. "I'll wager you enjoy it when you turn something to gold and ruin it for others, don't you?" she said, turning to Coral. "Tell the truth. It helps to tell the truth and be sorry for other people instead of just yourself all the time. You enjoy making everyone else just as miserable as you are, don't you?"

Corral pouted for a few moments, then utter weariness softened her face and she closed her eyes and nodded.

"It doesn't help to be stuck looking like a six-year-old when you know you're nearly a woman grown, and no one will take you seriously," Belinda offered. "I got rather snippy when I was twenty and looked like I was twelve. Is there any way to … I don't know, drain some of that magic that's keeping her childish, and help her grow up?"

"Send her to Bergomass and our orphanage friends," Bryan said. "I'll wager Coral hasn't had any real friends her own age. If she's surrounded by other children, and she has nice parents for a change, that might help. Or at least soften the magic binding her."

"I'll have to consult the other magic books," Bib said, "but that sounds like a workable theory. If we can make some progress in turning back the bear aspects of the house, more of the magic books should wake up, so I can consult them."

Captain Garan had the sense not to come rushing in when Bryan called for him to join them in the clearing. He did have his sword out, and his sword hand shook a little the first time Corwen spoke. Merrigan's admiration for the captain grew stronger when he shook off his astonishment and focused on the challenge ahead of them. How to help the bears make some large steps forward in becoming human again? How to get Coral to the orphanage and under Bergomass's supervision without someone realizing she had the golden touch and trying to take her?

While the soldiers got to work on the large job of turning the mound of rocks into a visibly human home, Merrigan and Belinda took Lucinda and Larch aside to deal with the task of dressing them as people. Bear paws and claws weren't made for sewing, but Lucinda had made wonderful progress in fashioning clothes for her family from what they had on hand. Corwen had taken to traveling to the nearest villages to scavenge for worn out items such as broken dishes and cooking pots and discarded sacks and rags. On the days when his hands were more human, he had tried to make repairs.

They were limited to taking castoffs because they had discovered that stealing reversed what little progress they had made. Every time they slid backward toward bear bodies and minds and hearts, they forgot themselves and often broke their few possessions, which set them back even further.

"And then Coral came along, and you made wonderful progress by helping her, but then she started breaking things, and that started you sliding backward again," Belinda theorized.

Lucinda nodded. Huge tears spilled down her furry face. Merrigan couldn't recall if bears were able to cry, but she was willing to wager that tears were a good sign of progress toward being human again.

Bib, do you have a moment? I have an awful idea, and I don't want to speak it aloud, Merrigan said, as she and Belinda worked on combining several suits of clothes to fit the bear family.

Are you wondering about Coral's mean old grannies? the magic book asked after a pause long enough to make her impatient.

Exactly.

The awake books noticed when Coral arrived. They heard women's voices outside the cave, and the sound of slapping, and the girl crying.

Then they did drop her here deliberately, to destroy the bears' chances of becoming human again. Why?

There's a wet spot, far back in the cave. Just a tiny trickle, but the scent of magic is strong. If Corwen and his family entirely lose their humanity, then the magic holding this jumble of rocks together into a home will disperse and the cave will collapse, revealing the source of the water.

It's a majjian spring, isn't it?

What's left of the majjian spring and the queen's garden.

~~~~~

Coral's temper improved greatly when they explained their plan. Once they got the bears on a more human footing, they would send her to the orphanage and to Bergomass to try to cure her of the effects of drinking the golden touch water. When she understood that the sooner the bears were dressed and their home repaired, the sooner she could be on her way, she threw herself wholeheartedly into helping. Her body was still that of a six-year-old, and her fingers didn't take well to sewing. She ran errands and helped keep little Larch out from under everyone's feet by playing with him. She nearly purred like a cat when Belinda, with her hands gloved, brushed and braided her unruly, wiry hair. Merrigan wondered if part of the child's nasty temper was that she didn't dare let anyone touch her. How much did the child ache to just be held, to have a hand to hold, and a shoulder to cry on?

Captain Garan had his doubts over the plan to send her to Alliburten. Not putting the girl into the care of the warehouse orphanage parents but choosing soldiers to escort her. He only had twelve soldiers to act as escort for the three royals in his care. Reducing that number meant fewer watchful eyes as they traveled, and longer turns at sentinel duty when they made camp at night.

And there was the temptation of a child with the golden touch. He trusted his men, but they had only been tested and proven in battle, not with the lure of great wealth.

"We're only two days over the border of Williburton," Bryan reasoned, when they discussed the dilemma around the campfire that
~~~~~

evening. "Perhaps the wisest course of action would be to turn back." His mouth twisted, as if those words had been difficult to say. "I'm sorry, Belinda. I know every delay in getting some kind of answer from your sisters has to hurt—"

"Don't pretend it doesn't gnaw at you, either." Belinda patted his hand and tried to smile. "Perhaps Bergomass will have made some progress and he'll have suggestions for interrogating them about Bayl, and we won't have to wait until they face Father."

~~~~

Shortly after midnight, a soldier on sentinel duty encountered a troll trying to sneak into the bears' cave home. The ruckus brought Corwen out in full roar, fangs bared. He ripped the troll out of the hands of the two soldiers who caught it, and smashed the ugly, foul-smelling creature to the ground. The struggle not to bite the troll's head off was visible on the bear prince's face, and his fur dripped with sweat.

"What do you want?" he finally said, after fighting for calm.

In the shadows and flickering light cast by the torches, Merrigan could have sworn the bear face had flattened and seemed less furry, and gained some cheekbones and a higher forehead.

The troll squeaked and wriggled and whimpered, and turned to her and Belinda with a pleading look that was almost pitiable. Merrigan made out "pretty ladies" and "nice ladies" and "feel sorry." The ugly, slimy, hairy, rotten-smelling thing was begging her and Belinda for sympathy.

Then Coral came from behind them and stepped between her and Belinda, rubbing her face sleepily. A whimper escaped the girl that was part fear, part disgust, and she pressed her face into Merrigan's cloak, leaving a smear of golden dust in the sturdy fabric.

The troll's expression shifted from pitiful to avarice. He reached out both hands, as if he could make Coral come to him.

"Get her away," Corwen growled.

Merrigan didn't have to be told twice. She picked up Coral and hurried her away, out of the clearing, back toward the wagon and the soldiers' side of the camp.

Bryan and Corwen and Captain Garan didn't have to wait long for the troll in its greed and fear to snarl and spit its thoughts at them. And confirmed all their suspicions.

Coral had been dropped on the bears' doorstep to wreak havoc in their home and set them further backward in their struggle to become human again. When they were fully bears, the trolls intended to come hunting and feast on bear meat. When Prince Corwen and his family were dead, the ground under the collapsed cave home would burst open and the foundations of the magic in this lost kingdom would crack. Or so they had been promised. Merrigan had her doubts about the majjian springs
~~~~

being so easy to uproot and control. When the old women took away the kernel of the majjian spring, Coral with her golden touch would belong to the trolls, to make them rich. Supposedly.

Prince Corwen's restraint in dealing with the troll did indeed go a long way in pulling him and his family back toward their humanity. In the morning, when everyone gathered for breakfast, all three bears were much smaller, their faces a rather lumpy combination of bear and human, and their head fur had changed color. Merrigan reflected that it was good she and Belinda had worked so hard to create full suits of clothes for them, to protect the modesty of their restored bodies.

Coral had nightmares that night, apparently spawned by things she had overheard. She had a nasty habit of sneaking and hiding to listen to conversations. Belinda woke up to cuddle the girl, dry her tears, and have a heart-to-heart talk. When the bears came out for breakfast, Coral met them with a curtsey and a stammering, tearful apology. She knelt and wept more over the rag horse that had been turned to gold and promised little Larch she would learn to sew and try to make him a new one.

One tear dropped on the nose of the golden horse. It hissed. Another tear dropped, and a soft chiming rang through the clearing. Several more tears, more chimes, a few tendrils of smoke. Larch dropped his horse, backing away in astonishment to hide his face in his mother's skirts.

The golden horse was partially rag again.

Coral stopped crying, stunned at what her tears had done.

"Hurry," Merrigan said, and gestured at the toy. "Before your tears dry, wipe the rest of them on the toy, finish the job."

Coral did so, and soon only a few spots remained golden on the horse. Larch huddled behind his mother for a few moments, staring, as she held the toy out to him. Then he hurried forward and snatched it up and flung his stubby, partially bear arms around her. Both his parents gasped in understandable fear. Coral wept more and hugged the little bear prince. Merrigan saw tears in more than a few pairs of stern soldierly eyes as they all settled down to enjoy their breakfast.

The light of day showed more transformations in the bears' home. It looked less like a rock pile and more like a cottage needing repairs. The door was solid wood, rather than a slab of bark that might fall inward with a strong gust of wind. Since their company had decided to turn around and take Coral to Alliburton, they handed over more of their traveling supplies to the family; dishes, pots and pans, blankets, and tools to repair the wagon. Merrigan and Belinda went to help Lucinda put away the new belongings and discovered the rough shelves of branches had transformed into cupboards. The beds were no longer nests of grass and rags but had frames and mattresses.

They were all in good spirits as they headed down the road, back the way they had come. Merrigan held her breath until she saw spots in her eyes, waiting for Clara's curse, prohibiting her from retracing her steps, to tear her away from her friends. Despite the return of her own face, and proof the curse on her had been broken, she was still afraid.

A trickle of irritation ran through her, when she suspected no one had noticed she was afraid. She caught herself before her thoughts turned into that familiar cycle of complaining and blaming. When would her reformation be complete?

When I find Nanny Tulip, I don't know what I will do to her, but she will like none of it, she vowed. *No one has the right to twist a child's heart the way she did mine. There is no justification for it, no cause worthy or noble enough. How I made my family suffer. I deserved far worse than to be called the Brat.*

Mi'lady? Do you need to talk? Bib's voice wrapped around her thoughts, soothing and calming her. She sniffled and wiped surreptitiously at her face, hoping she hadn't been crying. What kind of a self-pitying idiot had she been?

Bib, my dearest friend, thank you. I'll never be alone again, will I?

As long as my pages are bound to my spine, I am here for you, Mi'lady.

Bryan dropped back from the front of the line, where he had been riding with Garan. He reached across the gap between their horses and rested his hand on Merrigan's, on the front of her saddle. "Crystal says I've been neglecting you. I'm sorry."

Merrigan shook her head, sniffling to hold back more tears. She really had turned into a sentimental, sloppy mess. How she had despised girls who wept over what Nanny Tulip had taught her were inconsequential things. There were so many simple, pure, good things she had learned to consider unworthy of her time and consideration, because as a royal she was called to "higher" things. Clara had been incredibly kind with the curse she had laid on Merrigan, humbling her until her heart softened.

"I've left you alone with unhappy thoughts for too long. I'm sorry, Merrigan."

"You have responsibilities. Don't apologize for being a good man." She reluctantly let go of his hand, because it was rather awkward, after all, to make him lean out of the saddle to hold her hand as they rode.

"Looking after you is my highest responsibility." He shrugged, his smile going crooked. "That sounds rather sappy, doesn't it? Well, it's true, no matter how it sounds. Would it sound better if I said it is my favorite new hobby?"

"You are adorable. I'm sorry for all the time I wasted."

"Don't start in on that again. Please."

"My cure seems to be ongoing. It's a good thing we are waiting until we reach Avylyn to marry, because I am nowhere near ready to be a good wife." She blinked hard and tried not to flinch when several tears ran hot down her cheeks.

A figure stepped out onto the road ahead of them. A small, modestly dressed woman, clutching a market basket with both hands.

After the encounter with the bear family, only a fool would assume a woman appearing out of nowhere on a road miles from any village was an ordinary peasant woman. And Captain Garan was no fool.

"May we be of assistance?" he called and stopped his horse a dozen paces from her.

"It is I who can be of assistance to you." The woman tugged back the hood of her cloak, to reveal her pale, wizened face like a dried apple. She smiled, her lips tightly pressed together, and her gaze traveled up the column of their company until it landed on the wagon, where Coral rode next to Gorman. "That child is trouble waiting to fall on unsuspecting souls. She needs containing and taming and training."

"Yes, we know." Merrigan sat up straight and tall to fight the trembling deep inside that tried to fold her into a small package in her saddle. "We have promised to help her."

"You can help her, and yourselves, by handing her over to someone who knows how to deal with troublesome brats before they grow into large problems."

For just a heartbeat, something sour lingered in the air.

Bib, Crystal, do you know what she is? Hedge witch? Godmother?

No answer. She was tempted to reach over to Bryan's saddlebags and flip the top one open to find them. Had they accidentally left the book and the mirror with the bears? Or worse, Coral had played with them and turned them both to useless hunks of gold?

"Before they grow?" Bryan said, speaking slowly. Cautiously.

We are in enormous trouble, aren't we?

"That ... sounds ... reasonable." Captain Garan nodded at the old woman. "It would save us time, wouldn't it, Highness?"

From behind her, Merrigan heard Belinda gasp. Bryan glanced at her, moving his head just a little, as if all his joints had gone stiff. His eyes widened, then he frowned, his gaze going distant in deep thought.

Captain Garan had addressed Bryan as Highness. They had agreed before they started their journey, they would not reveal their royal blood or their quest. They would be simply My Lord, and My lady.

Was Captain Garan trying to warn them? Or was he being moved like a puppet, and someone else's words came out of his mouth?

Merrigan shook her head and widened her eyes, to convey to Bryan the peril she sensed. She couldn't seem to connect her head to her tongue, to speak. She felt as if her head were filled with half-frozen honey, slowing her thoughts.

"No." Bryan turned to face the woman. "We are responsible for her."

"But you don't need to be, gallant young prince." Her smile widened, still with her lips pressed together.

Merrigan shuddered, imagining the tight smile hid pointed teeth.

"We made a promise, and we won't break it."

"Coral doesn't mind, do you, sweet thing?"

Belinda let out a raspy bubble of laughter. "You don't know her very well, do you? And how do you know her name is Coral?"

"You can't have her." Merrigan felt as if she wrenched all the muscles on that side of her body to reach for Bryan's saddlebags. Warmth streaked from her fingertips up her arm as she fumbled with the flap of the saddlebag and touched the corner of Bib's cover. The thick coldness fled her head with the sensation of coming up out of icy water in a gush.

Well done, Mi'lady! Bib cried.

"Interfering fools!" the old woman snarled. She darted down the column of riders, swinging her basket to hit the horses and make them shriek and rear.

Bryan fought to get his horse back down on all four hooves.

Silence fell over the company. A Fae faded into being, blocking the old woman from reaching the wagon and Coral. She was all shades of green, even her skin, looking more like fresh young plants than the icy gemstones of other Fae Merrigan had encountered. The old woman let out a raspy shriek as she began to shrink. She flung herself at the Fae, barely tall enough to reach her knees. All her kicks and punches didn't even disturb the long, semi-transparent green layers of cloak and dress.

"Enough of you, who won't play by the rules." The Fae bent and picked up the old woman by the back of her collar.

Belinda muffled a shriek and Merrigan flinched when the old woman hissed and her features took on a distinctly weasel look. A forked tongue flicked out between pointed teeth. The Fae shook the weasel woman twice, with a loud crack of her spine, then tossed her high up in the air, where she vanished with a flash of sour yellow smoke.

"What rules?" Bryan's voice was harsh, like he needed to cough and clear his throat.

"Anyone she meets on this particular road are her lawful prey, if they agree to trade with her. If they let their greed control their decisions. She allied herself with the council of hoarders, to have the power to influence her prey so they obey her, unable to choose or think for themselves." The Fae woman shuddered.

Merrigan caught her breath, chilled suddenly by this sign of weakness in a Fae. She didn't exactly have charitable or admiring feelings toward Fae in general, thanks to Nanny Tulip's warped teaching. No matter how she felt, Merrigan expected and needed Fae to be confident and strong, not fearful or suffering revulsion or uncertainty.

"You have done us a great service, by your simple refusal to accept the easy solution, and pausing to think," the Fae woman continued. "How are you feeling now, my friends?" She waved her hand. Bib and Crystal rose out of Bryan's saddlebags and floated toward her.

"Didn't like that at all," Crystal said, her voice not quite as shimmery as usual. "I thought my glass might start softening and rippling in a few more minutes."

"She was trying to make me feel like my pages were on fire." Bib flipped open and his pages rippled in very visible uneasiness.

"Oh, Bib, I'm sorry. How awful." Merrigan reached for the book, then she drew her arms back. She fought a moan, fearing the Fae woman was taking Bib and Crystal from them. Had she done something wrong, and forfeited Bib's guidance and friendship?

"You have come a very, very long way, Princess Merrigan." The Fae woman flipped her fingers, sending the book and mirror back.

Merrigan and Bryan snatched the two magical items out of the air. She clutched the book close.

"Now, as for you, golden child…" She turned to the wagon where Gorman held Coral tight to his side, a sword in his free hand. She grew, so in two heartbeats she stood taller than the surrounding trees.

The soldier flushed bright red, offered a crooked, apologetic smile, and sheathed the sword. He didn't let go of the girl, who clung to his side and half-hid behind him. Merrigan admired him for that.

"The water you drank was stolen from me."

"I didn't know. I'm sorry!" Coral blurted.

"Isn't it amazing how much easier it is to say you're sorry, and to actually be sorry, the more you say it?" she mused. She tipped her head slightly to the right and her eyes narrowed.

Merrigan shuddered, knowing that assessing look. Despite knowing the girl's true age, she still felt as if a great injustice were taking place. Little children were constantly taking and touching and tasting. That was how they learned. She had learned that from living in the orphanage warehouse. A six-year-old could be forgiven, but a fourteen-year-old, not so easily. What could she do to protect Coral?

"Those old women made you thirsty on purpose, and left you alone with the pitcher, and kept telling you not to drink it so you would get angry and drink it, just to spite them. They're very good at twisting minds and hearts to do the opposite of what they know is wise and right." The Fae's eyes sparkled as she turned to meet Merrigan's gaze. "As you yourself know."

"Please, can't you help her?" Merrigan said. "I know I say it too much, but this time it really isn't fair. If she was tricked, then much of this isn't her fault. Yes?"

"Perhaps."

"Please, I don't want this. Can't you take—" Coral gasped as a flash of light erupted out of her, through skin and clothes. It swirled up in the air and condensed into a blinding brilliant golden spark, then shot into the Fae's chest.

The green tint of clothes and hair and skin and eyes deepened, so golden streaks and veins spread through her. Golden wings lifted from her back. Not the butterfly-style wings Merrigan expected to see in Fae, but wide, feathered wings, arched like a hawk's, semi-transparent, so the golden bones could be seen through the glassy feathers.

"Are you feeling better now?" Warmth touched her windy sort of voice. "All you had to do was ask. So many people nowadays demand instead of ask. That makes all the difference in the world."

Coral burst into tears and nodded and grinned between gulping sobs. Her hair was chestnut, her pale golden skin now was milky, dotted with freckles, and her eyes were hazel, not amber.

"Thank you," Belinda said. "She's going to be so much happier now, and probably much safer. Once we get her to the orphanage."

"Oh, turning around won't do. And no, Princess Merrigan, that part of Clara's curse doesn't apply to you anymore."

Merrigan tried not to be irritated by that flicker of amusement in the Fae's eyes.

"I know Coral's family. Her Fae family. They've been very concerned about her but all the trickery and twisting that contributed to her inability to grow kept them from finding her." The Fae woman held out her arms to Coral. "Will you trust me to take you where you'll be safe, and learn to use the magic sleeping in your blood?"

"I have magic?" The girl sat up and blotted her tears quickly on her sleeve. "To do what?"

CHAPTER FIVE

"We won't know until we have you freed from those ugly roots those old women wrapped around you. Those who are finally realizing the danger this land faces have noted the gradual decline in numbers of majjian, who should be helping the people in the territories assigned to them. That, Coral, is the first lesson you must learn as you explore your heritage. Majjians are born to duties and responsibilities. The Unseen who stands above us all holds us responsible. Gifts and powers are given to be used, and they are always stronger and purer and more pleasing to the Unseen when gifts are used for the benefit of others, rather than ourselves. Majjians and magic are increasingly scarce because we are busy patching all the tiny holes that we never noticed until nearly too late. Someone, many angry, judgmental, scheming someones, have been piercing thousands of tiny holes and draining the majjian springs, redirecting them so their waters are stored elsewhere."

The Fae's face twitched for a moment into something hurting and frustrated. Merrigan felt a momentary surge of pity for her.

"We did not realize what was happening, because it was all so tiny, so inconsequential, and we became busy dealing with huge problems that arose out of nowhere. When we traced the roots of the troubles, we discovered that children with magical potential and large parts to play in the future have been warped and twisted from their destined paths for years now. Frogs and swans have been disappearing, their homes going dry. Queens' gardens have been slowly, quietly filling with thorns." She shook her head. "We wasted time, looking for huge, evil causes, while the drain on magic continued and more majjian springs went dry. More people were hurt by our absence. And the more people who learn to distrust and blame majjians, the less freely we can move about and attend to our duties, and the less power we have, if people don't believe in us."

"So you can't just step in and help anymore?" Bryan asked. "You have to be asked?"

"And things like that weasel woman can trick people into giving her power over them?" Belinda added.

"What can we do? You said time is running out? What do we need to do?" Merrigan said.

"Command us." Captain Garan pressed his closed fist to his chest in salute. "Who is the enemy?"

"Oh, brave, loyal, and true." The Fae smiled, spreading warmth over the entire company. "Your part has always been to search and learn for yourselves. I would give you all the clues I could, if I could."

"But you don't know yet," Bryan said.

"We are learning. And every day that choices are made like you have made, to help and to question and to seek the truth and to do right, the tangles are unknotted and the light can penetrate a little further to the center of the darkness, to reveal the faces of our adversaries."

"Do you know what they want?" Merrigan said. "We have ideas, but we could do more to help if we knew for certain."

"They do not agree among themselves what they want, and that is a blessing, the Unseen's grace protecting us. If they were united, then we would be in grave peril indeed. At the base of all their muttering and whispering and complaining, the root is simple. And entirely false. They believe there isn't enough magic to go around, and that makes them angry. They complain about waste, and unworthiness."

"It's just like Bergomass's books say. They want to decide who is worthy," Belinda said. "My sisters were constantly muttering about that, before I had to flee. Bithia and Barbarina are involved in this whole ugly tangle, aren't they? The hoarding of magic, and deciding who is worthy?"

"I believe so."

"Then what can we do?" Bryan said. "Give us marching orders." His voice cracked a little, as if he found it hard to say the words.

"Ah, my brave, generous, noble prince. So determined to do what is right and aching with every sacrifice. I can hear your heart cracking, and your soul apologizing to your brother, so fearful you must abandon him. No, you shall not abandon the quest to find and free him. You must not abandon that quest, because your enemies who twisted your sisters from their destined course, Princess Belinda, and took Prince Bayl, are in league with the ones who worked so hard to keep you, Princess Merrigan and Prince Bryan, from joining your hearts and magical potentials. You have found each other. Do not let anything separate you again. That is a blow that threatens their foundations."

"Should we marry immediately, rather than waiting?" He reached for Merrigan's hand.

"Waiting patiently will give you much strength. And yes, wait for the king's blessing. You must find and open the sealed door of Queen Daylily's garden, bring it back to life, and marry there. The majjian springs connected to that garden touch all the majjian springs of Armorica. Free them, bring them back to life, and begin the final battle and healing."

"So … go on as we are?" Bryan said, after several moments of ringing silence.

"Perhaps." She smiled and held out her hands to Coral. "Are you ready to go to school, little one? Are you ready to meet your family who have nearly despaired of ever finding you?"

"I don't know. I'm scared," Coral admitted, and looked up at Gorman, who she still clung to even though she had stopped crying.

"Ah, there, see how much wisdom you have gained already? And we must find you some new clothes." The Fae chuckled when Coral stood up on the wagon seat and spread her arms, her mouth dropping open in astonishment. Her skirt was above her knees, and the sleeves of her dress barely went past her elbows, and the dress looked tight enough to pop seams.

"We gave away most of our supplies to the bears," Captain Garan said, "or we could clothe her. Should we return to Alliburton and start over?"

"Continue down this road until you find the roses. If they will talk to you, ask politely and they will help you."

Bryan and Merrigan and Belinda hurried to thank her. Merrigan felt a little wobbly with relief that they wouldn't lose days of travel, going back to replenish their supplies. The Fae inclined her head regally, and her features warmed. Merrigan had the oddest feeling that she wasn't used to being thanked. Or perhaps more accurately, she wasn't used to being thanked without having to threaten or frighten or scold someone into having good manners. Merrigan had certainly learned that lesson, both in giving and receiving thanks.

When the Fae beckoned for Coral to come to her, the girl hesitated. Gorman caught her around the waist and lifted her off the seat and jumped down to the ground. She looked up at Honk, who had been sitting quietly on the back of Merrigan's horse. The swan honked softly and leaped down, to waddle over to the girl. She hugged him. Then she laughed and tugged off the gloves Merrigan had given her. They were still golden and crinkled a little.

"Your first lesson, little one." The Fae gripped her shoulders and turned her to face the company. "Always be polite and grateful. Always look for reasons to be grateful. It delays and smothers complaining."

The tiny frown on Coral's face was almost amusing, except that Merrigan had a good idea of the struggle in the girl's mind. What horrid things had those nasty old women done to her? What awful, selfish lessons had they taught her, to warp her inborn magical heritage?

"Thank you for helping me." Coral bit her lip and looked at the ground for a few heartbeats. "Thank you for helping the bears. And fixing the mess I made."

"Very good." The Fae patted Coral's head. "Now, let's see about finding you some proper clothes that will grow with you. I pray the Unseen's blessings on you all in your quest. May you be invisible to your enemies, our enemies ..." She sighed. "Find them and earn the gratitude of our entire land."

She and Coral went transparent for two heartbeats, before vanishing on the cool breeze.

"Well," Gorman muttered, "wasn't that something? What sort of fun will we have, the farther we move along?"

"Anyone who doesn't like this sort of thing happening had better turn back now," Bryan called, standing up in the stirrups. "I suspect this is going to happen quite often, until we untangle the whole mess."

He waited. The soldiers looked at each other, exchanging glances up and down the short line. Then Gorman laughed and saluted the three royals.

"Not on your life, Mi'lord. Might be enough to knock a man off his feet once in a while, but what's the fun of life without some surprises to test his balance?"

The other soldiers nodded and exchanged grins and muttered comments. Bryan and Captain Garan nodded to each other, visibly pleased. In moments, they were turned around, the line straightened out, and they continued down the road the way they had been headed before encountering Coral and the bear family.

"I hope this wasn't the only reason you came to get me, to get us, Honk," Merrigan murmured, glancing back at the swan settled on the back of her horse. "I hope you'll be staying with us for the entire journey."

The swan honked softly and stretched his long neck to rub her arm with his beak.

"I think I will need you there to help me, when we look for the door to my mother's garden." She shivered deep inside, remembering the explosion of thorns that filled the center of the palace of Avylyn, and forced the doors and windows looking down into the former garden to be shut and barred permanently. All because of her. Because of her and Nanny Tulip and refusing to follow the rules.

~~~~

After more than an hour of riding, Merrigan thought she saw brambles filling the undergrowth along the road. She wondered if she simply had thorns on her mind too much. The more they traveled, the thicker the population of thorns of all types. She really didn't know that much about plants, which was sad, and rather embarrassing. After all, she had spent most of her childhood in the queen's garden in Avylyn. She should have absorbed her mother's lesson on herbal lore and the magical properties of plants, like drinking water. But her lessons had ended when her mother died and Nanny Tulip took over her life and trained her mind and soul in selfishness and cynicism and distrust.

That teaching was like the thorns, Merrigan realized. What would it
~~~~

take to rid such complaining and self-pity from her heart?

"Stop thinking about them altogether," she murmured. "But how can I stop thinking about them if I'm constantly telling myself not to think about them?" Her face warmed as she realized she had said that aloud.

Glances to right and left showed Belinda reading and making notes, and Bryan riding ahead of her, deep in conversation with Garan. She glanced over her shoulder, and muffled a chuckle to realize Honk was sound asleep. How did he manage not to slide off the back of her horse, with those hindquarters gently rocking like the tide?

That image got her thinking about her travels on the sea, and the friends she had made. She really did need to write to her friends in Seafoam. Rosa and Quincy, Myles and Elli the mermaid, Dulcibella and Warren, King Devon and Queen Adele, and the Chancellor, Morton. They knew about the damage done by shutting up the queen's garden, and the blessings that had spilled through the tiny kingdom of Seafoam once the royal family took back their responsibilities. Merrigan shuddered at the thought of those nasty women, all with Nanny Tulip's face, going to Seafoam to attack the queen's garden, and steal the refreshed magic. She needed to write to them and warn them.

"Could you take a letter for me, Honk?" she said, more thinking aloud than actually asking the swan. He was asleep, after all. Smiling, she nudged her horse to move up next to Bryan and Captain Garan, and ask them how long of a ride they had to the nearest town. She needed to get that letter written and sent as soon as possible.

That thought fled her mind when she saw the two men pointing at a break in the wall of forest on the left side of the road. A tunnel cut through the trees, formed of a solid arch of thorns, thick enough to keep snow from carpeting the ground. The road was paved with cobblestones, barely visible through a dusty carpet of leaves and dead thorns, and shriveled rose petals.

"I think we've found the roses," Captain Garan said.

"I suppose there's some sort of test we have to pass," Merrigan said, still more thinking aloud than joining the conversation. "The important thing is to be polite and not just rush in. This is their home, after all. Do you suppose they would appreciate some work done here? Pruning and watering and sweeping? Do roses resent being trimmed? Mother always said they were healthier, stronger, if they were pruned regularly, and it was like trimming nails and hair to cut them back."

"That depends on who does the trimming," a thin, rustling sort of voice said from somewhere in the darkness ahead of them.

Bryan and Garan and Merrigan exchanged questioning glances, and she nearly laughed when she realized none of them wanted to take the lead. Probably in fear they would say the wrong thing. At what point did politeness give way to cowardice, and discretion became laziness?

Garan moved his horse up, keeping its front hooves several steps back from the line where road gave way to cobblestones. He bowed from the saddle.

"Good morning to you. Please forgive the disturbance. We were sent here by a Fae. She didn't give us her name, but she was green like springtime, and gold, and she told us to ask for help here, if you were agreeable." He glanced at Merrigan. "If we met your approval. What do you require of us?"

"Well, that's a refreshing change," another voice said. It was much like the first, rustling, maybe two notes lower in the scale. "You soldier types are usually the ones who lunge forward, swinging a sword. Not the right tool at all, when dealing with roses. You, girl, you have some experience with roses?"

"Only what I saw and heard from my mother." Merrigan tried not to bristle at being called "girl." Perhaps that was part of the test. Did roses tend to make everyone prickly? "I fear I am the last person you want to touch you. I violated the rules of the queen's garden and caused the door to vanish altogether, and thorns to overtake the center of the palace."

"Oh, yes, we know all about that. Rose roots travel the length and breadth and depth of the land, much as the majjian springs do. We have heard whispers from the queen's garden in Seafoam, and we grieved when the roses in Avylyn went into their deep sleep."

"Does the entire land know my stupidity and selfishness?" she blurted.

"Just the ones who matter most," another voice, several notes higher, responded with a touch of prickly laughter.

"Can you tell me how to make up for my crimes?"

"It is not a crime to be young and trusting and make honest mistakes," the first voice said. "What matters is that you wish to make amends and you have learned the joy of caring for others. The frogs like you, and the swans speak up for you, and we approve of the awakening roots deep inside you. Continue as you are, and you will someday burst forth in blossoms and grace the world with sweet, healing perfume."

That sounds ominous, Crystal commented. *I wouldn't doubt it means they aren't going to give any more guidance or encouragement than that. We're on our own. At least, until we find someone else more willing to speak clearly.*

Silence rang like a bell from the dark, thorny tunnel. They waited. Behind them, their small traveling party made the usual noises, horses snorting and stamping. Belinda moved up next to Merrigan, and her saddle creaked as she leaned sideways to look around her.

"Excuse me," Belinda finally said, when the four of them looked at each other, with questioning eyes and slight shrugs. "May I ask ... what do we need to do to earn your assistance in our journey?"

"What do you want to do?" the first voice said.

"Your highest priority. We must warn you that your tasks will continue to grow, the further you travel," the third voice added.

"My highest priority?" She shrugged, offered a weary smile, and rested her gloved hands on top of the closed book on her saddle. "I don't really want to, but it is my duty to take my sisters home to face our father, learn how they went bad, who influenced them, make sure my other sisters are safe ... and then find some clue to what happened to Bayl. Although that probably won't please Father at all."

"To do that, we need provisions. If you don't mind assisting us in that matter," Garan added quickly.

"Hmm ... no, not flashy enough," the first voice said.

Merrigan wondered just how many roses were talking to them at one time. She had an image in her head of three or four enormous roses, as big as cottages, sitting in the darkness, their petals moving like enormous, multi-layered lips.

"Flashy?" Bryan looked like he wanted to laugh but wasn't sure that was wise.

"Don't misunderstand us," the second voice said. "We're enormously grateful for the assistance you've given Corwen and Lucinda and Larch. We're part of the castle garden, and we long to see it restored. Those trolls were despicable. Constantly coming here and eating at us, trying to make themselves sweet-smelling and pretty. They've been utterly defeated now. We owe you. Provisions aren't good enough."

"We will do much more and better for you," the first voice said.

A rustling sound rose into a growl. The opening of the tunnel filled with swirling debris and dust and thorns. Long ones, that fit Merrigan's mental image of cottage-sized roses. She imagined those thorns would do more damage than swords.

"Step through." All the roses in the tunnel spoke in unison, commanding them.

"And ... do what?" Garan said, when no more instructions came.

No response. Merrigan sensed a tightening of agitation in the swirling of leaves and thorns and dead rose petals ahead of them. She glanced at Belinda. Her friend nodded, pressing her lips flat together. Belinda tugged up her hood as far over her head as she could, nearly covering her eyes. Hunching her shoulders, she nudged her horse forward, between Garan and Bryan.

The horse didn't hesitate. Merrigan caught her breath, wondering if that whirlpool of debris and sharp, pointy threats was an illusion. Her father had always said that animals had far more sense than humans. Especially when it came to magic. Taking a deep breath, she urged her horse forward, trying to catch up with Belinda, just as her friend's horse stepped into the swirling cloud of darkness. And vanished.

Merrigan closed her eyes and pressed her heels into her horse's sides and bowed her head. Just in case some of that flying debris was real and solid. Behind her, Bryan called her name. Then … silence.

No, not silence. The rustling of the thorns and leaves and dirt stopped. She raised her head and opened her eyes. Her horse moved down a pathway through a snowy garden, following Belinda's horse. She looked around in wonder, seeing the walls and benches half-buried in snow and the shapes of sculptured bushes and trellises and archways. Belinda tugged on her horse's reins to stop it.

"Where are we?" she asked, seeing the stunned, wondering smile on the other princess's face.

"Home." Belinda's voice cracked. "The roses sent us—sent me home."

"Flashy, indeed," Bryan said from behind them.

Merrigan turned quickly enough she nearly twisted herself out of the saddle. Honk bobbed his head and leaped off the back of her horse, launching himself into the sky. His wings sounded like a thunderclap as he flapped hard, gaining altitude to soar over the towering pines that ringed what had to be the palace garden.

"The swan pool is that way," Belinda said, pointing in the direction Honk had gone.

In just a few minutes, the rest of their traveling party joined them, coming out of a shimmering arch in the air that made Merrigan think of a shallow, sun-filled pool set on its side. That shimmering vanished as soon as the last soldier rode through.

"Thank you!" Belinda called. "This is an enormous help. You've saved us days of travel." She shuddered, and her face twisted slightly, caught between tears and excitement. "All right … if nobody else thinks of it, I would like to formally welcome all of you to the palace of Danishoor and the kingdom of Aryslean."

Merrigan exchanged grins with Bryan, then she turned to look around at the garden. It was smaller than the public gardens of her father's palace, but she recognized the style, the feel of a place intended for the royal family and the court to be available to the populace without feeling as if their privacy were being invaded. Sharing such beauty helped remove one of the walls of privilege that, according to her father, often led to ridiculous uprisings. The kind that put self-righteous, destructive people into power, to inflict on everyone else twice as much abuse and injustice as they imagined had been inflicted on them.

A cry rang out from the area of the highest wall and the gates that she assumed led into the palace.

"Is that a good sound, or bad, Princess?" Garan said, glancing at Belinda.

"I'm not sure. It's been so long since I ... well, let's be honest, I ran away. Angry and afraid and sick of always having to be the good girl and put everyone else's dreams ahead of my own." Belinda sighed and offered a crooked smile to her companions. "It feels rather odd, but good, to confess."

"Rehearsal for what you'll say to your father?" Merrigan reached across the gap between their horses to clasp her friend's gloved hand. "I've been practicing my speech in my mind. I have so very much to apologize for. You have very little."

"Other than insisting on true love when very few royals seem to be allowed to have it?"

"Very few people, period, find true love," Bib offered, his voice somewhat muffled by the saddlebag. "You should see the thousands of books I've traded information with, all recording the same sad stories. Magic is strengthened and clarified when true love triumphs."

"Could that be part of the nasty old women's plan?" Merrigan said. "Interfering, making snots out of royals who should find true love to reinforce and purify the majjian springs of their kingdoms?"

"It's a good theory," Crystal offered. "Here they come. I do hope we get a chance to spend some time out in the open, out of these saddlebags. You don't happen to have any magic mirrors in your father's kingdom, do you, Belinda dear?"

"Since magical items weren't on the list for my education, who knows?" Belinda murmured. "Great-Aunt Sophie might have one, but she's been gone for years." She took a deep breath and pulled her shoulders straight, and nudged her horse forward, to put herself at the front of the small group as the gates into the palace swung open.

The first people to come out through the gates weren't mounted, and Merrigan took that as a good sign. Even better, they weren't visibly armed. Someone had taken time to consider that a small group of travelers suddenly appearing in the public gardens without passing through any of the guarded gates had to have some sort of magical help. Unless the situation here in Aryslean had turned incredibly grim since Belinda fled, hopefully the people coming to meet them expected good news.

Merrigan nearly laughed aloud as she realized she was studying the clothes of the men walking at the front of the group as a seamstress, not as a princess assessing the status of the nobles sent to greet them. She had certainly come down in the world. Or perhaps she should see it as learning to see things from a proper perspective?

Belinda let out a cry and swung down from her saddle. Garan hurried to follow her.

A man in the center of the group pushed his way past the others and ran, arms stretching wide. No, that wasn't a man. That was a woman in trousers.

"Hopefully that's a sister," Bryan said, pitched just loud enough for Merrigan to hear.

A man hurried after the woman, a few steps behind, heavyset even discounting the fur coat, and limping slightly. Several others in the group started to follow him. He gestured for them to stay back, just as the woman met Belinda and they embraced, laughing.

"Belinda?" the man shouted, skidding to a stop right in the middle of a small pile of snow. "How? This is good news, but it should be impossible." He spread his arms. "Please tell me this isn't a dream?" His voice cracked with tears, and his shoulders visibly shook.

"What do you want to wager that's King Horace?" Bryan said.

"At least he seems happy to see her," Merrigan said. "Shocked, but happy."

Less than an hour later, they were ensconced in the king's parlor. King Horace sat in an enormous chair that provided room for Belinda and her adventurer sister, Bronwyn, to perch on either side with their father's arms around them. They had had a little difficulty freeing Belinda from the king's embrace long enough to take off her cloak and boots.

CHAPTER SIX

King Horace had long suspected Bithia and Barbarina weren't using their magical abilities to bring Belinda home safely. When evidence indicated they had far more power than their majjian tutors had detected, he had employed several favors owed him to wrap spells around the two sisters to reveal what they were really doing. When the two enchantresses left to hunt for Belinda three months ago, King Horace's majjian friends had used those spells to track the sisters' magical work. When the separation spell had torn away Bayl, and the two sisters had invaded the orphanage warehouse with their cursed apple, the king and his majjian advisors had feared the worst. Especially when several restraining spells they had been weaving around the two sisters incinerated. Chances were good they knew what their father had been doing to block them. All he knew was that a powerful sleeping curse had wrapped around Belinda, and all hope for awakening her had vanished with Bayl.

"We have hope, Father." Belinda patted her father's hand. She turned to Captain Garan, who insisted on staying by the door to the king's parlor instead of taking a seat in the circle with the rest of them. "Captain, Bryan, do you think it's safe now?"

The two men exchanged glances, then nodded. Garan had charge of the enchanted box, keeping it tucked under his arm. He brought it forward and set it on the carpeting between the table where they all sat and the fireplace. He stepped back and glanced to Merrigan and then Bryan, visibly turning everything over to them.

"It's your box," Bryan murmured.

"But it was your idea." Merrigan muffled a chuckle and went to kneel in front of the box and unbuckle the straps that held it closed.

Bronwyn let out a gasp that turned into a decidedly nasty chuckle, when Merrigan brought out first Bithia, then Barbarina, and the two women grew from dolls the size of her hand to their normal size, and just lay there on the carpeting. Snoring. Bronwyn turned to Belinda and wriggled like a little girl one-third her age, eyes sparkling, not at all the trained fighter and explorer and commander. Merrigan suspected that being the sixth of the seven daughters, she had been somewhat put upon by the older girls, and she especially didn't like the two enchantresses.

King Horace tapped a glass disk on the arm of his chair. It shimmered and an answering shimmer appeared in the only open spot in the wall that wasn't covered with either portraits or bookshelves. A hunched, elderly woman with traces of red among her tangled white hair stumbled into the room, holding a book in front of her face with one hand and six more books tight against her side with her other arm.

"Hmm? Oh. Yes. Well." The woman blinked and straightened up a little, visibly stunned by the sight of Belinda. "That's a surprise. A very nice one. How did you manage to escape the nasty tricks those rotters were trying to weave around you? Never mind. Silvy was recording everything for me, so I can catch up later. Weren't you?"

"Of course," a piping little voice responded.

Belinda flinched and sat forward, and Merrigan realized the voice came from the glass disk. Not a glass disk, but a small magic mirror.

"Crystal," she began.

"Already working on it," the magic mirror called from the saddlebag hanging from the arm of Merrigan's chair. "Might I suggest putting all our coins on the table? We'll get a lot more done and spend far less time going over details that don't really need to be discussed."

"Huh," the woman said, turning unerringly to focus on the saddlebag. "Common sense. I like that."

"Usually I do also," King Horace said, after letting out a deep, exasperated sigh. "But could someone explain to me what everyone else seems to understand?" He pointed at his two sleeping daughters. "Start with what we're going to do with them and how long they'll sleep."

By the time Merrigan had Bib and Crystal out of the saddlebag and set out on the table, and the sorceress-scholar Sophie had put Silvy on the table, Belinda explained about the reversible sleeping cap that kept her sisters controlled. Then she explained about the magic box with the odd assortment of magical items that had proven very useful. Then Merrigan had to explain how she came into possession of the box.

Around that time, Belinda's three remaining sisters had heard the news that she was home. They came hurrying in to welcome her with hugs and a few tears and not a small amount of nasty laughter over the fate that had caught up with Bithia and Barbarina. Merrigan was relieved to hear, among all the chatter of the reunion, that Sophie had been working to mend King Horace's relationship with his daughters and protect the magic at the core of the kingdom. She was his great-aunt. That gave her the right to slap some sense into him when he needed it, Horace admitted with a chuckle and a bit of a red face. Soon, the happy reunion settled down enough to let them enjoy a long dinner full of talking and sharing stories.

"Unfortunately, during the time all the nasty influence came to bear on the family," Sophie explained, "I was away from the kingdom, pursuing some studies with a group of like-minded friends."

"It was supposed to be a short trip, maybe five or six years," Horace said, pausing in cutting his enormous venison roast into bite-size pieces. "She was gone so long, I wasn't quite sure it was really her when she finally walked out of her tower."

"Well, to be honest, the door had been sealed up so long and the tower had been rendered invisible so long, quite a few people forgot it was even there," Sophie said with a shrug. Her grin belonged on the youngest of her great-nieces, not someone of her decades. "Surely my stepping through a door that appeared without warning in the wall should have been some proof of my credentials."

"Yes, yes, keep bringing that up why don't you?" Horace muttered. He looked decidedly put-upon, especially when his five daughters chuckled and whispered among themselves. Then he winked at Merrigan and reached over to stroke Belinda's cheek. "We've all had some hard lessons to learn the last few years. It worked in our favor, though, that my girls forgot about Aunt Sophie. Those two schemers didn't expect someone to work against them from the other side of the wall."

"It was still a nasty shock for all of us when their spells unraveled, and some of the tracking and monitoring spells I was using just went up in smoke. And rather embarrassing to realize that some of my spells to try to restrain them and twist their nasty magic to work against them ended up working against us." Sophie shook her head, and a grim, hard expression came through the distracted, scholarly old woman mask she wore. Merrigan shuddered at the thought of coming against her when she was truly angry and determined. "We thought we had failed Belinda. To protect her and undo the magic her sisters were weaving around her. Failed to protect that dear boy who loved her so much."

She nodded to Bryan, apology visible in her eyes. Bryan sat up a little straighter and nodded back, accepting for Bayl.

"We thought Belinda had gone into that nasty, unending sleep, and we were honestly mourning her," she finished, spreading her hands.

"Auntie was trying to decide which of us she should try to train, to awaken the stronger threads of magic in our bloodline," Blossom, the youngest of the sisters, offered. "We theorized that if Bith and Bar had succeeded, then they were going to be heading home soon with some ridiculous lie and try to put themselves in charge."

"While I was testing the girls," Sophie said, taking up the story again, "I noticed something stirring and realized we had been distracted by the fireworks and all the shredding of magic and ... well, we weren't sure what had happened after all." She nodded to Blossom, and Merrigan suspected that the youngest princess would likely end up her student.

"That would be when Merrigan took the cursed apple in my place," Belinda said. "Or more likely, when Bryan shredded the curse when he kissed her."

Several of the princesses let out sighs. Merrigan marked them as hopeless romantics.

"The good news is," the old woman continued, "we might have some clues to what happened to your brother when that nasty bit of confundus spell snatched him away. The really vicious part of a confundus is to give the magic some self-control, so even the majjian who created it doesn't know the end result."

"As in?" Bryan's voice went quiet and hard. Belinda leaned forward, elbows on the table, studying her great-great-aunt while her cheeks lost a bit of their happy flush.

"It snatched the lad up and confunded him, first of all. Tangled his memories so he doesn't know who he is or why he's where he lands, or what he wants or how to get home. Or even if he has a home. Then, if it's really nasty, it will change his face and his voice, so even if he walked in this room in the next five minutes, you wouldn't know him."

She gestured at the door leading to the balcony off the king's study, rather than the door to the palace hallway. Merrigan choked on a chuckle when everyone at the table turned to look at the door. Did they really expect him to appear just because she said he could?

"Then, if the spell is especially nasty, the confundus erases its tracks, so it's nearly impossible to follow the path it scorched through the landscape when it dragged the young man away."

"That strikes me as a waste of a lot of majjian energy," Blossom said, her voice thoughtful. "Wouldn't it be easier to just kill him and leave his body lying where it would do Belinda the most harm? Sorry," she added, flushing, and looking rather startled at her own words.

"Yes, I've wondered that a few times myself," Bryan said.

"We discussed it," Merrigan said, reaching to catch hold of Belinda's hand. "We think, we hope, that they went to so much trouble because something or someone was protecting Bayl, or trying to protect him. And there was still hope of the two of them having their happily ever after."

"You have a great deal of experience with magic and all the consequences and permutations," Sophie said. "Have you considered an apprenticeship, becoming a majjian yourself?"

"No, thank you." Merrigan shuddered. The most she could manage was a thin smile. She definitely couldn't laugh. "I'm not as … as allergic to magic as I once was, but I don't think I will ever reform enough to want to have magic flowing through me."

"My dear, the entire reason you were targeted is because the potential for so much magic resides within you. The power can't help flowing through you. There has to be a great deal of magic within you, sleeping and waiting, to have had the spells and codicils wrapped around you that were used for your reformation. Indeed, what your friends have been telling me, about your theories and the things you have been learning … it supports some theories and suspicions I have been formulating ever since the great unraveling began." Her lips pursed in distaste.

"However, we have to awaken those two snots and interrogate them. From what I've discerned, following their magical trails, it won't be a pleasant task." She shuddered, eyes sparking with distaste. "But it won't take nearly as long or be as difficult as they could hope. They will be quite dismayed at the vast gulf between their estimation of their power and strength and cleverness, and the reality."

With a nod, she gestured at the deceptively plain wooden box with one hand and twisted the wrist on her other hand. The two sleeping women rose off the floor and bent into a seated position. The door appeared in the wall and opened. Sophie walked through, with the box and the prisoners floating after her.

"This will take a while," Silvy the mirror announced. "Only those most closely affected need to come. Or those who want to learn. Prince Bryan, will you carry me?"

"I'm honored." Bryan got up, bowed, picked up Silvy in one hand and Crystal in the other.

Merrigan scooped up Bib and followed Bryan through the door. King Horace held out his arms to Belinda and Blossom, who hurried to get up and link arms with him and follow.

Passing through the door was a little disorienting for Merrigan, and she was glad to have Bib to hold onto. From inside the study, the door looked like it led into a dark closet. As soon as Bryan's feet were over the threshold, he vanished. Merrigan faltered for a heartbeat.

"Onward and upward, Mi'lady," Bib said, sounding eager.

On the other side of the doorway, the dark closet became a stone stairwell winding upward. Wide enough for three to walk together, it still felt rather tight to her. Steep. Maybe because she couldn't see the top and she had an awful image in her head of climbing without ceasing. But she saw Bryan's back going up, vanishing behind the center pole around which the stones seemed to be anchored. Merrigan kept moving. After three steps, the slab of stone under her feet jolted and she hesitated, reaching with one hand to balance against the outer wall.

The stone rose under her feet, lifting her, turning on the spiral. She looked up, to find Bryan looking over his shoulder down at her, three steps ahead, and grinning. Merrigan grinned back, even though her heart raced and she had an image in her head, just for a moment, of reaching the top of the stairwell and being smashed against the ceiling.

Behind her, she heard King Horace let out a grunt, a giggle from Blossom, and a gasp from Belinda. No reactions from the other three princesses followed, so she assumed they had decided not to come into Sophie's tower. With her gaze focused on Bryan, to fight the slightly dizzy feeling from the wall sliding past her, Merrigan had warning when they reached the top. He stumbled as the stone step under him tipped, urging him forward. She braced herself and leaped forward, to avoid the stumble he made. The moment she stepped out onto the tiles paving Sophie's tower room, the stairwell turned into another closet.

The room beyond was far wider than any tower could be. This was more like the grand hall of her father's palace, with a vaulted ceiling and walls that vanished among shadows. The sight of rows upon rows of bookshelves comforted her, and she gladly took a few steps to the closest chair, to catch her breath even though she hadn't actually climbed those stairs. Merrigan turned as she sat, and surveyed the room, and only saw the emergence of Horace, Belinda and Blossom from the corner of her eye. What she had seen of Belinda's home told her this tower room was impossible. It was large enough to take up more than half of the foundation footprint of King Horace's palace.

"One of the nice things about being well along in years, when it comes to practicing magic," Sophie called to them, from somewhere among the bookshelves, "is that you learn how to use the truly convenient and useful spells. Like how to link a great deal of space to a comparatively small anchor and make it portable. I was able to take my tower room with me on my travels. It saved me a great deal of backache and bother, carrying clothes and books with me." She chuckled, emerging with a stack of books tall enough to stretch her arms. "And when I couldn't find a decent inn, I could just open up the door and spend the night quite comfortably in front of my own fireplace. Thank you, dear," she said, as Blossom hurried to take the books from her. "This way. No dawdling. Let's get this unpleasant part over as quickly as possible, so we can get some real work done."

She bustled away, leading them around several bookshelves, out into a wide open part of the room. Bithia and Barbarina lay on blankets on the plain white tiled floor. A long table stood horizontal to their feet, with Merrigan's wooden box sitting on it. Sophie spread the books out on the table beside the box, and beckoned for Bryan and Merrigan to join her, with the table between them and the sleeping enchantresses. Horace and Belinda took a padded bench to the right of the open area, with plenty of space between them and the sleepers.

"We need to make sure those two are properly restrained before I ask you to reverse that sleeping cap on those two, Merrigan." Sophie opened one book and set it beside the box. "Bib, would you be a dear and consult the other books, to make sure I'm not leaving anything out? This," she tapped the open book, "is my thinking book, where I make my calculations and combine the notes and advice from other books."

"Glad to help," Bib chirped.

Merrigan put Bib on the table among the scattered magic books. Bryan set the two magic mirrors on the other end in the open area.

"While I've been gone, those two spent a great deal of time trying to break through the guardian spells to get in here and access my library and my stockpile of helpful potions and powders. Their mistake was assuming the tower was abandoned, and the truly potent protection spells were never initiated. Still ... they did some damage. Likely with the help of whatever majjian was twisting them." Another sigh escaped Sophie, exasperation and disappointment combined.

"I've spent a great deal of time weeding out all the roots and whatnot they wove, to prepare against the day the true majjian of this tower returned. They hoped to have a nasty reaction like what took your sweetheart, Belinda, when I came home and opened the door. The problem is that it's nearly impossible to invade and set up boobytraps in an occupied house. And since, as I mentioned already, I was able to essentially take my tower with me on my travels, instead of leaving it locked up and warded ..." Sophie chuckled.

"They're going to get a very nasty surprise, to wake up and find themselves in here," Blossom said, "but not in control like they hoped."

"Exactly. And even more upset to find out you're more my heir than both of them put together," her great-great-aunt added, with a nod for punctuation. "Horace, what progress have you made on tracking down that sneaky twit of a nanny who misguided you in raising our girls?"

"It's like she's vanished into smoke," the king grumbled.

"Yes, well, the more I see of the damage she did to your daughters and your kingdom, misreading their talents and potentials and predilections, the more sure I am she's part of the whole nasty conspiracy. Highly convenient for her, that she decided to retire just before I came home. Her last attempt to pick the lock on my tower room alerted me, and hopefully stung her good and hard and left some of her magic useless."

"Conspiracy," Merrigan murmured. "Her name wouldn't happen to be Tulip, would it?"

"All the nasty, conniving, judgmental old women whose handiwork I've encountered in the last thirty or forty years have had flower names." Sophie harrumphed. "A silly, arrogant affectation, as if naming themselves after flowers somehow conveys a cachet of goodness and purity on their ridiculous plot."

"It sounds like you've been doing a great deal of work tracking them down and unraveling the scheme," Merrigan said. "Are you sure all the nasty tricks are quite related? What Belinda's nanny did to her and her sisters, and what Nanny Tulip did to me?"

"The methods and the immediate results vary greatly, as many different ways and means as there are kingdoms. However … the final result adds up to the same thing. A sabotaging and blocking and draining of the inherent magic that belongs to each kingdom. The different notes of the magical song, the threads of the tapestry of magic created by the Unseen, are tangled, pulled out of harmony, pulled out of the pattern, the warp and woof twisted so what is produced is useless. Ugly. The majjian springs are either drained or blocked so deep down, near the source, that all the magic is drained from the upper landscape. While that ridiculous insistence on rationing magic and setting up standards for who is worthy to use magic or be helped by magic is part of the reason, it is not the total reason. And there is no logic involved. It's ridiculous!"

"Who says selfish, scheming, evil twits have to make sense?" Crystal remarked, her chiming voice going sour.

"True." Sophie nodded salute to the magic hand mirror.

"Done," Bib announced. "Everything seems to be working together, no contradictions, no holes, with triple layers of protection and restraint."

"Thank you." She winked at Merrigan, who stood closest to her. "It's always wise to ask a fresh pair of eyes, so to speak, to give your work one more look-over, just in case there's some twiddly little mistake you don't see because you've gone over it dozens of times. In essence, the eyes see what the heart wants to believe is there."

Merrigan's hands shook a little when Sophie asked her to reverse the sleeping cap and put it on one sister, then the other, to end the sleeping spell. Who knew what nasty magic spells they might have ready to fling about them? People were often fuddled when they woke from a long sleep. If her thoughts and senses hadn't been overwhelmed with Bryan's kiss when he woke her from the apple curse, she might have awakened cross and ready to fight.

Don't worry, Mi'lady, Bib assured her. *Lady Sophie knows her trade.*

Merrigan removed the sleeping cap from the second sister and didn't care how undignified she looked as she scurried away from the long worktable where the two had been laid out. The table was, in fact, part of the restraint imposed on them. As one opened her eyes and turned her head, flickers of green and purple light danced over the sisters' prone bodies, like thin threads spun by a lightning-struck spider. The other one's eyes fluttered and she inhaled with a loud snort, earning a bubble of laughter from Blossom. That seemed to startle them both. They tried to sit up, turning to each other, and those threads flared all over their bodies, a net effectively holding them down.

"What is this?" the one on the right said.

Merrigan hadn't bothered to try to tell them apart. They were dressed alike in cliched evil enchantress garb: black robes and black hoods with red lining, their faces pale, eyebrows painted black.

"Well, Bithia," Sophie nodded to the one on the right, "Barbarina," a nod to the one on the left, "isn't this a fine mess you two snots got yourselves into?"

"It isn't our fault!" Bithia wailed. She sounded more afraid than nasty-snotty.

Of course, it could all be an act. Merrigan couldn't count all the times she had pretended repentance and amazement at the crimes others accused her of, just to escape punishment. At the time, she had thought it unreasonable and unjustified, but looking back, she could see most of the time she had deserved every unpleasant, humiliating moment. She wondered if the two sisters would learn their lessons quickly and start on the road to reformation, or they would prolong the struggle and make things really difficult for themselves.

"What exactly isn't your fault?" Horace said, stepping up next to his great-aunt.

"We were only doing what they told us we had to," Barbarina said. Bithia nodded and hit the back of her head on the table. She didn't wince. The hood probably padded her head, or it was simply that hard.

"Who told you, and what exactly did they tell you?" Sophie said.

Barbarina muttered something. Bithia snarled under her breath and tried to nudge her sister, but the magic threads holding them prisoner kept her from doing more than wriggling.

"Speak up, none of us can hear you," Sophie said.

"Us?" Bithia managed to lift her head enough to look past her toes. Her eyes widened when her gaze landed on Belinda. Her gaze slid to Merrigan, standing next to her, then turned into a scowl when it found Bryan. "Well, that explains partly how we got here. Oh, yes, very heroic, abandoning the old woman who bit into the apple to save you. I suppose you left her in the care of that horde of filthy little screaming orphans?"

Merrigan laughed. She doubted the enchantress had any concern for her. She was just trying to make Bryan and Belinda feel guilty.

"What's so funny, trollop?" Barbarina snapped.

"They didn't leave me at all," Merrigan said. "Bryan broke your silly little curse. Although he did overdo it a little with three kisses, but ... I don't mind."

"No," Bithia whispered, her voice cracking. "You can't be."

"Can't be what?"

Barbarina laughed. "Bith, you're an idiot. This works out perfectly!"

"But we agreed to help the old hags' plan by keeping them apart," her sister snarled, and wriggled more.

"Keep who apart?" Sophie said.

"Those two," Bithia snapped. "Bryan and his true love, Merrigan of

Avylyn."

"You know who I am?" Merrigan almost leaned forward to rest her hands on the end of the table, but that would mean putting her hands into those flickering, flaring lines holding those two prisoner. She didn't want to risk breaking the connections and setting them free.

"You're the whole reason we got help from the hags. Even more than from the Guild." That was definitely a spoiled brat pout on Bithia's face.

"Oh ho, now I understand a little," Sophie said. "The Guild is a particularly uppity and elitist group of dark sorceresses. Equal to, but entirely separate from the League, all evil majjian men. Too snooty to let women come play, because they're afraid of the stronger link women have to the majjian springs. So let me theorize, and you fill in the pieces. The Guild helped you, guided you, probably provided quite a bit of your dark arts education, with the proviso that you give them a strong foundation here in your father's kingdom, once you two knocked Belinda off the throne or turned her into a brainless figurehead, to take the blame for anything that went wrong. Am I getting warm?"

"Too warm," Barbarina grumbled.

"But their help wasn't enough? Or someone came along with a plan that suited your temperaments better than the stern discipline the Guild employs? Rather irritating that they do have some admirable qualities," Sophie added as an aside, with a resigned shrug. "Still getting warm?"

"The Guild was running up against opposition from a group of old hedge witches and minor faerie godmothers and grimy little grannies." Bithia heaved a longsuffering sigh. "Their ties with the majjian springs aren't as strong as they'd like, and the hags were interfering with it. Somehow. The deal was that if we learned what the hags were up to, we'd get more help dealing with Belinda and her prince."

"The hags offered us a different deal. They gave us the relocation and confundus spell to wrap around Bayl, to keep his little brother busy." Barbarina managed to turn her head enough to nudge her sister's shoulder with her chin. "Told you we should have just run for it, the deal was too complicated. We were doing just fine making Belinda miserable with the location spell that made her allergic to peas."

CHAPTER SEVEN

"So that was your idea?" Belinda cried. She raised her clenched fist, as if she might thump her sister. Merrigan gripped her arm to stop her.

"Why were you supposed to keep me busy?" Bryan said.

"So you wouldn't run into Merrigan, and true love wouldn't give a great leap forward on the reformation spell some seeress wrapped around her." Bithia snickered. "You should have heard the bickering among the old hags. Seems they're on the outs with each other, snarling back and forth. One of them made a great mess of the simple job to spoil the princess. And then they let her oaf of a husband get himself killed."

"Hah!" Barbarina grinned and nodded to her sister. "Any idiot knows you don't mess with magic apple trees. They blamed the one who had the temper tantrum and walked out in the middle of the meeting with us. What was her name? Utterly stupid, affected name. Why did they name themselves after flowers, every last one of them?"

"Tulip?" Merrigan asked, her voice cracking.

"That's the one. The old hags lost track of you once the seeress got her hands on you and you got sent over the ocean. Our job was to keep Bryan busy so he'd finally forget about you. Keeping Bayl away from Belinda and wiping his memory so he wouldn't even look for her didn't suit us. Honestly? We just wanted you two to suffer."

"Oh, yes, always be honest," Sophie muttered. The icy core to her tone made both nasty sisters go a shade paler. "Go on, what else did you learn from the hags?"

"Well … they convinced us that putting Belinda into the standard cursed apple sleep would put Father into a tangle, once he finally found her, and he'd be all repentant and weepy and dithering over waking her, and we could have great fun watching all those useless third and fourth and fifth-born princes lining up for a chance to kiss her."

"Then you had to go and decide the Guild was a better choice than the hags' offer," her sister said with a groan. "That's how we always make a mess of things. We agree on a plan, and then you change your mind halfway through."

"No, we never agree on a plan, you force your ideas on me and don't give me a chance to think of something better, and you think I agree with you because I don't argue loudly enough, and that's —" She stopped short, a band of green and purple writhing magic covering her mouth. Her sister started to laugh and got a second band across her mouth.

"Well, isn't that interesting?" Merrigan whispered, feeling dizzy.

Bryan was there, as always, when she reached for him to stop the vast room from spinning around her.

Sophie shooed them from the tower and scolded Horace for not treating his guests better. Wasn't it about time he ordered a grand celebration for Belinda's return? She was rolling up her sleeves and giving Blossom a list of books to find when the others left the tower. Merrigan was grateful for the steps that moved spiraling downward, carrying them, because she didn't think she could take steady steps. Try as she might, she couldn't shake herself free, or at least distract herself, from the weighty, rather terrifying conclusion deduced from Bithia and Barbarina's tangled, angry confession.

Somehow, Merrigan had a great deal to do with not just the drying up of the majjian springs across the land of Armorica, but potentially restoring the flow of magic. Otherwise, why would it be so important to keep her from reforming, from being reunited with Bryan?

"I don't know if that helps or not," she murmured, when another thread of thought came through the swirling in her mind.

They were back in King Horace's study, alone for a few minutes while the king followed Sophie's orders. Belinda had been swept away by her other three sisters, all chattering and laughing and hugging and weeping a little and generally acting as sisters should after a long separation. Merrigan wondered if she would have as happy a reunion with her sisters when she finally reached Avylyn. Would any of them be at home, or were they married and dealing with kingdoms of their own by now? She had deliberately cut herself off from contact with her family, believing they would only hold her back and destroy the future she deserved.

"What helps?" Bryan offered her a cup of some spicy-sweet herbal infusion Sophie had ordered up from the kitchen, according to the kitchen maid with delighted mischief dancing in her eyes.

"Everybody seems to know that we were destined for true love … except us. It was like we had the news written on our foreheads. You have to wonder who was laughing at us for being so oblivious."

"Well …" He grinned and reached to pour his own cup. "Look at it this way. If there was a sign, it was more like the label on bottles, and the two of us were inside the bottles. Kind of hard to read through the colored glass and read the label backward."

"Oh, now that describes me perfectly. Everything backward." She sighed and took a sip, and bubbled slightly as laughter escaped her. Then something cracked inside her chest and she fumbled the cup as she put it down, covered her face, and burst into tears.

Bryan scooped her up and cradled her on his lap. She buried her face in his shoulder and clung to him, and for the first time that she could ever remember, she didn't care if she cried herself ugly. She needed these tears. She rather hoped they washed away more of the ugly, gritty, stiff-necked, proud accumulation on her soul.

King Horace returned some time after she had cried herself quiet, while she was still cradled on Bryan's lap. She was quite content to let him keep holding her. As long as she didn't get too heavy. As long as his legs weren't starting to fall asleep. Wouldn't it be funny if, when they finally stood up, he wasn't able to because he couldn't feel his legs? A tiny snort of a giggle escaped her at that thought, just as the king returned to his study.

He put Bib and Crystal on the table so the book and mirror could report on what Sophie had learned from Bithia and Barbarina.

The group of minor godmothers and hedge witches Tulip belonged to had somehow discerned a way to not only block and divert the water of the majjian springs, but subvert the magical destinies guiding the lives of various royals throughout Armorica. They didn't want Bayl to marry Belinda because of the magical potential of their children. Making him wander for the rest of his life would also detour Bryan, and eventually destroy his magical destiny. The old women didn't know where Merrigan was. Until they could put her back on the path they had decreed for her, the next best tactic for them was to distract Bryan.

"It's utterly idiotic and … well, they sound like even worse brats than I ever was," Merrigan finally said.

Her whole life felt like an unsettled tangle, and she wouldn't be right again until she could find Nanny Tulip and not just give her a large, prickly piece of her mind, but inflict on her all the spankings she should have had herself, when she was a child.

"What about Bayl?" she hurried to add.

"That's the rather nasty part of the whole mess." Bib sighed, his pages riffling softly. "They used a modified confundus on Bayl. They have no idea what happened once the spell awoke. Nothing Sophie does can reweave their connection to the spell, to find Bayl's trail through them."

"The nasty grannies expected them to make a mess and be caught." Crystal snickered, a crackling sort of sound that made Merrigan fear for her polished surface. "What those nasties didn't count on was that Belinda and Merrigan would be friends, and Bryan would recognize Merrigan, and the two of you would be reunited. If they know, they're probably seething. I hope they're quaking in their boots."

"Our only clue is to be on the hunt for tales of a wandering prince," Bib added.

"That doesn't sound so bad," Bryan said. "Unless there are more pieces to the spell we have to look out for?"

"Exactly. I'm sorry, Mi'lady ... Sophie has advised us that the best tactic is to not be actively looking for Bayl. Thinking about him, searching for him, making him the reason for your actions and travels will push him to keep moving farther away. Even over the sea. The last thing you need is for him to take a ship and sail for parts unknown."

"If he takes a ship, at least we have friends who are sailors, who can be on the lookout for him." Merrigan felt rather breathless for a moment, as an idea coalesced at the back of her mind. "Better than sailors," she said, almost gasping. "The Sea King, all of Elli's mermaid sisters and cousins. Surely such a nasty spell wrapped around Bayl will be visible to them, or audible, or maybe they can even smell it. If they can keep him from crossing the sea ..." She trailed off, discouraged by how both men's mouths sagged open and their eyes widened. Did they think it was an absolutely stupid idea? Were they fighting not to laugh at her?

"I think Clara didn't weave that wandering curse on you to punish you at all," Bryan whispered. "I think she did it to make you into a kind of net to gather up magical friends and favors, against the day you would need them." He grasped her shoulders and pulled her close and kissed her deeply. It wasn't nearly long enough to suit Merrigan, but they were not alone, after all.

So they agreed, Merrigan would write to her friends in Seafoam and ask Elli to ask help from the Sea King, ensuring Bayl never left Armorica.

Sophie's advice was rather general, and flexible. They would leave Danishoor, and as she put it, "take care of necessary tasks." If they heard any stories of a wandering prince with no memory of his name or home, they would gather up those clues, but not actively go seeking him.

"The important thing is to help others, find what has gone wrong and make it right wherever you can. No matter how small it seems, no matter how limited the ripples from the stone you throw into the pool. Remember what the Fae woman said, about all the small things her people didn't notice or fix, and then discovering later, when they had grown large and spread out and connected, that those tiny things were vital. One princess who is taught to be a brat doesn't seem to matter, but if she isn't corrected, she becomes a wicked queen. Think of all the horrific things you might have ended up doing if you had followed in your husband's footsteps, if you hadn't asked Clara to help you lie and cheat." Sophie reached out to hug Merrigan, whose face was hot with shame.

"There, there, child, I am not criticizing you. Considering what was done to you, how you were hurt and lied to, and your sweet, innocent child's love used as a weapon against your father's kingdom ... well, you have done amazing things in your journey of reformation. You have chosen to do right, and to make things right. We must all do our part to make things right. These hags with their twisted, arrogant belief that they know best who should and shouldn't have magic ..." The old enchantress shuddered, her face darkening in anger. "They've twisted everything."

~~~~~

Sophie's plan for finding Bayl meant Belinda could not travel with them. The curse would constantly push him away from wherever she was. As long as she was with Bryan and Merrigan, the faster they moved, the faster he would be compelled to flee before them. The faster Bayl moved, the fewer the chances he would stop somewhere, act, and leave clues for them to follow.

Belinda reluctantly agreed that the best thing she could do to help find Bayl was to stay home with her father and work with Sophie, study Bergomass's books, and fix the damage done to Horace's kingdom. Then they would reach out to the neighboring kingdoms and fix what was wrong with them. The wider her sphere of influence, essentially, the larger the territory Bayl wouldn't enter.

"I'm not worried about you, Bryan, though I know you'll be thinking about your brother often enough to imperil the quest. You'll be distracted enough by other concerns to feel guilty about it, and that distraction will dilute the negative effects of thinking about your brother," Sophie had said, during one of their planning discussions. She nodded to Merrigan when she said "distracted." Then she laughed when Bryan blushed.

After all they had gone through over the last few years, who would have thought they'd still be able to blush about anything? Especially the sweetness and freshness of their rediscovered love?

King Horace wanted to have a grand feast to officially welcome Belinda home and acknowledge the help Bryan and Merrigan had been to her and the kingdom. Sophie talked him out of it. First, because it would just alert the Guild and the grannies, or as Blossom referred to them, the Worthy Warts, that their schemes had failed. If the destruction of their spells hadn't already done that. Sophie theorized that so many spells were involved, and so tangled together, chances were good the two groups might blame each other for the failure, and not know their mutual prey had escaped them. And second, because that would delay Bryan and Merrigan's departure for several days. They needed to move on. Their next task was freeing Sylvanglade from the sleeping curse.

The second morning after arriving in Aryslean, Merrigan went to the royal family's private garden, to find Honk and tell him what they had decided to do. She hoped her friend would agree to travel with them, and not just because the presence of a swan was always a harbinger of good luck. She missed her childhood friend, even if his presence reminded her of how blind and silly she had been. Then again, at the time, everyone thought he was simply an awkward, rather dingy little duck that didn't fit
~~~~~

in anywhere. How could they have been so blind, and not realized he was a cygnet, a baby swan?

"Because swans have grown so rare," she answered herself, as she stepped into the garden. That realization made her shiver more than the crystalline icy air of the early morning.

That was another symptom of the Worthy Warts' schemes. Just how rare had swans grown, and how long had this been happening? As far back as she could remember, swans were only heard, rarely seen. Swans usually made their homes in queens' gardens and enchanted pools hidden deep in forests. They only appeared for events of magical importance or to celebrate the breaking of dreadful curses. Their young were practically never seen. It made perfect sense that no one would have known Merrigan's ugly, grayish, loud little duck friend was actually a swan, waiting to grow into his beauty and grace.

She shuddered in fury at the certainty Nanny Tulip had known Honk was a swan. She had encouraged Merrigan to be ashamed of the waddling, loud little creature. How many times had she remarked that the clumsy gray duck wasn't an appropriate companion for a princess?

Merrigan's footsteps crunched on the ice-crusted path as she moved a little faster toward the pond where Honk was staying, sheltered from the public eye. After all, with the creeping awareness of a slowly growing famine of magic throughout Armorica, some desperate or greedy or even frightened idiot might try to capture Honk. She shuddered again when she stepped through the screen of tall, snowy bushes and saw the pristine, unbroken surface of the pond.

No Honk swimming in the open, breaking the crust of ice. No Honk sitting on the bales of straw providing shelter from the wind and snow.

No footprints approaching the pond, indicating someone had crept in to capture him.

She couldn't remember when snow had last fallen. If it was during the night, snow could have covered up the footprints of a kidnapper. Or worse, some large dog, maybe a wolf, or another large predator intent on a convenient meal.

"Honk? Honk, where are you?"

Merrigan took off her gloves and shifted the ring that let her understand birds from one finger to another. No, she was being ridiculous. How could she hear Honk better if the ring was on another finger?

Desperation prompted her to shift the ring to her left hand.

Merrigan dropped her gloves as strains of piping music spilled through the air. Touching only her left ear.

"Honk, where are you?"

Music that could only be heard when she put the ring on her left hand

… that was a bad sign.

"Honk?" She slid her gloves back on her cold hands and turned until she thought she had a good idea of where the music originated. Then she set off to follow that pipe and find whoever was playing it.

A low, rumbling, querulous sort of cry came from overhead and she ducked before she saw the shadow and felt the body swooping low through the air. Merrigan stayed bent down, turning to watch the massive owl gliding in for a landing. He scraped his talons on the top of the wall in front of her as he passed over, perhaps twenty paces away. She shuddered at the mental image of that huge body hitting her, or worse, trying to pick her up and fly away with her. The owl's wingspan was nearly twice as wide as her outstretched arms. What was such a huge creature doing out at this time of the morning? Where did it live? Was it hunting in the palace grounds?

The squawking of chickens and cries of geese and ducks arose from the other side of that wall. Her heart lurched when she thought she heard that distinctive honk amid the farmyard noises. She ran to the small door in the wall, skidding several times on the ice under the snow before she reached it.

The knob turned grudgingly, clogged with ice. Merrigan pushed the door and stumbled through, into a brick-paved area around a plain, utilitarian fountain with a wide basin. Likely the laundry yard.

It swarmed with ducks and chickens, pigeons, geese, and a veritable cloud of those little city-dwelling birds that never seemed to have the wits to leave for warmer lands when winter struck. Honk sat on the wide lip of the fountain, his neck outstretched, glaring regally at a young man who hunkered down under a long, slanted stone drying table. He continued to play his triple pipes, despite the thudding of the owl leaping up and landing hard, repeatedly, on the table.

Merrigan took a moment to catch her breath, bracing herself in the open doorway. The honking and quacking and cheeping and twittering had a sort of rhythm. As if all the different birds were trying to sing along with the piper. There was something slightly eerie about how they kept creeping forward, trying to get closer to him.

The piper's eyes were wide with what she took to be fear. He swept his pipes back and forth as he played, seeming to push away the birds with his song. Yet wasn't the music drawing them? Why didn't the idiot stop playing? He certainly didn't look like he enjoyed what he was doing. Especially not with that huge owl pounding on the table.

Something wasn't right here.

"Bother," she muttered. She marched through the living carpet of birds, trying to nudge a few aside rather than kick them or step on any, until she reached the lip of the fountain.

Honk trembled under his puffed-up feathers. His eyes weren't just wide with anger, but with fear. She wrapped her arms around him. She would carry him away from here if she had to, despite how large he was.

Stop him. Stop him. Stop him, he honked, gasping for breath between each honk.

"Who? The owl or the piper?"

"The piper, of course, silly girl!" the owl rumbled, and landed on the top of the drying table. The stone let out an ominous crackling sound.

The piper's song faltered. The encroaching ducks and geese and chickens and other assorted birds fluttered up in alarm.

"You, stop that noise!" Merrigan lunged through the squawking and quacking and chirping birds. She may have kicked a few larger birds aside, but they were all starting to scatter.

"I have to!" the piper wailed. He took a deep breath and brought the triple pipes back to his lips.

Stop him! Honk rose up in the air as if he would flee.

Seeing her friend so frightened made Merrigan furious. She went to her knees and slid the last few steps on the icy pavement. She nearly didn't duck her head in time to avoid braining herself on the edge of the table.

The piper yelped and tried to scramble away. She caught hold of his ragged patchwork coat with one flailing hand and managed a decent punch to the side of his face with the other hand. He squeaked and tried to twist free, and the cacophony in the laundry courtyard grew almost deafening as birds leaped into the air and some started fighting among themselves.

"Closer," the great owl rumbled behind her. "Push him closer to me."

The piper shrieked and flailed and the back of one hand hit Merrigan across the nose. The sharp pain just added to her fury. She tossed aside all ladylike dignity and clawed at him and grabbed and punched and managed to pull one leg out from under the table. He screamed as the owl reached with one massive taloned foot to grasp his ankle. The piper batted at her with his pipes. Merrigan snatched them from him. He shrieked louder as she flung them away.

CHAPTER EIGHT

"Good girl!" the owl chortled and darted away with surprising speed and agility for such a massive creature.

The piper scrambled out from under the table on hands and knees, sobbing, reaching for the pipes. The owl swooped back around with the pipes in one taloned foot, and with the other caught the piper by the collar of his jacket.

"Take these, girl," the owl ordered, as Merrigan got to her feet, somewhat winded from that highly satisfying tussle. He tossed her the pipes. The piper burst into tears and didn't resist as the owl backwinged, to sit on the stone table, and hold him in place, perched on the edge.

Merrigan, Merrigan, my Merrigan. Honk hurtled across the paved yard and nearly knocked her off her feet. She went to her knees and wrapped her arms around him. He was still trembling, and that made her furious.

"Just what did you think you were doing with these?" She waved the triple pipes in front of the ragged piper's face, far enough away he couldn't have snatched at them.

"I had to. The old ladies took my pipes away and threatened to break them if I didn't do their catching, first." He burst into tears.

"Old ladies?" Merrigan thought she would be sick. "Why did they— what did you do with your own pipes, before they gave you these?" She held the pipes out at arm's length, hoping her gloves would protect against any nasty magic coating them.

"I helped people. I made a good living luring away rats and mice and locusts and other pests." He gulped and tried to wipe his nose on his sleeve. He winced when the movement tugged on his coat, and the clear sound of tearing cloth stopped him. Merrigan almost felt sorry for him.

"Why did they want you to steal all the birds from the palace?"

"Not all of them." Another gulp. "Just the swan."

"Why?"

"I don't know. I don't!" His voice cracked and squeaked. "They just told me to follow the pipes. Anywhere they shine, I go into the palaces and gardens. I play until I draw away all the frogs and the swans and walk out into the countryside and play until they fall asleep. One of them comes and …" He shrugged. "I never wait around for them to come, so I don't know what they do."

Honk went to fetch Sophie, who came with the palace guard to take the prisoner.

"Well," she said, once Bryan had joined her, Merrigan, and Blossom in her tower room, "now we have a partial answer for the growing scarcity of swans and frogs."

"Why swans and frogs?" Blossom said, her voice somewhat distracted. She was bent over the triple pipes, which had been laid on the table, surrounded by a ring of iron filings and dusted with salt, to make their magic sleep.

The piper had grown paler and his voice had grown weaker, the longer the pipes were kept out of his grasp. Sophie had theorized some sort of binding spell on the pipes to ensure he didn't try to run away from the duty imposed on him.

"Not all swans and frogs have magic, but enough of them do, it's a sensible step to either eradicate or imprison any that might be in the area before you set about using magic for some negative purpose. To prevent their inherent blessing from interfering with your work." Sophie shrugged. "Just the little bit the lad told us about the old women, I'm inclined to think they're Bithia and Barbarina's Worthy Warts."

"Made the mistake of trusting them to keep their part of the bargain," Blossom said with a snort. A mischievous grin touched her face, the kind worn by younger brothers and sisters the world over when their overbearing elder siblings got their comeuppance.

"When he wakes up and he's more coherent, I'll have to find out how long he's been their unwilling servant. And how much success he's had. I can't imagine he's been capturing much of anything, at this time of the year. I could almost feel sorry for the boy."

"Almost," Merrigan said.

"I wouldn't be surprised if, once swans and frogs are eliminated, they start going after more suspicious and powerful creatures, more easily missed, such as talking dogs, cats, and horses. Theoretically ..." Sophie shook her head, lines forming around her mouth and eyes. "Well, eventually, as their power reserves grow, they'll have enough strength to start gathering up stronger magical beings, like basilisks and gryphons, unicorns, dragons, and my Silvy and your Bib and Crystal."

"We have to do something to stop them," Bryan said. "How? What do we do first?"

"I'll have to consult with my friends. This new information should give us a few steps forward. I will wager that your next step in the quest, to break the curse on Sylvanglade, will be a major blow for our side of this battle. Consider how much power is generated and collected by a sleeping curse slowly devouring an entire kingdom. That's a tempting target, especially for grumblers and complainers who want to be in charge. Don't be surprised, Prince Bryan, if you come up against stern opposition, the closer you get to your home kingdom."

"Well ..." Bryan sighed. "Should that be encouraging?"

"At least we are warned," Merrigan said.

I'll be on the alert. Honk pressed harder against Merrigan's leg. He had stayed so close to her, she found it a little difficult to walk from the laundry yard to Sophie's tower. Merrigan wasn't inclined to resent the closeness, when she considered how she had nearly lost her childhood friend once more.

~~~~~

By mid-afternoon, their traveling party was on its way again. Blossom had detected something approaching the city, and Sophie confirmed that the piper's attempt to capture Honk had triggered some magical reaction. Likely some sort of failsafe measure included in the spell wrapped around the pipes. That meant getting Honk as far from the palace as possible. They hurried away, taking back streets.

Merrigan was grateful for the speed of their departure, before the aching in her chest and her head turned into tears. Leaving Belinda behind to deal with her sisters and root out any nasty magic aimed at keeping her off the throne was essential. Especially if her presence made finding Bayl harder. Still, leaving her behind was hard. Merrigan hadn't had a real friend, someone who knew the whole truth about her and understood, for far longer than she could remember. She knew her brothers and sisters and father loved her, and Nanny Tulip had never loved her. Still, her family had a duty to love her, but she feared they had never *liked* her. Belinda liked her, when she didn't have to. Belinda knew the whole truth about her. Merrigan wondered if the friends she had made along her journey would still like her, once they knew the truth. She laughed at herself, remembering how she used to daydream about the revelation of her true identity, the awe and fear and wonder on the faces of the people who thought she was nothing but an old woman.

"I was a selfish little brat of the worst sort," she confessed to Bib and Crystal one night, after two days of ruminating on her past attitudes.

Their party had come to a nice village in the tiny kingdom of Frankengild, big enough to offer a choice of two inns. Honk didn't ride into the village with them but flew ahead to do some scouting. She missed him and worried about him. Brian must have sensed that and let her take both the book and mirror to her room when they separated for the night.

"You were, once," Crystal agreed. Soft greenish light swirled through the darkness from the magic mirror's surface. "You have come a long way. I can't wait to see the fury and despair on that despicable Tulip's face, when she realizes her most important tool has escaped her grasp."

"And remade herself," Bib added.

"Sometimes I feel like everyone else has been remaking me, and I've
~~~~~

just been sitting here, getting melted and twisted around and hammered with dozens of tiny blows every day." Merrigan sighed, ending on a little bubble of laughter. "I never thought I'd feel sorry for a lump of iron getting shaped into something useful."

"And refined and purified and turned into the purest gold along the way," Crystal added.

"Flatterer."

"Only because it's safe to flatter you now. Flattery won't corrupt," Bib pointed out. "We're very proud of you, Mi'lady."

"Thank you, Bib. And thank you, Crystal. Both of you, for all the help you're going to have to give me along the way until everything is made right. Sometimes I think people turn evil because it's so much easier to think only about themselves, and the weight of being responsible for others is so incredibly ..." She sighed. "Weighty."

"I know it's not very good advice," Bib offered after the darkness in the room seemed to thicken and the wind howled a little louder against the shutters. "But maybe the weight won't feel so oppressive if you don't think about it."

"You're right." Merrigan surprised herself with a chuckle. "Not very good."

"What I mean is, take the same approach to the problem of reparations and your destiny as the problem of finding Prince Bayl. Deal with the tasks immediately in front of you. Stop looking for clues far down the road. If you look too far ahead, you'll miss what's in front of you."

"I supposed that does make sense," she murmured. She was pleased to realize she felt drowsy, at long last. Philosophical discussions did tend to make her sleepy, after all.

Merrigan stumbled through her evening prayers, silently, and then tied herself into knots for at least half an hour, trying to remember when she had stopped saying her bedtime prayers. She still couldn't convince herself that the Unseen was listening to her, but at least she could say she had tried. With practice, she might get better, and maybe even start thinking of some prayers of her own, rather than repeating the ones her mother and Nanny Starling had taught her. She was very sure that constantly thinking, "Oh, please, Blessed Unseen who formed and guides our world, help us pound Nanny Tulip into dust, and help us find Bayl so he and Belinda can have their happily ever after," counted as real, worshipful prayers. Certainly not the mindset and heart of a princess who hoped to unseal the queen's garden and heal the majjian springs.

Just when her thoughts crept toward some kind of understanding or revelation, sleep overtook her. That was always how it happened.

~~~~~

A rapid tapping on Merrigan's window came just a few hours later.
~~~~~

She stumbled across the cold wooden floor in her bare feet and fumbled with the latch on the window. She nearly flung the shutters wide open before it occurred to her that she might hit whoever was outside, tapping.

She woke up enough to be afraid. After all, someone trying to come in her window couldn't have good intentions. What were they sitting on? She was on the third floor, and for the life of her she couldn't remember if her window looked out over a wing of the inn, or a straight drop from the window to the ground.

"Who's there?" She considered stepping back to the table where the nicely heavy pitcher and basin offered adequate weapons for self-defense.

Merrigan. Merrigan, Honk wheezed, and thumped on the shutters.

She lifted the latch, afraid he would hurt his beak on the sturdy wood. She carefully pushed open the left shutter. Honk perched on the slope of the roof beside her window on the right. He gave a great hop and leaped, folded his wings tight against his body and dove through the opening, nearly knocking her over. He landed with a thump she feared would rouse the people in the room below hers.

Swans in trouble. Princes are swans. His whole body shook so hard Merrigan feared his head would snap off his neck.

"Who? Where?"

She wiped out her washbasin and poured the last of her clean water into it, then set it on the footstool of the chair in front of her tiny fireplace, so he wouldn't have to bend his neck far to drink. Honk gave her a look so full of weariness and gratitude, she had to blink back tears.

"I fear the Worthy Warts have their hands in something nearby," Bib announced. "Swans in trouble."

She nodded and stroked Honk's back as he delicately scooped up water in his beak.

The thumping on her door made them both jump. It was the innkeeper's daughter. The man in the room below hers had indeed been disturbed by the noise of Honk's entrance. She feared Merrigan was hurt, or someone had broken in to attack her. Merrigan had liked the young woman when they came to the inn that evening. She seemed to have a lot of sense, competently overseeing all the inn workers. Well, that common sense would soon be tested. Merrigan took a deep breath and tugged the door open, and gestured for the young woman to step in.

She stood a little straighter when her gaze landed on Honk, and didn't scream or do something silly, like trying to drive him out of the room. That would have created an enormous mess, because although the room was comfortable, it was cozy to the point of being confining.

"Have you heard any unusual stories of swans hereabouts?" Merrigan asked, and returned to the chair, to rest her hand on Honk's back again. He gave the young woman one more glance and resumed drinking.

"My friend has returned here in some distress, but he hasn't had time to tell me exactly what is wrong with the swans."

"Told ... you?" The girl blanched, but didn't scream or flee.

Merrigan held up her hand with the ring. "This ring allows me to speak to birds." She could almost laugh at how the girl's color returned and she visibly relaxed. "Have you heard any stories?"

"Oh, yes, lady." The girl nodded. "The young queen is said to be beset with swans."

"Beset how?"

"Oh, it's said they keep trying to steal the baby princess."

"Why would swans try to steal a baby?"

They're not. Honk shook his head fiercely, again making her fear for his neck. The girl took a step back and gripped the edge of her apron.

"Bother," she muttered. "My friend says the swans aren't trying to steal the princess. Why is that story going around?"

"I don't know if it's a lie or not, lady." The girl cringed slightly. "I only know what we've been hearing for the past month. The king brought home a princess who'd been cursed to muteness."

"From where?"

"Nobody knows. Many people, especially the old queen, challenged him, but she had a gold ring that wouldn't come off no matter how the old wizard tried, and she was wearing fine clothes when he found her hiding up a tree. The wizard said she was a princess on a quest. Well, the king wouldn't be gainsaid, he had to marry her ..." She blushed brightly as her words trailed away. "Sorry, lady. Mustn't gossip. Pa says I'll get my tongue stolen one of these days if it wags too much."

"Let me guess ... soon the new bride was expecting a child, and she started acting oddly, but everyone shrugged it off because after all, she was with child, and women expecting their first often do strange things?" Merrigan tried to keep the sarcasm from her voice, but something knotted tight inside her, expecting the worst from this familiar tale.

Nanny Tulip had put her to bed every night with tales of the doings of faeries and enchantresses and other majjians, and the awful things they did with their magic to hurt good boys and sensible girls. Bib had been kept busy telling her the true versions of all those stories that had made her so distrustful of magic in her childhood.

"Exactly! She wanders the countryside every night of bright moonlight, gathering nettles. No one understood what she did with them at first, but the king assigned farm girls to help her with the gathering. Somehow, she breaks the nettles and spins thread out of them."

"And weaves cloth from the thread, and makes shirts from the cloth," Bib said in Merrigan's voice. "Always by the light of the moon."

"Yes." The girl didn't seem to notice that Merrigan's mouth hadn't moved. Perhaps she was nearsighted. "How did you know?"

"It's not a common curse, but it's used often enough to be known by those who study such things," Merrigan said.

"Are you versed in curses, and breaking them, lady? Perhaps you can help our poor king. He does love his wife, despite the awful things they've accused her of doing. Of course, they say the swans made her do it."

"What awful things?" Merrigan braced herself. She couldn't remember if this was the tale where the newborn baby was exchanged for a toad, and the baby vanished from her cradle and the mother, forbidden to speak until she broke the curse with the nettle shirts, was named an ogre because the king's stepmother had spread blood on her face.

"The princess keeps vanishing from her cradle, and she keeps reappearing with swan feathers in her little hands, and the old queen has horrid dreams of the mother throwing the child from the tower window. And every night, she keeps working on those shirts. They've been using the shirts as bait to capture the swans. Everyone thinks they're making the young queen throw her baby out the window because she isn't giving them the shirts."

Wrong, wrong, wrong, Honk cried, with furious honking and hissing that made the girl take another step back toward the door.

Footsteps pounded from down the hall. Merrigan looked up to see first Bryan, then Captain Garan skid to a stop in her doorway and look in.

"Highness, are you all right?" Garan said.

Merrigan and Bryan both sighed. They hadn't wanted to advertise their royal rank, certainly not until it was absolutely necessary.

Although, from the hope lighting the girl's face, perhaps this was one of those times?

Need the shirts to break the curse, Honk insisted. *They've caught six and there's only one more left. If they catch all seven, all hope is gone. And there's no one left to rescue the baby.*

"I assume the old queen is actually throwing the baby out the window?" Merrigan said.

The innkeeper's daughter gasped in horror, while Bryan demanded to know what Honk was talking about.

"Please, are you royal? Can you make the king listen to you and fix this awful mess? Everyone agrees that we've been having such trouble, with the singing river drying up and the owls vanishing from the oracle grove because the wizard insists on capturing the swans."

I wouldn't be so hasty to blame the old queen this time around, Bib said. *If you can get me into the palace, to talk to the books in the library and the king's archives, I can probably give you a list of people to accuse. And meanwhile, you talk to the king and queen and straighten out this mess and find some protection for their daughter. Any royal child has some magic potential, but a child born to a queen laboring to break a curse has even more magic potential. If the old queen is doing the throwing, someone is making her, to get their hands on the child and spirit her away, to harvest her magic as she grows up.*

Merrigan developed a headache, trying to listen to Bib theorizing in her head while dealing with the girl and assuring Bryan and Garan she was all right. And then there was the noise of several other guests in the inn who had been drawn by the running feet and the honking.

"Enough!" She drew herself up to her full height and was a little frightened, later, by how easily she returned to the icy imperious manner and tone of voice, from her days as spoiled, selfish Queen Merrigan. "I had hoped to pass through this land in peace, as I deal with matters of greatest urgency for my father, King Urson of Avylyn."

Several gasps and renewed muttering from the unseen people out in the hallway proved even in tiny Frankengild, her father's name had influence. She could only hope no one had heard about the shameful story of Merrigan of Avylyn.

"As a royal duty, I must intervene to help my fellow royals in their time of distress. Innkeeper … I am sorry, I was so weary when we arrived, I didn't hear your name. That is entirely too rude of me." She nodded to the girl, whose face lit up at the simple courtesy. Which she most likely didn't receive very often.

"Sunflower, Highness."

"Mistress Sunflower, in the morning, would you be so kind as to find a messenger to take a letter from me to the palace, asking for a meeting with your king, his wife, and his mother?"

Finally, Captain Garan and Sunflower got the gawkers to leave, and Merrigan was alone with Bryan, Honk, Bib and Crystal. She let Bib explain what had happened while she dug in her baggage for the handy little writing desk Belinda had insisted on giving her. Essentially it was a sturdy box with plenty of paper and quills, sealing wax and several pots of different colors of ink. She composed a polite, regal, but not too stuffy letter, offering her help in freeing the royal family from this magical trouble besetting them.

"Who is your choice for the source of this trouble?" Bryan was saying, as Merrigan set the letter aside to let the ink dry.

"Someone who doesn't want the queen to break the curse turning her brothers into swans," the magic book replied without hesitation. "Someone allied with the Worthy Warts, if this is part of the plot to capture magical creatures. Likely he or she has been promised the throne."

The sticking point was whether the king's mother was an accomplice or a victim. Sunflower had confirmed the pool in her garden had been drying up. That was part of the many small troubles in the palace, spreading blight through the kingdom. Some malady was blighting the roses and healing herbs. The young queen's actions were too easily interpreted to be dark magic.

"We have a growing tally of debt against the grannies," Bryan said, once they had agreed on their tactics.

He kissed Merrigan and left to go back to his room, once he made sure the sealed letter was given to a messenger to deliver to the palace in the morning. Merrigan heard his voice and Captain Garan's in the hall outside her door. Though muffled, she was very certain Bryan had asked the captain to post a guard on her door. Now that she had offered to help the royal family, their enemy might try to stop her.

Honk left through the window, to join the last brother of the young queen in guarding to ensure the baby princess wasn't stolen from her cradle. Rescuing her had been easy enough when there were seven princes on alert, but the baby was growing and heavier every time she came flying out the nursery window. Merrigan wished she could help them tonight, but all she could do was ask the Unseen for guidance and wisdom and try to get some sleep. She needed to be at her most alert tomorrow.

Her last thought as she finally dropped off to sleep was to be grateful she had listened to King Auberg and kept the crown he had loaned her in the plot to protect Belinda. She needed to look royal to ensure people listened to her.

~~~~~

A messenger from the palace met Merrigan, Bryan and Captain Garan midway between the inn and the palace gates. That was a good sign. They had feared the message from Merrigan would simply sit with all the other messages and petitions and reports that flooded the king's office every morning. Sunflower's messenger had managed to get someone to listen when he delivered the message.

When they arrived in the palace, they were separated from Captain Garan. While the parlor where they were left to sit was comfortable and provided with refreshments suitable for a royal visit at mid-morning, they were left to sit for nearly half an hour. By themselves.

That worked to their favor. Bib accessed the archives in the king's workroom, four doors down the hall from the parlor. Crystal bespoke Flecta, a magic mirror belonging to the king's mother. She was an elderly mirror, with the silver backing peeling away in spots, but still alert enough to give Crystal a good idea of the situation and fill in some pieces of the story. Dowager Queen Dorcas spoke to the mirror like children spoke to their favorite stuffed animal. Crystal was infuriated by Flecta's news.

"Either their enemies are sloppy, or more nasty than we feared," she said, her shimmery voice crackling in places. "The magic is slipshod, either way. Dorcas suspects she is the one tossing her granddaughter out the window, but she's terrified to speak her fears and ask someone to keep
~~~~~

watch, because she's been so unkind to Cygna. They used to be very close, until all the strange events began, and it was too easy to believe Cygna was serving dark powers."

King Frederick had been away on a diplomatic mission when the disappearances began. The palace servants who testified that they had seen the queen throw her daughter out the window and consort in the moonlight with swans were now out of their minds and locked up in the healers' hall. Frederick and Cygna used to communicate with hundreds of notes to each other, but now when she wrote, her handwriting was illegible, and often the notes burst into flames. Their notes to each other, collected over two years of courtship and marriage, were nothing but piles of ashes in the chests used to collect them.

Chancellor Domfries, the kingdom's wizard, was most sorrowful to conclude these were all signs that the queen's evil nature had grown foul enough to expose her. He feared for the baby princess and the prosperity of the kingdom, and urged the king to put her away, as soon as her conspirators in evil, the swans, had all been captured. They allowed Cygna to keep making the shirts, to lure the swans close enough to be captured. When winter came and the nettles stopped growing, Domfries had imported them from southern kingdoms, but they turned to ashes when Cygna tried to make them into thread. Domfries had taken to raging against the strictures of magic.

"And has said more than a dozen times now," Bib reported, excitement making his pages rustle nearly loudly enough to drown him out, "he agrees with those who teach that magic needs to be rationed. The people of Armorica have grown lazy, in his estimation, and depend on magic too much. It needs to be taken out of the hands of the uneducated majjians who let their actions be guided by sentiment. Not every goody-goody milkmaid and shepherd boy deserves magical help."

"Oh." Merrigan lost her breath for a moment, hearing Bib voice sentiments she had expressed quite often, at the beginning of her exile. Had she been taught to think that way, resenting those who received magical help because of the purity of their hearts?

CHAPTER NINE

King Frederick and Dowager Queen Dorcas entered the room. Both looked like they hadn't known a decent night's sleep in months. Merrigan felt some sympathy for the elderly queen, but shouldn't the woman know her legends and fables better, well enough to see the pattern and recognize what sort of tale enfolded their family?

A skinny, stooped, balding man dressed all in gray shuffled through the door behind the king and his mother. He leaned on a staff she considered rather garish, covered with carvings of all sorts of magical symbols, and topped with an enormous chunk of smoky crystal. His robes were heavily embroidered with magic symbols, in thread nearly the same color as the robes. The man obviously thought he was being subtle, but she suspected those symbols attracted all the available magic in the air and soil. What gave him the right to hoard magic and keep it out of the hands of honest hedge witches and healers and herbalists who were trying to help the people around them?

Crystal agreed with her. *I think he's the guilty party, or at least the focal point for whatever nasty magic is at work.* Bib agreed and Crystal reported a moment later that Bryan agreed.

"Princess Merrigan of Avylyn, Prince Bryan of Sylvanglade." King Frederick bowed. "We welcome you and thank you for your concern for our … difficulty." He glanced over at Domfries, who stared just a little too hard at Bib, sitting on Merrigan's lap. "Domfries?"

"Ah—er—yes, of course, Majesty. We are always grateful for new insight." Domfries turned his head, but his gaze didn't slide off Bib.

He knows what I am, Bib reported. *Oh, and he's made a major blunder. We have him now! The greedy snot is using a leach spell. I feel him trying to drain my magic into a cistern under the north tower. It's right under the cell where he's keeping the six swan princes, trying to suck away their magic.*

Flecta says everyone thinks the swans have been sent away to one of the royal farms, miles away, Crystal reported.

Merrigan could barely keep up with and respond properly to the formal welcoming words from Frederick and Dorcas. Her mind spun with ideas to take advantage of this new information.

The king and dowager queen took chairs facing Bryan and Merrigan. Domfries hovered at the doorway, shoulders hunched, gaze now focused on the secret pocket in the side of Merrigan's skirt where Crystal rode.

"Sir, you are rude, your gaze is too intimate." Bryan snapped his fingers, breaking Domfries' stare, startling both him and Frederick.

"Eyes up, Domfries," Queen Dorcas said. Two bright spots touched her cheeks. "I apologize for his ... familiarity, Princess Merrigan. If we didn't need his guidance so desperately in these ... well, these desperate times, I would have him sent from the room."

"In point of fact, he's been guiding you very badly." Merrigan slid her hand into the pocket and drew out the magic mirror, to put on her lap next to Bib. "He sensed Crystal's magical presence, and he's been trying to syphon away her power, and drain my friend Bib. Do you know, Wizard Domfries, that the most talented of magical books can access the stored knowledge of all the books around them, and sort through their secrets and find the most vital information in a matter of minutes?"

Domfries went so white, the gray stubble on his cheeks looked like mud and his robes seemed like charcoal in contrast.

"And Crystal can speak to any magic mirrors within several miles. For instance," Bryan said, nodding to Queen Dorcas, "your old friend, Flecta reports that you are quite distressed because you fear you have been enchanted to throw your granddaughter out the nursery window."

Dorcas wailed softly and struggled to stay upright, while her son rose slowly to his feet, his face flushing with fury.

This was the pivotal point in this meeting. He could either accuse them of lies and unwarranted attacks on his mother and wizard. Or he could be a clear and quick thinker and consider the possibility that those he trusted had been lying to him.

"The captured swans haven't been taken away," Merrigan added, to give the young king a push in the right direction. "They're being held captive in a room lined with runes of the nastiest sort, to drain their magic and keep them trapped in their swan shape. Domfries has a cistern under the north tower, holding the water stolen from the queen's garden."

"Impossible," Domfries croaked. His face flushed red. "They promised me no one would ever guess."

"I will wager their promise was that no *man or woman* majjian would ever see what you were doing," Bib said, speaking aloud. "They're rather sloppy, these people who convinced you to work against the royal family. They forgot to weave majjian creatures and objects into that warranty. Crystal and I are not man or woman but are magic ourselves."

Domfries raised his hands, sparkles gathering on his fingertips. Frederick shouted, leaped across the room and slammed Domfries into the door. The thud echoed through the room. The wizard slowly slid down the door, into a puddle of ostentatious gray robes on the floor. His staff toppled, clattering to the floor, and the crystal snapped off. Despite all its sharp points and flat surfaces, it rolled across the floor, aiming for the door. And it glowed.

"Get that before it escapes," Crystal shouted. "But don't let it touch your flesh."

Frederick growled and kicked at the crystal. A flash of gray-tinted light burst from it, and a clang like a dented bronze gong. It skittered sideways, bounced off a chair leg, then switched direction and again rolled toward the door. Bryan snatched up an ornately painted chamber pot from a curtained niche in the wall, turned it over and slammed it down on top of the crystal. It clanged against the inside of the pot. Merrigan reflected that they were lucky the pot hadn't been used yet, but the disgusting mess would have served the crystal right. Bryan put one foot on the pot that bounced from the crystal's attempts to break free.

"All right, Bib," she said, "now what?"

"I'll wager that despicable thing has been reporting to its true masters," Crystal said. "Until we find out how much they know, best to keep it entirely in the dark. Majesty, do you have a nice big, heavy chest, bound with lots of iron?"

Frederick thought for a moment, then grinned. It wasn't a nice grin. Merrigan sensed a need to return some of the pain he had been suffering.

Dorcas hurried from the room, head high and shoulders straight, visibly fighting tears. Merrigan thought about going after her. There was no telling what a royal woman would do when her participation in an evil scheme had been revealed, especially if she was someone's unwilling puppet. The king shouted orders and then he flooded her and Bryan, Bib and Crystal with questions. By the time that heavy chest arrived, and a guardsman with thick gloves picked up the crystal, wrapped it in burlap and dropped it in the chest and locked it, Dorcas returned with young Queen Cygna. The two women had their arms around each other and wept. Merrigan and Bryan retreated to a corner of the room while the royal family embraced for several minutes. It was rather refreshing hearing the king apologize, his voice breaking, and the sounds of kisses exchanged among the three of them. What they lacked, however, was Cygna's voice, both sobs and words.

That had to be remedied as soon as possible.

"You two need badly to talk," Merrigan said, once the tears had slowed and handkerchiefs came out. Frederick pleased her greatly when he settled on a sofa with Cygna perched on his lap. "Yes, I know finding the cure for the curse on your brothers requires you to be silent, but from what I heard, you two were communicating just fine in writing. Why didn't you tell your husband about the swans and the nettle shirts?"

Cygna looked around as she gestured as if writing.

"If I may be of assistance, Highness?" Bib said. He flipped open on the low table where he and Crystal lay, in the center of their circle of chairs. "Think what you want to say. I will hear you and show the words."

I tried to write it. I thought I was being discrete, with the nettles and shirts and meeting my brothers, because I knew how it had to look. There were so many odd rumors going around by the time Frederick found me and we fell in love. There were already strange stories being told about a witch in the woods who turned into birds and flew around, I didn't want people thinking I was the witch. So when I was caught with the swans, I tried to write out the whole story, but the pages caught on fire before I finished the first sentence.

"That wretch Domfries' doing, I'll wager," Frederick growled.

Someone tapped on the door. Before anyone could answer, the door swung open. A maid walked in, holding the baby princess. Cygna nearly broke her silence as she leaped off Frederick's lap and ran to her daughter. She covered the baby's face with kisses and wept again.

The debt Nanny Tulip and her cohorts owed to the world in general had doubled in size. There was no excuse for this misery.

"Under the circumstances," Dorcas said, watching the happy reunion with tears in her eyes, "it would be wise for me to retire to one of the country houses and leave them to heal without my ... well, my presence reminding them of what could have happened." She shuddered and looked down at her open palms. "When I think of all those nights of waking in the hall, wondering why I had started sleepwalking, and every time there was a commotion in the nursery, and the swan feathers in the crib or in the little one's hand ..." She closed her eyes and shuddered.

"I think some privacy would be kind," Merrigan said. "Shall we take a walk? Perhaps check on the state of your garden? Truth has a way of starting nasty magic unraveling."

From the new pallor in the old queen's cheeks, Merrigan half-expected to find the door to the garden hidden or stubbornly locked. She was relieved it opened easily, and the pool still had water in it. Dorcas confessed with new tears that it was only a quarter of its normal size and depth. The thorny vines clinging to the walls of the inner courtyard surrounding the garden had reached the windows of the second story. Merrigan remembered how the thorns had taken over her mother's garden, how quickly they had spread to cover the balconies and windows on the second and third floors, after she was tricked by Nanny Tulip to break the rules.

"I think we can solve several problems at once, Mi'lady," Bib announced, once Dorcas, Merrigan, and Bryan, carrying him and Crystal, had walked around the garden, and came back to settle on the benches by the pool. "It's encouraging that so little snow has gotten in here, and the remaining plants are still green."

"Is it?" Dorcas looked around and shuddered as she wrapped her arms around herself. "This place is too quiet. It's not the quiet of winter. In fact, it was never quiet in winter here, until the troubles came. I blamed poor Cygna for that. We all found her too easy to blame, when things started going wrong."

The first order of business was finding the north tower, to free the six swans. An illusion and forgetfulness spell enfolded it, enabling Domfries to go about his work without interference. There were several cracks in the spell, however, Crystal reported. The despicable man had been befuddling the servants. They came regularly to clean and cook, do his laundry and feed the swans, and then forgot what they had done as soon as they walked out the door of the tower. That had resulted in a large number of palace servants being dismissed from their positions, because they couldn't explain where they had gone or what they had been doing when they vanished for an hour at a time. The befuddlement spells interfered with the illusion spell. The resulting cracks allowed Crystal and Bib to unravel the spell.

Several of the guardsmen who came with Frederick and Bryan and Merrigan to deal with the situation quickly grew angry that they had so easily forgotten the tower was there. After all, the palace was nearly two centuries old, and the tower was four stories tall and had once held the royal library and schoolrooms for the nobility. Frederick soon discovered that Domfries had confiscated most of the truly useful books when he took over the tower, nearly thirty years ago. The paltry remains of the library, now in the east tower, had no useful books left to deal with the dilemma of the swans and nettles, and the baby princess vanishing from her crib.

The six swan princes acted with dignity and decorum when the door of their prison opened. They bowed to King Frederick and listened quietly as he apologized and explained and invited them to make themselves comfortable in the queen's garden. There they would be reunited with their sister and niece, while they waited to break the curse.

Cygna had to finish the shirts by herself. Domfries had done his best to eradicate nettles throughout the kingdom, but he had a private cache that he was trying to enchant to give him power over the princes. Bib and Crystal were suspicious as soon as the nettles were discovered and studied them for several hours to ensure they weren't laden with inimical magic. As soon as they declared the plants untainted, Cygna got to work.

The continuing sympathy for the young queen, despite the evidence against her, had contributed to frustrating Domfries' spells and his plans. The "old hags" he referred to in his journals couldn't get into the palace, so he had to get the baby princess out to them, before they could take her. They would keep her until she was sixteen, draining her of her magic. On her sixteenth birthday, Domfries would play the hero, returning her home. He intended to convince the king to let him marry the princess as his reward and become king in his place. Merrigan shuddered at the shock waiting for the girl if the plan had succeeded, learning she was royal and forced to marry the nasty old man.

Fortunately, the seven swan princes had intervened to protect their niece, each time the sleepwalking dowager queen had thrown her out the window. Unfortunately, they were blamed for the disappearances when the baby pulled their feathers, leaving evidence of what had happened.

While Cygna made the last shirt, Honk went out searching for the seventh swan brother. The six brothers were unable to fly, after spending so much time in captivity, constantly drained of the magic inherent in their royal blood.

Bryan and Crystal spent the day in the queen's garden, talking with the swan princes and getting their side of the story while Merrigan and Bib helped Cygna. They were from Peradyne, in the far north. The prime minister had convinced their father that turning the princes into swans would increase the inherent magic of the kingdom and cure the drought afflicting it. He thought he was helping the kingdom, and circumventing the king, who had a bad habit of marrying flighty girls. Four queens had given him eight children. Each bride had come under the influence of a group of old grannies who wanted access to the queen's garden. Each one died when a new blight struck the garden.

By the time the seventh son had been born, the door into the queen's garden had vanished entirely, and the thorns in the courtyard had become so thick that people bricked up the balconies and windows. Merrigan shuddered when Bryan related that information to her. Hadn't she done that to Avylyn, under Nanny Tulip's guidance?

Under the influence of old grannies, the king cursed his sons. The prime minister realized his error before the grannies could take the swans away. He helped the princes flee. While Cygna grew up, he wore himself out protecting her from the influence of the grannies and finding a cure for the curse. When the time was right, he sent Cygna out to find her brothers and break the curse.

The grannies led Frederick's hunting party to her and doused him in several love potions to ensure he became infatuated and carried her off, separating her from her brothers. Cygna showed great strength of character, defending herself from the king's advances, and earning the friendship of his mother, until the love potions wore off and real love took root. By the time the baby had been born, the grannies had recruited Domfries.

Merrigan told Cygna and Dorcas about the queen's garden in Seafoam and how apologizing had initiated the healing. They agreed that apologies and honesty were the most important ingredients in healing their family, the garden, and eventually the entire kingdom. Merrigan's face burned as she admitted how she had brought Clara's reformation curse down on herself. Later, she laughed as she realized how light and clean she felt afterward. Confession was as healing as apologizing.

By nightfall, Cygna had seven complete nettle thread shirts ready and waiting. She brought them to the garden, and spent some time sitting with her brothers, cuddling and weeping, until Merrigan had to leave. She didn't trust herself not to get snappish and critical if the tears and moping grew too much for her. So, she missed the moment when Honk arrived with the seventh brother, and the transformation by moonlight to become princes began.

The celebration that swept through the kingdom lasted for three days. When Merrigan and Bryan and their guards left on the fourth day, the seven princes insisted on flying escort for them. They had gained the ability to change into swans by choice, no need for moonlight. Several of Cygna's brothers admitted they had spent so much time in swan shape, it felt far more natural than their man bodies. They were unsure what they wanted to do with their lives. There was little reason to return to their father's kingdom. He was reported to be in his dotage, and his newest wife was a quite admirable, strong, sensible woman who was running the kingdom and making improvements. The people were happy and at peace, and the princes didn't know if they wanted to get into the whole ugly, sticky mess of proving who they were and then taking control out of those capable hands. They hadn't been raised to rule and weren't sure they wanted the responsibility.

"Yes, but they're born to responsibility. That's something my father always drilled into us. Royal blood means responsibility more than privilege," Bryan said, late in the afternoon on their third day of travel.

"Perhaps you should give them prince lessons," Garan offered.

A spark of mischief in his eyes belied the somber line of his mouth and his tone. Soon the three of them were chuckling softly. Bryan tipped his head back to search the sky for their flying wedge escort of eight swans. According to Honk, they were testing the air for magic currents and seeking signs of majjians in the landscape below. In unfamiliar territory, any majjian they ran into could just as easily be friendly as nasty, on the defensive and offensive if they thought their territory was being invaded. The dwindling of magic throughout the land might make them more difficult to deal with, expecting any intruder to be a possible enemy.

More important, within a day, two at the most, their party would cross the border into Sylvanglade.

The swan princes and Honk flew ahead to scout out the leading edge of the sleeping curse, so they wouldn't bumble into it and get themselves trapped, without the cure and defense within their reach.

Using the sleeping cap, reversed, to ward off the sleeping curse, was still only a theoretical cure. Merrigan had decided weeks ago she would wear it, just in case it didn't work. She quite trusted Bryan to be able to haul her out of the area touched by the sleeping curse and kiss her awake. She didn't trust herself to have the strength to haul him out, although she was quite sure her kiss would be just as potent for breaking the curse.

Better to be the one to take the risk that they were wrong about the sleeping cap. Bryan was born to be a hero, after all.

Finding the leading edge of the sleeping curse wasn't hard. Over the years since it fell on Sylvanglade, the people of the country had learned to live with it the best they could, and that meant keeping track of how quickly it spread. The king's counselors and advisors and scholars who had escaped the first explosion of the curse that enveloped the palace set up barriers around the affected area. Then they kept note of how quickly the soldiers patrolling the perimeter fell asleep at their assigned posts. The soldiers were there to keep people from going in, not to stop looting, but to keep the looters from being trapped. Far too many had been caught because they didn't believe the curse would touch them, until it was too late. The first few years of the spread of the sleeping curse were hectic because the perimeter had to be moved out several inches in every direction every day. Then the rate slowed and steadied, until the sleeping curse swallowing Sylvanglade grew at exactly half a mile every year. As the circle expanded, the speed of the line moving slowed and could be predicted. People had time to prepare to move, to empty their houses and shops and plan where to plant crops the following year, knowing they were safe at least that long.

The appearance of the eight swans flying escort for the small traveling party aroused interest and some hope. Within two hours of the swans being sighted, word had spread. A growing crowd came hurrying down the highway to meet their traveling party as they approached the first waystation on the main road into Sylvanglade. People shouted questions and begged for swan feathers to ward off trouble or sickness.

Merrigan let Bryan and Captain Garan deal with the people, answering their questions as vaguely as possible. After a while, they refused to answer any questions, except to ask the desperate people to let their traveling party through and promise answers would come.

CHAPTER TEN

A horn blared up ahead of them, just when the road had crested a small hill and they could see down into a valley, where the barrier stood. Several men in the dark green uniforms of Sylvanglade's army came marching out, escorting a man on horseback. More soldiers moved out from a long, low building and set about dispersing the crowd that blocked the road.

"Thank the Unseen," Bryan said, rising up in his stirrups. His expression brightened and he raised one arm, waving it.

"What is it? Who is it?" Garan asked. They had been riding three across, with Merrigan in the middle, ever since the leading edge of the crowd came out to meet them.

"Rulio! Chancellor Rulio!" Bryan waved once more, then dropped down into the saddle hard enough to make his horse grunt. "Make way," he called, and dug his heels into his mount, to move ahead of them.

He didn't need to rush, Merrigan reflected, since this Rulio was only a hundred yards or so away from them.

Or maybe he did, because he had been away so long, and to see a familiar face, someone who wasn't caught in the sleeping curse, had to be a relief. When they met, the two men leaned out far enough to clasp each other's forearms, they nearly pulled each other out of their saddles. Laughing, they slapped each other's backs, and then Bryan gestured back at their traveling party. Merrigan was close enough now to see the silver streaks in Rulio's red hair, and the hope and wonder that lit his face.

Then the murmurs swept through the crowd as people heard what the two men were saying. Someone caught Bryan's name, someone else recognized him. Soon his name became a cheer and a chant. Prince Bryan had returned, with hope, a cure, something to break the curse.

Merrigan wished Bryan had waited until they were indoors to reveal that much news. Of course, people might be speculating, once they recognized him. Still, she hated having hopes raised if there was a chance that the sleeping cap might not be the cure. She knew from bitter experience what it was like to have hopes and dreams and plans destroyed. Granted, many of her expectations had been unreasonable, but she still knew the bitter sting of disappointment. Expand that to hundreds of weary, perhaps even desperate people who were sick and tired of living under a curse and having to adjust their lives a few feet every year. That kind of disappointment could lead to disaster.

Rulio proved to be a sensible man. He had soldiers move out to enclose their traveling party and disperse the crowd, so they could complete their journey without obstruction. Soon, they were all dismounting and heading into the building that housed the current seat of Sylvanglade's provisional government. Servants took away their horses to stable them and more servants led them to antechambers where they could leave their cloaks and freshen up before convening in the council chamber. Merrigan reached the council chamber first, grateful to sit down and have a maid fuss over her and bring her tea and offer her a nice selection of cakes.

Thuds overhead announced the arrival and landing of the swans. They had agreed the seven brothers would stay together, in swan form, and Honk alone would join whatever meeting convened. Merrigan shivered at a new thought: as the only present member of the royal family, Bryan was de facto king of Sylvanglade. Who would see him as the savior and remedy for all their problems, and who would see him as an obstacle to claiming sole authority over the beleaguered kingdom?

A thudding on the far left door of three into the room announced Honk's arrival. Merrigan wondered how he had gotten from the roof to the door. Had he knocked a shutter open? She asked the maid to open the door and warned her to step back.

"How do things look?" she asked, once the maid had left. Best not to have a stranger hear her talking to the swan until she knew the attitudes in Sylvanglade.

Royals in tents beyond the trees. Bespoke a few owls. Don't like them, nobody likes them, throwing orders around. Honk settled down at the foot of one of the cast iron stoves radiating lovely heat from the four corners of the room.

"What kind of royals?" she asked, just as the door on the far wall opened and Bryan strode through.

"The worst kind," he said, nearly spitting. She had never seen his face so dark and his expression so disgusted, except for when he had to deal with Bithia and Barbarina. "King Steffan and Queen Arissia." His mouth flattened, like he fought not to spit. "Talithia's parents," he added, when she could only shake her head, unable to place the names.

"What do they want?" Merrigan's disgust for the duty-evading parents of Branwell's promised bride almost matched Bryan's.

Chancellor Rulio stepped into the room just then, and he laughed, a sharp, barking sound. "They're putting all the blame for this on Prince Branwell, of course." He gestured to take in the sleeping kingdom outside. "They won't admit that their daughter brought the sleeping curse with her. They've been working for years to convince people that Branwell caused it. They've grown rather vicious because they can't stop the rumors that they feared Branwell wouldn't be protected by the hero provision and break the curse within their kingdom."

"So if the rumors won't stop, what are they doing?"

"Oh, now they're trying to prove he was never hero enough to rescue their daughter. They've gathered a gaggle of princes eager to prove they're heroes, and will send them in, one by one."

"What do they do if one by one their princes fall asleep after only walking a few minutes?" Merrigan said.

Ropes, Honk said. *Long ropes.*

Bryan and Merrigan both laughed, and then had to translate for Rulio. He gave the three of them considering looks.

"Highness, you've had some adventures, haven't you? When did you learn the language of the beasts?" he asked.

"Just birds." Bryan held up his hand with the ring, for explanation.

"What do we do if one of them is a real hero?" Merrigan asked. "If one of them is protected by the hero provision in all magic spells, and he gets through to the palace and finds where Talithia fell and he kisses her and breaks the spell. What then?"

"With the twisting of the curse through the attempt to escape it ..." Rulio sighed. "King Steffan already has an entire battalion of advocates and barristers arguing that Branwell has proven he isn't worthy to be king. Since it's his fault the curse took their daughter, he should forfeit the kingdom. They want all of Sylvanglade annexed to their kingdom as recompense for the suffering their family has endured all these years."

"What about the suffering they inflicted on my family and the entire kingdom?" Bryan growled.

"You can almost hope the curse only releases Talithia when her hopeful true love kisses her, and the entire kingdom remains under the sleeping curse," Merrigan said. "No one will want it, and the people will be safe, protected." She sighed. "And sleeping forever."

"We need to get in there and free Branwell and give him a chance to be the hero."

"How?" Rulio said. "And how quickly can you do it?"

The sounds of voices in argument filtered down the hall.

Now, Honk said. *Go now. Don't let them see you.*

"He's right. If they see me, they might recognize me," Bryan said. "They're foolish and selfish and cowardly, but they aren't exactly stupid. They'll realize I'm here to try something."

"And they'll either stop you or try to confiscate whatever cure you've brought, using those same advocates and barristers." Rulio shuddered. "Please, Highness, we can catch up and you can explain things later." He gestured at the door Honk had come through. "That's the fastest way out."

"Do you have it?" Bryan hurried ahead and pushed the door open.

In answer, Merrigan pulled the sleeping cap out of the saddlebag that held Bib and Crystal, then tucked it back safely deep inside. Rulio hurried to shut the door behind them. With Honk leading the way, Bryan and Merrigan headed for the door out of the building.

Bryan took them on a circuitous route, to avoid being mobbed by relieved people who would want to know what their prince was going to do, and even insist on going with them. The sooner they tested the sleeping cap, the better for all of them.

Merrigan admitted she wouldn't mind seeing a trail of hopeful princes scattered down the road through the kingdom, sleeping, fallen within sight of Talithia's parents, and sending fear into the hearts of the remaining princes. It wasn't nice, and she admitted the useless third and fourth and fifth-born princes who had been chasing Belinda weren't representative of the breed. Quite a large number of princes who had no hope of inheriting a kingdom turned out to be heroes. After all, look how wonderful and heroic Bayl and Bryan were. So much inherent magic collected around the youngest royal sons and daughters. She shuddered a little, with a hot thread of anger at the core, when she wondered if that had been the first step in the Worthy Warts' plan: to convince the younger sons and daughters they were useless and despised, to stunt the growth of heroic minds and hearts and block the magic that should have come to them for heroic, magical deeds when they were grown.

"Please, Unseen, help me to repay another small part of my debt, and be heroic today," she whispered, as they approached the barrier that marked the beginning of the curse.

"What was that?" Bryan held out his hand. For a moment she thought he was asking for the sleeping cap, and she couldn't let him take that risk. He caught hold of her hand and they took the last dozen steps together.

The guards on either side of the opening in the barrier grinned and bowed as Bryan and Merrigan approached. Then their gazes landed on the swan waddling along several steps behind them.

"He's with us," Bryan said. "You will be immune, won't you, Honk?"

In answer, the swan took a few running steps and launched, tipping sideways to go through the opening in the barrier. He swooped upward and flew in a wide circle over their heads, several dozen yards within the area touched by the curse.

Hurry! I will look ahead, he honked down at them.

"That's clear enough." Merrigan caught her breath. "But let's do hurry, in case whatever magic protects him has a time limit. I should hate to see how much damage falling from that height could do him, if he falls asleep."

Bryan nodded and held out his hand. His smile faded and serious lines crinkled around his eyes and mouth. Merrigan had thought through this moment multiple times. They had grown so loud, Bib had overheard her thoughts. He didn't like her taking the risk, but he agreed with her reasoning. The only part of their plan that she sidestepped was wrapping a rope around her waist, so Bryan could retrieve her if the sleeping cap didn't protect her from the sleeping curse. There was no time. He would guess what she was doing and stop her.

Turning her back to the opening in the barrier, Merrigan pretended to fumble in the saddlebag, taking small steps backward. She pulled out Crystal and handed her to Bryan. Then she took several more small steps. Her foot went over the line. A tingle touched her heel. She nearly dropped the sleeping cap as she pulled it out by its silly tassel, when she couldn't remember for a moment which color was for sleeping and which was for waking.

"Doesn't matter, does it?" She took another step backward, going completely over the line into the curse.

"Merrigan, no!" Bryan shouted and reached for her.

She tugged the cap down past her ears and took another step back. If she slept, could she arrange for her leg to stick out far enough for him to grab her foot and drag her back?

Another step back. The tingle in her heel faded. Another step. The air seemed to hum around her, and she likened it to the far distant sound of hundreds of people breathing in unison. A giggle escaped her as she wondered if they all had sleepers breath, and what their mouths had to taste like after years of sleeping.

"I'm still awake." Another giggle. "Aren't I?"

"Merrigan ..." Bryan shuddered, and she thought he would shout at her. "Have I told you lately how much I love you? Despite how much I want to shake you until your eyes rattle right now."

"I love you, too, Bryan. Here's the real test of our theory." She faltered for just a second, then pulled off the sleeping cap. "Catch!" she shouted, stopping his protest. She flung the sleeping cap to him and took two more steps back. She didn't start to crumple. She felt more awake. Energized.

"It works." Bryan choked and jammed the cap down over his ears and hurried after her.

The green side of the sleeping cap cured the sleeping curse inflicted by the white side, and that cure was strong enough to fight the sleeping curse holding Sylvanglade.

The question was how long that cure would last.

"Well, if either of us feels sleepy, we can put the cap on again and refresh the cure," Bryan said, when Merrigan voiced that little dilemma. He handed Crystal back to her. "Were either of you in on this risky scheme?" he demanded, as she put the mirror back into the bag.

"Not exactly approving," Crystal said, her voice shimmering and prim, "but we understood her reasoning."

"Highness? Are you all right?" one of the guards called after them.

"Fine!" Bryan turned to wave at them. "Tell no one what we've done. Give us three hours, then …" He shrugged. What could anyone do to help them, if they didn't come back in three hours, unable to wake Branwell and Talithia and trapped here with the other sleepers?

The two guards stood tall and straight and saluted. Bryan caught hold of Merrigan's hand and they hurried down the road.

"Which way, Honk?" he called to the swan flying several hundred paces ahead of them.

"Don't you know the way? Don't you know where Talithia would have been when the curse took her?" Merrigan asked.

"She should have been in the guest suite, but there's no telling how the curse brought her and the spindle together. We weren't exactly given fair warning about the curse's details. As I recall … well, things warped, and there was some delay, like the curse couldn't find Talithia at first. We all started to relax, then Branwell and Talithia had that ridiculous shrieking, slamming argument. Some of us realized that just wasn't … natural." Bryan shrugged. "All we could do was run for it, and we nearly got caught when the curse enveloped the palace."

They made an effort not to look at their surroundings as they hurried down the road. Still, what Merrigan glimpsed wasn't anywhere near as awful as she had feared. After all, once the initial, rather violent explosion of magic took place, people still had time to figure out what was happening and get out of there. Some people had tried to go back into the cursed area to rescue loved ones or steal, depending on charms and magic potions to protect them. The general area outside the palace walls would be littered with people who had fallen, caught by the sleeping curse, but starting three streets out from the palace, everything was relatively neat, maybe some debris of dropped packages and personal belongings left behind in a hasty exit, but no people sprawled everywhere.

Merrigan had thought she was ready, but she wasn't, and she was glad of Bryan's hand holding hers tightly. She wanted to get into the palace and find Talithia and slap that sleeping cap on her head, and maybe slap some sense into the spoiled little twit while she was at it.

The sleeping curse affected animals, too. They were everywhere, curled up in the streets and sprawled on rooftops, and lying down in harness, wherever they were when the curse hit. The quiet was deeper than the stillness of a snowy morning after a heavy snowfall. That sense of shimmering promise that accompanied the snow as the sun rose was entirely missing here.

But … no. Merrigan held her breath and tried to listen through the hissing of her blood in her ears. She smiled as she caught it again: the sound of hundreds of people all breathing deeply and slowly in unison. This time she shared her thoughts with Bryan. He smiled and squeezed her hand tighter.

As they drew closer to the palace, the air seemed to thicken, making their steps slower. Merrigan could still breathe as easily as before, yet she had the sensation of wading through syrup that thickened the deeper they went. A whisper urged her to let go of their purpose and simply sit and let her muscles go limp, her mind blank. And sleep.

"It's likely part of the magic that preserves everything, and everyone. Those who have kept watch say that wind doesn't stir the trees inside the curse," Bryan said, when she shared her impressions. "Rain and snow don't fall inside. Which is good for those who were caught outside when sleep took them. I wonder if food that was cooking when the first explosion of sleep hit the palace is still good, after all these years."

"Let's hope the Unseen is kind, and we will soon find out," she whispered.

Whispering seemed the appropriate tone of voice, to avoid disturbing those who slept all around them.

Merrigan scolded herself silently not to shake Talithia when she found the silly princess. After all, hadn't she made even more foolish, selfish choices? No, the people to blame were her parents, just as guilty as Nanny Tulip, with their "we know better than anyone else" attitude.

Honk flew out through the open gates of the palace to meet them. He led them through two outer courtyards, and in through a smaller courtyard that Bryan named the family's private entrance. They went into the palace. The hall they followed curved with the tower it passed through, and they came out into another courtyard.

"My mother's garden. Not the queen's garden, but ..." Bryan muffled a moan and pointed with his free hand. His other hand tightened painfully around Merrigan's.

A man lay sprawled on the pavement, looking as if he had collapsed in the act of crawling, with one hand outstretched toward what looked like a massive tangle of thorny vines.

Huge, pointy thorns, as long as Merrigan's hand. She knew thorns, after the awful mess she had made.

"Branwell," Bryan whispered, and staggered the last few steps until he reached his brother. He rolled him over on his back and caught his breath. "He's still alive."

Merrigan bit back, "Are you sure?" before the words escaped her. She had feared a few times, as they contemplated this moment, they would find the people at the center of the sleeping curse were dead. Just what she would expect from an enchanter evil enough to set a curse on an innocent baby. Why not dig the knife in deeper and put a time limit on how long she could sleep, before she died?

"If we're both thinking the same thing ..." She gestured at the knot of thorns and vines. "He was trying to get to her, to break the curse. The hero provision helped him find her and get this far, at least."

"That would clear things up much quicker, and more easily and cleanly, if we let things progress as they were meant to." For several long moments, Bryan knelt next to his sleeping brother, looking back and forth between Branwell and the thorns that encapsulated Talithia.

Merrigan wondered if he felt the same temptation she did, just for a moment, to leave Talithia there, wake Branwell, then dig into the task of waking each sleeper individually. Then when all of Sylvanglade was rescued except the princess, whichever desperate prince actually woke her could have her. But not Sylvanglade.

That was the sticking point. If none of the hopeful princes managed to get this far, or wake her, then the curse might continue to take more of the land every year. Perhaps keep creeping across the landscape until it entirely devoured Armorica?

Merrigan thought of all the friends she had made in her travels, especially the warehouse full of orphans, all falling asleep, trapped in this same syrupy air ... because she and Bryan were irritated with the princess and her rule-bending parents.

"Let's get this over with," she murmured. Honk added a few honks that didn't translate as words but were clearly support.

Bryan shrugged, gave them a crooked smile, and pulled the sleeping cap out of his coat. He took a deep breath and leaned down to slide the cap onto his brother's head.

"I wonder," Merrigan said, as they waited for that first deep inhale of waking, "are you older than him now? How many of your brothers were caught here?"

Branwell groaned and one arm flopped outward and he smacked his lips a few times. Bryan watched his brother, not even blinking, until the older man's eyes fluttered open. Branwell blinked until his gaze landed on Merrigan. He frowned. He fumbled until he got an elbow underneath himself and struggled to sit up. Bryan reached to help him.

That startled an oath out of Branwell, who stared. Understanding swept across his face.

"Bry? Talithia—" He nearly knocked himself over, twisting to look toward the knot of thorns and vines. Branwell groaned again and rubbed his face with the heels of his hands. "Not a dream, is it?"

"No," Bryan said. "Sorry."

"Don't be. You and that mirror of yours tried to warn us." Another groan. "Help me up?" His gaze fastened on Merrigan once they were both standing. "Who might you be?"

"Merrigan." Bryan shook his head when Branwell frowned, visibly struggling to place the name. "It doesn't matter. What matters is hacking through those thorns to get to Talithia, so you can finally break this curse."

"What makes you think I want to?"

"Bran!"

"I know. I know. I've had … how long? Doesn't matter. Tell me later. From the looks of you …" He sighed and scrubbed his face with both hands. "Years. I've had however long to think, in my dreams, and figure things out. It's that stupid argument we had. And her idiot, arrogant parents, trying to circumvent the curse. The curse wouldn't have been slapped on her in the first place if they had taken some responsibility, shown some consideration or others.

"You want to know what's ironic? And poetic, at the same time? The celebration, when her parents realized they were finally going to have a baby after years of waiting and trying every magic potion and every hedge witch and faerie godmother and … the celebration woke an old sorceress who needed to sleep for precisely fifty years, to the day and hour and minute and second to complete a complicated spell to locate a lost library … and the celebration was so loud and so long, it woke her. And when she scolded the king, who was her great-great-nephew, for his rudeness, he laughed at her and told her reading and sleep were both overrated. So, she cursed the baby with sleep before she was even born. And knowing how King Steffan twists the law to his benefit, she probably added a few codicils, to cover any tricks he tried to play to escape his punishment."

He studied the thick bundle of thorns and vines where his sleeping princess lay. He shook his head, hard enough to make himself wobble. Then he turned to Bryan, his frown turning rather comical.

"How did you wake me?" His frown turned into a sheepish grin, and he snorted a little laughter, when Bryan explained the sleeping cap. "Clever. And embarrassing." He glanced at Merrigan. "So … you've been questing all this time? Trying to rescue our kingdom? Falling in love?"

"Is it that obvious?" Bryan grinned as he tucked the sleeping cap back in his coat.

"She wouldn't be here with you, risking the curse, if she wasn't in love, and you're too noble to let a girl trail after you if you didn't love her, too. Despite my stupidity and pride, I do know you, Bry." His smile twisted into a frown again. "Wait, where's Bayl? You two are a matched pair." He slapped a hand on his thigh. "Don't tell me. He finally convinced that princess of his—Belinda?—to marry him, and he's settled down and abandoned you to your own adventures?"

"We still need to find and rescue Bayl, and yes, reunite him with Belinda," Merrigan said. "As soon as you do a little heroic work yourself." She gestured at the thorns and Talithia.

"Why would I want to?" he murmured, turning to look again. "Why do I need to? Just use that cap of yours to wake everyone. Including her. Once she's awake, the curse breaks, you think?"

"Bran, that's not how to fix things." Bryan reached out to clasp his brother's shoulder and give him one good shake. "There's more trouble than you can imagine, twisting magic throughout all Armorica. As much as we can, we have to follow the rules, the patterns established through all the fables and legends that keep repeating. It's the only way to start straightening out the tangles. Be the hero we all need. Move beyond your own hurt feelings. Climb past your pride. Go get Talithia out of those thorns and kiss her and break the curse the way it's meant to."

"What if I can't?" His voice was so soft, Merrigan nearly didn't hear the words. He shrugged. "True love's kiss, remember?"

"The potential for true love," Bryan said, glancing to Merrigan.

Her face warmed, and he smiled, that special smile full of humor and shared memories.

"What are you talking about?" Branwell's voice cracked.

"Merrigan was under a sleeping curse. She took an apple meant for Belinda, and I had just recognized her, realized who she was, and I had no way of knowing if I loved her. We hadn't seen each other since we were children, but ..." Bryan shrugged. "I wanted the possibility. I couldn't leave her sleeping there, after the sacrifice she made. So I kissed her."

"Three times," Merrigan said. He grinned wider, blushing a little.

"Potential, huh?" Branwell looked back and forth between them. "There's a lot more to this story than you're telling me."

"Later." Bryan gripped his brother's shoulder again, turning him to face the bundle of thorns and princess. "Go be her hero, be our kingdom's hero. At least try, all right?"

"You're right, but ..." A raspy chuckle escaped him as he took a couple steps forward. Then glanced back at them. "I'd love to grab her parents and drag them in here and just leave them with her ... but I can't do that to Sylvanglade. What good is a kingdom with the palace swallowed up in sleep? Father's too thrifty to put up with having to build a new palace. How long has he been waiting for things to get fixed?"

"Nobody got out of the palace before the curse caught them," Merrigan said, fighting not to let her temper touch her voice. "While you've been sleeping, the curse has been spreading through the whole kingdom. In a few more years, it will be lapping at the borders, and then what will your people do?"

CHAPTER ELEVEN

"It's … not just the palace?" Branwell's expression grew stern.

He shook his head and seemed to shake off his irritation and uncertainty. He pulled his shoulders back, took a deep breath, and strode the last dozen paces to the bundle of thorns. Kneeling, he reached out to brush the thick barrier of thorns with the fingertips of one hand.

"How do I get in? Bry, do you have a sword?" He didn't look away from the thick barrier but held out his hand.

Bryan unsheathed his short sword and handed it to his brother. He and Merrigan held hands and stood back as Branwell made the first slash. The blade bounced off with a dull ringing sound, like metal on stone.

"This is … as much my fault as it is yours." He took half a step back and raised the sword higher and slashed down. "I should have stood up to your parents. I should have been there, in your kingdom, waiting for the curse to trigger, and then race in to rescue you. Maybe I was afraid." Branwell slashed again. "I used to dream about being a hero, traveling the land, rescuing fair maidens. Until I figured out that my responsibility as crown prince kept me tied to Sylvanglade."

Another slash. This time, the thorns crackled and sounded like wood under the blade, instead of stone. He slashed between every fourth or fifth word, chopping his sentences like he chopped the thorns.

"You know what's really strange? I've been dreaming about you. Angry at you, and then wishing …" He paused to glance over his shoulder at Bryan and Merrigan. "Wondering what it'll be like when we finally kiss for the first time. Wondering if we could have fixed things if we had kissed before your birthday."

He paused, gasping for breath.

"I'm sorry. I guess that's the important thing, right? I'm sorry. I hope you are, too." He reared back and stabbed down hard with the sword, jamming it between two thick vines. "I was scared." He leaned all his weight into the sword, twisting. "My father rescued my mother from a wyvern. All he knew was that people were in danger. He didn't know there was a princess involved."

A grunt. A gasp when his hand slipped and he nearly fell face-first into the thorns.

"He was surprised when the glass hill shattered and she stepped out. He wasn't ready to get married. He wanted to spend a few years questing and exploring, but he did his duty and took her home."

A chunk of thick branch snapped off and Branwell dodged aside, but still got clipped in the hip. He hissed at the impact, wiped his sweaty face, wiped his hands on his thighs, and went back to work.

"My mother didn't want to be queen of a tiny farming kingdom, but she had to follow the rules. If she didn't, calamity would fall on her mother's kingdom. So they were stuck with each other."

Another loud crack, and a soft glow spilled out through a gap in the vines. Branwell bent down and looked in. He wiped his face again.

"My parents didn't start out well. They both admitted they resented each other. My father had another princess in mind. More suitable for a farming kingdom. But they did what was right and they tried to work together, and soon they liked each other, and by the time I was born they were in love, and they've been very happy. And I got scared when they sat me down and had a long talk with me and warned me it wouldn't be all magic and wonder from the moment I finally kissed you. And ..." He took a step back, straightened his shoulders, took a deep breath, and grasped the sword. "I'm sorry. Probably most of this is my fault. Although I still want to put a lot of it on your parents."

A chuckle escaped him, turning into a grunt, as he put his whole body into the effort to wedge apart the two large branches.

A sharp crack echoed off the walls of the garden, then turned into dozens of sharp crackles and snaps, turning into a sound like sand rushing down a dune. The knot of thorns turned into dust. Light burst out, pulsing four times before fading away to reveal the princess, curled up with the broken pieces of a spinning wheel under her, and the spike still through her hand.

Merrigan swallowed hard, flinching in sympathy when she saw the blood glisten, still fresh.

"That's just not fair," Branwell growled, and went to his knees.

He scooped up Talithia and carried her away to the fountain in the center of the garden. He balanced her on his lap so he could pull out the spindle and then put her hand into the water. Talithia flinched. One eye opened, then she scrunched it closed again.

Merrigan saw and clutched at Bryan's hand. She hushed him when he started to ask what was wrong. Was she the only one who saw?

"Anyway, what I'm trying to say is ..." Branwell sighed and rested his cheek against the top of Talithia's head. "I'm willing to try as hard as I can, and I hope you are. My parents didn't even know each other before they had to get married. We've had time to get to know each other, and I already like you. I hope you like me, and you aren't just obeying because your parents—"

"Shut up and kiss her," Merrigan snapped. "What good is telling a sleeping girl all this, if you're going to have to repeat yourself?"

"I'm …" Branwell chuckled, and shifted Talithia around in his arms so she was sitting up more. "I'm practicing. I want it to be right when she finally wakes up. We have a lot working against us."

"Bran, just do it." Bryan interwove his fingers with Merrigan's. "Figuring things out and agreeing on things can be kind of fun."

"Thank you for your advice, oh master of vast experience." He winked at them, then cupped Talithia's cheek and bent his head so their lips nearly touched. Then he raised his head. "Three times, you said?"

"Do it!" Merrigan fought not to burst out laughing. Talithia's foot twitched, and if she wasn't mistaken, a slight flush crept across the princess's cheeks. Hopefully that was amusement and not temper.

"Here's to the chance of love and happily ever after," Branwell murmured, and lightly brushed his lips across hers.

Talithia flinched, inhaling with a soft gasp. Branwell bent his head for the second kiss, slightly longer this time. As he raised his head, Talithia's arm came up, hooking around his neck, and she lifted her head so their lips met.

Merrigan counted to ten before the kiss ended.

"I think they have a good chance," Bryan muttered. He cocked his head to the right, toward the entrance into the garden. Merrigan grinned, and they hurried away, still holding hands, with Honk waddling along beside them.

"Do you feel that?" Merrigan said, as they paused in the door leading back into the palace. She swept out one hand, pushing against the air. It didn't feel quite so thick.

"A breeze." Bryan grinned. "It's working. Come on."

He ran, tightening his grip, and at the first intersection of hallways led her to the right, deeper into the palace. The sounds of voices came to them, creaky and querulous, and loud as the air thinned and the background hum and whisper of thousands breathing in unison ceased. Merrigan caught movement as they passed open doors. Lamps flickered to life and she caught the distinct sounds of crockery and other items hitting the floor. She muffled a giggle. It shouldn't be funny. She imagined the confusion filling the minds of the people in the palace and throughout the cursed area right this moment. Yet at the same time it all seemed so ridiculous, the kind of nasty joke a very young child would play. Abruptly, Bryan stopped them at a closed door. The soft sounds of a man and woman talking came through.

"Here we are. This is where they always are at this time of day." Bryan let go of her hand to yank off his gloves, stuffed them in his belt, and raked one hand through his hair. He looked her over once and grinned. "They're going to love you."

Merrigan swallowed down several responses, some silly, some snappish, and fought a wave of nerves, as she realized just who was on the other side of that door. Bryan thumped hard on the door, and didn't wait for the man inside to call for them to come in. He pushed the door open and rushed in, to stumble to a stop after only four steps.

King Maxwell and Queen Violetta were sitting together in one massive, thickly cushioned chair, with the remains of afternoon tea still on the table beside Violetta. He had his arm around her. They stared at Bryan and Merrigan, and Maxwell slowly started to shake his head.

"Son, you're … you've changed." He shuddered once. "How long have we been sleeping?"

"It doesn't matter. Bran kissed Talithia and the kingdom is waking up—"

"The kingdom?" Violetta clutched at the front of Maxwell's coat. "Are you saying the entire kingdom has been sleeping? How? Why?"

"It doesn't matter now. It's been fixed. Although Steffan and Arissia are trying to put all the blame on Bran instead of —" Bryan shook his head. "What matters is you're awake and everything is going to be all right and …" He caught hold of Merrigan's hand and tugged her forward.

She wished she had stayed out in the hall.

"Mother, Father, this is Merrigan, and we're going to be married." He chuckled. "As soon as we find Bayl and as soon as we fix some problems in Avylyn, and maybe a few more kingdoms along the way."

"Merrigan of Avylyn?" Queen Violetta blinked, and Merrigan could almost hear the spinning of her future mother-in-law's thoughts.

This was likely the most frightening moment of her life. Even more frightening than the moment she swallowed the apple and thought she would sleep forever.

"Oh, welcome, dear." Violetta got to her feet and held out her hands. "I'm so happy for you. Bryan has loved you since you were children."

Merrigan burst into tears. It was ridiculous, and she managed to stop them after just a few gasping, unladylike sobs, but as it turned out that was a far better response than anything polite or flowery or courtly. Violetta embraced her and pulled a convenient handkerchief from the cuff of her sleeve to blot her face.

"Majesties? Are you all right?" A husky, red-haired woman dressed all in gray burst into the room.

"Auntie Ginger!" Bryan leaped to embrace the woman, and to Merrigan's surprise swept her up and spun her around once. "How wonderful to see you again!"

Ginger *ooph*ed and took a step back and tugged her clothes straight from the exuberant greeting. Merrigan shuddered in anticipation of the scolding she would get from the woman. This was the chatelaine of the palace, over all the servants, and according to Bryan had the entire king's council under her thumb. She had started out as nanny to the princes, but married the seneschal and her title was switched to Auntie, as the seneschal was a distant cousin and affectionately called Uncle Cobblestone. So named, Bryan had told her, because the big, gentle man had taught the princes important boy skills such as skipping stones and had had to use cobblestones because his hands were so big.

Auntie Ginger had been sympathetic yet had scolded Bryan to stop mooning over Merrigan when their friendship seemed to shatter. All his letters were returned, with notes written by Nanny Tulip warning him not to raise his sights so high, the princess of Avylyn was too good for the likes of him and if he didn't watch his steps he would fall and not be able to get up. Merrigan had been furious and ashamed at the same time, when Bryan finally admitted that he had written to her for years, getting the same response. She was very sure that the letters she had sent to Bryan had been stopped from even leaving the palace, much less the kingdom, and she was ashamed she had given up writing to him so easily.

"Well, look at you." Ginger exchanged a grin and a wink with the king and queen, and rested both hands on Bryan's shoulders, nodding with approval as she studied his face. "All grown up and tested, and ready for more tests. Are you well on your way to healing, Princess?" she asked, turning sharply and reaching for Merrigan's hand.

"Am I—" Merrigan choked and tried not to tug her hand free of the calloused, yet surprisingly gentle hand. She managed not to ask the ridiculous question: You know who I am?

After all, Bryan had warned her that Auntie Ginger was somewhere between a hedge witch and a faerie godmother. She might not have had as much education or power as the few resident majjians who advised and served King Maxwell, but her wisdom and insight were incomparable and the other majjians deferred to her.

"I have a long way to go, body and spirit. But I promise you, I love Bryan and I will do all I can to make him happy," she hurried to add.

"Ah … I knew I liked you. Even when I figured out what that rotter, Tulip, was doing to your heart, I had hope," she added. Then she took a deep breath, nodded twice, and looked around the room. "Let's get things cleared up, shall we? You're going to be deluged with messengers and petitioners and …" She paused and smiled. "And yes, a wedding very soon, if I don't miss my guess."

The sound of running footsteps echoed down the hall, and the sounds of people's voices calling Branwell's name. Moments later, Branwell and Talithia, holding hands and looking flushed and happy and nervous, skidded into the room, nearly running into Ginger.

"So, you fixed that problem, did you?" the woman said. "Good for you." Then she winked and side-stepped the happy, panting couple, and headed for the door.

"Not without a lot of good advice from Bryan," Branwell said. "Mother, Father, you're all right? Bryan tells me the curse spread beyond the palace. How long have we been asleep?" he continued, turning to his brother.

"We'd better sit down," Merrigan said, taking hold of Talithia's other hand. "This might take a while."

Queen Violetta caught Talithia's chin in her hand, while the three men fell silent, watching. She studied the princess's face for several moments, then bent her head to press a kiss on her forehead. "Everything will be all right, dear child. You have been tricked and hurt, and you have made bad choices, but ... let's consider this a fresh start, shall we?"

Talithia burst into tears. Merrigan didn't feel quite so silly now. She offered her the handkerchief Violetta had used on her, and Branwell had the sense to put his arms around her and let her soak his shoulder. Merrigan felt a little satisfaction when Talithia kept sobbing, gasping and sounding like a frog, and her eyes got red and her face swelled a little and got blotchy. A princess who looked too perfect was irritating, after all.

By the time Talithia quieted and apologized, sniffling, Ginger had returned with a fresh tea tray, followed by grinning maidservants carrying trays with too much food for a mid-afternoon snack. Merrigan discovered she was ravenous. Breaking curses was draining work, she supposed.

Interestingly, Talithia revealed as they ate that the enchantress who had created the curse had come to see her perhaps a year into it.

"She woke you?" King Maxwell said, stopping in the middle of pouring tea for Violetta. "Wouldn't that have broken the curse?"

"I wasn't really asleep." Talithia shuddered. "And she told me that a large part of the mess was my parents' fault. The curse was supposed to hit them first, and spread very slowly, to allow most of the people in the palace and court to flee. She wanted to punish the people who made the most noise at the celebration and laughed at her or got offended when she asked my parents to be good neighbors and show some consideration for others. The celebration lasted an entire week!" She sniffled, gave them a guilty look, and dabbed at her nose with the handkerchief. "Of course, many members of the court said the fact that the long-awaited child was a girl was punishment enough, so they thought there would be no sleeping curse at all.

"The enchantress told me the curse was intended to show my parents what it was like to want to sleep, to be unable to move, unable to sleep, ache for it, but not be able to sleep. Then they made such a muddle of things when they tried all the usual, worthless tricks like forbidding spinning wheels and spindles in the palace, and paid hedge witches for potions to protect me, and protect them and ..." She sighed.

"The enchantress apologized, but I honestly think she wasn't that sorry. She said she couldn't undo the curse because someone had come along multiple times over the years as I was growing up, and tangled things, and wove their magic into it. Then moving me to Sylvanglade to try to avoid the curse just tripled the knotting and tangling. The best option was to wait until everything took its course and the conditions were fulfilled. But how could it, when Branwell was right there, asleep? That was the worst part. There was a gap in the thorns, and I could see him, lying there, and I knew he had tried to come to me." Her voice cracked and she muffled a sob. "He tried to come rescue me, even after that horrid, ridiculous, childish argument. And we were both trapped. The entire kingdom was trapped, and it was all my parents' fault. I never want to see them again."

"Oh, I'm sorry." Ginger shook her head, and pulled out another handkerchief, which she handed to Merrigan, to hand to Talithia. "You're going to have to see them. They're camped just outside the perimeter, trying to convince a gaggle of hopeful young princes to risk their lives and wade through the magic to come kiss you and wake you." She sniffed, and then winked at the two princesses. "Seems the magic is being undone in the same order that it hit, so it could take a while until word of the cure reaches the outskirts of the curse. Oh, no, it won't take years, but it will take some time. Time enough for you to finish eating and then get a nice long bath and get into fresh clothes. The curse had a preservation spell, but I imagine you're tired of wearing the same things for six years now."

"Six years." King Maxwell shook his head. "I don't feel like I slept six years. You'd think I'd have more energy than this."

"Be grateful we didn't sleep a hundred years, Father," Branwell said. Then he frowned and sat up straighter and studied Talithia.

Merrigan had a hard time not bursting out laughing, as realization swept across his face.

"So ... when I kissed you ... you were already awake?" he finally said.

Talithia blushed deep pink and nodded. "And I heard everything you said. All of you," she added, looking to Merrigan and then Bryan. "I've had so very much time to think, and I hope I've learned my lesson, and I've promised myself a thousand times over I'll try to be a better person, and ... Branwell, I'm so sorry. I don't know how many times I can say it without being irritating, but—"

Branwell wrapped his arm around her shoulder and drew her half out of her chair and half into his lap and kissed her.

Bryan grinned and saluted Merrigan with his teacup. She saluted him back, and King Maxwell and Queen Violetta chuckled and tapped their cups together.

Talithia's parents arrived far too soon, although she did have time for that bath and a change of clothes. They brought with them the gaggle of hopeful princes, insisting that while yes, Branwell had broken the curse, it had taken him far too long to do it, and their daughter deserved better. They were going to take her and go home and choose a far better husband for her. She could do better than this table-sized little farming kingdom.

The meeting took place in the audience chamber, where King Maxwell and his council took petitions and met with ambassadors and generally conducted kingdom business. King Maxwell and Queen Violetta sat on the highest level of the dais, while Talithia and Branwell sat on the level down from them. There were only three levels. They didn't go for ostentatious or "putting people in their places" in Sylvanglade. Merrigan and Bryan had seats off to the side, where they could be observers but didn't have to participate. This was something Talithia and Branwell had to deal with themselves if they were going to have a solid foundation for their marriage.

"No," Talithia said. She didn't shout, she didn't pout, she didn't burst into tears, as Merrigan had half-feared.

"Now see here, young lady," King Steffan began.

"That's just it. I'm a woman now. In fact, I passed my eighteenth birthday and my twenty-first birthday under the curse that you totally muddled by refusing to follow the rules, and which you brought on these lovely people and on me because you don't have a lick of courtesy or sense of responsibility toward others. What kind of a selfish idiot irritates an enchantress, of all people?" Talithia stayed seated, her hand tightly clasped in Branwell's.

"Look here," her father began again, waving a long, pale finger at her. Merrigan had to wonder if he had done any work at all with that hand, other than feeding himself and signing proclamations that others wrote out for him. "You're coming home with us. You can do far better than Branwell of Sylvanglade."

"Really? You didn't think that when you were trying to find a dupe to break the curse. Of course, you did a wonderful job of keeping the curse a secret. I didn't even know about it, until you sent me here, two weeks before my birthday and loaded me with all sorts of contradictory instructions on how to deal with the problem that you created. It would have served you right if the curse stayed anchored in your kingdom and had nothing to do with me. I think I might have gladly gone my whole life without kissing my husband, if it would have left you two sleeping forever. The entire kingdom might have thanked me!"

"I wouldn't," Branwell said, glancing off to the side.

Talithia sputtered. Then she giggled.

King Steffan and Queen Arissia and most of the princes standing behind them were not amused. Three got startled expressions, looked at each other, seemed to come to some agreement, and turned and walked out. Merrigan speculated that they had just realized they hadn't been told the entire story and didn't appreciate being manipulated. She whispered her thoughts to Bryan. He proposed a wager on how long it would take the other princes to come to their senses and run for their lives.

Talithia's parents tried to argue that she was their daughter and they had the right to decide what was best for her and choose a more suitable husband. King Maxwell had his advocates and advisors waiting with all the documentation, signed by King Steffan, agreeing to the marriage. Unless he could prove that Branwell was unable to act in a heroic manner toward Talithia, he had no legal leg to stand on to break off the betrothal. Steffan stammered and stuttered when Maxwell asked why exactly he had used that specific wording, about Branwell being heroic. Another advisor brought up a translation of a large portion of the contract written in an archaic language. It had been explained away at the time as an ancient blessing on the betrothed couple, but just before the curse unfolded, had been translated as a codicil putting Sylvanglade under King Steffan's authority if Branwell failed to break the curse.

"The translation is taken from a larger document, an ancient agreement between two warring kings who had to work together to defeat a powerful sorcerer, in which they bound themselves to a mutual agreement. The phrasing here," Advocate Lord Symons said, pointing to a section of a long roll of parchment at least eight feet long, "clearly states that the agreement applies to the entire source document of the small quoted portion, meaning that you forfeit control of your kingdom to Sylvanglade if you fail in your side of the agreement."

"But we didn't agree to do anything!" Queen Arissia shrilled. She gave a triumphant look around the room. Her husband closed his eyes and bowed his head.

"You agreed to total honesty and openness and sharing between our kingdoms," Queen Violetta said. "Along with agreeing not to be interfering in-laws, you would allow Talithia and Branwell's children some choice in which kingdom they would serve when they were grown, and you would not demand their firstborn as your heir. Among other conditions we thought were almost too generous at the time."

Two more princes turned and quietly fled the audience chamber while Arissia sputtered and shrilled and denied any such agreements. She was very upset when Advocate Lord Symons showed her where she had signed the document in multiple places. Bryan caught hold of Merrigan's hand and got up. She gladly let him lead her from the audience chamber.

"Where would you like to go?" he asked, once they were outside, enjoying the quiet of the gardens.

"I don't know. There are so many places in Sylvanglade you told me about when we were children." Merrigan chuckled. "I would like to see just how accurate those pictures were that you drew for me."

"Umm, no, I wasn't much of an artist then." He sighed and leaned down to kiss her. A light, soft kiss, not nearly long enough for her. "I really meant, where do you want to go when we leave?"

Merrigan caught herself before she asked, "Do we have to leave?" They did need to move on. There was Bayl to find, and she needed to go home to Avylyn and try to undo all the damage she had done.

She feared facing her father and brothers and sisters, even as she ached to see them. She didn't so much fear apologizing, but a large part of her cringed in anticipation of accepting their forgiveness. Which was ridiculous, she knew. Maybe she feared that moment of confrontation because she feared she had hurt them all so deeply, they could never forgive her? A life of travel, constantly solving others' problems, didn't seem like such a bad life.

"We should probably stay for the wedding," Bryan said, when she had hesitated long enough to feel awkward. "And maybe we should let Bib and Crystal decide our route, once we leave."

"Could we?"

That evening was a family dinner, including Bryan's two remaining brothers, multiple uncles and aunts and cousins. The meal was a happy, loud, informal celebration. King Steffan and Queen Arissia and the remaining hopeful princes had huffed and threatened and argued as they stomped out of the audience chamber. They were still arguing as they headed down the highway out of the kingdom. Chances were very good they wouldn't be back for the wedding. Ginger advised Talithia and Branwell to send them the invitation anyway. And then advised them to be careful that they didn't climb so high on their moral high ground that they got dizzy and fell down into the mud.

CHAPTER TWELVE

Merrigan had time for solitude and quiet reflection during the weeks of preparation for Talithia and Branwell's wedding. She was amused and slightly dismayed when she realized she only enjoyed the first few days of others looking after her, anticipating her needs and desires. Her time of exile had made her independent. She liked taking care of herself. Even more startling, she liked taking care of others. She liked sitting back and watching others find their happiness.

"You like being on the sidelines," Bib told her, when she confided her discoveries to him and Crystal. "Having people watching you and knowing who you are prevents you forgetting your mistakes. Have you written to your father yet?" He sighed when Merrigan stiffened and took a deep breath to stop herself from snapping at him. "Yes, I know you wrote before we left Alliburton, but you promised details, and some idea of your path."

"I apologized. I told him I had been cursed and I deserved it, and I explained that we have to wander to complete a quest. And Bergomass said he would write a much longer letter with all the explanations and our theories and ..." Merrigan sighed.

She had a brief urge to pick up the magic book and throw him across the cozy little cottage Queen Violetta had invited her to use for her moments of retreat. It sat at the far edge of the family's garden, inside the palace walls, with several comfortable chairs and a table in front of the fireplace. It was kept provisioned with bread, butter and jam, cakes, and the makings for tea. Merrigan appreciated that no one would follow her to the little cottage. She hadn't wondered why, until now.

"Isn't that enough?" She tried not to whine. "It isn't like we've sat still long enough to expect any sort of reply from Avylyn."

"Such as if you're welcome to come home?" Crystal said softly.

"We're going to be here long enough to send a better letter, with quite frankly more apologizing, in more detail," Bib said. "And expect a reply. Who knows? Some of your father's majjians might come to help us."

"I should think with all our theories of what's happening across Armorica, my father wouldn't be able to spare any of them," she muttered.

"Imagine how much less talking and apologizing and explaining you will have to do, if you put everything in a letter now," Crystal said. "You'll simply be able to enjoy the reunion. You won't have to see their faces as you confess."

"Hmm, and maybe I need that punishment." She sighed and sank back in the chair to the right of the fireplace and stared into the flames. Merrigan chuckled briefly, reflecting that until she had run afoul of Clara, she hadn't known the first step in making a fire. She was rather proud of herself that she knew how make and tend a fire and brew her own tea. She didn't enjoy cooking, but baking had become rather fun, working with the girls in the orphanage warehouse.

She sighed, with a brief, aching throb in her chest as she thought about her sewing girls. She had become proud of those clever, imaginative girls, determined to make something of themselves, and so delighted to make pretty, sturdy clothes for others. Her mother and Nanny Starling had started her out so well, teaching her to be useful and giving, and find joy in making others happy. What kind of a woman would she be today if she hadn't listened to Nanny Tulip's teaching?

"Mi'lady?" Bib prompted. He wasn't going to let go, was he?

"Oh, very well. You're right, of course. You're always right. I simply … well, we have no idea how long it will take us, do we?"

Sighing, she settled her mind to at least start composing the letter. On the positive side, she had plenty of time to write the letter. Bryan needed time with his family, after all the years of separation. They hadn't felt his absence, locked in magical sleep, but he had. They could gather news of Bayl, if any came, and exchange letters with Belinda and find out how she was doing. And she could write to the friends she had made all during her long journey. Merrigan cringed again as she thought of their reactions when she had revealed her true identity. Would they want to write to her, once she had settled down somewhere? She had ached when she explained why she had been turned into an old woman. Well, that humiliation was all part of the reformation process, she supposed.

She wondered if the reformation and reparation included visiting Carlion and seeing what had happened to Leffisand's kingdom and his scattered, estranged family. Was anyone waiting for her to return? Did anyone care that their king's widow had vanished? Especially since she had proclaimed she carried his child, just before she vanished?

Oh, that was going to be painful and embarrassing, explaining that large untruth.

Talithia and Branwell chose to keep their festivities small, personal, for family and close friends. They wanted to be married as soon and as simply as possible. The kingdom would have a celebration, but they wanted it to celebrate the awakening of Sylvanglade and the reunion of families and friends who had been separated by the sleeping curse.

King Maxwell sent word to his allies, announcing the joyful news of the lifting of the curse. He thanked the neighboring kingdoms for their help in defending his people and borders during the creeping growth of the sleeping curse, and apologized for the fear that eventually, the curse would touch their kingdoms. Talithia's parents were notified of the wedding date and arrangements for them to attend, but no one made any pretense of hoping they would come. Least of all Talithia.

Merrigan enjoyed getting to know Bryan's family. After all, they would be her family eventually. She especially enjoyed the celebration after the lovely, joyous, simple ceremony. She decided it was her favorite wedding so far, of all she had attended. Her own wedding to Leffisand wasn't even on the list. She spent some time between dances reflecting on how styles of celebration perhaps were determined by the hearts of the people themselves.

Bryan's other two brothers, Boris and Baron, came to Merrigan perhaps an hour into the festivities and demanded she help save them. King Hubert of Duadock had arrived just before the wedding ceremony, with all twelve of his daughters. Now they all wanted to dance only with the royal sons. The two princes laughed about how furious Hubert's daughters would be that Bryan was taken, but there was some fear under their laughter, because that meant six princesses hanging on each of them. Before the sleeping curse, the princesses were young enough only five had come on the last visit. The thought of all twelve bearing down on them frightened the two princes, whom Merrigan considered rather sturdy and sensible, otherwise.

"Twelve princesses?" She understood now why Bryan held onto her hand and made sure everyone knew they were together. "Why aren't any of them married? What's wrong with them?" She cringed at this lapse. She should have known about Hubert and his daughters and their kingdom. Her father certainly would have kept up on the latest information about all the kingdoms of Armorica, not just the ones financially or militarily or politically strong enough, troublesome enough, to be worth his attention.

As it was, a king with twelve daughters certainly deserved some gossip, if only in fear for the princes of the neighboring kingdoms.

"They're not that old, if that's what you're thinking," Bryan said. He scowled at his two older brothers and gestured for them to take seats in their corner of the garden.

In Sylvanglade, they very sensibly held large festivals outdoors. If the weather was cold or wet, they simply spread massive sheets of canvas across the walls of gardens and between buildings. The tents and pavilions flowed from one to another, with tall, portable furnaces set up and tended by soldiers, to provide warmth. Merrigan thought the whole effect charming. It created a sensation of a large maze for adults to play in.

"King Hubert's daughters are all twins and triplets. The oldest triplets are twenty-four and the youngest twins are seventeen." Boris shuddered a little but tried to smile. "They weren't so bad when they were younger, and cute, but I'm afraid we treated them like pets the last time they were here. At least half of them think they're just a step away from being betrothed to us."

"Ah, and you don't like how they've grown up?" Merrigan tried not to smile or laugh aloud at the brothers' predicament.

"We haven't seen them yet," Baron admitted. "But they have a reputation. They love to dance. They won't stop. They've worn out the strongest men."

"And they're critical, the entire time they're dancing, like that horrific dancing master who tried to whip us into shape so we wouldn't embarrass Mother at her cousin Freesia's wedding, remember, Bryan? You were five at the time." Boris shuddered again.

"I remember." Bryan grinned. "I swore that if I had to dance when I got married, then I would never get married. Then we met and I decided girls weren't so bad after all." He caught up Merrigan's hand to kiss.

Boris and Baron laughed with them. Too soon, their respite ended. They all had duties as family of the groom.

In the press of the joyful crowd, Merrigan became separated from Bryan. While searching for him, she discovered King Hubert also loved dancing. The spectacle struck her as amusing and yet sad and fascinating at the same time. She couldn't resist lingering to watch him thump and spin and jolt around the dancing square. He never quite stepped on the feet of any of the ladies he swept out onto the floor with him. He did manage to step on the feet of many of the other dancers. How could a man huff and be so red-faced and yet not shower sweat on everyone with the force of his exertions? Heavy-set and half a head taller than most of the people around him, he was white-haired and wrinkled, with spots where his hair thinned.

Then Merrigan realized one rather large error on her part. Weddings were the prime hunting ground for widowers and widows. Bryan hadn't mentioned King Hubert's wife. He should spend at least half the dances with his wife, but Merrigan had been watching him through four songs now, and each had been with a different partner.

Then their gazes met. His gaze swept over her, head to foot … and lingered just long enough to be noticeable, on her crown. King Hubert winked at her. Merrigan wanted to run, but that would just attract attention, and let Hubert know she understood that look. She had seen too many men, in her father's court and in Leffisand's court, who never got the message that when a woman fled, she wasn't interested. They insisted women fled because they wanted to be chased. All women, no matter how terrified or nauseated their expressions.

Why had she agreed to wear that wretched crown? She should have left it with Belinda. Merrigan wished she hadn't showed the crown to Violetta, but she had been having such a lovely time getting to know her future mother-in-law, telling her about all she and Bryan had done and seen so far on their quest. How could she refuse when Violetta asked her to wear it for the wedding?

The song ended as Merrigan turned to find the nearest refreshment table. She desperately needed something to drink and calm herself. There was no logical reason to fear Hubert. She was betrothed to Bryan. There hadn't been an official, royal proclamation, but surely by now half of Sylvanglade knew about their adventures. King Hubert couldn't be so desperate for a new wife that he would ignore the publicly acknowledged bond between her and Bryan, could he? Well, considering how the man danced, how he swept partners out onto the floor without asking their agreement, maybe he could.

The last thing Merrigan wanted was to find herself tricked or confused into agreeing to be stepmother to twelve overbearing, dancing princesses. She had barely freed herself from being the royal brat. She didn't want to risk becoming a stepmother, and all the awful curses that came with the title. Even the kindest, most loving women hadn't been able to resist the transformation that often came on stepmothers when magic was insistent. Merrigan knew she was too vulnerable.

"Oh, stop being such a twitterhead," she scolded herself as she found the long table with rows of filled cups of wine and punch and tea. "Bryan will intervene long before—"

"So you are Merrigan of Avylyn," a booming, growling sort of voice declared as a hand grasped her left elbow.

She flinched and turned to free herself, and nearly splashed half the cup of punch across Hubert's chest.

"I am." A flicker of the royal brat surged up and she slapped the cup down on the table with a little more force than necessary. "And I know who you are, and no thank you, I have no wish to dance. I am saving all my dances for Prince Bryan."

Around them, several ladies gasped and twice as many chuckled. Merrigan thought she caught a few starting to clap. So, Hubert wasn't quite as popular as he imagined himself, with his chatting and grinning and bellowing laughter with and at everyone.

"Hmph. Know your own mind, do you?" His eyes narrowed for a moment, then he tipped his head back and laughed, four loud bursts like drumbeats. "Good for you. Wish my girls could speak up for themselves like you do. The only thing they're passionate about is dancing. I could swear there's a curse on them." He tipped his head toward the nearest doorway. "I've heard something of what you and the lad have been doing, and I think I can help."

"Help?" Merrigan feared she would regret it, but she let Hubert hook his arm through hers. He had very long legs and moved quickly. Several times, she thought she would get lifted off her feet as he swept them out into the next gathering space. Technically it was outdoors, but was quite warm between the walls of the buildings on four sides and the thick canvas roof and all the celebrating people.

"Not enough fresh air around here. Too many people breathing." He maneuvered them around clusters of laughing, chattering celebrants.

"What sort of help do you think I need?" she demanded, when they had moved down a lane with fewer people and came out from under the enveloping canvas roofs. "I do believe you're right. About the fresh air," she hurried to add, in case she had missed something else he had said, while they dodged conversations and loud music.

That was a trick Leffisand had employed numerous times in dealing with his council of lords. Make enough noise, have enough going on around them while he talked, change the subject often enough, and force people to scramble to keep up with him. Then publicly thank them for their agreement and support, in front of witnesses, and shame them into agreeing without knowing what they had agreed to. Merrigan muffled a bitter little chuckle at the realization that she had learned some useful things from Leffisand. Even negative lessons were still lessons, and she could use such things to defend herself. And perhaps defend others, too.

"That's better." Hubert tipped his head back and took several deep breaths. He gestured down another lane, still open to the sky above, with a long, backless bench sitting against a wall that ran along the front of a bakery. "Speaking of curses ... well, I was, you weren't, but you've been thinking about curses, haven't you?"

"Yes. Why?" She thanked him with a nod when he guided her to the bench and waited for her to sit before he settled down next to her.

"I think I saw young Bayl." His eyes narrowed as he studied her reaction.

Merrigan sat still, though part of her wanted to grab the red-faced, hefty old man by his collar and shake the story out of him.

"Why do you doubt? There has been plenty of socializing between your kingdom and Sylvanglade over the years. Bryan and Bayl would have had contact with you during their wanderings, wouldn't they?"

"That's why I think there's some additional curse involved."

"Have you told King Maxwell?"

"I was not sure of what I saw until I met up with young Bryan and heard something of his story. And when exactly should I approach my old ally and confront him, and taint the joy of this lovely occasion ... and add more concerns, in the middle of all the work of restoring the kingdom?" He chuckled. "Besides, I've been busy, having some fun frustrating that arrogant twit, Steffan. But none of that matters to you, does it? Ah, to be young and righteous and devoted to the happiness of another."

She snorted. "I am the last to call myself righteous. Self-righteousness is very different." Merrigan felt suddenly very weary. "But please, tell me when you saw Bayl and why you didn't recognize him."

"We see what we expect to see, don't we? And when someone shows up who looks somewhat familiar, but you haven't seen him in years, and he doesn't act as you would expect him to act ... well, you immediately doubt yourself. And then there was a sort of haze around him. Not just to obscure his features, but I suspect to obscure the memory of him." The old king shook his head. "At the time, I was furious. Here was a young man with the bearing of a prince, and all I wanted from him was his help discovering why my daughters' shoes were worn out every morning, as if they had spent the night dancing, and why they were always exhausted, and yet they never left their dormitory room."

"Dormitory room? You make twelve girls share one room?" Merrigan again fought the urge to shake him. "Men can be such ninnies."

"Come again?" Hubert blinked rapidly and leaned back, as if he heard her wish to shake him and wanted to get out of her reach.

"The inherent magic of royal blood. The inherent magic of twins and triplets. And you keep it all bottled together in one room? Forget about the arguments and fighting over the dressing tables and baths and mixing up shoes and borrowing each other's clothes and jewelry. Did you bring in any majjians to assess the situation and test for collected magic?"

"Well, yes, Sybellia came in and did measurements, but she said she couldn't discern anything unusual."

"Hmph. I'll wager Sybellia is a little old lady, a minor majjian, who grumbles about how others waste magic, and someone should be put in charge to decide who gets to use magic?"

"Why ... as a matter of fact ..." Hubert's ruddy coloring slowly faded. "Yes," he said, nearly on a whisper. "How did you know?"

"Did she tell you to keep the girls together in one room, long before the trouble started?" Merrigan got to her feet, needing to move. She needed to go back to her room and consult Bib and Crystal. She needed to tell Bryan what she had learned.

"What is going on?" He reached to catch hold of her hand, as if he thought she would run away.

"This Sybellia is collecting your daughters' magic. I wouldn't doubt there's a drain somewhere in their room, but it's not working very well. All that collected, condensed magic has attracted the wrong sort of attention. Like flies to spilled honey. Your girls are being whisked away somewhere to dance all night, collect the magic they generate, and likely drain away their energy and youth, too. Separate your girls, give them their own rooms, and you'll solve three-quarters of your problem right there. Now, about Bayl—"

"But what about the other quarter of the problem?" Hubert held tighter to her hand.

"Lock up Sybellia. Do whatever you can to keep her away from her magic books and her favorite tools. Especially staffs with crystals in them. Gray crystals. And consult with Sophie of Aryslean. She knows what's going on, and she's on our side."

"Our side?"

Merrigan sighed, the sound turning into a groan, and sank down on the bench again. Maybe Bryan would come looking for her. She was so tired. "There is a plot to block the majjian springs, to control the flow of magic throughout Armorica and put it into the hands of some very angry old women who think they know best who should have magic and who shouldn't." She tugged her hand free of Hubert's and massaged it. Who would think such an old man could have such a strong grip? "Now, tell me about Bayl. What did he do and say when he was in your kingdom?"

"Hmph. Well, he didn't stay long." He shrugged. "And I admit, I was angry that he didn't want to stay and accept my offer to marry any daughter he wanted, if he solved the riddle of the worn out shoes and exhausted daughters. They always loved to dance. Their mother always said that dance was a way to release their inherent magic, and the kingdom would be better for their dancing. They used to dance at all the festivals. The farmers always said the weather stayed fair for harvest, and the crops were more abundant in the spring, if my girls danced at their festivals." Hubert's face went even more pale. "Their magic power. How could I have been so blind?"

CHAPTER THIRTEEN

"Too close to the problem, and distracted by twelve girls." Merrigan shook her head. "So you were angry with Bayl. What did you do?"

"I threw him out. Had my guards march him out of the kingdom." A loud, gusting sigh made him seem to deflate. "Only later, when I finished fuming, I had the strangest feeling I knew him, but there was something odd about his face and his voice. And he didn't seem to know me."

"What was odd?" She muffled a little shriek of frustration. What was wrong with kings, that their first response to a puzzle with clearly magical elements was to give away their daughters, without checking to make sure the man with the remedy hadn't caused the problem in the first place?

How could she get into his memories, to have a better idea of how Bayl had been disguised? They sat in silence for a short time, as the music and chatter of the wedding festivities drifted around them.

Perhaps Crystal could somehow look into the old king's memories? When she proposed the idea, Hubert seemed to cheer up and regain some energy. They headed for the family side of the palace. She planned to settle Hubert in the parlor, and she would go to her room and retrieve Bib and Crystal, and the four of them would have a nice, quiet chat.

Halfway there, they met up with King Maxwell, and he did not look happy. Bryan and five of Hubert's daughters trailed behind him. Bryan looked frazzled and weary, and his boots looked like they had been trod upon and were scuffed and dusty as if he had been walking for weeks. The princesses looked absolutely mutinous.

"See here, Hubert, I know you're desperate to solve the riddle of your girls, and I'm sorry I wasn't awake to offer help until now, but to set your girls on Bryan, that's rather inconsiderate. Bryan and Merrigan are as good as betrothed. All they need is her father's blessing. I won't have anyone or anything coming between them, after all they've suffered."

"But Papa," the tallest of the girls said. The hint of a whine in her voice sounded far too familiar to Merrigan. Had the princesses come under the influence of another Nanny Tulip? "He said he wasn't betrothed and he wasn't in love the last time we saw him. He keeps telling us he never saw us, but he's lying. Papa, make him tell the truth! He's the one to fix things, I know it. We all know it!"

Her four sisters nodded. Merrigan felt slightly queasy to see them nod in perfect unison, like a series of mirrors set up to reflect each other.

"He won't listen to us," another daughter said. "Whoever he chooses gets to be queen and he'll be king. He won't be married to a younger daughter who won't inherit anything." Her lip curled as she gestured with a lift of her chin at Merrigan. "Except maybe trouble." Her sisters mirrored the expression. "Yes, we've heard about you, Princess Merrigan. If that's who you really are."

"That's enough, girls!" Hubert barked.

It was rather heartening to see them cringe in perfect unison. Merrigan would have laughed, except she understood the desperation that made them so insistent and unpleasant. And besides, there was Bryan, continuing to wilt.

"You don't know what has been happening," Maxwell said, his voice low and intense, vibrating through the room, yet going no further. Merrigan envied him that skill. "Only a fool interferes with the magic wrapped around Bryan and Merrigan, or discounts the heroic deeds they have performed and have still to perform. Already, they have been written into the great ledger of fables and legends—"

"And only a fool tries to take the pen from the Unseen's hand." King Hubert leaned forward, making his five daughters take a step back in unison. "Or tries to change the story when it is only half-finished. Besides, you're wrong. You didn't see Bryan at all. If I recall correctly, he hasn't been to our kingdom in more than ten years. The young man who looks so much like him was Bayl, his older brother." He raised a hand, silencing their responses. "Before you get your hopes up, the poor lad is under a curse. A memory curse, and a path erasing curse, if Princess Merrigan and I have theorized correctly. He's betrothed to Crown Princess Belinda of Aryslean and needs to be rescued. As for our uncomfortable problem ..." He bowed to Merrigan and offered her his arm. "Princess Merrigan has come up with wise advice to put us on the road to your cure. Starting with giving each of you your own room."

Shock froze the five princesses. Then they let out unison cries of delight and tried to hug Merrigan and thank her. She was nearly smothered. In moments, they ran off to tell their other seven sisters the good news, so only Maxwell and Bryan accompanied Merrigan and Hubert to the family parlor to work with Bib and Crystal.

Merrigan was glad to sit down. She didn't have to do anything more once she had introduced Crystal and Bib to King Hubert, and then explained her idea. She and Bryan held hands and listened, and watched, as Crystal explored King Hubert's memories, asking him questions to prompt recall, then displaying on her surface what she picked up from his mind. This prompted more memories. They were all quite encouraged to see Bayl hadn't been changed, physically. He frowned a great deal, and seemed to suffer headaches, constantly pressing his knuckles to his temples to rub them. Sometimes a haze passed over his features, likely the concealment spell to hide or erase his features from others' memories.

King Hubert apologized to King Maxwell, when his memories included the somewhat unpleasant and ungracious farewell, as he had Bayl escorted to the border of his kingdom and sent on his way.

"That's encouraging, I think," Bib said. He had been recording everything Crystal had displayed, the words and even sketches appearing in his pages, for study later. "He refused the offer to become king by marrying whichever princess appealed to him. That has to mean he has some memory, however dim, of true love and Belinda waiting for him."

"That's a rather incomplete and sloppy memory spell, then," Crystal said. "I don't think much of the majjians who cast it."

"Oh, it's not sloppy at all," Merrigan said. "They want him to suffer. Give him a fragment of memory, something that he can't quite pull out into light of day, and it will fester like a splinter. He can't accept a hero's reward and settle down somewhere for a happily ever after, because he knows there's someone waiting for him. He'll keep wandering."

"I'm sorry," Hubert said. "I should have recognized him."

"There's that memory fuddling spell, remember." Maxwell reached across the table to clasp his old friend's hand. "You've given us far more than we had before. I'm grateful." He sighed. "And I must apologize for my anger, earlier."

"No, no, quite justified. I know how I'd feel if one of my girls was in love and someone tried to convince her to choose someone else." He nodded to Merrigan and Bryan. "You two have been blessed by the Unseen. Don't give up hope. Although I do suggest you hurry home and get that blessing before someone else tries to come between you. They might have some far nastier spells at their disposal, to get their way."

~~~~~

Once the wedding festivities had ended, Maxwell gathered the family into the parlor and Crystal showed them everything she had gathered from Hubert's memories. There were tears, but being able to see Bayl and know he was healthy and active two months ago was some comfort. Violetta expressed some irritation with Hubert that he had allowed himself to be led into such a situation. Common sense said that magic gathered around twins and triplets. If he didn't have some way of controlling or draining away that magic, he was simply asking for trouble. She commended Merrigan for giving such commonsense advice for dealing with the primary cause of the problem.

"Now," she said, turning to Boris and Baron, "what are we as good neighbors going to do to help our friend, Hubert?"

Silence for several seconds. Maxwell's beard twitched as he fought a grin. First Boris's eyes, then Baron's widened as they caught their mother's
~~~~~

meaning. Then their mouths dropped open in matching, silent dismay.

"Mother ... no," Boris said.

"They're pests. They have screechy voices and messy hair and they go everywhere in clumps and ..." Baron frowned as his words trailed off, and a thoughtful expression replaced the horrified one.

"Is that the impression you had of Hubert's girls, dearest?" Maxwell asked Violetta.

Bryan chuckled and caught hold of Merrigan's hand under the table.

"I thought they were all quite lovely," the queen said, nodding. "Although, yes, they do tend to move around like a flock of ... well, swans, not ducklings. I'm sure once Hubert gets to work on following Merrigan's advice, they'll find they have separate interests and want separate lives."

"The girls have grown up while you two have been asleep," Bryan said.

"Tell us something we don't know," Boris said.

"Now that you've pointed it out," Baron added, and exchanged sheepish grins with his brother.

"I would be quite pleased to have one of my grandchildren sitting on Hubert's throne," Maxwell murmured, gazing up at the ceiling.

The rest of the family laughed.

They discussed the puzzle of how the princesses escaped their dormitory room and no one seemed to know or remember what had happened to them during the night.

"It makes sense to me," Bib offered, "that if someone set up the whole messy situation to generate more magic from the sisters and drain it away, they won't be very happy when King Hubert changes how things are done in the palace. If this Sibellia is involved, she's going to resist him. She might call in reinforcements."

"Good." Baron thumped the table. "If the same people are responsible who made Bayl vanish, then I want to face them. Give them some frustration and what-for."

"We're talking about majjians here, son," Maxwell said. "Conniving and self-righteous. Those are the worst kind, because they think they're justified ruining other people's lives. Such folk can be vicious when their plans are thwarted."

Boris nearly spat out the mouthful of tea he had just taken. He swallowed hard. "Justified? Father, how they justify suffering?"

"Such folk see all the hard work they're doing, scheming and threatening and punishing, and all the opposition from true heroes, and consider themselves badly used and abused," Bib said. "It happens quite often. Do you think that evil enchanters and kings see themselves as evil? Many of them start out seeing their actions as commonsense reactions to problems, and guiding people away from stupidity."

"I can attest to that," Merrigan offered. Her face warmed as she thought of how self-righteously angry she had been in the town of Smilpotz. She hadn't set herself to punish Judge Brimble because he was evil. She had been lashing out at the memory of all those nobles who had snatched away her maidservants. She had thought they were selfish, when the truth was that those kind lords and ladies had used their authority to rescue those overworked, cruelly treated girls.

Yes, you might have started out badly, Bib said so only she could hear. *But see how well on the road to reformation that first choice put you. We wouldn't have met, Mi'lady, if you hadn't decided Judge Brimble needed to be punished. And you honestly did want to protect little Fern. You knew he was a true lecher, and you were honestly furious on her behalf.*

Bib, you have always been my dearest friend, even when I helped you for selfish reasons. Where would I be without you?

"Merrigan." Bryan released her hand, so he could wrap an arm around her shoulders and press her snug against his side. "It's all right. So much isn't your fault."

"Yes, but some things are my fault, my choices." She took a deep breath and blinked hard to fight back the tears. Sometimes it really was a bother to be so damp and leaky nowadays. The queen she had once been would have scorned the princess she had become. "Now, can we get back to figuring out how Boris and Baron can become heroes? How do we decide which one will become king?"

That made Bryan's family laugh. They discussed what they knew of King Hubert's palace. The Sylvanglade palace library had architectural archives for several of the surrounding kingdoms. Trading such information had been seen as a safeguard, in case of damage from storms or invasion or earthquakes, so important buildings could be repaired. Crystal gathered up what information they could about Sybellia from the few magic mirrors she could reach to consult.

Boris and Baron agreed to take time to get to know the princesses in their home. They played with the idea of using disguises, to further ensure the princesses were totally relaxed around them. Merrigan didn't like that idea, but she held her peace. If her life had turned out differently, if she didn't love Bryan, she might have found the notion of a hero approaching her in disguise rather romantic. Having worn a face that wasn't hers for so long, she didn't like it on others.

When the puzzle of the dancing princesses had been solved, the two princes would let the princesses decide who would be queen after their father, and the prince who fell in love with her would be the nominal winner. If neither of them liked the princess who was best suited to take her father's throne, they promised their parents and each other that they wouldn't be disappointed. After all, if Bryan and Bayl could find true love, they had hope of finding it for themselves as well, and they wouldn't settle for anything less. Their parents had taught them that.

~~~~~

Five days after the wedding, Merrigan and Bryan left Sylvanglade and resumed their journey and their quest. The most direct route would take them through Carlion, which was unavoidable. Merrigan supposed she owed it to the people of Carlion to ensure that whoever of Leffisand's relatives held the throne was doing a good job. The people certainly had suffered enough under Leffisand. She had let him influence her, instead of being a good influence on him. A queen's duty was to be the champion of her people, no matter what kind of man the king was. Her mother had taught her that. Merrigan silently cursed Nanny Tulip for contradicting and then wiping away those precious memories and lessons.

More important, she and Bryan planned to visit Clara's cave and vision pool in Carlion. Merrigan wanted to confront the seeress who had put the curse on her, to thank her. And ask why Clara hadn't acted sooner. Why hadn't she put a curse of reformation on Leffisand, and intervened when he was a child? So much misery could have been avoided for thousands of people if Leffisand had been a better king, a better man. He might still be alive.

She felt a little surprise that despite everything, she did have some sympathy for Leffisand. She had been influenced away from the right path in her childhood, so couldn't the same have happened to him? From everything she had heard, his father had been a good, beloved king. So why hadn't the son grown up to be like the father?

"Why didn't someone see all this earlier and do something about it?" she asked on the second day after they left Sylvanglade.

"Distractions, I think," Bib said. "All sorts of little problems close at hand, that kept them from seeing the bigger issues farther away. And I daresay, in most instances when a king's evil destroys him, he didn't start out evil. It happened slowly. Need prompted people to close their eyes."

"And plenty of lies. And grudges against other countries," Crystal offered. "It's easy to do petty, nasty things if you see it as justice for someone who has hurt you in the past. Or who you've been taught will hurt you in the future. Think about how Tulip suborned you, turning you against your own family. Think how they reacted to the changes in you. No one realized until perhaps too late that there was something wrong. They just thought you were the brat."

"They excused me at the beginning, because we were all aching after Mother died," Merrigan said softly. "They let me get away with things, and then they were too busy with their own pain, and then irritated enough to let me hang myself. And maybe they thought I would go far enough to punish myself, and I would reform." She sighed. "But I didn't."
~~~~~

That conversation lingered in Merrigan's mind the next evening when they made camp, on the edge of a section of forest that Garan had been advised to avoid. It meant a slight detour to the east to get around it. Honk left them perhaps an hour before they stopped for the evening, so intent on something he heard or sensed ahead of them, he flew off without warning. When Merrigan called after him, he said, *Swan. Not a swan. Sad. Sleeping.* Then he vanished into the haze that had drifted around them since mid-morning. What could she do but ask the Unseen to keep him safe, and trust him to come back?

The weather was turning warmer, but still very damp. Merrigan took a stroll to stay out of the way as the men rigged several canopies of canvass among the trees, to provide shelter against the rain during the night. She tried to keep the camp in sight and was grateful for the small fires at the four corners, bright beacons of warmth through the gathering darkness. She had left Bib safely dry and covered in her saddlebag, and only took Crystal with her for company.

Do you feel anything stirring? she asked the mirror, when a shiver of something that wasn't chill or damp in the air brushed at the nape of her neck, under her hood.

We're being watched, yes, Crystal said after a pause just long enough to worry Merrigan.

"That's a pretty trinket you have there," a gritty sort of low voice said from the place where the shadows seemed thickest.

"Trinket?" Crystal laughed, the sound brittle. "I have been called many things, but never a trinket. I may be decorative, but I have never been a mere decoration."

The voice laughed, and something stirred in the thick darkness. "It's got teeth, it does."

"She," Merrigan said. "And yes, Crystal will bite, if necessary. What do you want?"

"Oh, dearie, it's not what I want, but what you want. You're a bit long in the tooth for me, but—"

"Excuse me?" She had to laugh. Was that gritty, creaky voice saying she was old?

"Let me finish! The sooner I get the compulsion over with—" There was a choking sound. "You want to be a princess, I know. You think all your troubles will be over, once you've got a prince wrapped around your little finger, and a crown on your head."

"Hardly!" Merrigan turned Crystal around, to face into the darkness. "What is it? Can you see?"

"It's a filthy, rumpled little stick-man," Crystal said after a few seconds, while the source of the voice sputtered and choked, and made thrashing sounds.

"Stick-man? You call me a stick-man?" A twisting, dark shape fell out of the shadows and rolled a few times, until it was only four or five steps from Merrigan.

She backed away and silently apologized to Crystal. If that figure leaped at her, she was going to have to hit him with her.

He seemed to be growing. Unfolding. The sputtering, choking sounds turned into weary laughter. He remained dirty-looking, and there were sticks in his tangled hair, and his clothes looked like a patchwork of different colors of leather. With a final gasp, he spread his arms and looked up at Merrigan.

"What do you mean, 'hardly'?" he said on a gasp.

"First of all, any ninny who stops to think for two seconds knows an offer that comes out of the darkness, from a total stranger, has to be a trap. Especially if it's an offer to make me a princess. And second of all ..." She sighed and took two more steps back, just in case. "I'm already a princess."

"Ah. No wonder." He nodded, frowned a little, and scooted himself around, pushing with one leg and pulling with the opposite arm, until he lay parallel to her and didn't have to look up at her upside down.

"No wonder?" Crystal said. "You said a compulsion?"

"Dratted inconvenient thing." He raked his mottled, dark hands through his hair and took a few more deep breaths. "Every time I encounter a girl who's got that look of burdens and quests on her, it makes me go through the whole nasty routine. I thought once I got away from the cavern and all those doubly dratted children, I'd be free. Thought the compulsion would land on the next unlucky fool and I could go on my way. It's been thirty years, after all." He pushed himself up so he was sitting facing her and crossed his legs. "Never ran into a genuine princess before. Or did the mirror make you one?"

"She was born one," Crystal snapped, "and it's not a tenth as wonderful as nasty little creatures like you try to make innocent girls think. The obligations that go with being royal, and all the nasty curses that try to attach to royal blood ... it's a wonder more girls don't leap on you and rip you to shreds for trying to trick them."

"Do you think I enjoy it?" the rumpled man spat, while Merrigan fought not to burst out laughing. The whole conversation was turning rather ridiculous.

"Merrigan?" Bryan hurried through the trees to her, holding a lantern aloft. "Are you all right? I thought I heard—who's this?" He put himself between her and the rumpled man.

"You," the little man growled, glaring up at Bryan. "What are you doing out here? Who let you out? How did you get out of the cavern? What have you done with the children?"

As he spoke, he rose up and floated a handspan off the ground until the final screech, when he dropped with a thump. He staggered and inhaled, visibly preparing for another volley of fury.

"What children? What cavern?" Bryan looked back over his shoulder at Merrigan and gestured toward their camp. "Run."

"You two have never met before!" Crystal shrilled, cutting off the rumpled man before he resumed.

"Eh? What?" He shook his head, fury battling confusion, and took two staggering steps forward, to peer at Bryan. His eyes widened. Some of the mottling seemed to fade off his face, and some of the stickish appearance smoothed out of his hair. "Well, what do you know? You could be his … well, not his twin. Are you sure, mirror?"

"I have been with Bryan since the day he fled Sylvanglade with the sleeping curse nipping at his heels. We have never encountered you," the mirror said, her tones cold enough to put frost in the air.

"Ouch. Sleeping curses are nasty things. Almost had a couple of those latch onto me. Relaxed too soon, got the compulsion …" He sighed.

"Wait." Merrigan stepped up next to Bryan, to get a better look at the man in the lantern light. "You said Bryan could be his twin? Whose twin?"

"The addlepated fool I tricked into taking care of the children."

"What children?" Bryan said.

"In a cavern, somewhere," Crystal said.

"Why did you have to trick someone into taking care of children?" Merrigan said.

"My boy. Those vicious old hags took my boy. Promised they'd make him a prince and he'd be the most powerful ruler ever if he'd just do what they told him. Promised him a princess, and they'd take over her father's kingdom too, along with the one they'd steal for him, just because he looked like the brat who wasn't working out like they planned."

"Someone stole your son?" Crystal said. "When? You said —"

"Vicious old hags?" Merrigan said. A new chill raced down her back.

"We need to get comfortable and have a long talk," Bryan said. "Dinner isn't quite ready yet, but you're welcome to join us."

That brought tears to the rumpled man's eyes. "You're *inviting* me to dinner? Do you know how long it's been since anyone offered to share anything with me?" A rusty sort of chuckle escaped him. "Do you know how long it's been since I wasn't the one cooking dinner?"

"No, but I have the feeling that's part of your tale," Crystal said.

The man chuckled again. He told them his name was Tangle as they headed for the camp. That was the only name he could remember. Quite a few things had been taken or hidden from him over the years, he said, as they settled around one of the fires to eat. Garan and his soldiers settled around the other three fires, to let them speak in privacy. He was clear on a handful of things, and they were the foundation for his anger.

Decades ago, Tangle was a simple man, living on the edge of an enchanted wood. He made a good living by gathering herbs and magical fruit for the local enchanters and hedge witches and healers, and carving figures out of enchanted wood to delight the children, because they could move and perform simple tricks. Young men on noble quests appeared quite often because of the heavy atmosphere of enchantment in the forests hereabouts. Tangle always volunteered to guide them onto the safe paths through the woods, because that was simply the right thing to do.

Then one day he grew quite irritated with a particularly spoiled young prince who gave up on a quest to free a princess from a black swan curse. Tangle slapped the prince out of his temper tantrum when his fourth attempt failed. Then to show him that it wasn't impossible, plucked the proper four feathers from the swan's wings to free the princess.

The princess chose to stay with Tangle, rather than allow the prince to carry her off to his kingdom. She had tired of waiting for princes in general to figure out the rather obvious riddle. She didn't want to go home. She had been gone so long, she knew her home and kingdom had changed. A grandchild of her cousin was on the throne by now. She had watched Tangle at work for several years and admired him for his honesty and solid work ethic.

I thought he said he didn't remember much, Bib commented in Merrigan's thoughts.

She had to muffle laughter.

"I heard that, book." Tangle chuckled. "Been soaked in magic too long. It's hard not to hear. And you're right. My life, what I remember of my life, starts with my princess kissing me and waking me out of my peasant dream, I suppose."

CHAPTER FOURTEEN

Tangle and his princess were happy for several years, but trouble struck after their son was born. Rumors of magic going astray filtered into their corner of the enchanted wood. Old women came to their cottage and convinced the princess that she had unbalanced magic by refusing to go with the prince, as she was meant to. Her son was meant to have a throne. They convinced her she needed to go seeking through underground chambers to the source of the majjian springs and change the course of one channel of water. It needed to go where it should have gone if she had let the prince take credit for rescuing her and married him.

"That doesn't make sense. That breaks the rules even more, basing a royal marriage on a lie." Bib's pages ruffled loudly in agitation. "No one can change the course of the majjian springs ..."

"Except that's what those old women are doing," Crystal said, taking up the thought he couldn't seem to finish speaking.

"So what happened? Where is your princess now?" Merrigan wondered if anyone else noticed that Tangle never said her name. She was always "my love," "my princess," and "my wife." She suspected the Worthy Warts had taken that memory away, along with his family.

Tangle shrugged. "She went with them to seek answers and fix things. She thought she might go to Carlion to confront her cousin's grandson and ask for his help."

"Carlion?" She was grateful she didn't have anything in her mouth, otherwise she might have spewed it across the fire.

"And that's why they took my boy." He bent over, pressing his clenched fists against his temples, shuddering with pain that sent ripples over his flesh.

"Crystal, Bib, do you have anything, know anything that can at least ease his pain?" Bryan asked.

"No. Nothing." Tangle sat up, shaking, and wiped his sweaty face with his sleeve. "They're punishing me. I'm so bound with curses, it's a gift I can move at all."

Merrigan bit her lip against the retort that such a gift was something she would give back.

"I'm just glad I can remember anything at all. I know I had my love, and our son, but I don't remember their names, or their faces. Everything I do remember, everything I do know, I have been given in small, torn bits and pieces, rewards when I obey them. I am a horrid, weak man." He bowed his head.

She reached out and caught hold of his left hand and held it tight in both hers. Tangle gasped and his head jerked up and he stared at her. Some of the darkness and mottling left his face, and the stick-like appearance of his hair settled.

Did I do that? There is some magic at work here, she said privately to Bib. *What just happened?*

Kindness, the book told her. *You were meant to do great good, and you were turned from that course. When you do kindness, when you hurt for others, you free more of your magic.*

"Those nasty old hags have a great debt to pay," she whispered.

"No one has touched me in years," Tangle said at the same time. He gave them a pitiful, crooked smile, and raised his free hand to wipe tears from his face. More of the dirty mottling faded. "I am a horrid man. I take children from their mothers. That's what they told me to do. I find kings and princes in trouble, and I maneuver peasant girls, sweet, innocent girls, into their paths. The magic grows around them as it's meant to do. But when they have children, and those children are full of potential for so much more magic, I take them away." He wailed and tugged his hand free and covered his face with both hands.

"What do you do with them?" Bryan looked at Merrigan over Tangle's head, his eyes wide with dawning dismay.

"The cavern," Merrigan said. "You kept the children in the cavern?" She caught her breath. "Where is the cavern? How long have the children been left alone?" An ache shot through her at the thought of even a few children alone in some dark, damp place. Her imagination put the warehouse orphans in some great, vast, dark, wet place, with no blankets, no food, no beds, no shoes, no adults to hold them and dry their tears when they woke with nightmares.

"That's just it," Tangle moaned, lowering his hands. He nodded to Bryan. "I left them with him. Or at least, the one who looks like him. To take care of them. I borrowed some of the magic I drain from the children, and I got away. I thought if I got far enough away, I would remember more. And I could find my boy. I was going to go to Carlion. To see if my love was there. Maybe my boy was there. They said he looked enough like the prince, he could take his place. My boy."

Merrigan caught her breath, chilled with an awful idea. Bryan looked back at her with the same dawning understanding and dismay she felt.

"Bayl," he said, at the same moment she said, "Leffisand."

"What?" they both blurted.

"Tangle got Bayl to take care of the children. That's why he was so angry when he saw me. He thought Bayl had abandoned the children."

Bryan's face twisted, like he wanted to laugh and be sick at the same time. "That is the last thing he would do. Bayl was never happier, those weeks we spent at the orphanage with you and the children. He knew Belinda was close even if he couldn't recognize her, and he had more hope than he had felt in years. And the children ..." He shook his head. "Bayl is ... he's close. How close is your cavern?" he said, grasping Tangle's shoulder.

Merrigan shivered as the pieces of her awful suspicion formed a torn but readable picture in her mind. Too many theories and suppositions would never be answered until she and Bryan confronted the old women interfering with the flow of the majjian springs for decades.

Had Tangle's son so much resembled the crown prince of Carlion, the boys had been switched? Maybe the real Leffisand had refused to be warped, as she had been, so they had taken the chance the peasant boy was more malleable and put him in the prince's place. Where was the real Leffisand now?

How could she tell Tangle what had happened to his son? Until she voiced her awful suspicion, Tangle still had hope of finding him. How could she take that away from him?

"Merrigan?" Bryan stood in front of her, holding out his hands. "Are you coming?" He frowned. "Are you all right?"

"Sorry ... my mind was wandering." She tried to smile and gave her hands into his and let him help her stand. "Where are we going?"

"The cavern." Tangle gave a little hopping, dancing sort of step, and smiled crookedly. His face brightened and he seemed even less stick-ish. "The book says maybe we can free the children. There are books in the cavern, although I never read them. The old hags left them there for me to guard. Because I couldn't read. The book says if he can talk to the books, maybe we can find my boy. Maybe my memories are stored in the books."

"Maybe," she whispered.

"If I know Bayl, he's been trying to read the books." Bryan shook his head. "Maybe his memory is coming back, if he agreed to switch places with Tangle and look after the children."

Merrigan nodded, and wondered how in the world she could keep Tangle from learning the awful truth, if she was right. He looked so happy. He looked so much more human now. Had hope done that?

Captain Garan didn't want to trust Tangle or break up their cozy camp and head out into the rainy weather. He wasn't mollified by Tangle's promise that the cavern was dry and they would be comfortable, with plenty of places to sleep. Bryan didn't order him but kept repeating the main reason for going with the little rumpled man: Bayl was close. Finally, Garan agreed. He left four men to take care of the camp, and the rest went with Bryan and Merrigan and Tangle, who assured them the cavern was only a short walk away.

"Short" turned out to be nearly an hour. Every time Tangle thought he recognized a landmark, he changed course. Several times, he forgot they were going to the cavern, and nearly ran away from them, eagerly calling out that he was near his old home. He muttered constantly, so sometimes Merrigan feared he had forgotten they were with him.

"Silly girls. Desperate girls. Silly, greedy, braggart princes. Trapped with promises and fear and desperation." He sighed. "Promised to help them. Kings were fools. Making demands not kingly at all. Enormous, magical things from silly peasant girls. What girl wants to marry a man who wants ridiculous things? Spin gold out of straw? What choice did she have? Spin gold or die? Oh, yes, wonderful reward. Marry the idiot who made the stupid demand. Maybe death is better." He shuddered and his face twisted, and he seemed a little more stick-ish, though Merrigan couldn't really tell in the shadows that surrounded them. "Should have made the girls' fathers spin the straw into gold. Braggart fathers. Tried to be a good father for my boy. Never bragged he could do magical things he couldn't."

"The hags probably arranged things to get the kings into a bind and put the silly fathers in a position to brag where the wrong person would hear them," Crystal said. "It's a classical move, calculated no doubt to generate circumstances where faeries or other majjians would have to step in and help, to protect the innocent girl caught between the stupidity of her father and the desperation of the king." She sighed. "Kings are always desperate for magically produced gold."

"Far too many instances of such situations," Bib agreed.

"Why would the hags do all that just to get hold of children?" Bryan mused.

"The magic of the children born of such marriages, and bound with magical promises," Merrigan said. She nearly stumbled, suddenly dizzy with the implications. "Just like Domfries, draining the magic of the six swan princes."

"That makes far too much sense," Bib said. "The hags are harvesting the magic that drains from captive royal children."

Tangle burst into tears, and they had to stop while Merrigan dug for a handkerchief so he could wipe his face and blow his nose. He nearly went to his knees, protesting that he didn't know, he wouldn't hurt children, it was the compulsion. He forgot more, the more he fought not to trick silly girls.

A familiar honking broke through the sighing of the wind through the trees around them. Tangle cried out and stumbled away, still clutching Merrigan's handkerchief.

"My love? My love? Is that you?" He wailed as a shape dropped through a gap in the canopy of branches and turned into Honk. Tangle went to his knees, wrapping his arms around himself, muttering about "wrong color," over and over.

That's him, Honk said. *The smell is right. Come quick!*

"Come where?" Merrigan demanded, and nearly hugged Honk, so relieved to see him.

The black swan. She can't get free. She needs him. Honk fluttered a wing at Tangle.

"Why?" Bryan said.

Garan and the soldiers, of course, couldn't understand Honk. When Bryan explained, Garan surprised them by laughing.

"Of course. Didn't he say his wife was a black swan, before he rescued her? What if she got turned back into a black swan?"

Tangle popped up from the lump he had collapsed into. "Where? Where is my love?"

Honk led them off the animal trail they had been following. Tangle trembled the farther they went, until Merrigan feared his ragged clothes would shake right off him.

"I know this place," he said, when she asked him what was wrong. "I don't know how, but I know this place. My poor head, how it hurts."

They came into a clearing, filled with ice. The trees were coated thick with it, and the ground, and the thatched roof of the neat little hut sparkled in the moonlight. Everything glistened, and a glow came through the gaps in the door that hung crooked on its hinges.

"There is a terrible spell inside," Bib said.

"It's a trap," Crystal said. "Made with anger and frustration."

She's trapped, Honk said. *She remembered. She came back. She hoped he remembered. They caught her.* He thrust out his long neck and hissed fury.

"Do you think?" Bryan said, after he translated for the others. "Tangle, is this your old home?"

The rumpled little man looked like he might burst into tears. He moaned and pressed his fists to his temples and slumped to the ground.

Honk hissed again, darting first to the door of the hut to peck at it with his beak, then to the little man, dancing around him, nudging him several times with his head.

"Bib," Merrigan said, "what should we do?"

"We shouldn't do anything. This is his knot to untie." The book rustled until she brought him out of the saddlebag and held him open in front of her.

"How?" Garan said.

Go. Go. Go! Honk nudged Tangle again. *She's waiting. She's crying.*

"Crying?" Tangle raised his head. He looked more stick-ish and rumpled now.

"The black swan," she said. "Your love. Remember?"

"I don't know."

"That's part of the nastiness of the spell," Crystal said. "It's infuriating. The spoilsport, brattish mindset. The closer he gets to freeing his family, the more tangled everything gets. There's a spell to steal his memories tied into this whole place. I can see it digging roots into him, and the longer he sits there, the worse it gets. I'll wager he's been trying to come back here for years, and every time he gets set back worse off than he was before."

"How old is this ice?" Garan slowly walked the perimeter of the clearing, touching the ice coating everything. "Considering how far along spring is, this ice shouldn't be here. The air isn't cold, did you notice? But the ice is thick enough to be the worst point of winter."

"Part of the curse. Part of the trap," Bib said. "I fear the longer we linger here, the better our chances of being trapped. Maybe our memories drained away too."

"Get up." Bryan hauled Tangle to his feet. "I know it's frightening, but you have to bull your way through. I'll go with you, all right?"

The little man nodded and Bryan wrapped his arm tight around Tangle's shoulders. He leaped forward, hurtling them at the ice-coated door. They bowed their heads as they hit it.

The ice shattered. The door vanished in shreds of broken wood, as if it had gone to dust with the weight of years. A chime rang through the clearing and Merrigan shuddered at the sour waves of something vibrating through the air.

"What is that?" she whispered and clutched at Bib to keep from dropping him. All their horses stood still, unaffected by the broken magic. Honk let out a joyful trumpet and darted through the door after them.

"He didn't give it time to bite him," Crystal said with glee in her shimmery voice. "Quick, pull me out. You need to see this."

Merrigan pulled the mirror from the pocket of the saddlebag, and turned Crystal so Garan could see the image that formed on the silver face.

The interior of the hut was coated thickly with ice. In the center of the room, a black swan struggled within a glowing egg of ice. She pecked at the thick coating imprisoning her, making cracks. Every time she paused, the cracks visibly healed.

Tangle and Bryan struggled to pick themselves up off the floor, but it was slick and there was nothing they could grab onto, to keep upright. In any other situation, it might have been amusing to watch, but Merrigan felt as if a fist clutched tight at her heart. She hated her helplessness, but what could she do to help them?

Tangle raised his head and saw the black swan and let out a wail. She tipped her head back and let out a trumpeting sound, muffled by the ice. Tears glistened in her eyes. Fury twisted the little man's face and he leaped from Bryan's side. He landed against the side of the ice egg and climbed up it, struggling and gasping, until he was even with the swan's head. Weeping, he pressed his lips against the ice.

Merrigan opened her mouth to cry out, to warn him, envisioning him trapped there, as she had seen silly children trapped by licking frozen metal.

A massive crack thundered through the clearing. Garan cried out and flung himself at Merrigan, throwing her to the ground, and taking Bib with them. He flung his cloak over her as the ice filling the clearing shattered in a shower of diamond dust. The horses screamed and bolted.

"Bryan!" she shrieked, envisioning him shredded by all that ice exploding inside the hut. She tried to get up, to run to him, but Garan was on top of her.

Something heavy lay on top of him. He mumbled what sounded like an apology.

Merrigan pushed against the cloak covering her, until she found an opening. They were buried in snow. Very wet snow. It melted as she pushed at it. Gasping, she clutched at Bib with one hand, trying to keep him out of the rising water all around her.

"I'm very sorry, Highness." Garan got to his feet. He stepped back, then bent to help her up. She was soaked nearly to her knees.

Most of the soldiers were gone, probably chasing the horses that had fled. Ice and snow cascaded off every surface, water running everywhere. Terror choked her as she turned to where the hut had been. She cried out for Bryan. The sound caught in her throat as he stood up, shaking off snow and meltwater. The hut was entirely gone, leaving a cup of melted stone where everything had been scoured away, smoothed by the force of the shattered magic.

Two people huddled together in the middle of the cup of melted stone. The woman was dressed in black, her hair silvery gray, the man dressed in roughspun and leather, with a woodsman's axe hanging from his belt. He was broad-shouldered and lean and looked strong despite the deep gray of his hair and the weathering of his features. He looked nothing like Tangle, being twice his height, and yet the shape of his mouth, the wideness of his eyes marked him the same man. Restored.

"My dearest love," the woman said, raising her head to look at the others in the wet clearing.

"I'm sorry," he groaned, and slowly got to his feet, drawing her up with him.

"Sorry?" She laughed. "For rescuing me a second time?"

"How long were you trapped this time, waiting for me?"

"Not long. Just a few months. I regained my memories and came looking for you, and they caught me. No, my darling, don't blame yourself," she said, as Tangle wept and buried his face in her shoulder. "We've both been safe."

"Both?"

"Our son and I. We've been together many years, trying to find our way home to you."

"Your son is alive?" Merrigan's face burned as everyone turned to look at her. This was the moment for Tangle and his wife, not her relief that their son hadn't been turned into the horrendous brat that Leffisand had been.

The Worthy Warts' plan hadn't worked. They hadn't substituted Tangle's son for Leffisand after all. That would likely be a fascinating tale, but they needed to get to the cavern and find Bayl, first. Then they would have time to sit and exchange stories.

"You know my son?" The former black swan shuddered. "Why would you think he was dead?"

"They failed," Bryan hurried to say. "That's the important thing. The hags' plan failed. We have ... theories." He wrapped an arm around Merrigan. "We're glad one of them was proven wrong. If you regained your memories, who are you, and what is Tangle's name?"

"Tangle?" She chuckled. "You, my true love, are Adlar. I am Carran, crown princess of Carlion. Or rather I was, until my cousin conspired to have me cursed so he could become my father's heir." She shrugged. "I am much better off, despite ..." She spread her arms, indicating the clearing, the remains of the hut that had been their home.

"You found our son?" Adlar wrapped an arm around her waist. "When? Where is he? I'm remembering more, in bits and pieces."

"There are very few spells strong enough to interfere with a mother's love for her child," she said, her smile fading. "They reawakened the curse that had kept me trapped as a swan for decades, and tried to make my memory sleep, but I regained enough to know my child was in danger. I found him, struggling with another boy in the palace nursery. My palace nursery." She shuddered.

CHAPTER FIFTEEN

"The nurse was asleep. Both boys were crying," Carran continued after a moment. "Those vicious old women were pulling the magic from my son, the magic trying to return a child to the path he should have been on … I could see the magic threads at work, trying to reweave the whole cloth. It created energy, power, and they used that power to … to change my baby's face, to make him look like the other boy, and put him in his place. I threw myself through the nursery window and fought them. The nurse woke and the old women fled when guards armed with magic rushed in. I took my son and we flew away. We flew until I collapsed from exhaustion, and I didn't know where I was. I didn't even know who I was. All I knew was that my boy was safe."

"Mi'Lady?" Bib said. "Bryan, she's about to fall off her feet."

"Merrigan?" Bryan tightened his arm around her.

She tried to laugh, tried to tell them she was all right, but she could hardly breathe. Everything seemed so dark around her. She clung to Bryan, struggling to regain her breath. He was warm and she felt so very cold. Leffisand's voice rang in her ears, the words fading in and out with the struggling beats of her heart, as she remembered.

"They tried to get him to kill you," she blurted. "It had to be them." She pressed her face into Bryan's coat and clung to him until the need to weep and shriek fury passed.

By then, Garan and the soldiers had returned with their horses.

Merrigan didn't want to tell the story. This was Adlar and Carran's moment, and they were just standing there when they should have been hurrying to the cavern and Bayl and the stolen children. Yet, everyone was looking at her and they clearly wanted an explanation for her moment of revelation and sorrow and anger, a little fear and a large dose of guilt.

"I … was married to Leffisand, king of Carlion," Merrigan forced herself to confess. "The hags tried to steal him from the palace nursery, to put your son in his place."

"So that's why …" Bryan hugged her close and pressed a kiss on her forehead. "She thought your son was dead, because Leffisand … well, he was turned evil by the hags and got himself killed."

"One of his favorite sports was to hunt …" She swallowed hard. "Black swans. And I was foolish enough to encourage him. I thought I was being a good wife …" She shuddered. "One time, when he fell ill, he wouldn't let anyone near him but me. He was feverish, with nightmares. He dreamed of a black swan breaking through the walls and attacking him. When he woke, he was so relieved not to be alone, he told me the story behind his nightmare. About a black swan breaking into the nursery when he was a baby and trying to eat him. And he remembered another boy. He believed for years he had a twin brother, stolen by the swan. And all this time, he was hunting black swans, hunting you."

"And all this time, I have been guarding my son, advising him, coming to him at night and helping him, working magic." Carran shuddered. "Keeping him away from Carlion, when I finally knew where we were, and where Carlion was."

"Where are we?" Adlar shuddered and looked around, as if waking fully. "What a wretched, weak, selfish creature I have been. You would be ashamed of me, love."

"You were not yourself. None of us were ourselves." She wrapped her arms around him and tucked her head under his chin. "But now we are free. Because you hoped and you kept hunting and trying to remember."

"And stealing children. Tricking their parents. Helping the hags drain magic from children." He shook his head and gently freed himself from her arms. "We have to go to the cavern and free the children and start making things right."

On the journey to the cavern, they introduced themselves to each other, comparing what they could remember of the hags, what Bryan and Merrigan and their friends had learned and theorized. They came up with a plan, which was by necessity simple until they had more information. Hopefully the books stored in the cavern would contain information on the stolen children. He was relieved to report that there were only five in the cavern right now, but he thought he recalled at least forty over the last thirty years, stolen from royal parents through trickery. Adlar had no memories of the hags ever reading those books, but they had been careful to lock them up and keep them out of the hands of the children, and away from him. They threatened him with torment if he tried to read them.

"When I had my moments of clarity, I always wondered why they were so adamant that I should not read those books, because I can't read," Adlar admitted.

"But you can read," Carran told him. "We saved our coins for the great spring and fall fairs, so we could search the books that the traveling merchants brought to town. It was our favorite thing to do in the evening, curl up together in front of the fire and read to each other."

"Vicious, cruel creatures," Merrigan spat. "To take that away from you, too."

"That's proof of dangerous information stored in those books," Bib said. "If they were so fearful of Adlar reading them."

"But why store the books there and then threaten him not to read?" Captain Garan said. "It doesn't make sense. Wouldn't it have been simpler to put the books somewhere else?"

"The stress of it all, the prohibition, the lost memories," Crystal said. "That generates magic energy, too. Just like the stolen royal children. Oh, I can't wait until you face down those Worthy Warts and give them a taste of their own nasty poison. I'd like to tie them up and hang them upside down and drain some of their magic, too."

Her vehemence made them laugh. Maybe it was the late hour and the strangeness of the day, and the anticipation of finally finding Bayl. Merrigan wondered how difficult it would be to give him back his memories. Would just seeing his brother be enough? Would they have to take him home to Sylvanglade? Or would it require true love's kiss to break this spell? Would they have to reunite the sweethearts?

When Adlar announced they had arrived at the cavern, there were no rock faces, no cave mouths. It was a simple clearing, silvered by moonlight, surrounded by huge, ancient trees. One massive oak tree that filled one side of the clearing could have replaced a castle tower. Adler released Carran and stumbled across the clearing. Each step seemed to make him a little shorter, a little more crooked. He looked back once, and the fear wrinkling his face made the breath catch in Merrigan's chest.

"No, my love," Carran whispered. She darted after him and caught up with him midway into the clearing.

Adlar didn't see her, his gaze focused on the base of that oak. A dark blot of shadow crept up from the roots until it was man-height, wide enough for two to walk side-by-side, and it deepened until it was a doorway through the oak. When Carran caught up with Adlar, he let out a cry of despair and tried to push her away, back to the others. She caught hold of him, and as her arms wrapped around him, the shrinking and twisting of his body reversed. The astonishment and relief on his face choked Merrigan. She wanted to laugh and cry at the same time. She made no sound, stopped by a sudden sensation that something hovered in the trees high above, keeping watch over this entrance to the cavern. She shivered, but not from the chill of the night.

"It's all right," Bryan whispered, as they started across the clearing after Carran and Adlar.

"Are you sure?" she whispered back, glad of his arm around her. This was not a clearing to cross alone, or a doorway to enter by herself. She imagined teeth hiding in the shadows, ready to bite her in half.

Carran and Adlar vanished into the inky depths of the mouth of the oak. The quiet felt so very wrong.

"We expect noise everywhere, at every time of the day or the night," he said, when she told him that. "Even with just a handful of children, there's always some noise. They can't help it. Even when they're sleeping." He chuckled, quietly. "The stack where Bayl and I slept had three boys who snored and chirped and whistled in their sleep, in chorus. We wished we could record the sounds, for them to hear when they were awake, because they never believed the other boys' complaints."

"You're ridiculous." She sighed and tightened her grip on his arm as they approached the oak to step inside. "I do adore you."

He brushed a kiss against her cheek as they stepped into the darkness.

The ground sloped downward immediately, and they nearly stumbled. Bryan stretched out his free arm ahead of them. She heard his gloved hand brushing against the wood. They turned every few steps, walking downward in a spiral.

"I don't trust ..." Bryan let out a sigh of laughter. "Crystal, would you mind?"

"I wondered when you would remember," the mirror responded.

"What?" Merrigan flinched as Bryan released her and tugged on the saddlebag holding Bib and Crystal, slung over her shoulder.

Soft, bluish-silver light spilled out of the saddlebag when Bryan lifted the flap. He reached in and brought out Crystal. The light came from the mirror. It grew stronger as Bryan faced her forward.

"Highness?" Captain Garan called from outside.

"The rest of you stay up topside until we call for you. I have no idea how large it might be down here. One man's cavern is another man's root cellar," Bryan said. "There might be another way out that's easier on the children."

The captain sounded reluctant, but he agreed. Merrigan and Bryan continued downward, with Crystal lighting their steps. The walls of the passageway were smooth, solid wood, when she would have expected them to turn to packed dirt or even stone after a certain depth. In twenty steps, she estimated they were three stories down in the ground. Light appeared ahead of them.

Adlar let out a cry of dismay that became a howl. Bryan let go of her and hurried down and around the last two turns. Merrigan clutched the saddlebag holding Bib and raced after him. What would they find? Had some enemy got there ahead of them? Was Bayl hurt? What about the children? She had a momentary vision of the orphanage warehouse, devastated by a fire or by robbers or even a tornado that had swept through the city. Then she stumbled out into the cavern.

It was empty of all but Adlar and Carran.

The place rang with emptiness. No echoes of voices raised in laughter and tears, quarreling, begging for stories, and the clatter of children doing chores.

Merrigan and Bryan crossed the floor, plain wood smoothed by the passage of many feet. Adlar and Carran stopped in front of a cluster of tables, each surrounded by benches and stools. There were crumbs and scraps of the usual debris of children on the floor under and around the tables, and Merrigan found that comforting. Adlar shuddered, staring down at a piece of paper that had been tacked to the center table with what looked like sewing needles.

"That's Bayl's handwriting." Bryan's voice cracked a little on the end. He looked to Adlar, who nodded and gestured for him to pick it up.

Merrigan took Crystal from him since the mirror's light wasn't needed anymore. She wasn't sure where the light filling the cavern came from, because there were no lanterns or lamps, and the four stone fireplaces embedded in the walls of the cavern were dead and cold. She shuddered, imagining that the light was fed by the magic that had been slowly drained from the stolen royal children all these years.

Curtains the color of the wood covered niches in the wall, with a series of narrow steps cut into the walls and curving upward, leading to the niches. She supposed if she looked inside one, she would find storage rooms or larders, and likely bedrooms for the children. In some ways it was like the orphanage warehouse.

"Alliburton." Bryan sighed, a frustrated sound. "Bayl is taking the children to Alliburton. He remembers enough to know there are people who will take care of them."

Merrigan sat down, to get a closer look at the note. Adlar and Carran sat facing her and didn't look quite so distressed now.

"How long ago did he leave? That's the question. When did you leave him with them?" He made a strangled sound when Adlar just shook his head. "You don't remember?"

"That's part of the tangle they made of him." A dry, dusty, thin voice came from behind one of the curtains.

"Fenndrake?" Bib yelped. The book leaped inside the saddlebag, banging against Merrigan's hip.

"I know that voice. Who's out there? You're all so thick with magic, all swirling around you, untamed, so many spells shattered, I can't make heads or tails or bobbins of anything."

Bryan was two steps ahead of Merrigan, striding across the floor to the curtain that took up maybe ten paces of wall space.

"The books are back there," Adlar said. "They tacked the curtain down so I couldn't get to them. When the books talked to me, they were punished."

"The nasty harridans burned some of us. A page at a time!" Fenndrake said, his wail ending on a rasp.

"You had talking books … and they made it impossible for you to get help or answers." Merrigan shuddered and nearly dropped Bib as she pulled him out of the saddlebag.

Bryan grasped the curtain and yelped as greenish-black sparks whirled around his hands. He scowled and pulled out his riding gloves, yanked them on, and reached for the curtain again. Merrigan flinched at the smell of scorched leather. His muscles flexed, visibly straining. With a flash and a sharp cracking sound, ending with a *whoomph* like a hard wind had knocked a door open, the curtain came free. Bryan fell backward.

Adlar shouted. Merrigan tasted scorch as she held back curses worse than anything the sailors of Quincy's ship had ever let fly in her presence.

The shelves were empty. Scorch marks and piles of ash showed where books had sat and, according to Fenndrake, had burned. All but for one book, a good handspan wider than Bib, and thicker than a stairstep, flung open, with loose, scorched pages scattered around him. Dust and ashes covered his pages.

"Can we fix him, Bib?" Merrigan cried and clutched her friend close to her chest.

"Bib? Is that really you?" Fenndrake the book riffled a few pages, sending up a cloud of ashes.

"It's me, you ragged old cookbook." Bib sounded like he might weep. "How are you? How long have you been here?"

"Another friend from the enchanter's library?" Bryan asked, once he was back on his feet.

"Our masters were friends. For a short time." He sighed as Merrigan put him down on the shelf close to Fenndrake, but out of the pile of ashes and dust. "Thank you, Mi'Lady."

"They quarreled bitterly and were disciplined. Their trinkets and libraries and tools were scattered as punishment," Fenndrake said.

"Did the hags … " Bryan swallowed audibly. He looked like he might be sick. "Burn all the other books?"

"Oh, no, no, the lad took them with him. He promised me he would give them to an enchanter he knew, who would repair them and give them a good home. Lovely boy. He felt quite bad about leaving me alone here, but what can you do?"

"Bayl remembered?" Merrigan caught her breath. "Bergomass. But how could he take all the books and the children?"

"Oh, Swinny, a bestiary tome, had some magic rings hidden in his binding. The hags never knew they were there. We used to laugh about it. The magic rings were for transportation. Easy enough to control, but a one-way trip, and only one trip to each ring."

"So the children are safe?" Adlar and Carran joined Bryan and Merrigan in front of the shelves.

"Well, Tangle, you're looking much better. I hardly recognize you." Fenndrake sighed. "You had the worst of it. They punished you ten times more than they punished us, when we tried to talk to you and help you. We quite admired you, how you kept trying to remember, and how well you took care of the children. They quite loved you."

"They did?" Adlar staggered, his eyes wide with shock. "I thought they were … well, not entirely afraid, but I thought they really didn't like me."

"Children, especially children with magical potential, can see far more clearly than adults." He sighed. "Or old books of magic who have outlived their usefulness."

"Why were you left behind?" Merrigan asked.

"Punishment, of course. Any attempt to lift me off this shelf of my imprisonment results in …" Fenndrake riffled his pages, sending up puffs of dust and ashes. "I'm half the book I used to be."

"I'm sorry," Bib said. "I wish I could help. Crystal, can you see any way to break the curse imprisoning him?"

"Well, hello there. Delighted to meet you, lovely lady," he said, as Bryan set the mirror down on the shelf on the other side of him.

"This could take a while," Crystal said. "Anything to frustrate those nasty hags. You're right, Merrigan. The tally against them just keeps growing, longer and more bitter."

They left the three magic objects to confer and retired back to the cluster of tables and chairs. Adlar sighed and looked around and his eyes glistened with a threat of tears.

"It looks much larger without the children. I don't like it so quiet."

Carran held his hand and asked him what it was like, raising the children. How many children at a time? Who was easier to raise, boys or girls? How old were the children? What did he teach them?

Merrigan listened and thought about the children in the warehouse. She felt as if she had left them behind a lifetime ago, and yet it wasn't even half a year. Her eyes burned, and sometimes her throat closed up, torn between tears and laughing at herself. The woman she had been three years ago would have scorned the woman she was now, aching for all those orphans. Cast-offs of society. Dregs, she would have called them, when she was queen of Carlion. When had she ever decided, or been taught, that children who had lost their parents were a burden and a blight? Who had decided that the children were to be blamed and punished for the sins and failures and loss of their parents?

This world is a cruel place in so many ways, so much unfairness. Would it be better if no one had magic, if magic can't be used for the good of all? I always thought all those stories Nanny Tulip told me were so unfair, with so many undeserving people being helped with magic, their wishes granted when they certainly weren't smart enough to use them properly.

Merrigan caught her breath. Was that how the whole ugly scheme started? Someone decided there had to be a better system of judging who was worthy of having magical help?

Let the magic flow where it will, let the majjian springs trickle through the land unseen and unfelt until they well up and work and bless, her mother had said. *The Unseen made magic to be wild and free, its pathways invisible until it has passed by.* Then she had told the story of how someone decided a stream wasn't deep enough to suit their needs, so they built a dam to collect all the water. The farms downstream were deprived of water and became dusty plains. When the rains came in the winter, the water caught behind the dam and spilled out over the land and washed all the good soil away. The lesson had been that trying to control freely flowing things like magic and water might seem wise and even prudent, but in the end, trying to change the courses and the channels they had made for themselves ended up harming everyone.

"You would have been welcome at the warehouse in Alliburton," Bryan said. "It's easy to see you cared about the children."

"Yes, Alliburton," Carran said. "You said that before. What warehouse? Why did your brother take them to Alliburton?"

Bryan explained about the warehouse that had been turned into an orphanage, and a little about Aubrey, who had been hidden from his family by an enchantment that made most of the people of his country forget him. He held Merrigan's hand and his eyes were warm and happy as he told how he and Bayl had come to the warehouse, following rumors of a princess in hiding there. Carran and Adlar laughed when he recounted how Merrigan had worn a borrowed crown and scolded Belinda's unwanted suitors and sent them away in apparent defeat.

"If you have nowhere to go," Bryan said, when their laughter had faded, "I can't think of a better place for you than to join the people raising the children at our warehouse. If Bayl realizes they are all stolen, he will ask Bergomass for help in reuniting them with their parents."

"That sounds lovely," Carran said. "A safe place, hidden, with no one knowing our story. But I want to go back for our boy. He has to be worried, I've been gone so long."

"Our boy." Adlar's voice broke. "Tell me about our son? What kind of a man has he become? How did you rescue him?" He brought her hands to his lips. "No, first tell me what happened to you. When did they turn you into a swan again?"

"I was always a swan. From the moment I crossed the border into Carlion, the same curse that stole me away from my family caught me again. I was so confused it was too easy to give in and become a swan. I remembered enough to want to get to the palace. I remember being pampered and adored, because I was a black swan, and so rare." Carran shuddered. "Then one day, an old woman came to the pond in the royal gardens and she was furious when she saw me. I was still myself enough to understand when she tried to bribe one gardener and guard and servant after another to capture me and give me to her. I was frightened enough I wanted to fly away, but I sensed I was safe there. If she could have gotten hold of me there, she wouldn't have been bribing them to give me to her.

"I might still be there if I hadn't heard our son's voice. Heard him crying. Heard him calling for me. A mother always remembers. I went looking for him, but I was afraid because how could I hold him and comfort him, as a swan?"

"And you followed the sound to the nursery, where the hags were trying to put your son in Leffisand's bed, and take away Leffisand, but he fought them, and he fought your son," Merrigan said.

Carran nodded. "I got my boy on my back, and I flew away with him and we hid and … he understood me, when I talked to him. I couldn't find my way home. I couldn't remember where our home was. It was all I could do to protect him. What we were, our strange circumstances, my royal blood, my being a swan … it generated magic. That magic tried to force us into a story, make us visible, when we needed most to hide." She shuddered and hid her face in Adlar's shoulder.

"The magic gathering around you was like a bonfire," Bryan guessed. "It attracted majjians to you? Ones who wanted to help, and ones who wanted to steal your magic?"

She raised her head enough to nod. Adlar made a soft moan of comfort and wrapped his arms tighter around her.

"They kept finding us. The old women. And we kept fleeing. Until the swineherd found us and knew what we were. He used to be a prince, but he chose a simpler life, with a girl who loved him just for himself, and not because he could give her a palace to live in. They were older, getting on in years, so they adopted our son and raised him, and taught him well. I couldn't be around him in the daylight, because people would remark on a black swan spending time with a swineherd's boy, but I came to him at night, and we would speak in the moonlight, and make plans to find you, when he was a grown man." A sob escaped her. "But I forgot so much, in all those years of waiting."

"Where is he now, our son? What kind of a man is he?" Adlar said.

"Oh, he is a good man. He is a swineherd, and he makes trinkets and toys and fills them with the magic that tangles around us like threads. Pots that let you know what others are cooking when you breathe in the steam. Music boxes that play your favorite song. Mechanical birds that sing all the languages of the birds. And whenever someone grows suspicious of the talented swineherd, he sells the toys and we move on to a new place, and he starts all over again." She smiled and wiped her tears. "We have to move when the magic grows too thick around us, and a spoiled princess gets suspicious and accuses him of being a prince in disguise, and wants him to take her away to his father's kingdom. Princesses ... I never realized what trouble we are to the world, until I was on the outside looking in. Unless we're born to some destiny, a service to perform, we really are self-centered, rather brainless bits of fluff."

Merrigan had to laugh at that because she did agree. Bryan gave her a thoughtful look. She wondered what he would say if she suggested they cast aside their royal status and go somewhere far away and live a simple life. Would they be allowed to do that? Or had destiny and fate claimed them, giving them only two choices: solve the problems around them, or be someone else's problem to solve?

They found some food stored in magical boxes. Merrigan complained privately to Bryan, as they dug through boxes and bags and tallied what had been left behind. The hags had made sure the children were fed and clothed, but there was no surplus or luxury. Their entire purpose for this cavern was to house and drain the stolen royal children until the hags found other uses for them and keep Tangle busy and unable to search for his family. Carran had more sensitivity to the working of magic than they did, and she had a disturbing conclusion to share, as they sat down to a simple meal of bread, fruit and some eggs they hesitated to fry and eat.

"This place is draining our magic. It's slow, like little nibbles, but if we stay long enough we will lose enough of ourselves, we'll be unable to leave. I suggest we leave in the morning."

"I suggest we not spend the night here," Garan said, before he even sat down. He had just joined them, after checking with his men. "We've only been down here a few hours, but a whole day has passed by up top."

The others agreed. Merrigan couldn't finish her portion, having no appetite, even though she had felt ravenous by the time they had sat down to eat. From the remains left on the others' plates, they felt the same.

CHAPTER SIXTEEN

They debated whether to go above ground to spend the night in the camp, then come down in the morning to search the cavern for anything useful before they left. Crystal let out a shout.

"We've found it!" The mirror fumed as the five crossed back over to the shelf where she, Bib and Fenndrake sat. "It's rather insidious, but you have to give them points for cleverness. Nasty, but clever."

"What is it?" Bryan said, on the edge of snapping.

"Well, we discovered something interesting about Adlar," Fenndrake said. "Did you know you were a prince?"

The surprise lighting Adlar's face brightened everyone's spirits slightly.

"Well, at least you have enough royal blood to qualify you as a prince. Which confirms our theory that this place has been draining magic from him, as well as the children," Crystal said. "The spells to keep Fenndrake bound to this shelf simply state that no grown man or child of royal blood can free him from his prison."

"That's it?" Garan said.

"That's it. Adlar got stung when he tried to pick up Fenndrake, and whenever a child tried to pick up the book, pages burned. It was a lesson that had to keep being learned over the years. Bayl tried to pick up Fenndrake to take with the rest of the books, and pages burned. All we need is for an adult woman of royal blood to take him off the shelf and break the spell."

"A princess," Bryan said, smiling, and taking a step back to bow to Merrigan.

"Clever," she said, nodding, "if rather nasty."

Despite trusting Bib and Crystal's judgment, her hands still itched slightly as she reached to pick up Fenndrake. He was rather heavy, despite the pages burned away over the years. She supposed he had regenerated slowly, just as Bib had during the many incidents when Judge Brimble's uncle had tried to destroy him.

She held Fenndrake out at arm's length to avoid the dust and ashes and crossed the floor to the nearest table. Merrigan set down the book, and Adlar stepped up to pick it up and test if the spell had truly been broken. He went rather pale and muttered an apology to Fenndrake as his hands closed around the edges of the book.

They were all silent for several heartbeats as he picked up the book and nothing happened, except a slight puff of ashes rising up in the air, disturbed by the movement. Then a moment later, they all burst out in cheers and cries of relief.

That night, safely above ground, they made their plans. Garan sent half his men with Carran and Adlar, to take them and Fenndrake to Alliburton, to seek help from Bergomass and King Auberg. Fenndrake had all of Bib and Crystal's knowledge of Bayl and would do all he could to restore Bayl's memories. Bryan wrote a letter to his brother, given into Fenndrake's care, urging him to go to Aryslean, where Belinda would be waiting for him.

~~~~~

"How many more places are there like this?" Bryan mused, standing in the opening in the massive oak, looking down into the darkness of the spiral tunnel.

"We should seal it up somehow," Merrigan said. "I can imagine the hags coming back and trapping someone else like Adlar and starting the whole mess all over again."

The soldiers, Carran, Adlar and Fenndrake had ridden away maybe half an hour ago. They took the wagon for Carran and Adlar to ride in, and half the supplies and luggage. The eight who remained would travel lighter and more swiftly now. Garan and the soldiers were busy repacking the remaining supplies and luggage on the three spare horses. Bryan had a pensive expression, and Merrigan had let him wander, frowning, until he came to a stop in front of the oak. She shuddered now, imagining what it must have been like for Bayl, to start to remember small details of his life. He wouldn't have been able to abandon the children, once he understood what was happening.

The cavern was designed to drain away magic. She wondered if Bayl had felt his small portion of magic from his royal blood being drained away as well.

"It needs to be destroyed utterly," Crystal said. "This is another of those horrible, warped spots, where natural, wild magic has been twisted for the profit of a few instead of benefiting many. This was once a majjian spring. The oak grew as large as it did because of the magic and abundance of water, and the wood was used for amulets and shields, all sorts of magical tools, and enchanted chests. No matter how much was cut off, it grew back. When the spring at its roots was diverted, it became thirsty, making it vulnerable to the hags' twisting."

"How do you know this?" Merrigan asked.

"Fenndrake told us. There was a great deal he learned when all he could do was sit there and watch and listen and try to talk to the oak. It's very unhappy," Bib said. "The departure of the children broke some of the
~~~~~

spells the hags put on the place. The oak has started to wake up and remember how it used to be. We can't destroy the oak. Even if we had the kind of magic needed to entirely uproot it and turn it to ash, it would be wrong to punish the oak for being sick and enslaved."

"Can we bring the water back?" Bryan said.

The book and mirror were silent long enough, Merrigan wondered if he had finally asked a question neither one could answer. She caught hold of Bryan's hand and intertwined their gloved fingers. He sighed and smiled down at her, and leaned slightly so he could tip his head to rest against hers.

The silence was nice. Peaceful in some ways. Despite the early hour and the brightness of the morning sunlight and the freshness of the cool air, she felt weary and worn thin in places. Other than the months in the orphanage warehouse, and the winter she had lived at the Bookish Mermaid in Wylder-by-the-Sea, she hadn't spent much time in any one place since Clara had cursed her.

"There is a chance," Crystal finally said. "A small one. The paths of the water from the majjian springs have shrunk, some have closed entirely, some had been blocked deliberately, and this changes the flow of the water so it collects where it should not and flows away from the places where it should be."

"That doesn't tell us how to bring it back." Bryan lifted his head. "What do we need to do? How do we help the oak, so it's strong enough it doesn't become a prison again?"

"We need to fill that cavern in its roots with magic water," Crystal said. "But it could take us a year to divert enough majjian springs to do the job. And doing so would deprive other areas that are already suffering drought as it is."

"Oh!" Merrigan thought she might just throw herself at the tree and bang her head on it a few times. "Bib, the bottle of water from Morton's chest. Do we still have it? Please tell me we didn't leave it with someone who we thought needed it more?"

"The bottle of ..." The book laughed, hard enough he made the saddlebag bump a few times. "Brilliant, Mi'Lady."

"Garan, where is the chest?" She kept hold of Bryan's hand as she turned and ran to Garan and the remaining soldiers. "Please tell me I didn't leave it on the wagon?"

Bryan laughed, and his smile said he was proud of her. Merrigan liked making people proud of her. This feeling was clean and warm and freeing, rather than the pride she had felt when Leffisand approved of her nasty tricks and schemes.

Please, please, let Carlion be a much happier, kinder place, now that Leffisand and I are no longer ruling there.

The chest was on top of the baggage loaded on the second of the three horses, and easy enough to get to.

"How quickly does the water spill out?" Garan asked, once Merrigan explained the magical qualities of the little leather water sack, and what she hoped it would do for the cavern. He shrugged when she gave him a slightly confused look. "I have seen and read about how magic responds to the need. That is an enormous space to fill. I would not like so much water to come out that you are drowned and washed away before you can get up the tunnel. Perhaps you will let me do it? I can certainly run faster than you, hampered with your skirts."

"Hmm, yes, you might be right, but ..." Merrigan shook her head and tried to smile away the little chill that curled through her belly. "I think this is something I need to do, simply because I have done so much taking in my life. I need to give, and take a risk, I think."

"*We* will take the risk." Bryan caught hold of her hand and interwove their fingers.

"Highness, I promised His Majesty—" the guard captain began.

"Did he actually tell you to keep us from risking drowning from a magical water sack?" He held out the little sack. The opening, currently corked and tied shut, was no wider than his thumb. "I think if the magic was so eager to come out, and so eager to drown us, there would be no way to stop it. The pressure would be so great, it would have escaped the sack ages ago. And Merrigan is right. This is a risk we need to take. That is why the Unseen made some royalty. To lead and take risks and carry burdens for the people."

"Too many royals have forgotten that. My father would be the first to insist that power means responsibility." Merrigan held onto her smile, though she shivered. "It's about time I started making him proud of me."

"How quickly do you think it will come out?" Bryan asked, once they were walking back down the spiraling tunnel under the oak, still holding hands. "You've used the sack for water before, haven't you?"

"Several times, when I was traveling, by myself." She sighed, remembering those quiet days traveling by cart. She missed her sweet little donkey and the cart of supplies to set herself up as a seamstress. The protective cloak, the harness that hitched and unhitched the donkey for her. The solitude. The long talks with Bib, and the stories he told her to pass the hours. Missed that simple life, when she was securely hidden from the world behind the mask of an old woman. Most of the time, nobody noticed an elderly woman traveling alone, except for those cowardly brutes who attacked her. Now, restored to her own face, her youth, and yes, the bearing that proclaimed her royal blood, she needed defenders. Why had she ever thought that being royal made her better than everyone? It made her vulnerable, it made her needy. She admired

Bryan and Belinda even more. They had learned to make their way in the world without servants and soldiers and gold and baggage. She should be glad for Clara's intervention, no matter how much it had hurt.

"Merrigan?" Bryan squeezed her hand. "Are you all right? You've been too quiet, and your eyes seem to be looking somewhere else."

"Oh?" She caught her breath and realized they had stopped, with the cavern spreading out before them. "Yes, of course."

"You were telling me how fast the water flowed out?"

"Oh. Yes." She squeezed the water sack. It didn't slosh, it didn't feel like it held anything at all. It never had, all the times she used it. Maybe part of its magic lay in the fact that she *believed* water would flow out every time she opened it. "When I used it to fill my little pot to boil water for tea, it took maybe a minute. It didn't gush like a river trying to squeeze through a small gap in the rocks. Then again, all I needed to fill was that tiny pot." A shiver ran through her. "Garan is right. Magic grows to suit the need. But what if we're wrong? So much water, filling this huge space … what if we're doing more harm than good?"

"The hole needs to be filled, so the hags can't come back and use it to trap others. And it might be good if this is just ordinary water, obtained through magical means, rather than magical water. We don't want to give them a never-ending supply of magic."

She grimaced. "Oh, now you're making me doubt this whole plan even more!"

Bryan laughed and kissed her. "Faith, my Merrigan. Trust in the Unseen and the gifts of magic that were put into your hands, perhaps for needs like this."

They decided to test the flow of water, first with a bowl large enough for a child's serving of porridge. Then a cooking pot. Then a tub large enough for a child to bathe in. The water trickled out for the bowl and spilled out with more force for the pot. When Bryan held it over the tub, the opening doubled in size, so the stream of water gushed out. His eyes grew so wide with shock that matched what she felt, Merrigan had to laugh.

"I wonder …" he said, as the tub filled rapidly, so it was half-filled in a minute. Bryan took a deep breath and plunged his hands into the water. He waited. He held his breath. After Merrigan had counted to fifty, then fifty again, he slowly grinned.

"The water isn't rising any more, is it?" she whispered, though she wasn't quite sure why she whispered.

"Magic not only grows to fill the need, it has some common sense, and some safeguards," he whispered back. Then he leaned forward across the tub and kissed her. "Were you afraid too, of starting a flood that would never stop?"

She laughed. "I didn't think that far."

"Help me tie this up before I pull it out of the water. We're going to need something to fasten it in place ..."

Merrigan realized something, as they searched cabinets and chests. The hags, for all their self-righteous determination to have everything their way, had ensured the children were taken care of. They hadn't been deprived, in terms of food and clothing and basic comforts. They had plenty of food, even if plain and limited in variety, provided by magical cabinets and pots. Plenty of clothing, and shoes, and even simple toys, and a cistern to provide water for washing and drinking. And there were tools to make repairs. Specifically, a hammer and a box of nails.

They climbed halfway up the spiraling tunnel. Bryan nailed the sack to the wall, upside down, by the straps made to tie it to a belt. The sack writhed and swelled as she untied the string. The opening widened, tripling in size the moment Bryan pulled the cork out. He caught hold of her hand and with the other hand tossed the cork behind them, down the tunnel. Merrigan squealed as they fled upward as fast as they could run. She remembered when they had been children, adventuring, running wild together through the forests and fields of Avylyn.

Laughing, breathless, they darted through the opening in the base of the massive oak and nearly fell to their knees. Behind them, distance softened the sound of water roaring, cascading down the spiraling tunnel.

"We should really seal the oak," Bib said, when Merrigan picked him up to put him in the saddlebag with Crystal.

"That makes sense," Garan said. "How? We don't have any tools or boards."

"We did," Bryan muttered. He muffled a chuckle, and snorted louder when Garan gave him a quizzical frown.

"Fortunately, I have the power to influence anything of which I am made," the book announced.

Merrigan laughed when the two men just shook their heads, clearly confused.

"Bib first made himself known to me when he was still unable to speak, by helping me with a very large sewing task. Once I had used thread to bind some of his pages together, he could control thread. He is made of paper and thread, cloth and leather, and wood." She turned, so the book clutched in her arms faced the oak. "Yes, Bib, you're right. We can't allow anyone to go down in there. At the very least, we can't allow someone to make a mistake and get trapped, maybe drown."

"And take the chance someone will find the cork and seal the sack, maybe let the water drain away," Bryan added.

The effort took much persuading on Bib's part, to get the oak to awaken and grow so it filled in the hole in its base. They camped there two days before the opening visibly shrank, and Crystal assured them the healing would continue after they left. Bib was unable to speak for three days, exhausted by the effort and the magic he had spilled out of himself to help the tree.

He wasn't able to talk, not even privately in Merrigan's head, until they were nearly to the border of Carlion. By then, she had some questions and even doubts about what they had done. How much damage would the force of all that water do to the interior of the cavern? Would it wash away the roots of the tree, and cause it to fall in? Would the water work its way down to the dried channels of the majjian springs, and somehow reconnect them, bring them to life again? The questions and fears in her mind were so strong, Merrigan swore sometimes she could hear water bubbling, trickling through the ground below her, in her dreams. There was something reassuring and even calming about the sound, and that sensation somehow worried her at the same time.

Bib had no way of being sure what the water would do. He could guess the impact on the water channels under the tree, both natural and majjian. At the very least, the natural water sources would benefit. They had dried up when the majjian channels were diverted or blocked.

"There is some hope that the entire cavern, once it is filled with water obtained from a magical source, might become a majjian spring. We can only guess and hope and ask the Unseen for blessing," Crystal said, when they discussed the possibilities in the privacy of a parlor in the inn in Wayfair Crossroads, where they had stopped for the night.

"But what are the chances the hags will come back and try to take it over again?" Bryan mused.

"If only we could use it as a trap," Merrigan said. That earned a snort and a grin from Captain Garan.

"How close are we to Clara's pools?" Bryan said after several moments of thinking silence among them.

"I honestly don't know. I'm sorry." Her face warmed when both men frowned slightly at her. "When I went to consult her I was … well, I was selfish Queen Merrigan. I didn't bother myself with details like maps, except for big maps showing how Leffisand's plans of conquest were progressing. I got in my carriage and told my driver to take me to the seeress, Clara, and then I ordered my servants to entertain me so I wouldn't notice how long it was taking to get there."

"I suppose we can ask, once we cross the border," Garan said.

"What will happen when we cross the border?"

"Well …" Bryan rested his hand on hers on the table, and narrowed his eyes slightly as he studied her.

"What's wrong? What have you thought of?"

"I'm just trying to calculate how well your people knew your face.

Will they recognize their queen when she rides past them? Is a hood enough to hide you?"

"I'm not their queen any longer." Merrigan fought not to squirm. Bryan had triggered an avalanche of worries she had been trying not to consider for several days. "Besides, I never would have let myself be seen in sensible, plain clothes, or traveling with such a small company. And no jewels. And while I much prefer riding, I would have been in my carriage because that is much more dignified." She shuddered, anger easing some of her discomfort. "How easily Tulip controlled my thoughts and values! Everything I loved, she took away from me by telling me 'that's not how a real princess should act,' 'that's not how a real princess should think,' 'that's not something a real princess would enjoy.' On and on and ..." She tugged her hand free of Bryan's, and hid her face in her hands, taking deep breaths until she could tamp down the fury and shame.

"Tulip and her kind have no idea of what 'real' means, or what royalty should be like, I'll wager," Garan said.

That wrung a choked little chuckle from Merrigan. She wiped her face on her cuff, deliberately, because she knew Tulip would scold and demand she use a lacy handkerchief.

"My mother knew, and I was silly enough to forget all the things she taught me when Tulip said otherwise. What an idiot child I was!"

"You were lonely and you missed your mother and Nanny Starling, who, I might add, approved of me." Bryan caught hold of her hand again, to interweave their fingers.

"Yes, Starling did approve of you. Do you remember ..." Merrigan's face warmed. She shook her head. This was too intimate a memory to share with Garan there to hear, though she did consider the guard captain a friend, after all they had gone through.

"Our betrothal rings?" Bryan whispered. He turned her hand so he could brush a kiss across the back of it.

"That's actually a very good idea, Mi'Lady," Bib said.

"What is?" Garan asked.

"How do you know about our rings?" Merrigan asked.

"The boy told me, and I told Bib," Crystal said. "It's very elemental, simple magic, like a hedge witch would use, but often the simple things are the strongest. Yes, I approve."

"It would be another layer of protection for you," Bib said.

"What would be?" Garan said.

Merrigan sighed. "Nanny Starling showed us how to braid our hair to make rings, to seal our friendship and make sure we remembered each other until Bryan's next visit to Avylyn. She called them our betrothal rings, and we were young enough that the idea seemed lovely."

"We weren't in that silly phase where boys thought girls were useless and girls thought boys were disgusting," Bryan added. "The thought of being together for always, having adventures like we had shared, exploring the countryside and creeping through all the secret passages in the palace, that was very appealing."

"Might I suggest that you braid your hair together around the rings you're already wearing, to add that magic as a foundation?" Bib said.

"A simple binding and promising would be helpful, too," Crystal added. "A promise to be betrothed, with enough hope and devotion woven into it to draw on more magic."

Merrigan didn't know whether to be amused or irritated that Bib couldn't help them braid her and Bryan's hair together around the rings that let them speak to birds. She made a note to herself to ask Honk if he noticed any change in the magic of their communication, when they were far enough from the town that he could rejoin them.

That night, she clenched her fist tight as she slept, protecting the hair ring. Her dreams undulated between the sensation that someone tried to shred her new ring and get it off her finger, and feeling the water trickling through the ground below the inn.

When she woke, she heard the distinct sounds of boots and hooves splashing in the water covering the cobblestones of the inn courtyard. Merrigan laughed at the fancy that the water followed her.

Yet when she stepped outside to go to the stables and mount her horse to resume their journey, the courtyard was dry. Even dusty. She shivered a little and wondered if perhaps with all they had gone through, she was losing her mind. Just a little bit. Did a guilty conscience put images in her mind to haunt her?

"It's all right," Bryan said, reaching to take her saddlebag from her. "The border of Carlion is only four hours away. We'll have a leisurely ride today and stop at an inn just inside the border and take our time, get a feeling for the spirit of the kingdom before we go any further. No rush."

Merrigan blinked several times, wondering what he was talking about. Then she had to yank her thoughts to the present moment. She nearly laughed aloud. When she told him about her dreams of the water, he frowned.

"That's funny. I dreamed about water last night, too. I thought it had rained, when I woke up, but ..." He looked around the courtyard as they approached the stables door and shrugged.

"Bib? Crystal?" Merrigan pitched her voice low. With their reduced numbers, it was even more important now that no one guess they had two very strong magical beings in her saddlebag. There was no telling who would try to take them. Bib and Crystal had the strength and ability to return to the people they wanted to stay with, but that was little help in stopping people from attacking and trying to steal them. "Do you sense water?" Whispering, she described her dreams from the last several nights.

Both book and mirror were silent, as their party went into the stables. Merrigan feared the question was a hard one, and the answer even harder to come by. The two didn't respond until their party had left the town behind, and the other travelers on the road had either moved ahead of them or had fallen behind.

"Channels of majjian water are awakening," Crystal said, startling Merrigan. "It's loud, perhaps it could even be described as violent —"

"Desperation," Bib said. "The land hereabouts has been dry for so long, affected by the drying up of the majjian springs in Carlion. Majjian water follows you, Mi'Lady, and the land hereabouts is so desperate to soak it up, you're feeling or hearing something of a battle to pull it in."

"Things will just get worse, the closer we get to Carlion?" Bryan said.

"I fear so," Crystal said.

Honk agreed, when he spiraled down out of the sky to join them less than half an hour later. He had been delayed in rejoining them by the exhausting hunt he had been carrying out, trying to locate swans in the area. Carlion hadn't had swans since Leffisand's mother had died. That drought in swans had affected the surrounding kingdoms, because whatever had been either killing them or sickening them or simply tainting the ground and water to drive them away, had been spreading outward from Carlion like oily poison rippling through the water.

The swan grew restless, and unable to sit still on the back of Merrigan's horse, the closer they got to the border of Carlion. She wished there was something she could do for him, to calm him, soothe him, maybe even make him sleep. It was very clear, to her at least, that the swan's discomfort came from magic. Disturbed, upset magic.

CHAPTER SEVENTEEN

Their party approached the last rise in the landscape before the long slope down to the valley and the border of Carlion. Honk's restlessness drew more attention from fellow travelers than if he had simply stayed perched on the back of her horse. The sight of a swan constantly leaping into the sky, circling a dozen times overhead, then coming back down to land on the horse again, drew attention. And curiosity. And the chances of someone unpleasant confronting them.

Merrigan breathed a prayer of thanks that the seven swan princes had left them in the quest to find other swans and protect them from the Worthy Warts' plans. Eight swans would be impossible to hide.

"Isn't anyone else worried by this?" she finally burst out, when their traveling party had passed a group of slower travelers, and they had the road to themselves for perhaps half a mile in either direction. "Honk, what can we do to make you more comfortable?"

"Forgive me, Mi'Lady," Bib said, "but it's only going to get worse. Honk and I have discussed this, the possibility of it. We were unsure if there was some sort of repulsion spell at work, to keep swans away from the kingdom, or perhaps some spell to lure them in to be captured."

"Then what are we doing, intending to cross over at all?" she said. "We should change our route, go around Carlion utterly. I won't risk Honk's safety, or his freedom."

Not me at all, Honk said.

Bryan translated for the others, then asked, "What do you mean?"

This was utterly ridiculous, that only she and Bryan could understand Honk. She was half-tempted to yank the ring off and not hear her childhood friend at all, rather than have this foolishness. Who ever heard of being able to talk to birds at all? What was the use of it?

Gasping, Merrigan sat up and looked around, hoping the landscape would ripple and melt and change, and she would find the last few minutes, perhaps the last hour, had been some strange, warped dream.

"Merrigan?" Bryan reached for her. "What's wrong?"

"It's me, isn't it?" she blurted, without really thinking. "You said you were unsure, past tense. Something is affecting me. I'm all tight and ... I don't know, itchy, inside my head. I was thinking and feeling like I used to. In Carlion." She gestured with a tip of her chin, down into the long sloping valley ahead of them.

The border crossing station straddling the road was clearly visible, despite the distance. She found it rather ridiculous, all of a sudden. Huge and ostentatious and a wasteful display of power and wealth. That was Leffisand's thinking, needing to show off and control everyone around him. How had she ever thought him clever and far-sighted?

"I'm afraid so, Mi'Lady," Bib said, from the confines of the saddlebag, which tended to muffle his voice even with the flap open. He sounded somewhat crestfallen.

Magic wraps around you, Honk said. *Gathering.*

"Waiting to pounce," Crystal added. "I imagine that's an uncomfortable feeling for a fellow like Honk. The nature of swans, needing to be free to move."

"Pounce on me?" Merrigan shuddered.

"Excuse me." Corporal Anders nudged his horse up closer. He was the youngest of the soldiers. "If the magic is gathering around Her Highness ... maybe the swan would be more comfortable riding with someone else? Where he won't feel it?"

Bryan laughed, just a few short, sharp chuckles. Garan nodded approval, making the young soldier flush.

Honk let out a hissing sigh that was pure relief, no need for translation, as he settled down on the back of Bryan's horse. He bobbed his head, and Merrigan tried not to feel unjustly treated. She knew she should be glad for her friend, but those cranky little complaining thoughts kept trying to make themselves heard. She fought them for the next hour or so, as they rode down the gentle slope into the valley.

"Bib, distract me? I have the most awful feeling I'm going to fret myself into a headache and then start spilling bitterness on everyone."

"That's the magic gathering around you," the book said slowly.

"I know that!" Merrigan sighed and closed her eyes and rubbed the center of her forehead with her knuckles. That didn't seem to bring any relief. "It's the most uncomfortable feeling. I can't believe—well, yes, I can, but I don't want to—I used to live like this, have this awful feeling, this cranky discomfort, irritation, like sand between every layer of my clothing that I can't get out no matter how many times I change my clothes. How could I have gone through life so miserable, and thought it was normal, and I was fine, even happy?"

"What does the magic want from her?" Bryan asked.

Queen. Honk leaped up from his perch, to dart out ahead of them, heading toward the tower of the border crossing station.

Merrigan thought her heart had leaped up to the back of her throat, choking her. She had the most awful vision of a bored guard seeing the swan coming and pulling out a crossbow to shoot him down, for sport.

"What does he mean by 'queen'?" one soldier asked, when Bryan translated for them.

Their company sped up without any conferring among them. As if they knew it was vital that they keep up with the swan.

Garan snapped his fingers, and turned to Merrigan, his quietly somber expression darkening. "The magic is pulling you back because you're the queen of Carlion."

"But I'm not," she protested. "Leffisand and I never had a child, so the succession goes to the next closest male to the throne." A sigh that tried desperately to be a chuckle escaped her. "That's what started me on my humiliating journey in the first place. I was so desperate to stay queen, I lied to his family and to the lords and to the people, and I lied to a seer, tried to get her to support my lie."

"That's it, then," Bryan said. "With so much magic woven through Carlion to make it what the hags want it to be, it's trying to turn you into the queen you used to be."

"No." Merrigan fought the urge to yank hard on her horse's reins and turn around and go back up the slope. Away. Put Carlion forever behind her. Take an extra two weeks of riding and go the long way around to Avylyn. "I refuse. I will not be that horrible woman, that nasty royal brat, ever again."

For a moment, she thought she could see the tightening bands of magic arching through the air to capture her. They rippled and tensed and thickened in response to her declaration.

"I swear by the Unseen," she called, and hoped at least one of the hags was listening, infuriated and feeling powerless. "I will not be that brat again. Unseen, help me. I swear by the Unseen, and I swear on the magic of my mother's garden, no matter how buried in thorns it is."

Something snapped, inside the back of her head and in the very air around her. Merrigan yelped and nearly threw herself out of her saddle, expecting something to come flying through the air to smack her.

"Merrigan?" Bryan leaned far enough out of his saddle he risked falling flat on his face. He caught hold of her hand, then reached up to cup her face. "What's wrong?"

She released a shuddering breath and sat up straight. The tightening in the air had eased.

"Is that all it took?" she said, more thinking aloud than asking.

"I am not sure, Mi'Lady," Bib said. "All we can do is keep moving and be ready for the next attack."

"Oh, pooh, you're such a pessimist." She muffled a ridiculous giggle. The sense of freedom, the release from the pressure, was delightful.

Bryan scowled at her, making her laugh more. She leaned out of her saddle and snagged hold of his collar and managed to smear a kiss against the corner of his mouth before she started to slip. He yelped and nearly knocked himself out of his saddle in the effort to push her back upright. Giggling, she bent over her horse's neck until she could catch her breath. Bib said something, probably explaining what had just happened.

Really, their enemies were such self-righteous prigs, so sure of themselves, they did seem to make mistakes right and left, didn't they?

"That does it," Bryan said, his scowl darkening. Or was that the air darkening around him, like a storm cloud solidifying into rain? "The rings aren't enough to protect us. I don't care what stronger magic we'll have by waiting to get your father's blessing, we're getting married immediately. It's the only way I can think of to protect you."

Something flashed in the corner of Merrigan's eye. She turned, looking for the source, and looked right at the gate crossing into Carlion. It was like a ripple of sunlight across water. She shuddered, recognizing that flash somehow. But from where?

"Merrigan?" Bryan caught hold of her hand. His scowl had faded, but now several lines dug furrows between his eyebrows. "Don't you want to be married?"

"To you? Of course. We could have avoided all this trouble if—" Merrigan shuddered again, remembering.

It was the moment she faced another gate crossing into Carlion, when she had fled Avylyn, so sure of her rightness, of her greater wisdom. There had been that flash, distracting her from her one last moment of regret, wishing Bryan had defied Nanny Tulip's judgment. Wishing he had come for her and swept her away on a silly, foolish, romantic life of wandering and adventure. Then she had listened to the beckoning of the flash and rode across the border, to where Leffisand waited to make her his queen.

She turned back to Bryan, just in time to see something swirl around him. Something dark. Dangerous. Magic.

A curse?

It was coming from Carlion. Part of a curse that had wrapped around her, too? When she defied her father and embraced the creature Nanny Tulip and her hag friends had tried to make of her?

"We can't cross," she said. "Not yet."

"No, of course not." Bryan caught hold of her hand again. "We have to get married first. It's the only way I can protect you."

"Protect me from what, exactly?"

He shook his head, confusion fighting the darkness.

"Captain Garan?" She turned her horse, looking for him.

"Here, Highness." Garan nudged his horse so now he was on her left and Bryan was on her right. He looked at Bryan with some concern wrinkling around his eyes.

"There's some magic attacking us, from over the border. Isn't there, Bib? Crystal?"

"I'm afraid so, dear," Crystal said, her voice muffled from inside the saddlebag.

"What is it?"

"No idea, except that I didn't feel anything until you broke its hold. It was building up so gradually, there was no clue until it sort of snapped, and latched onto Bryan on the rebound."

"I fear it was something that was already there, but gaining strength as we approached Carlion," Bib said.

"I thought all of Clara's curse was resolved when I took the apple for Belinda." Merrigan fought the urge to stomp or kick something. She was in the saddle, after all. Kicking her horse wasn't wise.

"What are you talking about?" Bryan shuddered and shook his head, and the darkness she had sensed around him seemed to shred like a particularly noxious mist.

"Bryan, I will not marry you until we stand before my father and he can put the marriage bands on our wrists himself," she said, speaking slowly, her voice raised so whatever nasty majjian might be listening or whatever magic might be lingering in the air, it would understand clearly and give up.

"Well, of course, that's what we—" His voice caught with an audible click. Bryan shook his head again. "I was just insisting ... what happened?"

"It's gone," Bib said. "That's odd. I didn't get a clear look at it, but I could have sworn this curse wanted you to be married, Mi'Lady." The book's pages ruffled violently enough it made the saddlebag bump slightly. "And some sort of dark design seemed to be trying to wrap around you, Prince Bryan. Odd."

"How could marrying Merrigan endanger me?" Bryan said. His voice strained like he wanted to laugh but couldn't.

"That does it," Merrigan said. "Captain Garan, we are not entering Carlion, which I suspect is the source of that new attack, until we can be sure of going straight to Clara the seeress. I know her pools were near the border, but I don't know where. If we have to ride all the way around Carlion until we find the right spot, to make the journey as short as possible, that's what we're doing." She took a deep breath, hating what she was about to say, but knowing it was the right thing to do. "And then, when we know what we're facing, we have to go into Carlion. Even though I would much rather go straight to Avylyn. I need to make it very clear to whoever is manipulating me that I do not want the throne. I was wrong to lie about carrying Leffisand's child. Carran and Adlar's son is more the rightful king than Leffisand ever was."

"Did you feel that?" Crystal said.

"Feel what?" Bryan tipped his head back and looked up at the sky. "I thought I saw something ... not sure what."

"Whatever you did," Bib said, laughter in his voice, "you did what needed to be done, Mi'Lady. You should really consider pursuing a career as a majjian. Or at least a breaker of curses."

Merrigan shook her head, holding back the declaration that she wanted nothing whatsoever to do with magic. Common sense said she would have a great deal to do with magic for some time to come. At least until everything was set right in Carlion and Avylyn. Wisdom said not to make declarations and vows that she would have to break.

Garan went with one of his soldiers to the gate crossing to ask for the way to Clara's pools. Merrigan was glad to dismount and sit on a fallen log some paces back from the road, wrap her arms around Honk, close her eyes and just be still. Bryan paced in front of her several passes before finally dropping hard on the log next to her. He nearly knocked Bib and Crystal off the log, where Merrigan had placed them so they could be out in the open. Mirror and book both enjoyed feeling the sunshine and open air on their surfaces, even if they couldn't actually breathe.

"That was ... disturbing," he said, followed by a gusting sigh.

"Contemplating finally taking the dreadful, irreversible step?" She smiled, eyes still closed.

"Step for—oh, no." He managed a rusty chuckle. "Not talking marriage, but the feeling sort of churning through me. It was like being in a fever dream. I knew something was wrong, but I couldn't figure out why it was suddenly such a good thing to demand you marry me. At the same time, I could hear these voices. Snarling sort of voices, and nasty laughter. I couldn't hear them clearly, but if I could, I would know why they were pushing me to marry you right away. And why that was so bad."

"Now that it's over," Crystal said, "I can see some residual effect on your rings. I fear something wants to get you to remove them."

"Why?" Merrigan blurted, opening her eyes.

"They don't like the promise of those rings, I suppose."

"Then why influence me to go against what we planned?" Bryan said. "I had the most awful urgency to get married before we crossed the border."

"There's some awful curse on me, when it comes to marriage." Merrigan tried to smile, wanted with a sick, churning feeling, to turn it into a joke. "Leffisand was certainly a ..."

"What are you thinking?" Bryan caught hold of her hand and wrapped his free arm around her. "You look like you're going to be ill."

"What if Leffisand put a curse on me? I thought we were partners. But what if he didn't trust me, despite everything? What if he was determined that I never ... never find love, never find happiness, if anything happened to him?"

"It could just as easily be a curse his relatives sent after you when you vanished," Crystal said, her tone sharp. The sunshine flashed across her surface, emphasizing the anger.

"Then why urge us to marry? Shouldn't the curse keep us apart?"

"It is perhaps reacting to Prince Bryan's royal blood. If you marry royalty from another kingdom, that perhaps weakens your claim to the throne of Carlion," Bib offered.

"I have no claim, because I didn't produce the heir."

"No one ever said curses or those who fling them at people are reasonable or logical or are even required to make sense," Crystal offered.

That got a snort and a lopsided grin from Bryan.

Garan came back with directions how to find Clara's pools. They would add an extra day to their journey by going west and north around the border of Carlion, rather than going in at the gateway ahead of them and following the road at a slight north-northwest angle. But taking the longer route would give them less time inside Carlion itself before reaching the seeress.

"One of the guards did remark that chances were even that we won't find Clara. The royal family has been regularly consulting her and she has been spending more time at the palace than at her pools," Garan said. "The guard captain seemed irritated that the man offered me that information. He offered his opinion that a seeress who didn't stay with her pools didn't seem to be much good to anyone."

"That kind of thinking is probably what helped with Carlion's downfall in the first place," Merrigan snapped. She surprised herself with that observation. "Think about it," she hurried on. "If they expect her to stay at her pools all the time, then she isn't advising the king and she isn't influencing his heir, or anyone else in the government. Besides, what kind of wisdom depends on … on humid air to be worth anything?"

That got a chuckle from Bryan. He stole a kiss when he helped her climb back into the saddle, and then their party headed off, away from the gate. Merrigan's good humor fell when she looked back and saw a man in the scarlet and blue uniform of Carlion ride out through the gate and take the same road. Was he following them?

Just minutes after she noticed the man, who stayed far enough back she couldn't make out any details except his uniform, Garan dropped back from his position in the lead, to ride next to her.

"It might be wise if you kept your hood up, Highness," he said, his voice pitched softer than usual. "In case the people we encounter on the way recognize you."

Merrigan nodded and did as he advised, but she thought it was a waste of effort and caution. When she did go out in public, she had always been regally dressed. The difference between the woman she had been and the one she was now ensured no one would ever suspect she was their king's widow, much less royalty. Still, she didn't argue with him, and she kept her hood up until that night, when they were safely inside their semi-private parlor at the nicely large, comfortable inn within sight of the border. If someone did recognize her, Merrigan wouldn't be surprised if the reaction was negative. She and Leffisand had been selfish rulers. There had to be a great deal of resentment remaining even after Leffisand got himself killed and she vanished.

She silently apologized to the people of Carlion for the damage she had done. There was so much she should have done to protect them.

Their soldiers took turns walking the streets surrounding the inn and sitting in the public square, enjoying the dancing and singing, and looking for the soldier who had followed them. Merrigan thought of all the information Leffisand had used for his profit, and wondered for the first time how he obtained it. How he knew so much and used it so well to force the stubborn nobles and merchants and military to his will. Perhaps he had spies, and this man was one of them? Just how loyal had those spies been, and could they be bought? Were they perhaps already vowed to his cousin, the healer Rafal? He had a reputation as a generous, kind, compassionate man. Although, how could anyone be a healer without possessing those qualities? Still, Merrigan knew from experience how power and the need to defend his throne helped a king justify actions that he might not have approved if he weren't sitting in that seat. What kind of a man had Rafal become? How easily had he won the loyalty of the military and the nobles? How many could justify killing Leffisand's widow if she returned?

Merrigan left her window open when she went to bed. Honk came to her after moonrise and kept her company. She gladly curled herself around him in the quite comfortable bed. She didn't think she would sleep, with all the thoughts and fears in her head. Somehow, she did, and those thoughts and fears and questions affected her dreams.

None were clear, and none lingered in her mind when she woke. She simply had that strong impression that she had dreamed long and deeply, with that nagging certainty that the dreams were important.

"The odd part is that I have this overwhelming memory of hearing water, all through the dreams," she told her companions the next morning, over breakfast in their private parlor. It was the only way Honk could be there without raising an uproar. Swans were such a rare sight anywhere, his presence would generate too many questions.

"Calling to me," she continued, after giving Garan and Bryan, Bib, Crystal and Honk time to consider what she said. "Trickling down the pathway behind me. And somehow hearing it under the ground. Like a stream digging its way through the ground below my feet. Following me."

The water is following you, Honk said. *You freed it, you healed it, and it wants to rejoin the other underground streams that have been dried up or blocked.*

"How am I to do that?" Merrigan nearly shouted, but her head was starting to throb.

The swan shrugged, which was an odd sight to see, because she didn't think he had shoulders enough to complete the gesture.

"Bib, Crystal, what do you think?" Bryan asked, after he translated Honk's response for Garan.

"I only know what is written in the books I have consulted regarding water, and especially magical water," Bib said. "You can understand that I would try to avoid water."

"There are some similarities and linkages between me and water," Crystal said. "It's the reflective qualities. However ... I think the wisest course of action is to go to an expert in magical waters. Don't depend on those who are only a few steps ahead of you on this journey."

"Clara," Bryan said with a sigh, and reached to squeeze Merrigan's hand.

"Clara," Merrigan said, nodding. She wasn't sure if that odd, twisting, sort of settling and expanding sensation in her chest was relief, or dread at facing the seeress again.

~~~~~

When they stopped at a picturesque village for a late lunch and to replenish provisions, Bryan purchased a set of boy clothes to disguise Merrigan when they crossed the border. The place where the border came closest to Clara's pools was a little less than a day of riding away, now. Merrigan would change clothes before they crossed the border at the gateway. They would make a mad dash to reach the seeress and pray the Unseen's mercy that no one would see them, and if anyone did, they wouldn't ask any questions.

Their small company was in better spirits, because the man who had been following them had vanished.

An hour away from the village, they came to a convenient spot with plenty of trees and bushes on both sides of the road, and no one visible behind them. They discussed whether they should stop and have Merrigan change into her disguise now. Then Bib riffled his pages hard enough to make the bag around him thump against Merrigan's leg.

"Strong magic at work just ahead of us, Mi'Lady."

Honk extended his long neck and hissed. He leaped off Bryan's saddle and glided ahead of them, aiming for a thick clump of bushes that extended out from the cover of the woods and almost touched the side of the road. Merrigan thought he would fly into it, but at the last moment veered aside, wings flapping like he would batter something aside. The swan landed and hissed at the bushes. She shuddered, imagining all sorts
~~~~~

of horrid, dangerous things hiding there.

The bushes rippled as if with a heavy wind, as their company stopped. But there was no breeze, let alone a wind strong enough to make the bushes sway and shake. Merrigan muffled a yelp of surprise as the leaves changed colors, and suddenly there were no bushes, but five mounted men. Four were in the uniform of Carlion.

Garan urged his horse forward and turned it slightly to block the five men from Merrigan and Bryan. He rested his hand on his sword.

"What do you want?" His calm voice offered neither challenge nor fear.

"Peace," the fifth man said, moving ahead of the soldiers a few steps, and raised his gloved hands.

He didn't smile. Merrigan thought she would have been more worried if he had smiled. Especially if the new government of Carlion continued her late husband's rather aggressive policies. She mentally slapped herself again for blithely approving all Leffisand's actions.

The soldier on his right moved up next to him and Merrigan felt his studying gaze like a physical weight. She refused to look away. She found it hard to meet his gaze, however, and was relieved, her face warming, when he turned to the leader of the small group and nodded.

"You're sure?" the man said. The soldier nodded again. He gestured, and the soldier moved his horse back a step. The man bowed from the saddle. "Welcome home, Queen Merrigan."

"Princess," she said, trying not to snap and not let her voice tremble. "I am not the queen of Carlion, and whoever you are, you know it."

"Indeed? And what of the child you told the nobles you carried, Leffisand's heir?"

She choked, her belly cold and her face hot.

"Is this really the place for this conversation?" Bryan nudged his horse forward, partially blocking her view of the man. Merrigan appreciated his protectiveness, even if it was far too late.

"How did you find us?" Garan said.

CHAPTER EIGHTEEN

"Enchanted thistles, well hidden in the tails of your horses, to let us track your path. Once we determined where you were going, it was easy enough to get ahead of you." The man moved his horse forward a few more steps. "You're returning to Clara of the Pools, aren't you?"

"Are you here to stop us from entering?"

"I'm here at the behest of Prince Regent Rafal, seeking the welfare of his cousin's widow and posthumous child."

"Didn't Clara tell you?" Merrigan blurted.

"She has been frustratingly quiet." A bit of amusement touched the man's eyes and tone. "All the advice she would give was to wait and see, and not worry about you and your child, Highness. She said that when the time was right and all had been repaired, you would return. Please, Highness, where—"

"There is no child! I lied. I was afraid. I wanted to keep the throne. I came to Clara to make her help me cheat." Merrigan gasped for breath, dizzy with the sudden evaporation of a weight she hadn't even known was there until it was gone. Bryan reached for her hand. "She cursed me, until I learned my lesson."

"And what lesson is that, Highness?"

"I am not the center of the world. Leffisand was the worst sort of king for Carlion, and I was most certainly his perfect queen. I hope Rafal has had a chance to start making things right for the kingdom. Please assure him I only wish him well. I'm here to show Clara her curse worked, and to thank her." She caught her breath, surprised at the spill of words. "And to ask for her help. Not for me, this time, but for all of Armorica."

The man's smile widened. He nodded, and Merrigan wondered if he was a majjian of some sort. Not as strong and possessed of knowledge like Clara but entrusted with helping Prince Rafal protect the kingdom from undeserving claimants like her.

"Why still prince and not king?" She clutched the question to pull herself out of another imminent whirlpool of self-condemnation.

"Many nobles insist on waiting until they are sure of your fate and the child's before they fully acclaim Rafal the heir and new king."

"Now that's not fair. Certainly not to Rafal or the kingdom."

"Indeed. You have changed greatly, Princess Merrigan."

"I have been sick, in my heart and mind. Clara's cure threatened to kill me. Please take my regrets and my apologies and my wholehearted support, if that means anything, to Rafal and Naomi. She is here with him, isn't she?"

"Indeed. And we fear she has need of your help."

"Why Merrigan's help?" Bryan said. He let go of her hand and again put himself between her and the man.

"What is your name? I should hope since we seem to be on the same side now, you'll at least give us that much?" Merrigan said.

"I am Trevor, advisor to the Prince Regent. And yes, a majjian of middling strength." He sighed, and weariness touched his face. "Enough to tell that the late king wove several curses around you, somehow tying you and Princess Naomi together. Untying them and freeing you both could be difficult."

Honk let out a loud trumpet call and jumped up and down several times, calling, *Trust and talk. Trust and talk. Time is speeding away. The closer you get, the stronger the danger.*

Trevor shook his head, staring at the swan. "And why did you not speak up sooner, friend, and let us know you were a wise beast?"

Merrigan is my friend, and I must protect her. Honk waddled off the road, into the cover of the trees. *There is a clearing where we can talk. Battle strategy!*

Trevor chuckled. "Indeed. That would be wise. Well, Highness, will you trust me enough to listen, and to tell me your story?"

"Who is he?" she said to delay the answer while she considered. She pointed at the soldier who had seemed to confirm her identity to Trevor.

"Maxil, son of Lord Amaxin." Trevor seemed to expect her to know.

She remembered and her face warmed. Lord Amaxin was one of the few nobles who had enough courage and ethics to stand against Leffisand when he went too far. He was intensely loyal to Carlion, an honorable man who chose compassion over expediency. He had enough power and wealth to allow him to stand against Leffisand and escape retribution. She couldn't remember ever meeting Maxil, but he had probably been there, in the background, ignored because she and Leffisand judged he was neither useful nor a threat. But obviously he had seen her enough to be entrusted with identifying her.

"Honk says to trust him," Bryan said. "We obviously aren't going to be able to sneak across the border and visit Clara without being seen and recognized. And sneaking implies something to hide."

"I do have much to hide," she blurted. "My foolishness, for one thing. My selfishness. My wrong choices." A soft sound that threatened to become a roaring filled the back of her head. "Oh, would someone please stop that water! Why must it follow me?"

"Water, Highness?" Trevor's pleasant expression sharpened. "Do you hear water, spilling through the ground under us?"

Freed and healed. Freed and healed, Honk cried.

She shuddered as an image from her dreams pierced the haze in her memories. "Trevor … I never saw the queen's garden. I never wanted to see it, after what had happened with my mother's garden when I was a child. Is there a queen's garden in the palace?"

"No one knows, Highness." He sighed and his eyes narrowed, as if he saw something new when he looked at her. "Indeed, that lack is tied into the magic tangling Princess Naomi, and if I am any judge of the ties and crossroads of magic, that problem ties to you."

"I promise you, I did nothing to the queen's garden."

"Oh, I believe you. There has been no queen's garden since Queen Lorellia died.."

"Then how—"

"The water that follows you is desperately needed in Carlion. This is no place for a conference, though I had planned to make sure of your mind and heart before allowing you across the border. Will you ride with me now, all the way to the palace? The sooner we reach it and the water follows you and reawakens the sleeping majjian springs, if they can be awakened after so many years of drought, the better for all of Carlion. But especially for Princess Naomi."

"Is she dying?" Merrigan whispered.

"Worse, Highness. She is besieged by suitors." He gestured for everyone to mount their horses.

"But … isn't she married to Rafal?" she asked.

"Yes, and there is at least one assassination attempt every day, to free her to marry again. Cruel magic and tied to you in some way."

"Do you think it's the same magic that urged me to marry you immediately, rather than wait for your father's blessing?" Bryan said.

"Did it?" Trevor frowned. "That is something new to consider and add to the tangled knot."

"Excuse me, but I can offer some hope," Bib said. "Mi'Lady, bring me out so I can be heard more clearly?"

Merrigan hurried to open the saddlebag, and propped Bib up on the front of the saddle. For fairness, she brought out Crystal, and wedged her handle into the strap of the saddlebag.

"Please correct me. I am sadly behind on the news of Carlion, as there have been few books or public bulletins to consult. How many children do Rafal and Naomi have?"

"Three."

"Once Prince Rafal is confirmed as the rightful king of Carlion, Naomi becomes queen mother, and their children are his heirs. If he dies, she remains queen."

"And those kings trying to marry her would gobble up Carlion, adding it to their kingdoms, and then make sure Naomi and her children died in sad accidents that no one can prove weren't accidents," Bryan said.

"No." Merrigan shuddered, feeling both queasy and chilled to her marrow. "Worse. Carlion gobbles up one kingdom after another, through marriage alliances and the sad, inexplicable deaths of their kings. That's just the sort of nastiness I would expect of Leffisand, if he died. He would expect me to continue his plan to take over all of Armorica."

"Indeed, Highness," Trevor said, his expression growing grimmer. "We have found references to the grand unification plan in Leffisand's hidden journals. There is an entire labyrinth of hidden rooms under the palace, all accessed through his private chambers. And no entrance through your former apartments. He kept secrets from even you, despite how much you formerly supported him."

She nodded her thanks to him. She felt rather breathless from this sign of his belief in her words, and even more his belief in her reformation.

"Prince Rafal has been increasingly ill since entering Carlion. One spell wants him dead, and another spell is already maneuvering powerful kings into place to snatch up the widow. It explains quite a few of the diplomatic tangles we're in, all the protests from ambassadors who have been caught plotting assassinations, proclaiming their innocence, claiming they were coerced by magic, that they would never do such a thing. Or worse, their kings have come in person, against all common sense, contradicting themselves, supporting Rafal one day and the next day trying to seduce Naomi."

"Why not throw them all out of Carlion until you get the throne established and secured? Just tell them you believe them, there's nasty magic at work and they're all safer at home with their own majjians to defend them?" Garan said.

"If only it were that simple." Trevor nodded to the captain, one side of his mouth quirking up in a grim smile. "Diplomacy is an ugly, complicated thing by itself. Add in magic coming from multiple directions with all sorts of conflicting spells. No wonder Prince Rafal is ill."

"Multiple directions, did you say?" Bib said. "What do you think, Crystal?"

"Oh, I agree." The mirror's surface flared bright with excitement. "Our theory is being proven with each new clue and problem."

"Theory?" Trevor said.

"It's the hags again. They want things done their way. It doesn't matter what mortal laws say, and they don't care who is hurt. They're tripping themselves up with their impatience. I just don't understand, though," the mirror continued, "why they're so supportive of Leffisand's conquest plans."

"Maybe he was an ally all along, and knew what they were doing?" Merrigan said.

"I'm sorry, but you've entirely lost me," Trevor said, raising both hands in both surrender and a plea for explanation.

"We're wasting time just sitting here," Bryan said. "Can we talk and explain what's been happening to us, what we've learned, as we travel? You did say time was of the essence, and Princess Naomi and her family were in danger?"

"Indeed." He gestured to his four guards, who had been conferring quietly with the remaining soldiers from Merrigan and Bryan's party. They spread out to surround Trevor, Merrigan and Bryan, and their horses turned back onto the road.

"Mi'Lady, if you don't mind," Bib said, "we might save time if Crystal and I ride with Trevor and explain the chain of events and what we've learned. Just to lay a foundation."

She agreed, though she didn't like handing the book over to someone else. Bib had been her only ally and friend and confidant for so long, and she still had nightmares from time to time of some powerful person tearing him away from her.

"Forgive us, dear," Crystal said, "but I think we need to start with your story, because it is so interwoven with what we've found, what the hags are trying to do."

"Of course." Merrigan's voice cracked a little. She just hoped she didn't look as white and cold as she felt. It was one thing to confess her foolishness and selfishness to people who knew her. Trevor only knew what he had been told by the people of Carlion. She supposed someday she would find something humorous in her desperate need for a total stranger to think well of her.

Trevor leaned over the book, propped up on the front of his saddle, and paid no attention to the road ahead of them. Merrigan was grateful that as a majjian, Trevor could hear Bib speak directly into his mind. No need for the soldiers to hear all the uncomfortable details of her story. She focused on the sound of their horses' hooves and the singing of the birds, the rustling of the breeze through the budding leaves, and the trickling of melting water in the ditches along both sides of the road.

Bib wasn't done speaking when their party came to the border gateway. The guards there stood at attention and waved them through, no need for stopping. Merrigan fought the aching need to hunch her shoulders and pull her hood down lower over her head. She knew no one would recognize her even if her hood had fallen back, exposing her face to the world. After all, she wasn't wearing jewels or makeup, her clothes were simple, sturdy traveling clothes, and her hair was a plain braid. There was nothing to connect her to the former queen of Carlion.

She prayed silently for what felt like several miles that there truly was nothing to connect her to Carlion ever again.

They were more than an hour on the grand highway, leading directly to the capitol, when Trevor sighed and straightened up and looked around. He met Merrigan's gaze, and he smiled. It was a warm expression, and he gave her a respectful nod.

"Princess Merrigan, I wish you all the happiness you deserve, after all you have gone through."

Merrigan laughed. She couldn't help it.

"Now I have a better understanding and quite a few theories for dealing with the problems facing Carlion. I am grateful. I truly believe the Unseen has been guiding you, and the timing is too perfect to be mere coincidence."

"Is there any chance I can consult with Clara?" she asked. "I would like to thank her for cursing me, if I do nothing else."

Trevor paused, his expression unreadable, caught between several emotions. Then he smiled.

"Yes, I can see how you would consider her spell a curse. But often, aren't cures, temporarily at least, worse than the disease they conquer?"

"Disease is a very good description for what Tulip and her hag friends have been doing to children and kingdoms, and the majjian springs." She shuddered and fought the urge to nudge her horse forward and snatch Bib from Trevor's hands. Just being able to hold her book friend again would help her feel better. Bib had loved her and encouraged her into being a better person. The person her mother wanted her to be.

"And in answer to your question, yes, you will be able to consult with Clara. She is at the palace, helping to untangle the royal family from the snares left behind by their predecessors." He cocked his head to one side and narrowed his eyes. Merrigan felt the intensity of his gaze. "The same snares that are thickening around you, the closer we draw to the capitol. If you would be so kind as to move back among the rear guard? I want to test a theory. The less you are visible, the more true the reaction."

Merrigan chose not to ask what he referred to. She had the awful feeling she would understand very soon. Bryan caught hold of her hand and squeezed it in silent encouragement, then let her slow her horse, so soon she was riding nearly in the rear of their little group. Garan and Bryan rode on either side of Trevor, then their soldiers alternated with Trevor's escort. Merrigan rode second to last in the short column of horses beside Trevor's third man.

Bring me out so I can see better, and show you what I see, Crystal said, after they had ridden another mile or so. *Those threads of magic are thickening and vibrating. I can guess what Trevor has in mind.*

More proof of Leffisand's nasty spells and whatever curse he placed on me?

Merrigan dug into the saddlebag and rested the mirror on the front of her saddle, angled so the sunlight didn't reflect off her face and give away her presence. At least, she hoped so.

If someone knows you're a princess without any visible clues, yes.

The traffic on the road grew thicker and slowed, but people moved aside readily enough with very little prompting. Merrigan frowned, noting how people showed some annoyance, but not the resentful fear that she had seen whenever she bothered to look out the carriage windows.

What an utterly selfish, arrogant little twit I used to be. Please tell me I've improved greatly since those days, Crystal?

You're an entirely different person. But would you mind a little helpful criticism, dear?

Yes, of course — I mean, yes, please tell me, but no, at least I hope I won't mind.

Crystal's sigh in her mind was somehow comforting, even as Merrigan detected a bit of laughter behind the sound. *Merry, dear, you really do need to stop thinking about yourself so much. Repentance is good for the soul, but you're verging on being somewhat maudlin. And whining. Renounce your foolishness and move forward.*

For several moments, Merrigan couldn't make herself breathe, and her mind seemed frozen in place. She wanted to let out one of her infamous shrieks of outrage. Nanny Tulip had always scolded her that a queen did not shriek like a fishwife, and royalty never gave in to heated emotions. Cold fury was always a sharper and more potent and terrifying weapon than heated anger.

Then something cracked inside her. Merrigan let out a little squeak, and suddenly the pressure in her head and chest evaporated. She took a deep breath …. And laughed. Softly.

Thank you, Crystal. Have I truly been so nauseating?

Not yet. But getting there. I thought you could use a nudge back onto the solid path. And distract you.

From what? Merrigan raised her head and gasped at the sight of the group of riders charging down the road to meet them.

Their perfectly matched black horses and ebony saddles and other equipment, and the glossy black and silver livery told her exactly who they were, even before the thickset man in the lead stood in his stirrups and bellowed.

"Halt in the name of Prince Schendrake of Pittarm!"

"Oh, please, not him. Of all the insufferable …"

"Problem, Highness?" the soldier beside her murmured and reached for the sword at his side.

"No need to fight that pumped up, self-important …" A sigh escaped her. "A good joke would destroy him much more easily than a sword. Although I wouldn't doubt he'd explode like a bladder filled with hot air, if you managed to get through his guards and puncture him."

The Carlion solder behind her muffled a chuckle. She glanced over her shoulder, glad to turn her attention off the prince and his party as their two groups met.

"Have you had much trouble from his royal self-importance?"

"He takes his dialog from ancient ballads and expects women to swoon in delight, even when they can't understand half of what he says," the soldier said. "Prince Rafal keeps offering him various potions to untangle his tongue and help him speak clearly."

Merrigan muffled a chuckle. "Good for him."

Interesting, Crystal said. *Turn me a little, Merry, and raise me so I'm facing them.*

Merrigan complied. "What do you see?"

The strings of the spells are thickening, pulling on him, and trying to thicken around you, to pull the two of you together. Wave your hand in front of yourself. The hand with your betrothal ring. The mirror *hmm'd* a few times as Merrigan obeyed. *Interesting.*

A moment later, Bryan looked over his shoulder back to Merrigan. Their gazes met, then he did the same thing, moving his ring hand in the air in front of his chest.

"What is it doing? Are our rings affecting the spells?" Merrigan whispered.

Some of the strings have snapped, and others thickened, but not the same ones on each of you. I'd wager your betrothal is protecting you from some of the spells and making others more knotted and thick. Most likely the ones that want to kill Bryan to free you to marry someone else.

"What?" She managed to muffle her shriek in time.

I was right. Look at Schendrake, how he's focusing on Bryan and on you. His head's turning back and forth so quickly, it threatens to snap off his neck. The mirror sniggered.

Merrigan stared for a few heartbeats and was glad that she was partially hidden in the column. Schendrake leaned slightly to the right, trying to see around the soldier, urged by the spells to look for her. Yet every few seconds, he turned to glare at Bryan, very clearly ignoring what Trevor was saying to him.

"Oh, Leffisand, if you weren't dead already, I would dearly love to find a spell to slap you against a wall like a dirty rug," she murmured.

"Bravo, Highness," the Carlion soldier behind her said, just as quietly.

She muffled a squeak of laughter.

"Enough!" Schendrake roared. He pointed at Bryan. "Have that man arrested for conspiracy against the throne of Carlion and against my august personage."

"No," Trevor said, his voice calm. Merrigan heard boredom in it.

"How dare you? I will soon be your king, and when I am—"

"You are not, and you never will be. You are a visitor to our kingdom and have pushed the bounds of hospitality past the breaking point far too often." Trevor stood in his stirrups and pointed downward. Schendrake dropped into his saddle with an *ooph* and a grunt of protest from his longsuffering horse. He went noticeably paler.

"My lady, my love," Schendrake whined, and reached out a hand to Merrigan. "Can't you see that I am here to rescue you from this unworthy boor?" Another disgusted glance at Bryan.

And the theory is proven, Crystal said. *I wonder just how embarrassed and offended this overblown grandee will feel when the spells are unwound and he is set free. How badly has he been making a nuisance of himself?*

Merrigan asked. The soldier gave Schendrake a disgusted look.

"We've caught several of his people trying to poison Prince Rafal's food and medicine, and others trying to slip all sorts of love potions into Princess Naomi's food, or in gifts of perfume and sweets, and even her bathing water. They're all visibly bespelled, half-asleep or dazed. We have to believe them when they say they don't know what they're doing when they're caught."

"This needs to stop," Merrigan said.

"Maxil," Trevor called, raising his voice to be heard over Schendrake's renewed bellows of outrage. "Take our guests to the palace while I deal with the prince." He raised both hands and magic visibly gathered around his fingers, streaks of silver and pale blue sparks.

The swirls of magic spun outward, expanding to surround Schendrake and his entire party. His shouts suddenly stopped as he froze, his mouth open. Merrigan gladly turned her horse to follow the soldier. Bryan rode next to her, and she wanted to shout for him to turn west and head for the border and never come near Carlion ever again.

Yet she knew they couldn't escape just yet. She had a duty to Carlion. Despite everything, she had been their queen.

Merrigan heard the soft trickling of a shallow stream over pebbles. Yet when she looked on either side of the road, all she saw were houses and then fields. Some showed the soft green of the first haze of spring growth, yet most of them were the dry, dead brown and dull yellow of winter's sleep. She shuddered at the contrast of the dryness of the land, while the sound of water teased her.

"Maxil," she asked the man riding beside her, "where is the stream?"

He frowned and shook his head. "There is no stream for dozens of miles in any direction, Highness," he finally said. "The land is dry."

"But I can hear water," she said.

It is following you, Honk said, circling down and around to settle on the back of Bryan's horse again.

"The water is underground," Bryan said. "It's following us."

Maxil shook his head. "That would be a blessing if there was water underground, but useless, if we can't get to it."

"How long has it been this dry?" Merrigan asked.

"As far as anyone can remember."

"If we can lead the majjian water all the way to the palace," Bryan said, "maybe that will help untangle the spells troubling Rafal and Naomi, and free us of whatever curses Leffisand wrapped around you."

"How?"

Go. Go, Honk said.

"Go where?" She caught the confused twist to Maxil's frown, and a bubble of strained laughter escaped her. "I'm sorry ... We have rings that let us hear the language of the birds. Honk is helping us."

"Your pardon, Highness, but ... what sort of bird is that?" the other Carlion soldier said.

"You don't know what a swan is?" Bryan said.

"That's a swan?" He and Maxil stared at Honk, who regally nodded to them, then set to work smoothing his feathers.

"No, we never had swans around the palace the entire time I was here, did we?" Merrigan said. "I don't suppose you know anything about the queen's garden?"

"Princess Naomi has been searching for it," Maxil said. "We're not quite sure what she means or wants, because there are several gardens at the palace. She talks about hidden doors and rooms where the windows to the inner courts of the palace are blocked with thorns. Some fear —" He glanced at the other soldier, then seemed to brace himself to speak. "Some fear she is cracking under the terrible pressure, the assassination attempts on Prince Rafal, and attempts to force her to marry other princes."

CHAPTER NINETEEN

"The queen's garden is the heart of the kingdom," Merrigan said. "It was brutally attacked at one time, and thorns grew up to defend it. Other magic has wiped the garden from memory, and disguised the windows blocked by thorns, so all anyone sees are blank walls. No one sees the door into the inner courtyard of the garden. Naomi should be able to see the door, even if no one else can. Her heart is purer, her magic is stronger, than anyone else in this benighted kingdom." She shuddered. "Bryan, how am I to make up for the harm I did to this place? Those hags must pay for what they have done, what they warped me to do for them."

"One step at a time, love." He turned to look back at Honk. "Are the horses rested enough to run again?"

Honk tapped the root of the horse's tail with his beak, then made a rattling noise, ending on a honk that certainly sounded like a question. The horse whinnied and shook its mane.

Run, yes, the swan said.

Bryan's horse whinnied again, and all their horses leaped forward as if they had heard the trumpet to start a race. Merrigan gasped, laughing a little raggedly, and held on. She was grateful for the thundering of the hooves, to muffle the sound of water. When they slowed maybe twenty minutes later, the musical trickling had turned to a louder gurgling, as if the water flowed faster. The spires of the grandiose towers of Carlion were faintly visible streaks rising above the horizon, far ahead of them.

Twice more, they galloped the horses for maybe fifteen minutes, then walked for half an hour. That got them to the gates of Carlion.

When their party slowed because of the traffic on the road approaching the city gates, Merrigan couldn't hear the water at all. Had they lost the majjian water? Or was it so deeply underground she couldn't hear it? She lost her breath for a few moments at the choking fear that she had already failed in this task she had no idea how to accomplish.

Bib, what do you sense? Have I lost the water?

I do not know, Mi'Lady. Everything is so very dry, the land so hard. And I am not good with water.

I am, Crystal said after a moment. *Reflective things are more my specialty, you old ink blotter.* She chuckled, but Merrigan sensed the mirror strained just to tease Bib and raise their spirits. *There is a feeling around the palace, going deep down, through the rock. Something waits. A sensation of prowling. I don't know if it's like a sentry waiting to welcome a long-missing ruler home, or to drive away an invader.*

"I can't imagine any magic welcoming me back, either the queen's garden or the old hags. I fought one and failed the other," Merrigan whispered.

Then the sentries at the gate called out and Maxil responded, in some odd military cadence Merrigan didn't understand. They passed through the gates without stopping. She felt the weight of curious eyes following them, following her. She fought not to hunch her shoulders and duck her head. Her hood, which kept her face in shadows, was depressingly flimsy shelter.

I'm sorry, she silently told the city as she rode through the shadow from the wall. *If I can do anything to restore you to what you should have been all along ... I will do what I can. Unseen, please help me? Give me guidance?*

Do you feel that? Honk cried, rising up and raising his head to the sky.

"Feel what?" Bryan said.

The swan launched hard and fast from the back of the horse, so it grunted and tossed its head in momentary protest.

"Where is it going?" Maxil asked, as their whole company stopped their horses and watched the swan flap hard, rising above the rooftops.

"To the palace, I hope." Merrigan's heart seemed to rise up through her throat and follow the swan. She watched, refusing to even blink, willing safety to her childhood friend. Certainly, even in a city as densely populated as Carlion's capitol, there were people whose first reaction would be to try to knock the massive bird from the sky, and feast. If the palace soldiers didn't know what a swan was, how could she expect the ordinary townspeople to know? They wouldn't know that the hope of magic returning to Carlion might just rest on Honk's wings.

"Yes, the palace," Maxil finally said, as Honk vanished behind a tall tower of gray stone. "And so should we. As quickly as possible."

Despite how quickly they moved, it wasn't quickly enough. Maxil led them around to the entrances once used by the common people when they had free access to the royal gardens. Merrigan had heard about those days only because some of the lords like Maxin regularly petitioned Leffisand to re-open the gardens. He had closed the gates to the common people soon after his father had died and proclaimed he was protecting the royal gardens in his mother's memory, because she had so loved them.

Merrigan silently scolded herself for never asking about either of his parents. There was not a single portrait of them anywhere in the palace. Not even in Leffisand's private rooms. Merrigan had discovered small caches of books in the neglected library with Queen Lorellia's name inscribed in them, and notes written in the margins in delicate handwriting. She had enjoyed reading them. The books had vanished after she mentioned her delight in finding her predecessor's treasured books. She wondered now where the books had gone. Had Leffisand taken them? If so, why?

Where was the queen's garden? Where were other possessions that Queen Lorellia had used and blessed? What kind of a woman was she? Where were her clothes and journals? What had happened to those books when they vanished from the palace library? And why hadn't she persisted in searching for those books and asking why they had vanished?

"Because I was a flighty little twitterhead who let herself be distracted," she muttered. "I believed Leffisand adored me, but he was just tugging on the reins and offering me treats to get me to do and think and believe as he wanted." She sighed. "Not what was right."

You are learning, Mi'Lady, and sometimes learning is painful. What matters is that you do want to do right, and fix what was wrong, and atone for your errors, Bib said, his tone gentle and soothing in her mind.

"Yes, but what price will we all have to pay for atonement?"

"Are you all right?" Bryan looked back at her. Their horses walked single file now down a narrow lane. They had to leave room for other travelers.

"Memories are not always kind." She mustered a smile for him.

"You have no good memories here?"

"Oh, I have many pleasant memories, but ..." She sat up straighter, when she wanted to hunch over, bracing for something to fall on her. "I'm afraid that every pleasant memory, every happy moment, will be revealed as another crime I committed, if only by being selfish and demanding."

A shout echoed down the narrow lane, bouncing off the buildings. Merrigan looked back, and the soldiers escorting them turned. Maxil raised his hand, signaling a stop. He shouted to his man who brought up the rear.

"Prince Oris, sir," the man called.

Maxil muttered something that Merrigan suspected was a curse. Yes, it was indeed a curse. The same spell that had brought Schendrake to confront her had brought this new prince. He probably didn't even know who she was yet.

"Highness." Maxil flung a large black key to Bryan. "The gate is just ahead of us, around two more right turns. Whatever it takes, get her through the gate and lock it. We'll delay them as long as we can." He nodded to Merrigan, then gestured for the remaining Alliburton soldiers to come with him. Garan saluted her as he turned and followed Maxil.

Bryan tucked the key inside his jacket, then dug his heels into his horse. She followed suit, leaning low over her horse's neck. The clatter of hooves on the cobblestones echoed off the stone faces of the buildings but couldn't drown out the sounds of men's voices and the demand in a deep, resonant voice for them to halt.

No. That man shouted for her to halt. She shuddered, hearing the poetic words. Prince Oris. Of course. Now she remembered him. Who could forget that richly cultured voice, even raised in near-desperate shouts? Oris, third-born son of King Rufus of Ostengarde. A swaggering dandy who fussed over learning the newest dance steps and redesigned armor so it was comfortable for daily wear. Leffisand had said the prince might look the part of a war hero, but the first time someone came at him with a sword, he would shriek like a little girl faced with a room full of spiders and faint, if he didn't soil his leather trousers.

I hope we are able to laugh about this soon.

One more turn. There. The buildings halted abruptly, leaving a wide-open space with a fountain in the middle and a high wall. There was something wrong with the colors of the wall. Merrigan nearly didn't tug on the reins to slow her horse in time. She was too busy trying to figure out what was wrong with the wall and gate.

"Oh, Leffisand, what a selfish ... idiot you were," she murmured, as she tipped her head back and looked at the wall.

It had been added to, with a different color of bricks. Visibly newer than the original wall that surrounded the palace garden. It was double the original height, so that only the people on the third and fourth floors of these buildings could look over the wall. That was just the sort of selfish, petty, vindictive tactic she would have expected from Leffisand. He likely excused it as defending the privacy of the palace gardens, protecting the sacred spaces his dearly departed mother had adored.

"Merrigan!" Bryan's shout woke her from her contemplation of the gates.

She urged her horse forward, through the gate once Bryan had it open. On foot, he urged his horse through the gate, and pulled it closed behind him. It swung slowly, ponderously closed, groaning, likely from lack of use. If she were still queen, she would have the gates taken down, to allow the people free access to the palace gardens day and night.

But I'm not queen, and that's good. Naomi would do that, once this whole ugly tangled mess is settled. She's just that sharing, trusting kind of person. Bib, remind me to apologize to her?

You were never unkind to Princess Naomi, the book said after a moment, during which the lock groaned and squeaked as Bryan turned the key.

No, but I mocked her in my head and my heart. I thought she was a silly goody-goody who deserved all the cruel things smarter, more realistic people did to her. More realistic, perhaps, but certainly not smarter.

"We need to keep moving," Bryan said as he climbed back into his saddle.

She flinched at the sounds of hooves and men shouting and the clash of bodies and horses colliding. Lots of grunting and gasping and cursing.

Something hard slammed into the gates, making both of them flinch.

"My darling! My dove! My treasure! Call to me, and I will tear this wall down and rescue you!" Oris cried. "No, unhand me!"

His next few words were lost in a shriek that rose up through two octaves.

Merrigan burst out in giggles. She couldn't help it. She barely got herself under control by the time she and Bryan had ridden into the palace gardens far enough she couldn't hear Oris shriek any longer.

She slumped in her saddle, breathless and sputtering. Bryan stopped their horses and helped her dismount. He led her to a nearby bench and sat her down, and knelt in front of her, holding her hands. Merrigan took a few deep breaths, and that calmed the thudding of her heart.

"Oh, Bryan, I'm sorry. You probably think me an utter brainless twitterhead, don't you?"

"I think you're holding up admirably, considering the gauntlet you likely ran through to get here," a woman said from behind them.

Merrigan turned so quickly, she nearly twisted herself completely off the bench. She hiccupped in shock, and that seemed to be the cure for the giggles.

"Hello, Merrigan." Princess Naomi came around a low hedge. She smiled, as if she were actually pleased to see her.

That felt like a slap across Merrigan's face with a cold, wet cloth.

She stared, seeing Naomi in an entirely new light. The wheat-colored hair and blue-gray eyes and golden, sun-kissed skin that she had mocked, calling her a milk-and-water farmer princess, now proclaimed Naomi as strong and level-headed. A far better queen for Carlion.

"Merrigan?" Bryan tightened his arm around her. "It's all right, you're safe now."

"No, I don't think so," Naomi said. "I'm sorry. I'm grateful that you've diverted those arrogant idiots from hounding my every step, but that won't be much comfort for you." She sighed. "Unless we can figure out what exactly has been done, and how to untangle it."

"Trevor thinks that some spell to attract kings to Merrigan latched onto you, because she wasn't here. The fact that Prince Rafal hasn't been officially crowned yet has been protecting you two. The illness plaguing him should have killed him, if he had officially become king," Bryan said.

"Why would Leffisand want Merrigan to remarry?"

"It has something to do with the hags, no doubt." Merrigan wiped her face again and finally felt like she could take a deep breath, for the first time since the ridiculous chase started. "Naomi ... I am truly sorry."

"For what?" The other princess laughed as she settled on a bench facing them. "This idiotic spell sending all those overdressed, overdone poets chasing me and now you certainly isn't your fault."

"All the awful things I've said and thought about you. The nasty things I helped Leffisand do, to you and your country and your family. The trap you fell into because I tried to cheat and got sent on a quest to fix my mind and my heart." She shook her head. "I have no doubt I will keep apologizing for ... years to come, probably."

"Did you help Leffisand pursue and seduce Fialla, and then grow disgusted with her and kill her and try to blame her death on someone else, to start a war so he could take over her father's country?" Naomi's expression was somber, but there was a sparkle of something in her eyes that hinted she found some amusement in all this. "Did you help him with his plan to try to kill my brother, and force me to marry him, so he could take over my father's country? Did you help him become so vile that even a magic apple tree couldn't cleanse his heart?" She shook her head. "Merrigan, you were a child when Leffisand instigated so many of his plans, and from all the entries in his journals, he corrupted you, for a purpose. He considered himself a sculptor and you were his masterpiece. The two of you would someday rule the world, if not by sitting on the thrones of every kingdom, then through the sons you would raise together." She sighed. "And that brings me to a question that the council of nobles will want to ask as soon as they know you are here."

"No, there is no child. I lied." Merrigan caught her breath, feeling as if something in the air had paused and grown painfully still, listening and waiting. "I lied! I tried to cheat. There is no child. Leffisand wanted children but we never had any, and I'm glad. Thank you, blessed Unseen, for protecting the world from that!" She half-rose to her feet as she called out the last few sentences.

The ground rippled faintly under her feet and another ripple moved through the air. A soft, brief glimmer came from somewhere to her left. Merrigan shuddered, suddenly able to orient herself to where she was in the garden. That shimmer was the spot Leffisand had enclosed with a thick brick wall, two stories high, to imprison the magic apple tree he had tried to corrupt to serve his purposes. The apple tree that had ultimately killed him.

Merrigan exhaled slowly, feeling as if she deflated slightly. Bryan's arm tightened around her, and she nearly burst into tears again with the depth of her gratitude for his love and support.

"I'm sorry. I lied. I was afraid and greedy and desperate, and I thought I was completely justified in cheating and asking Clara to give me a child of Leffisand's through magic, so I could hold onto the kingdom. I convinced myself it was for the good of Carlion, when it was really for my own good. My pride. I refused to go home to Avylyn." She inhaled sharply, as Naomi's words seemed to reverberate in her head. "So you have proof? He wrote in his journals all the things he did to ... to change me? Train me? Make me like him?"

"Leffisand liked to brag about all the things he had done, and gloat, I suppose, over all his great and glorious plans." The sparkle of mischief in Naomi's eyes drew an answering, weak smile from Merrigan. "He had hundreds of journals. It's been quite educational, going through them. And exhausting. He repeats himself constantly. But we've been able to untangle so many events, and put names and blame on the right people, and exonerate others, and start making reparations for all the damage Leffisand did."

"Have you found the queen's garden yet?" Merrigan said.

"Highness? Naomi?" a woman called from the general direction of the palace.

"What's wrong?" Bryan said, when Naomi's serenity cracked into concern. She leaped to her feet and turned toward the voice.

"Rafal." Naomi glanced at them, then the palace. "Come." Then she ran.

Merrigan held onto Bryan's hand as they followed Naomi up the sanded paths to the palace.

A woman hurried down the grand, formal stairs from the palace to the garden, reaching the bottom of the steps at the same time Naomi did. She gestured up at the palace, and Merrigan was close enough to see the astonishment on her face. Happy astonishment. Naomi reached out and hugged the woman, then leaped up the stairs, sometimes taking two steps at a time.

"What happened?" Bryan called, as they raced across the pavement to the stairs.

"Prince Rafal is awake. His fever has broken." The woman wrapped her arms around herself. "We were so afraid this time it was poison, not illness, and he wouldn't awaken. He's worn himself out, using his own healing magic to fight the illness. It's a gift from the Unseen."

"Yes, a gift." Merrigan shuddered and was glad to finally slow down and try to catch her breath. She clutched harder at Bryan's hand, wondering when this part of Leffisand's curse would latch onto him. Would the unofficial nature of their vows protect him or make him even more of a target?

Too much thinking. It was making her head hurt.

Then she let out a gasp.

"What?" Bryan asked.

"Bib. We left Bib and Crystal behind."

"Shall I send for them?" the woman asked.

Honk dropped from the sky, startling the woman into jumping backward. She nearly tripped on the bottom step. Neck outstretched, Honk let out a triumphant trumpet blast of sound and waddled up to

Merrigan. He butted her hip with his head, making her turn. A sputter of laughter escaped her tight throat when she saw their horses come trotting up the sanded paths of the garden.

Water coming, Honk said. *Apologize. Confess. It comes faster.*

"Merrigan's apology to Naomi is helping the water?" Bryan asked.

The swan bobbed his head. The woman stared. Merrigan muffled a few sputters of laughter. She feared she was losing what little balance she had left.

"Bib, what should we do?" she called, now that the horses were only a dozen steps or so from the stairs. "Are you able to talk to the other books of the palace yet? Any clues? How can we break this spell?"

Bryan hurried to retrieve Bib and Crystal from the saddlebag. The woman excused herself, mumbling about needing to check on Rafal. Merrigan felt only a brief regret that she hadn't been polite enough to ask her name. And wasn't that proof of how much she had changed? The queen she had been believed no servant was worthy of the courtesy of knowing her name.

"So many books." Bib sounded rather breathless the moment Bryan pulled him from the saddlebag.

That frightened Merrigan, because as a book, Bib didn't need to breathe. "What are they doing to you?"

"They aren't doing anything to me. They are suffering." He gasped again.

"They're imprisoned," Crystal said. "Their voices are smothering him, calling for help. Pull me out, I can show the way."

Bryan gave Bib to Merrigan. She clutched the book to her chest, holding him tight, feeling the rippling of his pages inside the wood and leather cover. She envisioned the book's torment, shared with the imprisoned books, twisting and turning him until he tore to pieces.

CHAPTER TWENTY

Not if I can do anything about it, Merrigan promised him silently. *Don't you dare waste all the hard work I did, putting you back together the first time.*

Bib chuckled, and his twisting eased for a few heartbeats. Bryan had Crystal out now, and her glass showed a pathway through the gardens. He looked to Merrigan, she nodded, and he went ahead of her, consulting the mirror and studying the sanded paths and awakening flowerbeds all around them. They hurried, their boots sometimes splashing through small puddles in the pathway, where the last of the snowmelt had collected. Merrigan fought dozens of memories that swirled around her, of gala events filled with noise and hundreds of torches to light the night sky, the roar of people's voices and music and elaborate dresses designed to rival the flowers and trees. Of silent days when Leffisand had banished everyone from the palace gardens but her, and he raged and sulked and screamed at the magic apple tree. Naomi's magic apple tree, meant to be a blessing, but turned to poison by Leffisand's lies and schemes. Not even the enchanted wall he had ordered built around the tree could contain the poison that seeped out from the apple tree's roots. He was the true source of the poison, not the tree.

"I don't understand," Bryan said, and came to a halt so quickly Merrigan nearly ran into him. He turned, showing her Crystal's face. "She brought us here, but that path isn't here."

"Yes, it is." Merrigan swallowed hard, fighting an icy fist catching around her throat. The path currently ran between two hedges, rising higher than their heads. The image in Crystal's surface showed a narrow, arched opening through the hedge on their right, and sunlight spilling down on another passageway lined with hedge, going perhaps twenty steps, before it opened into a courtyard still touched with snow, and a simple cottage, shuttered and dark. By the piles of debris littering the courtyard around the cottage, obscuring the cobblestones, Merrigan guessed that no one had come in here to simply sweep and cart away broken limbs and leaves, for several seasons.

Maybe since Leffisand died? Merrigan nudged Bryan aside and stepped up to the arched opening, and leaned in, to look down the path.

"Merrigan!" Bryan clutched at her shoulder, but stopped short, his mouth open. "That's … impossible."

"What is?" She didn't want to say what she suspected but wanted him to say it.

"You vanished, into the hedge. "

"An illusion spell," Crystal said.

She shook her head. "Bib, do you sense any spells, other than the ones hiding this place?"

"None. Hurry, Mi'Lady. They're getting rather frantic, now that they know someone knows they are there. Nothing hurts a book more than to be locked up and unable to share the treasures hidden in him."

"Keep holding on," she told Bryan. Then she took a deep breath and stepped through the archway. His hand tightened on her shoulder. He inhaled sharply but followed close enough he nearly trod on her heels twice.

Something rippled through the air, stirring the hedges on either side of her, as they went down the narrow path. Merrigan refused to quicken her pace, just in case something nasty, some last trick of protection, waited to pounce when she stepped into the courtyard.

Bryan gasped as they came out into the light and he let go of her shoulder. He turned to look back the way they came and nodded. "From the looks of things, no one has been in here for several years."

"Since Leffisand died." Merrigan frowned at the door. "I wonder why he left the spell open so it didn't affect me."

"He likely intended you to carry on his plans, or at least find whatever he left in there," Crystal said. "Anything besides books held prisoner, Bib?"

"Letters. Maps. All sorts of charms. It's like a minor majjian's war storehouse," the book said after several moments. Merrigan was quite happy to just stand there.

"All right," she said, and finally relaxed her hold on Bib, to let him fall open in her outstretched arms. "What should we do first?"

"Besides open the door?" Bryan brushed a kiss against her cheek, then went ahead of her and reached for the doorknob.

Merrigan braced herself for some flash of magic, an ominous voice calling warning, a cloud of dark magic to come bursting out through the open door. Or at the very least, for the door to refuse to open. But the knob turned easily. It wasn't even locked. Bryan pushed the door open. It creaked slightly from disuse.

"You over-confident idiot," she muttered. Of course, Leffisand would feel no need to lock or otherwise protect this hidden little cottage. If no one could find the way into this courtyard, why would he take any further effort to keep intruders out?

She hoped that would prove true. She held her breath, expecting some delayed attack, as she stepped through the door after Bryan.

He had put Crystal down on the first table he found, just inside the doorway, and now walked around, opening the shutters on tall, narrow windows. The room was lined with bookshelves up to the ceiling, with three long tables down the center of the floor, and shoulder-height shelves creating a maze-like feel through the rest of the building. It was all one room, with a fireplace at the far end and lanterns hanging from the ceiling every four or five steps.

"Well, he spared himself no expense, didn't he?" Crystal muttered. Light flashed on her surface, becoming a ball that shot up in the air and ricocheted off each lantern, leaving a bright golden glow. "Majjian lights. No need for flame in here."

"Considering the amount of paper and parchment?" Merrigan shuddered, imagining a stray spark landing on a pile of papers and turning quickly into an inferno.

She turned slowly, surveying the piles and boxes and bundles of papers everywhere, sitting on top of the shorter shelves, in crates under the tables. And the books jamming the bookshelves or sitting on the floor in semi-tidy piles. She shuddered as she stepped up to the second table in the center of the room and saw the maps in haphazard piles, with notes and pins and markers, and Leffisand's bold, jagged handwriting.

This was his war room, hidden even from his most trusted advisors and henchmen. Because Leffisand truly trusted no one. Not even her, obviously. He had shared his dreams with her, during those seemingly blissful early days of their marriage. She imagined now that he had considered her a pet and indulged and rewarded her for performing her tricks properly. Leffisand intended them to take over all of Armorica, sending their daughters to marry heirs to powerful thrones, to put their grandsons on those thrones, and send their sons to win the hearts of princesses who became the heirs when their brothers died in tragic circumstances.

And now, if the spell trying to tangle and strangle her and Bryan, and Naomi and Rafal had been interpreted correctly, it appeared Leffisand had left some contingency plan to fall on her, to take over other kingdoms through marriage, if anything happened to him. Nothing had happened to him, she countered silently, as she turned away from the war table. Leffisand had done it to himself. He hadn't taken into account how the lack of a son born through her uprooted all his plans.

"Mi'Lady?" Bib riffled his pages. "I think you need to start there. That chest tucked under the table closest to the fireplace. The letters in there promise to be … interesting."

Crystal dismantled the cloaking spell, so when Naomi came looking for them an hour or so later, she had no trouble finding them. It helped that her herbalist magic guided her, by simply asking the trees where the strangers had gone. By then, Bib had interrogated most of the journals and magic books there, and Merrigan and Bryan had read enough of the letters in the chest to have a good idea what all of them contained, who they were from. And to be furious.

And oddly, to feel a little sorry for Leffisand, of all people.

"This was Leffisand's schoolroom," Bryan announced, once Naomi had taken a seat and they explained a little of how the books and letters and maps were organized. "Those two chests are copies of all the letters he wrote to Merrigan during the years he was training her, in league with her Nanny Tulip." He shook his head. "And he wrote every letter at least twice before he sent it to her. Because he had his own version of Nanny Tulip, who went through each letter and corrected him."

"She wasn't kind." Merrigan shuddered. "She constantly scolded him, how he was running ahead of the plan, that he wasn't as smart as he thought he was. She warned him regularly that if he wasn't careful, Carlion would end up being swallowed up just like all the kingdoms that he was supposed to swallow up, that he would be a footnote rather than a chapter in history." She sighed. "Every compliment, every bit of advice he gave me, every friendly question to make me think ... all planned out, coordinated with Nanny Tulip's training, to make me feel unloved and alone and desperate for their approval as I turned into the brat."

"You threw a major roadblock in the Hyacinths' path," Bib said, "when you gifted Leffisand that apple tree to protect and bless the kingdom. It threatened to heal Carlion and bring back the majjian springs that had been blocked since the death of his mother. Quite a lot of his energy was spent trying to warp the tree to serve him. There are hundreds of letters of advice on what to do, and lots of scolding that he should have burned the sapling and never brought it into Carlion."

"You protected Carlion through the tree," Merrigan said. "You kept the Hyacinths out of the palace gardens, and then out of the palace, then out of the capitol, as the tree grew."

"Wait. Who are the Hyacinths?" Naomi asked, shaking her head as if she were waking up from a confusing dream.

"That is what they call themselves. The minor majjians and half-blood Fae who have joined together to force the rationing of magic."

"They decided generations ago that the distribution of magic throughout the world is entirely unfair," Bryan said, "and people they considered undeserving fools got far too much help. They decided magic should be put in the hands of those with common sense. Their idea of common sense. So, they have been working to control the flow of the majjian springs and enslave frogs and swans and corrupt royal children, to use their inherent majjian gifts and ..." He shrugged and dropped down on the bench next to Merrigan. "It will take far more time than we've spent here, just digging through the records and following up all the connections. This is just what Leffisand left behind, and it appears he was just one of many kings who had fallen under their sway."

"The irony," Crystal said, "is that the Hyacinths are just tools of someone even more despicable. Do you know the legend of the Dragon's Teeth?"

"There are so many stories of dragons' teeth," Bib said. "Be more specific, please."

The mirror's surface flashed, and she wobbled a little bit, where she was propped up next to Bib on the central table, with books and papers and maps piled up all around them and underneath them.

"You're right," she said after a moment when Merrigan considered picking up the mirror to keep her from wobbling right off the precarious pile and off the table, onto the slate floor. "The Dragon's Teeth Mountains."

"Where are those?" Bryan said, speaking the question that was clear on Naomi's face and poised on Merrigan's tongue.

"That's the puzzle. They aren't mountains anymore. They're the Archipelago. The king who controlled them wanted to gather all the water of the majjian springs to the many deep valleys and canyons of his kingdom, so he could control the magic of the entire world. Interfering with the flow of water eroded the foundations of his mountains, and they fell, and the water that he had imprisoned already turned bad. It became part of the sea, and his mountain peaks became islands. He uses up all the magic that he can siphon out of the sea to keep himself alive. According to the bits of information the Hyacinths dribbled out to Leffisand, his dream is to bring all the majjian water of the world to surround his islands, replacing the salt water. When he holds all the majjian water of the world, then he can restore his kingdom."

"And make all the Hyacinths his ministers and nobles," Merrigan guessed. "So they can ration all the magic of the world to those they consider worthy. To accomplish that, they need to stop up all the majjian springs, fill all the queens' gardens with thorns, drive away all the frogs and swans and other magical beasts?"

"And consolidate all the kingdoms on each continent into one kingdom, with one king under his control," Naomi said, speaking slowly. "By killing off the kings, one by one, with their queens inheriting from them and marrying other kings." She shuddered. "Which explains the spell that was attacking both of us. And trying to kill Rafal."

"How is he?" Merrigan hurried to say, with a guilty start.

"Much better, now that you've deflected the spell. I actually came to find you, to ask you to come see him. He's been holding council meetings in his bedroom, whenever he's been able to sit up, so the council of lords are used to …" Naomi shuddered and covered her face with her hands while she took several deep breaths. When she lowered her hands, she tried to smile. "This is rather a shock, but … I think I will eventually be grateful to know all this. To understand. Maybe not feel so guilty about all the mistakes I made."

"You didn't make any mistakes," Bryan hurried to tell her. "Everything you did was a blow against the Hyacinths and their overlord's plan, and you didn't know it."

"That's not very encouraging when it certainly feels like we're walking into battle with no weapon but a tiny herb harvesting knife, and a straw hat for protection."

"I think it's entirely encouraging," Merrigan said. "It's a very long story, but we're on a quest to find Bryan's brother, who was snatched away by a nasty complicated tangle of spells. As part of the overlord's plan, it turns out, to keep us distracted and stop … well, that can be discussed later. The important thing is the advice we were given. A wise majjian told us to keep moving, as we had already been moving, helping when we saw a need and keeping our eyes open, but not go hunting for clues. We did just that, and we've had an amazing journey so far, snapping the threads of the nasty, tangled net of spells and curses that apparently are part of the Hyacinths' plan. We've helped awaken sleeping magic and freed people from curses and brought majjian water back where it hasn't flowed in years. And I think that's what we need to do here. Awaken the queen's garden and bring back the majjian spring. Honk will look for more swans to come inhabit the garden again, and there have to be some frogs around here somewhere, despite what Leffisand and I did."

She caught her breath, fighting another surge of nausea, thinking of all those frogs' legs she had eaten. Would Viridian, prince of frogs, ever truly forgive her? Even knowing she had been manipulated by their enemies so thoroughly?

"We just need to do what we can, small things that add up."

Before they moved from the cottage, Bib identified ten books of magic and four journals that would be useful for Trevor and the other majjians who had returned to Carlion in an attempt to bring healing. The spells attacking Rafal's health and drawing princes and kings to Naomi had been applied in layers, over time, the weight of them tangling and interfering with each other and warping each spell slightly from its original intention. Once they were identified, it would take some time to uproot them and dissolve them, but once the process had started, there would be a cascade effect, making each successive unwinding and uprooting easier. In theory, at least.

Trevor snatched up the books once Bib explained what they were. He and the other majjians got to work immediately. He warned that once the warping began to dissipate, there might be some fluctuations when the spells went back, or tried to go back, to their original intentions. When that happened, it might feel as if the situation had grown worse. Having Rafal, Naomi, Bryan and Merrigan together in one room was already thickening the threads of magic around them. He promised to have several majjians waiting to cut those threads of magic to protect them from rebound. When the time came. If they weren't distracted with larger problems.

Apparently, several theories he and the other majjians had been exploring were proving true, and the rebound of several spells breaking could cause physical harm to Carlion. They needed to protect against floods and gale force winds and surges of animals reacting to the spells that had been set up decades ago to drive away swans and frogs and a dozen other species of minor magical animals.

"That is the warping effect we detected," Bib explained, once Trevor had left the massive sitting room that had been turned into the council room.

Merrigan thought she could breathe a little more easily, once Trevor and the eight other majjians had left. She didn't recognize this room at all, because she had never come into this wing of the palace. From the older style of decorations, she suspected this had been the quarters of Leffisand's father.

She was grateful to be in a place she didn't remember. If only she could have changed her face, and her voice, so she didn't remind these nobles gathered around Rafal's bed of the days when she had been their spoiled, demanding queen. She could see it in their faces, no matter how calm and business-like their expressions. It showed in the sideways looks, the effort not to look at her. Like they expected her to suddenly start throwing orders around, usurping Rafal's authority. Maybe they thought that if she had effectively returned from the dead, Leffisand would walk through the door any moment and reclaim his throne?

No, she realized, as she heard the whispered word, "child," from one noble, and another saying, "heir to the throne," and "how old?" and "prince or princess?" from another. They were waiting for her to bring out Leffisand's child and start a massive fight over who would be regent.

"I'm sorry," she cried, determined to resolve that problem immediately, and do what she could to solidify Rafal's claim to the throne of Carlion. Even pale and thin, reclining in that narrow bed, with tables full of papers around him, evidence of how he tried even in his illness to fulfill his duty, Rafal was a better king than Leffisand had ever been. "I lied. I never carried Leffisand's child. Thank the Unseen for that large mercy. I lied, to hold onto the throne. Rafal is the rightful king. I renounce any claim I might have. I'm sorry. I'm so very sorry. You have no duty to forgive me anything—but I'm sorry."

She shut her mouth with a snap of her teeth, as she realized she had started babbling. She trembled, but she couldn't make herself sit down. She kept her gaze focused on Rafal and Naomi, who sat on the side of his bed, holding his hand. She prayed that heat in her eyes wasn't tears. If she started crying, she would be an ugly, loud, drippy mess, and there was too much work to do to waste time on her weakness.

"Merrigan," Bryan whispered, and wrapped his arm tight around her. He kissed her cheek, right there in front of all those staring, whispering, astonished nobles, and guided her to settle into a chair.

"And the last thread is snapped, the last root is killed and pulled free," Clara announced, emerging from the bright spot by the windows. Merrigan had honestly thought that was just sunlight glaring bright in the glass. The seeress smiled and stepped through the circle of chairs, holding out her hands. "Well done, Princess Merrigan. You are your mother's daughter indeed. Daylily bequeathed the greatest share of her legacy to you, and you honor her with your strength and courage."

"No, I haven't done anything to honor her," Merrigan whispered, trying not to burst out in sobs. She didn't care how she looked. She hid her face in Bryan's shoulder and prayed his sleeve would dry up her tears.

"Well, that does change everything, doesn't it?" Lord Maxin said, as he slowly got to his feet.

"You need to investigate a hidden cottage we found in the garden," Bryan said. "There are records there of much of Leffisand's work, his plans, his conspiracy with a group of majjians who called themselves the Hyacinths. Probably guides to the curses and constraining spells he put on the kingdom."

"Yes, please," Naomi said. She and Clara exchanged glances. "We need to extend hospitality to our returned cousins. They have been on a long journey. You may interrogate them tomorrow."

"Come." Clara held out her hand to Merrigan, and her smile was so much like Daylily's, after a long, difficult day of lessons and small triumphs, it was all Merrigan could do not to throw herself into the woman's arms, weeping.

And didn't that just prove how terribly upside down the world had become, or perhaps had been up until now? The longing to be embraced by the woman she blamed for all her trials and travels and struggles for the last two years.

To Merrigan's dismay, Naomi led her to the suite of rooms that had been hers when she had been queen of Carlion. The door was open, and servants bustled about, removing sheets to protect the furniture from dust and sweeping the floors. Merrigan knew if she looked in the closets she would find everything exactly as she had left her possessions when she headed out on that fateful carriage ride to badger Clara into making her lie reality.

"No, please—I can't. This isn't mine anymore." She looked first to Naomi, then to Clara. Surely the seeress would agree that she didn't deserve to spend one minute in her former place.

"Yes, it is," Naomi said. "Although perhaps your tastes have changed? Would you and Prince Bryan prefer something ..." She shrugged. "On the other side of the palace?"

"We?" She looked to Bryan. He grinned, even as his cheeks flushed.

"We're not married yet," he said. "We decided it would be wise to wait to get her father's blessing. Just to start things out right."

"Ah. And that decision has helped to deflect some of Leffisand's curse. Or rather ..." Clara frowned and stepped up, lightly pressing her fingers to Merrigan's temples and looking deep into her eyes. "How sad. It appears Leffisand didn't trust his co-conspirators, and they didn't trust him. There are several curses, actually. To sicken the king, to sicken the queen's consort, to force powerful men to fall in love with the queen, and to ensure that Merrigan finds no happiness if she should marry again."

"What?" Merrigan's voice cracked. Then she startled herself by laughing. "Oh, that does sound like Leffisand."

"The curses battle each other for dominance, it appears, and that is perhaps what is protecting you and Rafal and Naomi. I believe I need to see what you found in that cottage."

~~~~~

Lord Maxin and the other lords of the council spent two days going through the contents of the cottage. Trevor and Clara and the team of majjians spent much of their time going through the knot of spells anchored in the cottage, untangling and identifying them, and nullifying them one by one.

Merrigan, Bryan, Naomi, and Rafal had a miserable time the first day, when some spells dominated as others were destroyed. Rafal's illness grew worse for several hours, and Naomi and Merrigan had to lock themselves in their respective rooms to keep from racing through the palace, seeking out new suitors. Or fighting each other like alley cats, struggling for dominance. Merrigan was rather impressed by how sly Naomi could be with her insults, and the accuracy of her aim when she threw small objects, to knock out her rival for the throne.

When the last spell in that particular direction snapped and faded, with a distinctly sour aroma that lingered around its victims for several minutes, the change was visible before the smell had entirely faded away. Rafal's color improved, and his breathing, and the aches that kept him immobile eased. When Naomi and Merrigan could finally be civil to each other again and were enjoying a quiet cup of tea, a minor prince managed to scale the palace wall and stumble through the private gardens to an outside stairway, to find them. He stopped short, his mouth open in the
~~~~~

middle of a deluge of flowery love poetry and looked at both women as if he didn't know who they were. He seemed surprised to find himself in the small parlor where the two princesses had taken refuge. At the same time, loud voices that had been in argument several corridors away stopped short. The silence was almost deafening in and of itself. The prince, whom neither princess recognized, bowed and excused himself, and left through the door.

By nightfall of the third day, all the royal suitors and their entourages and particularly unpleasant, demanding ambassadors had all vacated the overcrowded guest quarters in the palace. Rafal was well enough to dress for dinner. The two royal couples had a pleasant, private dinner in the summerhouse in the center of the palace gardens. Bib and Crystal spent the evening entertaining them, answering questions and providing information liberated from the many volumes found in Leffisand's cottage. Bib turned the conversation to the most pressing topic, right after the sweet course had been served: the queen's garden.

Finding and awakening the queen's garden and bringing the majjian spring back to life would be a large step in healing Carlion and protecting it from the machinations and influence of the Hyacinths.

The answer lay in the letters and journals of Leffisand's mother, which had been found packed away in a chest covered in spells, to keep it nearly invisible and nearly impossible to open. Once Bib made contact with those journals, the spells began to unravel, just enough to reveal the chest. With time, they would unravel completely, but Carlion and Naomi and Merrigan didn't have that time to wait. All those precautions to keep the journals locked away were a clear sign that something dangerous to Leffisand's plans lay inside that chest. Something powerful enough to be protected, so he couldn't destroy it. Trevor and Clara spent two hours untangling the spells.

CHAPTER TWENTY-ONE

Even before the chest was physically opened, Bib got to work condensing the journals' hidden knowledge. Merrigan found it heartbreaking, revealing the great love Leffisand's mother had for him and his father. She had essentially died to protect them.

The Hyacinths had contacted her, early in her marriage, which was a diplomatic, arranged one. She came from Carathoris, across the sea, and was lonely. King Elfrid made no effort to get to know his bride, who needed a tutor to continue learning the language of Armorica for the first year of their marriage. The Hyacinths were sympathetic and offered her all sorts of little tactics and minor spells to win the attention and affection of her too-busy husband. They initiated a private correspondence for her with Acheron, king of the Archipelago, who claimed a historic alliance with her father's kingdom, and wished to help her. He provided help with learning about Carlion, about Armorica, the language, and understanding of the political currents that King Elfrid struggled with. The partnership between Armorica and the alliance of major kings on the continent of Maranbourne wasn't turning out at all as King Elfrid and her father had hoped. Queen Lorellia earned the respect and then admiration and trust of the council of lords with her insight and advice, provided by the Hyacinths and the Archipelago. She finally earned the friendship, then the love of her husband, and they were devoted to each other by the time Leffisand was born.

Then Acheron went on the attack. He flustered her by a sudden insertion of love poetry and flowery language into his letters. She tried to be kind and noble when she declined his protestations of love. He grew demanding, then threatening. She turned to the Hyacinths for help, and discovered her mentors were divided. Some scolded her for being foolish and not seeing that she could have the love of both kings, and she had a duty to use them to her advantage. The others offered her advice and minor spells to protect all of them.

She didn't realize what she was doing until the frogs, then the swans vanished from the queen's garden. Then she became desperate, and Acheron changed his tone, becoming her mentor and teacher again. His advice went against everything her heart and instincts told her to do, but it paralleled what the Hyacinths advised, to protect her family and kingdom. They kept her busy, traveling the kingdom, and away from the queen's garden, until one day she discovered the majjian pool had shrunk, and thorns climbed the walls.

The Hyacinths came to her with proofs that King Elfrid had been tricked, and certain items he considered protections for Carlion had actually opened the kingdom to infiltration and slow poisoning. The drying of the pool and the thorns in the queen's garden were just the most recent signs of trouble. The old women guided Lorellia in slowly, carefully finding the majjian talismans where they were hidden throughout the kingdom and among her husband's possessions, and removing them to purify the kingdom and strengthen it.

Then Leffisand fell deathly ill. He became her entire focus and she neglected everything. Until one day her ladies in waiting reported that the door into the queen's garden had vanished. Worse than that, a growing number of people, when asked, couldn't remember where the door had been.

New attacks came in rapid succession. A black swan tried to steal Leffisand out of the nursery. Then the Hyacinths came to her, weeping, with proof that King Elfrid was unfaithful to her. He blamed her that they hadn't had any more children. Acheron sent her copies of letters from Elfrid, seeking a new royal bride and asking for help in removing her, quietly, so no one would suspect murder.

The Hyacinths insisted she had to strike first, to protect the kingdom and her son, who would be murdered by the new queen so her own son could inherit. She had to arrange for the same kind of accident her husband wanted for her. Then, she needed to make alliance with a better king. One who could find the majjian springs and drive away the thorns.

Lorellia refused to believe them.

Her journals detailed her growing desperation and fear. None of her messengers seeking help from majjians inside and outside the kingdom ever returned with answers. Acheron urged her to join him as his queen, to purify Armorica and protect the people from magic gone wild and unruly and destructive.

She refused. When she warned King Elfrid, she discovered other majjians had uncovered all her secret activities. The king and his council of lords believed she was physically and mentally ill, rather than accusing her of treachery.

Her last month of journal entries bewailed the complete disappearance of the door to the queen's garden. Thorns grew across the windows and balconies that looked down into the inner courtyard, until those places were first covered with curtains, then with furniture, then forgotten altogether. A check of palace records showed Queen Lorellia had died only three days after her final entry.

"We need—" Merrigan shook her head. "No, Naomi, you need to

find that door. You are the rightful queen of Carlion now. You need to awaken the garden and free it of the thorns."

"No, consider that the troubles with the kingdom started long before the Hyacinths started influencing Lorellia. Maybe the true bloodline needs to be restored. That means Carran is the rightful queen, and her son is the rightful heir to the throne," Bryan said.

"Who is Carran?" Naomi asked.

They laughed, somewhat bitterly, when they realized they hadn't told that part of their story. When Bryan related how they had found the black swan and Tangle, and the cavern where he had raised the stolen royal children, Rafal and Naomi were first astonished, then rightly angry at the cruelty and scheming. Then they were relieved.

Carran and her son were the rightful rulers of Carlion. Rafal and Lord Maxin gladly sent to King Auberg, asking for his help in bringing Carran and Adlar and their son to Carlion. Hopefully their presence would begin correcting many things that had been going wrong for generations.

"I'm relieved," Rafal admitted, when their small company finished up their work, writing letters and going through the last of the reports from the majjians and nobles investigating Leffisand's cottage. "I never wanted to be a king. I'm a healer, and that's what the Unseen made me to do and be. If I can turn the kingdom over to the rightful heir, then we can return to our healing hall."

"Herbal lore magic is more suited to healing than to living in a palace," Naomi said, nodding.

There was something bitter-sweet in knowing their lives might soon return to what they considered normal. The lives they wanted to lead, rather than the roles thrust upon them. Merrigan had much to think about as she and Bryan bade the other couple goodnight.

They held hands and were silent as a maidservant led them to their rooms. Her head was still spinning with the revelations of the long, busy day. She wanted so very much for him to hold her for a long time, but they were royals, and she was the former queen of this place, and the maid was watching them with great curiosity. Servants loved to gossip. Especially when they had no love for their masters. Merrigan wondered how long it would change for the servants here in Carlion's palace to respect her, forget about liking her.

"Soon we'll be free, and together forever," she whispered, as Bryan let go of her hand and reluctantly stepped back. "What do you want to do? Once we find Bayl and make sure he and Belinda are together, and we free my mother's garden, where do you want to go?"

"Let's ... wait until morning. Or dream about what we want to do," he said. "I'm too tired to think straight."

Merrigan nodded, and stepped backward through her door, and let him walk away. The palace was far too big, the guest wing was the size of an entire village, and she missed the days when Bryan was just one door away from her in a crowded inn. Away from Carlion, they could again be anonymous travelers on the road, surrounded by Garan and his soldiers, who had become their friends, and Bryan could steal kisses and Honk could ride on the back of her horse again.

"Open the window, please?" she said, as she crossed the sitting room and stepped into the bedroom. Bib and Crystal were busy with the contents of Leffisand's cottage, so if she couldn't have Bib's company during the night, at least Honk was free to keep her company and offer his advice.

"Oh, now, that's not healthy," a creaky, slightly off-tune voice responded. That couldn't be from the maidservant who had just brought in a pitcher of steaming water and put it on the washstand with an aromatic bar of herbal soap.

A wrinkled little woman perched on the stool next to the massive bed, piled so high with mattresses and quilts, it required a three-step ladder to climb into it.

"Pardon me?" For a moment, she felt slightly dizzy, and wondered what the old woman was talking about. Merrigan shook her head and clenched her fist tightly enough to feel the braiding of her and Bryan's hair around her ring. She caught her breath and remembered. Yes, she needed Honk to keep her company. "I'm sorry, but I—"

"Oh, dear child, you're too tired to think clearly. Let Nanny Iris take care of you. Just sit right down and relax and you'll finally be treated like the queen you are." Iris smiled brightly and hopped down off the stool. She gestured at the cushioned chair next to the washstand.

"No, I really need to have the window open. It feels rather stuffy in here." Merrigan started across the room.

For a moment she panicked, unsure where she was. Had her quarters been moved? Had Naomi put her in an interior room, where the windows had been lost years ago to the thorns, and there was no way for Honk to get to her? She backed away from Iris's reaching hand, through the door into the sitting room. There was the window. She darted across the room to pull back the curtains and reach for the latch for the shutters.

"Oh, now, what's this ugly old thing?" Iris reached to catch hold of Merrigan's hand on the latch. Her tiny hand was incredibly strong as she tugged, and three fingers wrapped around Merrigan's ring finger. She hissed and yanked her hand free, and there was a smell like singed hair.

The smell jolted Merrigan fully awake. Her ring hummed on her finger. A thud against the shutters startled a yelp out of her.

"Nasty interfering—"Iris caught herself, but the creaking, angry rasp of her voice pushed Merrigan to move faster. "No! Stop! Don't let it in!"

Merrigan yanked on the latch. Another thud just as the latch lifted, and the shutters banged inward. Honk tumbled into the room. He knocked Merrigan back, turning in midair to hiss and flap his wings hard, hitting Iris. Honking loudly enough to make the walls shake, he leaped on the old woman, knocking her to the ground, pecking at her and bouncing and earning shrieks from her. And that singed hair smell continued.

Bryan burst into the suite of rooms, followed by several maids and a palace guard, with Clara and then Naomi after them.

Iris struggled out from under Honk's assault, spitting fury, sparks streaming from her fingertips and eyes. Her rage darkened her face and her simple, worn black clothes changed to a severe, purple-black robe and hood. She opened her mouth and drew back her hand, and the sparks coalesced into a spinning reddish-black ball.

"Silence!" Clara shouted. Pearly-blue light shot from her fingertips, to knock Iris flat and encapsulate her.

Your ring, your ring! Honk cried. *She wanted your ring.*

~~~~~

Naomi insisted on Merrigan sharing her suite with her that night. No one protested when Bryan camped in the sitting room outside their bedroom door, and Honk settled in a nest of pillows at the foot of the bed. Merrigan guessed quite a bit of the story before Clara and Trevor hauled away Iris and interrogated her. She was grateful for the sleeping charm Naomi insisted on wrapping around her, and hoped she wouldn't dream anything, especially not this very clear evidence that the Hyacinths had found her and were trying to control her again.

Common sense said the informal betrothal rings she and Bryan wore protected them. Iris had sensed the interfering magic and came to remove the ring. She had probably sensed Honk waiting to come into the room to stay with Merrigan and tried to prevent the window opening. Honk was furious, and before the sleeping charm took effect, demanded Merrigan come out to the garden with him, where he could protect her better. Indoors was a trap, and there was too much mean, nasty, dark magic woven into the walls.

Knock the whole nasty place down to rubble, he said several times before she slept, and several more times when she woke the next morning.

Naomi and Clara and Trevor could understand what Honk was saying, and Merrigan suspected they agreed with the swan's judgment and antipathy toward the palace.

"What did you dream?" Clara asked, when she stepped into Naomi's sitting room the next morning, to join them for breakfast.

Rafal was feeling strong enough to walk in under his own power and join them. Merrigan wished she felt brave enough to insist that she and Bryan leave Rafal and Naomi alone to enjoy a meal together, in privacy.
~~~~~

She was still shaken by the attack, and numbers provided safety.

"I didn't dream. Not that I can remember," Merrigan said, after thinking for several moments. "But I have this strong impression of hearing water running. Getting louder. I could smell it. So sweet. And an impression of light, as the water got closer. Does that make any sense?"

"Considering how you've heard water before, following you?" The seeress smiled, nodding slowly. "A very good sign."

"What did you learn from Iris?"

"Such a sweet face hides a devious, nastily self-righteous mind. She was stunned that we knew so much of the Hyacinths' plans but kept trying to gloat and frighten us. She tried to read our minds, to find out who betrayed them. We didn't realize what she was doing until she had a temper tantrum and started ranting about how they should have killed Queen Lorellia much sooner. The Hyacinth sent to train her had been an incompetent fool, and she deserved her punishment." Clara shook her head. "So sad when an army executes its wounded, rather than trying to heal them."

"So she confirmed everything that Leffisand's mother only theorized, as well as what she learned from their mistakes?" Rafal said.

"Unfortunately, yes.

"Between us, do Merrigan and I have a chance of finding and awakening and freeing the queen's garden?" Naomi said.

"The question isn't if you have a chance, but if you have time. The Hyacinths suspect many spells are failing, if not already destroyed. They surely must be rallying their allies and preparing for war. All I can see in my visions is that you must be alert for the sound and smell of water."

So that was what they did. Merrigan and Naomi had a vague idea of where inside the palace to search, what rooms might have once had balconies and windows looking down into the queen's garden. They went room by room, slowly, because so many were locked and required a search of the housekeeper's massive, multiple rings of keys each time. Too many of those rooms were stale and full of dust. Too many rooms had been simply locked up, abandoning the furniture and possessions left inside them.

Long ago, in Carran's grandfather's day, the royal family of Carlion had been large and healthy and several generations lived in the palace. That was before her uncle wove his plan to take the throne, and the royal family began to die from accidents or illnesses, or disappeared on quests. They hosted ambassadors and diplomats and took turns with the other major kings of Armorica in hosting the bi-yearly conclaves of allied kingdoms. Merrigan wondered if the emptiness of the palace came from Leffisand's distrust of other kings. Or perhaps more humiliating, no one trusted him enough to travel long distances to be his guests. After the suspicious deaths of his father, several powerful nobles, and his first wife, Fialla, Carlion's relations with many kingdoms had all but ceased.

Merrigan and Naomi opened and searched ten rooms. They tapped on and pressed their ears against the walls should face the interior courtyard of the palace. They took deep breaths despite the dust and stale air, seeking the perfume of sweet water.

Then Trevor joined them, bringing Crystal. She felt she wasn't contributing anything to the ongoing search of Leffisand's records and letters, and her affinity for water might be helpful. This necessitated going back over the rooms the two princesses had already opened up and investigated, just in case.

"It makes sense," Merrigan offered, when she wanted to sit down and cry, and maybe have a temper tantrum at the very thought of retracing their steps. "We could have missed something."

Honk accompanied them on their searches after lunch. By the fifth room, Merrigan learned to watch for his response as soon as a door opened and the imprisoned air seeped out to greet them. He settled down in the hallway just outside the door each time a room had nothing to offer. Their search went faster, because they knew just by the swan's reaction they would find no hint of the thorns on the other side of the wall.

Honk stayed perfectly still, neck extended, inhaling loudly when the third door opened. He never sank down to the floor, but he also never moved from his position in front of the door, which made getting into the room to take Crystal around to study the walls somewhat difficult.

On the seventh doorway, Honk followed them into the room, taking four steps and staying right there. He stared at a corner of the room, and Merrigan was tempted to not just tap on the wall, trying to determine if it was a thin veneer over thorns, but call for a manservant with a sledgehammer to try to knock a hole in it.

At the ninth room, Honk went all the way to the wall and tapped his beak against it.

Smell. Smell. He honked loudly, almost gleefully.

"Yes," Naomi whispered. "I smell it. What do you hear, Merrigan?"

They tapped on the wall. It sounded hollow. Perhaps an empty space behind the wood paneling? Naomi sent a manservant to fetch someone with the right equipment to pull the paneling off the wall, and they went to the next room.

The smell of water and a light breeze greeted them as soon as the maidservant pulled the door open. The girl let out a squeak and pointed at the far wall. In the shadows, Merrigan glimpsed movement.

"What is it?" Naomi asked.

"The tapestry." The girl backed away. "It moved."

Naomi and Merrigan exchanged questioning looks that turned into smiles. They stepped into the room and went down the narrow aisle between all sorts of haphazardly stacked boxes, then came out into an open space, with chairs set up in a circle, as if people used to meet there in hiding. The feeling of breeze grew stronger. Together, they grabbed hold of the slightly rippling tapestry, and the maidservant let out another squeak.

"What if there are rats behind it?"

"Pull," Crystal said, triumph in her voice. "Courage has the power to break any wicked spell, and this is not a wicked spell but a defensive one."

"Just like the thorns coated the walls of my mother's garden," Merrigan said. "When the magic of the garden was attacked, by breaking the rules, the thorns made it impossible for people to sneak inside through the balconies and windows." She shuddered and tightened her grip on the tapestry. Then she stopped and frowned. "Why is there a tapestry on this wall, when all the others are paneled over?"

"Oh, the wall was so ugly," the maidservant said. "And my granny, who served here before me, said that good Queen Lorellia loved to sit in this room, and she made this tapestry. When His Majesty ordered everything that reminded him of her taken away and burned, Granny made everyone bring it in here, to protect it. She used to sit in here with other servants who remembered and loved the queen."

Love, Honk said.

"Yes, indeed," Crystal said. "Their love for the queen, and the presence of her remaining possessions has been fighting the magic. Pull, girls. Pull for all you're worth. Today the victory comes!"

Grinning with determination, Merrigan and Naomi took double handfuls of the tapestry and pulled hard, putting all their weight into the effort. Merrigan flinched at the sound of tearing, but almost instantly the tapestry started to fall. She realized it wasn't the tapestry tearing, but a cord strung across the top of the wall, with the wooden rings that held up the tapestry. The heavy wall of thickly embroidered cloth slid down with a rushing sound like a wave hitting the shore and a clatter of wooden rings and a cloud of dust. Honk hissed and honked and flapped his wings hard, driving the dust away. The maidservant shrieked for the two princesses to flee, they would be covered and smothered.

Light spilled through gaps in the wall. Honk leaped through the clouds of dust and pounded his beak against it. More gaps appeared.

Break! he honked, and tapped several times, then cried, *Break!* again.

Merrigan raised her fists and pounded. In moments, the thudding turned to a thin, crackling sound, and what felt like wood changed to something brittle and flaky, like paper that had been soaked and stuck together. More light came through as the cracks grew. The cries of the maidservant turned to wonder, and she joined them to pound on the wall, breaking it down. The noise attracted the attention of the two manservants who had come with axes to break down the wall in the previous room. They stared with wonder for only a few moments, then stepped up and raised their axes. Merrigan and Naomi laughed and moved aside. In moments the wall disintegrated into dust as it fell and blew away, revealing an opening the size of the room, looking through a screen of twisted vines.

The vines did not fall to the blows of the axes. Merrigan shivered, sick at the sudden change from jubilation to frustration.

"Of course, there's magic at work," Crystal said. "Layers upon layers of spells, built up over the years. I wouldn't doubt that if Trevor comes in and examines this, or Clara, they will tell us that the Hyacinths took advantage of the defensive magic of the thorns and warped it, trying to make it unbreakable. So not even the rightful queen could make them go away when she came to claim her heritage."

"Carran and her son's wife?" Merrigan shook her head before the mirror could respond. "Naomi has just as much claim as they do. Shouldn't the queen who is present have stronger magic? Shouldn't a pure heart have more impact? Didn't Trevor say Naomi and Rafal were already bringing healing with their presence?"

"Yes, but ... well, I hate to say it and discourage you ..."

"What?" She fought a sick twisting in her stomach. Crystal was usually so forthright and blunt, it was a worrying thing when the mirror hesitated.

"You could be tied to the warping magic. After all," Crystal hurried on, when Merrigan muffled a moan, "you were queen here, wife of the king in residence. And you were poisoned by the Hyacinths, to ensure you strengthened whatever damage they did here."

"I'm sorry." Naomi wrapped her arm around Merrigan's shoulders. "It is so unfair, all the things they did to you. You're not to blame for even a tenth of the nasty things you did. Putting the blame on you for this as well, that's so entirely wrong."

"But I am to blame, even when I didn't know what was happening, because I made my choices," Merrigan whispered. "I caused this, just like I caused the door to vanish for my own mother's garden." She shrugged herself free of Naomi's arm and stepped up to the screen of vines and wove her fingers through the openings. "I'm sorry." She tightened her grip, so the sharp tips of the thick, hard thorns pierced her fingers and palms. Tears touched her eyes, but not from the itchy pain. "I'm sorry," she whispered, and closed her eyes, and leaned forward so several thorns touched her forehead.

"Merrigan," Naomi whispered.

"I'm sorry." Merrigan inhaled, shuddering, choking on the need to break down weeping as she hadn't done since her mother died. "Mama, I'm sorry. I failed you."

Tears streamed down her cheeks, but she didn't sob. She heard the trickling of water in her head. It merged with her deep breaths and the thudding of her heart until it felt like a storm surge and sounded like waves pounding on the shore. She wished she was back in Seafoam, designing pretty dresses and making common girls happy, and the weight of the fate of many kingdoms didn't rest on her aching shoulders.

"Merrigan," Naomi said again, louder. She gripped her shoulders with both hands.

A cry caught in Merrigan's throat as the thorns turned to dust in her hands. Naomi's grip helped her stay upright.

Merrigan opened her eyes, momentarily blinded by the dust filling them. She scrubbed with her fists and choked on the dust in her mouth. Naomi guided her backward, into a chair.

A shower of dust fell down into piles like brownish-silver snow on the deep balcony before her. The maidservant cried out, her fear turning to wonder. Crystal laughed. Honk launched himself off the balcony, his wings stirring up the piles of dust that turned to a shimmering smoke in the air and then vanished. Merrigan caught her breath and watched the swan fly in a wide circle around the perimeter of the courtyard.

Overhead, a dome of thorns turned to dust and smoke. The walls of the inner courtyard lost their layers of black thorns, melting into silvery-gray dust that sheeted downward, turning white, shining in the light that broke through the evaporating dome, as it vanished. Balconies and windows became visible. In too many places, the backside of paneling and plaster and even large cabinets and chests showed where the blocked walls had been hidden from sight and then forgotten over the years.

CHAPTER TWENTY-TWO

Merrigan remembered how her father's office had been on a wide balcony on the second floor of the palace, with stairs that let him come down into the garden to spend time with her mother every day. That balcony had been filled in with thorns, the windows and doors blocked, and in his grief and growing despair, he had chosen to move his office to another wing of the palace altogether, rather than sit there in darkness and remember what had been lost.

She wondered if the same had happened to Leffisand's father, at the death of his wife. Merrigan didn't want to look, but she made herself get up and cross the balcony and lean on the railing to look down. The next step was to find the pool fed by the majjian spring and search for healing herbs and other plants to replace what had gone to dust over the years of sleeping imprisonment and neglect.

"This is amazing," Naomi whispered. "It's so huge."

She laughed and hugged Merrigan, and that wrung tears from her. Who would have thought she would enjoy being hugged by the princess she had despised as a too-sweet, brainless little goody-goody? Who would have thought she would want Naomi to think well of her?

"Is it?" Merrigan bit her lip against saying the queen's garden here seemed small to her, compared to her mother's garden.

Then again, she had been so small herself the last time she saw the garden in Avylyn.

There were no stairs visible from any of the balconies. Merrigan and Naomi didn't have to speak to agree. They needed to get down there and explore the garden and see what needed to be awakened next. Naomi looked into the previous room and told the manservant with the axe to leave off, they could redecorate the palace another day. She sent him to find Rafal, Trevor and Clara and give them the news, although she and Merrigan were sure the majjians had felt the release of the garden, if no one else in the palace had.

"I don't suppose you have any clue where the doors should be?" Merrigan said, as they moved down the main staircase to the ground floor.

Naomi stopped short, eyes wide in surprise for a moment, then she tipped her head back and laughed. "No idea at all. I've been wandering these halls for months, trying to find the doors, but they didn't even make a shadow on the wall for me."

"They might appear on their own. I know no one expected it when the garden awoke in Seafoam." Merrigan turned Crystal around, so the mirror faced forward ahead of them. "Crystal, do you have any clues? Any sensation of magic awakening?"

Soon, however, it didn't matter if the doors appeared.

An elderly seamstress named Flax had tried to free Nanny Iris the night before, but Trevor had caught them. He suspected that Iris hadn't been working alone, and he had set up a trap. He had ordered them locked up securely behind wards and left alone to seethe and hopefully argue and reveal who else was working with them in the palace. They fell to arguing and blaming each other late in the morning.

Trevor had been meeting with Rafal and the other majjians, discussing what little they had overheard, the small bits of magic the two Hyacinths had attempted, which had been blocked easily, when the dome of thorns evaporated. The two old women went into screaming fits, terror alternating with fury. Trevor had them brought to face Naomi and Merrigan in the council room. Iris and Flax clutched at each other and hissed and snarled and muttered, their words incoherent. Merrigan feared they were trying to rouse a spell in some archaic, foreign language. Before she could cry out a warning, Clara stepped into the room.

"They're afraid of drowning," the seeress announced. Her words struck the two old women silent. They cowered down before her, hatred gleaming in their eyes, their faces pale and gleaming with fear sweat. "Listen. Smell. The water is coming. Multiplied a hundredfold by the tears you shed, Merrigan."

The silence rang, so it muffled the gasping sobs of the two old women. They opened their mouths to start in again. Naomi gestured and two of the four guards clamped their arms around the women, pressing their arms to their sides. The other two guards pressed their big, muscular hands over their mouths. One yelped.

"Sorry, highness, but she bites," he said, flushing bright red.

Then the sound of bubbling water, the smell of sweet spring water, heavy with the scent of stone, filtered through the room.

Clara tipped her head back and laughed. "Oh, well done. Healers and queens by right and deed. Go and see your handiwork, and what healing is brought by tears." She gestured to Merrigan and Naomi to go.

The smell of water and the sound of bubbling grew stronger, like music and fresh, sweet perfume, as they reached the top of the stairs and turned down the hallway to lead to the room where they had broken through. The breeze freshened and it was damp and sweet and cool. Merrigan took deep breaths as she ran. Naomi got there first and she let out a cry of wonder. She hung halfway over the railing of the balcony when Merrigan joined her.

The garden looked twice as large as it had been just an hour ago. The shapes of the beds of healing herbs, the hedges and the bare, skeletal trunks of the trees were visible, sticking up through a heavy, dry mat of grass and debris. In the center of the garden, like the iris of an eye, water sparkled, silvery and blue, with flashes of gold, in the center of a circle of white and blue stones. Merrigan leaned on the balcony railing and watched as the water bubbled up, the geyser visibly reaching higher into the air, the puddle of water expanding and widening as the majjian spring refilled the pool. Honk sat on the edge of the circle of stones, his neck stretched out, his gaze focused on that geyser of magical water.

Merrigan trembled, remembering how Dulcibella had knelt in the dry depression of the former pool in the queen's garden in Seafoam, and apologized and wept, and the water returned. Had she somehow helped to bring about this miracle and blessing of healing? She thought about Leffisand's mother, and imagined the woman's despair and sense of guilt, that she had allowed herself to be used as a tool to destroy the kingdom. Merrigan wondered if she would have liked her mother-in-law, and if the woman would have liked her. Perhaps the woman she was now, but certainly not the woman who had run away from her father's kingdom to marry Leffisand. She hoped Lorellia, and her own mother, Daylily, knew what had been accomplished here, and they were proud of her.

She and Naomi stayed there at the balcony railing, and she told her about Princess Dulcibella and how the queen's garden in Seafoam had been restored. She was only halfway through the tale when Rafal and Bryan and Trevor joined them. Merrigan started over but got distracted when she saw how Trevor's amazed smile slowly, visibly faded as he stared down at the filling pool.

"Is there something wrong?" she asked, once she related how Dulcibella stood up, startling everyone with the mud on her dress.

"That's filling too quickly," Trevor said.

"The water spout is taller," Bryan said, nodding. "It was only halfway to the bottom branches of that tree behind it when we got here, but now it's bubbling higher than the second limb on the right."

"Honk, is something wrong with the water?" Merrigan called down to the swan.

Wash away! the swan cried on a long, triumphant trumpet call with his head tipped back. The song echoed off the walls of the courtyard.

The spout of water doubled in height, so it reached above the balcony directly across the courtyard from them. The stream of water tripled in width, and a rumbling went through the ground. Everyone turned to Trevor, who gripped the balcony railing, his face going pale.

In that short span of time, the water crept past the white and blue stones ringing the pool.

"Everyone evacuate the palace!" Rafal wrapped an arm around Naomi and hurried her off the balcony.

"Crystal?" Merrigan asked, bringing the mirror out and turning her so she faced the garden and the spreading pool.

"I'm sorry, dear, but there's only so much I have in common with water, after all. A great deal of magic has been stoppered up and held back all these years," Crystal said. "It's flowing where it's needed. Maybe the swan is right, and all this needs to be washed away. Start over again."

After the first burst of panic, the evacuation of the palace proceeded in an orderly fashion. The housekeeping staff and the seneschal and footmen and other authorities among the servants organized everyone and focused on the rooms closest to the courtyard, to empty them first. Several known water majjians were sent for, to consult and to try to brace the walls against flooding. The door into the queen's garden had yet to appear, and Merrigan was grateful. There were no windows on the first floor of the palace that opened into the queen's garden, and never had been. That provided a little comfort and offered a little leeway for emptying the storage rooms and clearing away furniture and linens and emptying the files of all the offices of the ministers and secretaries and records keepers and scribes and counselors.

By the time the water majjians arrived, just before dusk, five more balconies had been opened, and several secretaries had been assigned the task of tracking the growth of the water spread and monitoring the walls when the water touched them. The majjians were astonished by the sight of all the water, but not surprised. They had felt the flow of water under the surface of the ground for days and had been backtracking the path of the flow to its source, which explained why it took so long for them to come. They recommended that swans and frogs be found and persuaded to come inhabit the garden, to help control the waters. They cast spells on the walls of the first floor of the palace, to prevent leaks, and admitted they had no idea when or if the water would stop flowing. Then they cast defensive spells on both sides of the walls surrounding the palace grounds entirely, to protect the capitol city from flooding.

"Can you bring swans here, Honk?" Bryan asked.

Invite us, Honk responded after several long moments of wagging his head back and forth.

"We need to invite you?"

"A royal invitation," Clara said. "Princess Carran is the bridge between swans and the throne. She can circumvent and even break the threads of any lingering spells to prevent the restoration ..." She trailed off, studying Rafal and Naomi, who sat opposite her around the oval table set up in the palace gardens far from the threat of flood.

"I have said already I would gladly yield the throne to someone with a greater claim," Rafal said. "Carran was the rightful heir generations ago, and she was stolen away, cheated, so a minor branch of the family took control. The throne is hers even more rightfully than it is mine. If her presence will not only put the magic back in balance but help restore swans and frogs and other magical creatures to the garden ..." He spread his arms, and he grinned. "I must be honest and say that I am relieved to be free of the burden of royalty. I was raised to be a healer, to use my gift for others. Naomi and I will gladly go back to the healer house we were building, and give my cousin and her heir all my support."

That was settled almost too easily and simply for Merrigan's peace of mind. She welcomed the mental tussle that followed, when Trevor and his team of majjians brought Iris and Flax to stand before the council of lords. Iris reminded Merrigan too much of Nanny Tulip, her apparent sweetness hiding a cunning mind and twisted truths. The sparks of anger in their eyes made a lie of their sobs and shaking and whimpering voices.

They protested that it was all a mistake, they hadn't come to do anyone any harm, they were being used by nasty majjians who were out to destroy the kingdom. No, they liked the pretty princess and just wanted to help her, and it was all a mistake, a misunderstanding. Then Clara stepped into the sheltered garden, into the light of the torches burning with enchanted oil to hide the meeting from magical sight and magical hearing. The women's true natures blazed forth with venom in their voices and spite in their faces.

She carried two pitchers sloshing with water. It glowed a pale silvery-blue. Water from the growing pool in the restored queen's garden.

Clara walked up to the two spitting, cursing, hunched women and studied them for several moments.

"Such language is unbecoming to women of your years," she announced. "Have some decorum."

Iris straightened up, her mouth open as she inhaled, likely preparing to spew another volley of filthy words. Clara swung the first pitcher, sloshing the entire contents over her. Iris shrieked, the sound drowned out by hissing as blackish-green steam rose off her. Flax tried to leap away from her, to avoid the spatters of sparkling water, but they were tied together, her left wrist to Iris' right wrist, her left ankle to Iris' right ankle. In a graceful, swift turn, Clara picked up the other pitcher and doused the seamstress, and she went down, shaking and steaming. A sour smell wafted through the garden.

"Who is your leader, and where is she?" Trevor said, when Clara nodded to him.

"Kill us. We'll never tell," Iris whimpered.

"The water compels the truth," Clara said. "Is she with Acheron of the Archipelago?"

The two old women twitched and whimpered as if they had been struck. They huddled in on themselves, slowly shrinking visibly.

"He will not succeed in calling all the majjian waters to his control. The sea is salt to fight his foul, poisoned magic, and it will always stand as a barrier between him and the majjian springs." Clara turned to Bryan and Merrigan. "I would ask a great favor of you two."

"Anything," Bryan said, when Merrigan just squeezed his hand and nodded for him to speak for both of them.

"You should learn not to make vows like that so easily. Even to someone you trust." Clara's smile turned weary. "The box that held the two enchantresses. Would you loan it to me, to hold these two, asleep, until we have fully dealt with the enchantments on Carlion, and we can confer with the other majjians dealing with this plague of domination?"

"Gladly."

"And ..." She put the pitcher down on the table with a thud. "Go home to Avylyn. Merrigan is needed there. She is indeed Daylily's heir, meant to bring healing to the heart of this land. This battle to heal the majjian springs could still take years, but time is of the essence, now more than ever."

THE END

About the Author

On the road to publication, Michelle fell into fandom in college and has 40+ stories in various SF and fantasy universes. She has a bunch of useless degrees in theater, English, film/communication, and writing. Even worse, she has over 100 books and novellas with multiple small presses, in science fiction and fantasy, YA, suspense, women's fiction, and sub-genres of romance.

Her official launch into publishing came with winning first place in the Writers of the Future contest in 1990. She was a finalist in the EPIC Awards competition multiple times, winning with *Lorien* in 2006 and *The Meruk Episodes, I-V*, in 2010, and was a finalist in the Realm Awards competition, in conjunction with the Realm Makers convention.

Her training includes the Institute for Children's Literature; proofreading at an advertising agency; and working at a community newspaper. She is a tea snob and freelance edits for a living (MichelleLevigne@gmail.com for info/rates), but only enough to give her time to write. Her newest crime against the literary world is to be co-managing editor at Mt. Zion Ridge Press and launching the publishing co-op, Ye Olde Dragon Books. Be afraid … be very afraid.

And please check out her newest venture: Ye Olde Dragon's Library, the storytelling podcast. Interspersed between the chapters will be interviews with authors of fantastical fiction. Listen to the podcast on your favorite podcast app or listen on the website: www.YeOldeDragonBooks.com, and click on the Ye Olde Dragon's Library link.

www.Mlevigne.com
www.MichelleLevigne.blogspot.com
www.YeOldeDragonBooks.com
www.MtZionRidgePress.com

NEWSLETTER: Want to learn about upcoming books, book launch parties, inside information, and cover reveals? Go to Michelle's website or blog to sign up.

Thanks for reading!
If you enjoyed this book, would you help Michelle by posting a review on Goodreads?
Are you a member of Book Bub? If so, please follow Michelle on Book Bub, and you'll get alerts when new books are coming out.

As a way of saying thanks, Michelle invites you to the Goodies page on her website. It will change regularly, offering you a free short story, a sample audiobook chapter, sneak peeks at new cover art, inside information on discounts and new release dates, etc.

Please go to: Mlevigne.com/good-stuff.html

Also by Michelle L. Levigne:
Guardians of the Time Stream: 4-book Steampunk series
The Match Girls: Humorous inspirational romance series starting with **A Match (Not) Made in Heaven**
Sarai's Journey: A 2-book biblical fiction series
Tabor Heights: 18-book inspirational small town romance series.
Quarry Hall: 11-book women's fiction/suspense series
For Sale: Wedding Dress. Never Used: inspirational romance
Crooked Creek: Fun Fables About Critters and Kids: Children's short stories.
Do Yourself a Favor: Tips and Quips on the Writing Life. A book of writing advice.
To Eternity (and beyond): *Writing Spec Fic Good for Your Soul.* A book defending speculative fiction.
Killing His Alter-Ego: contemporary romance/suspense, taking place in fandom.
The Commonwealth Universe: SF series, 25 books and growing
The Hunt: 5-book YA fantasy series
Faxinor: Fantasy series, 4 books and growing
Wildvine: Fantasy series, 14 books when all released
Neighborlee: Humorous fantasy series
Zygradon: 5-book Arthurian fantasy series
AFV Defender: SF adventure series
Young Defenders: Middle Grade SF series, spin-off of *AFV Defender*
Magic to Spare: Fantasy series
Book & Mug Mysteries: cozy mystery series
Quest for the Crescent Moon: fantasy series
Steward's World: fantasy series reboot and expansion
The Enchanted Castle Archives: fantasy series